THE Q
CHAIR

CHLOE GARNER

A HORSE CALLED ALPHA

ISBN: 9798795499017

THE QUEEN'S CHAIR

Isabella Gabriella Angelina Aurora Renata Anastasia Fielding-Horne stood at the top of the grand stairway and looked down at the ball going on below her.

She'd dawdled in her room for as long as she could, but her father had told her that she actually did have to attend the banquet being held in their honor for arriving in Verida, and Alyssia had sent servants up to check on her three times now.

Stasia didn't hate parties, normally.

Normally parties were an opportunity to shower her friends with invitations and they would steal off into an un-tended part of the house to drink wine and laugh and tell stories until her father came and sent her up to bed with the select few who got to spend the night. The rest he would shepherd out to carriages to take them home with great, dramatic calls of goodbye from the courtyard to the cluster of nightgowned girls up at the balconies.

No, she hated this party because she hated Verida.

No.

No, that wasn't true, either.

Verida was a port town, and all port towns stunk, but it was the *worst* port town because they didn't have any inland. The whole place was one foot above the swamps, ports on all sides and mud in the middle.

But even that wasn't why she hated it here.

She hated it because it wasn't home.

She'd hated it from the moment she'd set foot off the boat and laid eyes on Port Verida, as her father had overseen the unloading of the cargo, half gift for Alyssia to mark her wedding success, and half for trade at one of the city's many, many markets.

Everybody traded at Verida.

Her father hadn't sold the manor outside of Boton, so there was hope that they would go home again someday, but Stasia had left behind a shuttered building with two groundskeepers, the only ones remaining behind, and all of the rooms cloaked in white sheets to keep the dust off the furniture. Verida was supposed to be home for a long time.

Half the household staff had traveled with them, and the other half had gone looking for new work. The Fielding-Horne name was picking up roots and finding new soil, and Stasia was just going to have to adapt, as Minstrel had told her every time she had argued for turning back to Birch, the cozy little hamlet outside of Boton where she had grown up, during the crossing.

Minstrel Fielding was one of the most widely-known merchants in Boton, a kind man who had doted on his youngest daughter from a very young age, indulging her every whim and interest. Stasia had heard the staff refer to her as the spare daughter more than once, and she obviously knew what it meant.

Meglyn, the eldest Fielding daughter, had married very, very well while Stasia had still been so young that she couldn't remember her sister ever living at the house. Alyssia, Minstrel's middle daughter, had been shopped around in a wider net, fetching a very handsome match in one of the richest merchants in Verida about three years hence. With two wealthy merchant sons-in-law to take on his business when he retired or died, Minstrel had had the luxury of allowing Stasia to do as she pleased with her time and energies, much to Meglyn's dismay.

Well, at any rate, now Meglyn's dismay had been replaced with Alyssia's.

Stasia's sister came charging up the stairs, holding her skirts up with both hands as they dragged along behind her.

"What do you think you're doing?" Alyssia hissed. "You can't wear *that* to my coming-out party for you."

"No," Stasia corrected, adjusting her mask. "Daddy told you that there wasn't going to be a coming-out party, because I'm not on the market for courting. So I can wear whatever I want."

Alyssia looked pointedly from Stasia's face to her breeches and back, then two or three more times for effect, but whatever shame Stasia had for not living up to expectations had long worn away under Meglyn's constant application of guilt.

Alyssia huffed and went charging down the stairs, likely to find Minstrel and try to force him to do something about it.

He was even more immune to the manipulation than Stasia was.

Stasia went slowly down the stairs, watching the couples dance in their strange, anti-touching ways, everyone holding little masks on sticks.

Yes, there had been one sitting on Stasia's dresser when she'd gotten back from her walk that afternoon, but the one she'd brought from Birch was *better*, and it matched her clothes. So she'd gone with it.

A young man walked over to her, holding a little mask in front of his eyes and smirking. Stasia rested her hand on her hip, watching him approach.

He licked his lips and smiled.

"You're Alyssia's little sister," he said. "The merchant's daughter."

"Amazing," Stasia answered. "You must be a nobleman's son. We don't even need introductions. How very efficient of you."

The smile disappeared, and Stasia raised an eyebrow, daring him to say it wasn't true.

"Everyone says you're sour and difficult," he said, and she pressed her mouth into a line, the pique and outright temper she'd been holding down all week threatening to boil over.

"And I don't even *need* anyone to tell me that you're boring," she answered.

"You're new here," he said. "And you don't have any friends."

Stasia flashed him a short grin, unbothered.

"When I go looking for them, I assure you, they'll be absolutely fascinating. I only spend time with *interesting* people."

"Does your father know that you're insulting the son of one of the most powerful men in Verida?" he asked, and she shrugged.

"I'm sure it will make it to him eventually," she answered, looking over her shoulder and wondering if she'd put in enough of an appearance to go back up to her room, now.

The young man waited for another moment, as though to see if she'd crumble under the withering weight of his ambiguous threat, then he wandered off again, going to console himself at the food table.

Stasia saw Alyssia waving her over from across the room and she briefly entertained the idea of cutting straight through the dancing couples before going around the dance floor. It wasn't *actively* their fault that they were uninteresting.

"Daddy, you can't permit this," Alyssia was saying as Stasia got close. "In Birch, it's one thing. You were a big fish in a tiny pond, there, and they'd put up with anything. Verida is different. We can't afford for her to get us ostracized, here."

Minstrel put his arm out and Stasia came to stand under it, trying very hard not to look smug as her father took her side.

The way he always did.

"It used to be that clothing being as expensive as hers *made* it fashionable," Minstrel said, then held up a hand to forestay

Alyssia's argument. "Do you know *why* I was a big fish in a small pond in Birch, Alyssia?" he asked.

"Because you made more money than everyone else combined," Alyssia said, braced for whatever he was *actually* going to say.

"Because I acted like their opinions of me didn't matter, and I had the success to back it up," Minstrel said.

"Daddy, having a wayward daughter is not *fashionable* here. They don't understand the *idea* of a spare daughter," Alyssia said.

"And I was the one who invented it, in Birch," Minstrel said. "If she were a son, she would be considered perfectly acceptable, if odd. Why should it be different, just because she's a daughter?"

"Because she's embarrassing me," Alyssia hissed.

"Are we really going to spend the whole night talking about how I'm *dressed*?" Stasia asked. "All I want is an interesting conversation with someone who knows something I've never even thought about before."

"No one is going to *talk* to you, dressed like that," Alyssia said.

"Why?" Stasia demanded. "Why is it *so* important to be wearing the *exact* right dress?"

"Stasia, you're wearing *pants*," Alyssia answered.

Minstrel sighed, putting up a hand to interrupt them.

"Very well. Stasia, because tonight is our welcome party, I am going to ask you not to attend it as you are presently dressed. Out of consideration for your sister."

Alyssia raised an eyebrow at Stasia, who saw the cart-sized loophole that her sister had missed.

"Yes, Father," Stasia answered.

She looked around the party once more, then changed her mind about what she wanted to do with her evening and went for the front door.

She heard the outraged noise Alyssia made when she figured out what Stasia was planning, but she didn't turn back, going out the front door and turning to follow the path the carriages would take toward the stables.

There was a field full of carriages with horses-in-harness being tended by stablehands. They'd get feedbags when they got here and buckets of water every few hours to keep them comfortable and patient, though a few of the carriages had unhitched their carriage horses because the animals had been selected for look and spirit rather than tolerance to hours in the traces.

Off to the side of the barn there was a small paddock that they'd split up with ropes to keep the high-strung beasts away from each other for the evening as they trotted about and showed off their spirit. Stasia leaned on the fence for a few minutes, watching a particularly handsome pair of onyx-black stallions who were even in that moment lining up kicks on each other. It was a terrible choice for pulling animals, those two, but they were beautiful. Needed to be cut, from the look of both of them, though it was a shame to lose breeding stock just because they'd been conscripted into labor like they had.

"Miss Fielding-Horne," a servant said, and Stasia looked over at him passively, impressed that he'd recognized her.

"Yes?" she asked.

"Your father came down earlier and said to leave your horse tacked," he said. "He said to keep an eye out for you and make sure you didn't steal a strange horse instead."

Stasia frowned, wondering if she actually would have done that.

Maybe, if she'd thought that she could get out of here without anybody saying anything to her.

Anything was possible.

"Is she ready to go?" Stasia asked, and he dipped his head.

"Yes, miss," he answered. "She appears to anticipate you."

Stasia smiled.

The cargo for the crossing had been limited, but if she'd only had one thing she was allowed to bring, she would have brought Schotzli and nothing else. Everything else was replaceable.

She followed the stableman down the wide middle aisle of the barn - it was much bigger than the barn back home, designed to be able to work on two carriages next to each other without the horses being able to reach them from their stalls and leaving enough room in the middle to walk another horse in between.

Schotzli stood, tied to a ring against the wall outside of her stall, looking over her shoulder at Stasia. She was tacked elegantly, and for a moment Stasia considered asking them to re-tack her in more common gear, but she wanted to be gone and she didn't want to explain why she didn't like the highly-decorated saddle and bridle.

"May I give you a leg up?" the stableman asked. Stasia respected that. Most of the men she had come in contact with in Verida were vaguely uncomfortable with a woman sitting astride a horse, and even more uncomfortable with the premise of them getting up onto said horse.

He cupped his hands for her, squatting, as she unclipped Schotzli, and Stasia gave him an eyebrow.

"Is that how you do it around here?" she asked, and he looked down the barn aisle, then straightened. Stasia bent her left knee, offering him the toe of her boot. He grabbed it and tossed her up onto the saddle as she straightened her leg.

"You can clip her up anywhere in here and someone will see to her when you come back," the young man said. "Are you sure you don't want company, Miss?"

"Are you offering?" Stasia challenged, and he shook his head quickly.

"No, Miss," he said. "Simply that the roads are dark and not entirely safe in the daylight. Would be a shame for you to get thrown and no one know where you are."

"Then I'd better not get thrown," Stasia answered. "Thank you."

She gave Schotzli a big boot, not unkindly, but with the goal of encouraging the mare to take off as fast as she liked.

And she didn't have to tell Schotzli twice.

The mare jumped, leaping off of her hindquarters and breaking out into a long-legged lope out of the barn and past the stationary carriages, down the driveway and out onto the road, Stasia's cape flying along behind them.

The roads in Birch were better, the cobbles filled in deeper to make for a smoother road, but Schotzli handled the surface like a goat, only easing to a trot when Stasia asked her to, far enough away from the house that she was confident no one was going to come after them.

Iron horseshoes made a lovely clopping on the clean stones, though, and she couldn't begrudge them that.

They slowed to a walk as they got out of the more residential portion of the street, the castle coming into view above the rest of the buildings. The streets became more full with more people walking or pushing handcarts. She passed uniformed soldiers or guards and gentlemen on their horses. Some of them gave her odd looks, but most of them simply nodded or touched their hats.

She reached the castle wall, looking up at the towers that were only just visible over it, at this proximity. There were more guards, here, but the feel of the place was relatively relaxed. There was only the one gate in the wall on this side, and it was narrow and closed at this hour, so unless someone was so foolish as to try to climb *over* that wall, there wasn't anything of that much interest that was going to happen.

Now, Stasia couldn't help but calculate how she *would* get up and over the wall. They had done a good job dressing the stones, and there was a dearth of handholds if you were expecting them to be obvious, but with the right running start… or, better yet, starting from Schotzli's back… Yeah, she could find it. The wall had been built in stages, and she could see the joints where one overseer had stopped and the next one had started, and those were the weak points. She could stick her fingers in to those joints and get just enough lift as long as she kept moving…

Yes.

Yes, she could crack that wall.

She rode on.

The river was ahead of her, not as pleasantly noisy as the ocean, but sort of surging along in a watery way that she enjoyed. Up here by the castle, the smell wasn't so bad as it was down at the docks and along the ride from the docks up to… here, whatever they called this district or that. They'd passed a very decent-looking market along this way somewhere, and she had half a mind to look for it, even as she knew that the sellers would have shut down at dusk, for the most part.

Hard enough to keep sticky fingers off your goods in broad daylight.

She got to the river and let Schotzli drink out of one of the public troughs as she watched the night's remaining bustle. People out to visit or to drink, crowds enjoying the very end of the day and the reprieve from their labors.

These were the people who knew things.

A man just such as this had taught her how to pick pockets and locks. Another how to climb and roofjump. A soldier had taught her swordplay and an old man in a bar had taught her to fight with her fists.

Her father's coin could unlock a trove of knowledge that Alyssia and her high-society peers couldn't imagine, even as they sneered at it.

And there was magic here. Real magic.

Stasia didn't know what that meant, even, but everybody knew that there was magic in Verida. She could learn magic.

She could learn anything else.

She rode slowly along the riverwalk, a section of cobble that was frequently underwater by the look of the side of it, then climbed back up a short, steep slope to cross the wide river at a bridge that touched down on a permanent island in the middle and then finished the crossing.

The city on this side of the bridge was decidedly more industrial. She passed blacksmiths and potters, a small-scale smelter and a man making quicklime. Schotzli moved like the way was less reliably clear, undoubtedly finding bits of industrial debris that would accumulate through the night and sweep away again before the crowds.

Stasia considered a few turns, but decided against it, in case they got into winding streets that made it harder to find her way home again. She wasn't *that* concerned about getting lost, really, because all she had to do was find water and go upriver. Eventually she would inescapably find the castle again and then she could find her way back to her sister's house.

Even so, she wasn't exactly looking to *invite* a mugging, and narrow streets where the street lamps were few and far between was just asking for it.

The old man at the bar had made clear to her that, while being able to fight was certainly better than *not* being able to fight, no one was ever guaranteed a win, and it was better to avoid the fight entirely, if she could.

Even brawlers were pacifists, down somewhere in there.

People were complicated.

She came to a livery stable and went in, giving the oat bins and water troughs a careful look, then handing the liveryman her coin. The rest when she came back. Basic business.

That one was her father. Keep both parties financially invested until the transaction was completely done, and you never had to worry about trust, so long as murder was off the table.

Keep them financially invested *enough*, and murder never *was* on the table.

She took the two daggers out of the saddle bags where her father never failed to stash them no matter how many times Alyssia seized them and complained that Stasia had no business carrying them. They strapped on to her belt in a convenient but unobtrusive way, and she went on, tucking her purse away.

She passed another bridge, but didn't cross over again, enjoying the sounds of men working and serious people talking about serious things. Eventually, she found a river-facing bar that she liked the look of well enough and she went in, going to sit on a stool at the very end of it and ordering a beer.

The bar was most of the way to full, mostly men at tables playing cards and drinking. A huge majority of them were in uniform.

There were three different uniforms represented, and they were clustered around the bar in groups that Stasia sensed would fall to conflict if they did much more than look at each other. A man in black leathers came up to the bar to get a flagon of beer, and one of the red leathers stuck out a toe as he returned to his table. It wasn't enough to make the black leathers fall all the way to the floor, but he stumbled two good paces before regaining his balance and sloshed beer all down his front. The red leathers laughed amongst themselves and the black leathers bristled, but that appeared to be the end of it.

"This is the kind of place that replaces the window glass a lot, isn't it?" Stasia asked a barmaid as the woman came to stand across from her.

"He put in pane glass in hopes of not having to replace all of it every time," the woman agreed. "I like your cape."

Stasia smiled.

"Thank you. I do, too."

"And your mask," the woman said.

"Oh," Stasia said, putting her fingers to her face. "I'd forgotten I still had it on."

Someone jostled her elbow landing on the stool next to her. He slapped the bar.

"You ever see a bar fight?" he asked and Stasia looked over at him, wondering if it was possible he was talking to her.

"Yes," she said. "Many."

He grinned as the barmaid handed him a pint with a bit of an offended sigh.

"Wanna see another one?" he asked Stasia. He had a profound dimple that made him seem even more absurdly cheerful.

"Ambivalent," Stasia said. He took a huge swallow of beer, struggling it down and grinning again, then pointing with his thumb over at the corner.

"See, 'cause me and my buddies over there, we were taking bets whether you're here *to* see the fight or because you haven't got a clue it's coming."

Stasia tipped her head as someone coughed funny and a chair screeched across the floor. Her eyes didn't leave his face and his eyes didn't leave hers as he continued to grin that absurd grin.

"Which way did *you* go?" she asked.

"Oh, I figure you like 'em," he said. "The bloodier the better."

She snorted, turning forward again as a body landed against a table and more shouting happened.

"Sorry to disappoint," she said. "But the house wins. Third option."

He laughed.

"Suit yourself. Was gonna offer you safe passage if you wanted it."

"Don't need it, but full credit for chivalry."

He laughed again, downing more beer and standing.

Someone stumbled back into Stasia at a decent speed, pinning her against the bar, and she braced her hands against the front edge of it to push the unseen stranger back into the fray.

"That'll be my cue then," he said. "Enjoy your third option."

"Enjoy your fight," Stasia answered, genuinely surprised at how amused she was by him.

Chair shattered.

Glass broke.

The barmaid came back and topped up Stasia's drink.

"I know you didn't ask, but that's gonna be the only mug in the whole bar that'll hold beer after the likes of this one," the woman muttered. "May as well pour it before it breaks, too."

"Why does he let them in, if they're predictably this violent?" Stasia asked.

"No other bar this side of the Wolfram will have them," the woman told her, watching with resignation over Stasia's shoulder. "Thieves and murderers are better customers. So they pay through the nose if they want to drink, and those that want the house discount come back in the morning to help put it right."

Stasia finally looked, finding just the chaos that the sound had suggested, leather-armored men pounding each other and throwing each other about. She looked at the barmaid again.

"Don't the police do anything about it?" she asked.

"You not from around here?" the barmaid asked. "Fellas in black *are* the police."

Stasia drew a half a breath, then frowned.

"Huh. Hadn't guessed that."

"Reds are soldiers, browns are guards," the barmaid informed her. "Drink that down and I'll fill it again if you want. Gonna need more… everything, tomorrow."

"He really makes a profit like this?" Stasia asked, looking over at where the bartender was watching like a bald, stony mountain as the men destroyed his bar.

"Bar's been here three generations," the maid said. "He runs it same as his father and his father before him. I guess it keeps the family in beef."

Stasia frowned, sipping her beer, then putting a hand over it.

"I don't need any more than I've got," she said, and the maid shrugged, taking the half-empty mug that the dimpled man had left and filling it back up, then leaning on her elbows to drink it.

"Shame wasting it," the woman said, and Stasia smiled, settling over the counter and drinking with the barmaid convivially as the men trashed everything.

There was the sound of breaking glass and they made eye contact. The other woman winked and Stasia laughed.

Finally, the energy level of the fight dropped. Men were leaving, men were groaning, men were dragging about. Stasia looked over her shoulder once more as a pair of black-leathered men dragged out a third and a pair of red-leathered men leaned against each other on the way out.

The room was in complete disrepair.

The barmaid sighed and straightened.

"No rest for the weary," she said and went back down the bar, presumably to get something to clean with.

The table in the corner still had three men in brown leather sitting at it. Two others also in brown - including the dimple-man who had offered to escort Stasia out of the bar - stood in a newly-cleared space. Stasia tipped her head to the side, trying to figure out exactly what they were doing.

No, it was exactly what she'd thought at first.

They were sword-fighting with imaginary swords.

Quite dramatically.

Their actual swords were still in sheaths at their sides, but the men shuffled their feet up and back forth through the bits of broken pottery and glass, a few loose table legs, dodging and swinging like their lives depended on it, though neither face held the remotest sense of tension.

Magic swords?

Magic *invisible* swords?

She didn't know what was and wasn't possible in Verida.

"Cowards," a man Stasia hadn't been able to see before said, stumbling from behind an upturned table. "Cowards and buffoons."

The man who had spoken to Stasia sighed, sheathing his imaginary sword, his opponent just allowed his own to evaporate as he turned to face the red-leathered man staggering up off the floor.

"He's all yours," the dimpled man said, coming to throw himself onto the stool next to Stasia again. "I'm going to finish my beer."

"You already have one over there," his sparring partner said, stepping back, away from the red-leathered man and across the quasi-clearing, his hand on his actual sword. As he backed yet closer to Stasia, she admired the detailed work that went into his facial hair. Mostly men went bare-faced in Verida, and those who didn't wore full beards. The dimpled man's sparring partner rather had a very elegant goatee and a narrow ridge of hair that went from his chin to his ears. He must have had the world's tiniest pair of scissors to make that work.

"Two is better than one," the dimpled man said, grinning and peering into his mug. "And this one is fuller."

"Only because you haven't sat there for more than a minute," the goateed man said, still tense, watching the red-leathered man who hadn't yet found his feet. Stasia looked over at the other three brown-leathered men at the front corner table, but while they were *watching* what was going on, they appeared to be having a completely unrelated conversation.

The red-leathered man shook his head as if to clear it, then drew a dagger and staggered forward.

"Cowards," he said once more.

"Come on now, Locus," the goateed man answered him. "Let's not let it get that serious."

"Can't draw on him," the dimpled man teased, indicating the drunk man's dagger. "That wouldn't be a fair fight."

"I'm not carrying anything that *small*," the goateed man said, and Stasia frowned, then shifted.

"I am," she said, pulling out one of her own daggers and flipping it to hold it by the point-end. She held it off to the side so that he could see it in his peripheral vision, and he shot her a very, very quick look, then gently took it from her and held it out defensively.

"This what you guys do for entertainment?" Stasia asked the grinning man.

"No, typically we try to stab each other for fun when we get really bored," he said, turning his back against the bar and sipping his beer comfortably. "This is just a Tuesday night."

"They seem awfully unconcerned," Stasia said. "Not much for friends."

The grinning man grinned wider.

"Oh, no. If he were in any danger of losing this, they'd be up and breaking it off. It's just a shame you gave him a blade. I'd have made him fight using just his belt."

"Belt," Stasia said, and he nodded, content with that for an answer.

The red-leathered man lunged at the brown one, and Stasia finally took a moment to truly size him up. She'd been *aware* of all of it from the beginning, but now that he was actually engaged in a fight that she was going to watch, she became consciously aware of the things that had just been passive observations, before.

He was a lean man, light on his feet and in lighter boots compared to basically everybody else there at the bar, probably including the barmaid. He moved up on his toes more than Stasia would have done - power went down through your heel, she'd been taught - but it made him quick and it made him seem… ephemeral in a way that she couldn't put her finger on. Like you could swing at exactly where he was, where you *saw* him to be, and he simply wouldn't be there anymore.

Stasia confirmed, now, that his facial hair was of a style she hadn't seen before in Boton or Birch, but it suggested a meticulous man. Probably one who didn't get in a lot of fights, but who - given the way he moved - was very specifically aware of how to get out of it.

The grip on her dagger was a bit peculiar, more like a musician's than a soldier's or a brawler's, but she admired it with a sense that he was a master of this kind of thing, and it made her want to get the other one out to see how it felt with her own fingers, holding a dagger like that.

The red-leathered man was bull-shaped, red-skinned, and angry, but drunk to the point of seeing double, and unlikely to remember any of this in the morning.

"Oh, this isn't hardly a fair fight," Stasia observed, and the grinning man shook his head cheerfully.

"That's what makes it so fun to watch, right up until you armed him *fair*. Once made him fight a guy off using a meat skewer."

Stasia glanced over at him, wishing she might have seen that.

The drunken red man slashed the air and the goateed man slid sideways, dagger out, just watching.

"Why does he call you cowards?" Stasia asked, and dimple opened his mouth to answer, then held up a finger and pointed.

"After the show," he said with a wink.

The red man attacked three or four more times, then the goateed man stepped sideways as the red man overcommitted to a charge. He kicked the red man with his heel on the way past, sending him charging head-first and windmilling into the wall.

The dimpled man stood, peering over, then sat down again.

"Could have killed him like that, man," he said, turning around to face his beer. "Could have stabbed himself on the way down."

The fighter watched the man on the floor for a moment longer, then turned his eyes to Stasia's dagger.

"This is a gift of a blade," he said. "Who made it?"

"I don't know," Stasia answered. "But you're right that it was a gift."

He put it across his palms and offered it back to her with a small bow, then he went to sit next to the grinning man at the bar.

"Name's Colin," the dimpled man said. "This is Sterling."

The fighter lifted two fingers in greeting to Stasia, then leaned over the bar slightly.

"Marigold, darling, have you guys got a bottle of wine hiding away back there?" he called.

"I'm Isabella Gabriella Angelina Aurora Renata Anastasia Fielding-Horne," Stasia answered. "But you can call me Stasia."

Colin lifted his head to engage the table in the front corner.

"Guys," he called. "Meet Stacy."

Stasia pursed her lips, but the grin that came back around made it evident that he'd done it on purpose, and she wasn't going to wrangle with that. He hunched over his elbows, taking a long drink of his beer, then hunched over his elbows again, always on the verge of starting a story, but never... quite. He took another drink, and Stasia frowned.

"Are you damaged?" she asked.

"Dramatic timing," Sterling muttered. "Sometimes we find that a sharp blow to the back of the head will accelerate it."

Stasia smiled at this.

"So you're the cleanup crew," Stasia observed, looking back at the bar.

"It's our bar," Sterling said. "They just invade it in flocks."

"She said no one else would let them drink there," Stasia said, and Sterling nodded, spreading his hands with wide fingers as the barmaid materialized with a bottle of wine and a genuine glass. "Marigold, I swear, you work miracles."

"I'm getting there," Colin said moodily. "Yes. The reds, the blacks, and the browns. The reds hate the blacks because the blacks abuse the city. The blacks hate the reds because they abandon the city. And they both hate us…"

"Because of your mouth?" Sterling suggested.

"Because they say that we don't do anything about either problem, we just sit up at the king's table and drink *wine*."

"If you know what you like and have the coin to pay for it, I don't see why what a man drinks is any business but his own," Sterling said. Colin took another long drink of beer, then settled on his elbows again, looking at Stasia.

"So what are you doing in our bar?" he asked. "Come for the show?"

"I told you, it was the third option," Stasia said, unable to *not* smile at him. He was so absurdly… everything that it was just disarming. He wasn't hitting on her because he would have been trying harder, and he wasn't taking her for granted because he would have shown more ego. He was his own self and completely delighted with the situation.

"And what is this magic third option?" he asked confidentially.

"I wanted a beer," Stasia answered, smiling. He tapped his mug against hers where it sat on the bar and he nodded.

"Mission accomplished. You're awfully fancied up, for a bar like this, though. Why didn't you go find the capes and masks bar instead?"

"You guys got one of those?" Stasia asked. "I would love to see it."

"You are exquisitely dressed," Sterling said.

"Yeah," Colin said. "Aren't you worried about messing up… whatever that is?"

He waved a hand at her, and she snorted.

"Not at all."

"Because it's dragonskin," a calm voice said from behind them. Stasia turned to look over her shoulder, finding one of the men from the corner had risen, coming to lean against a post in the middle of the room, his arms crossed and ankles crossed.

"Really dragonskin?" Colin asked. "Or is it just called that?"

"Oh, it's real," the new man said. "And unthinkably expensive. Where are you from?"

Stasia lifted her chin.

"Birch," she said.

"Where's that?" Colin asked, clearly unconcerned as he returned to his drink.

"Outside of Boton," Stasia answered, a bit offended.

"Where's that?" Colin asked again, snorting.

"Forgive his ignorance," the leaning man said. "He's been rewarded for it too often."

Colin grinned and Stasia turned, finding that the other two men had finally risen from the corner table and were approaching the bar, picking their way through the rubble. Stasia glanced at Colin, intrigued by the other three men, but unwilling to let the opportunity past.

"Boton is the capital of Kirfall, the closet landmass to Verida across the Sorbine. Birch is the part of Boton where all of the richest people went to get away from the worst of the city," Stasia told him.

"Like the taxes," the leaning man observed nonchalantly, and Stasia shot him a look.

"Bad city for a rich girl to be wandering around after dark on her own," the big man from the corner table said.

"I can take care of myself," Stasia answered, turning her back to the wooden bartop.

"Minstrel Fielding just relocated here from Boton," the leaning man said.

"So he did," Stasia said, uncomfortable for the first time. Yes, many, many people in Boton knew who her father was, but they rarely associated Fielding-Horne with Fielding, and even more rarely recognized her dragonskin for what it was.

"The king is eager to see you happily settled in Verida," the leaning man said. "A man of your father's standing in the merchant community is a significant asset to the city."

"So he is," Stasia said.

"Oh, come on, Stacy," Colin said. "Don't be like that. Remember? We hang out with the king all day and do no work. We haven't got any problem with rich kids."

She looked over at him, and he looked chastened, but he also looked like it tickled.

"I'm no one's asset," Stasia said, turning to face the leaning man again.

"I'm glad to hear that," he said, dropping his arms and coming to sit at the bar. "I don't like it when the place that I come to drink turns out to be interesting."

"Jasper," Sterling said. "Stacy. Stacy, Jasper."

She *should* have corrected Sterling, but she didn't.

There was no telling why.

She watched Jasper for a moment as the barmaid found a mug and set it down in front of him, then the bartender walked over to lean against the back wall of the bar.

"Any news from the king?" the man asked.

The two men behind Stasia began cleaning things up, dragging the unconscious red-leathered man out and then pushing broken bits along the floor behind bigger bits of broken things. The barmaid went to join them.

"Nothing you won't hear from the right newspapers," Jasper answered.

"There's no news on the queen…?" the bartender asked, and all three men at the bar went still.

"No," Jasper said slowly. "There's no news on the queen."

Stasia sipped her beer, recognizing quite suddenly that the King's Guard would be men who knew a considerable number of useful things.

"So what is dragonskin?" Colin asked Stasia confidentially. "Is it just *called* dragonskin, or is it actually made out of dragon hide?"

"I didn't ask," Stasia said, considering cutting him off there, but deciding to open the door instead. "It'll stop a knife unless it's made of black steel and sharpened specifically to do it. It's impervious to heat, and it basically lasts forever."

"That's neat," Colin said, leaning back with a visible temptation to touch it. She sighed and offered him her wrist.

He felt the tough material between his fingertips and whistled.

"Not too tight?" he asked. "Hasn't got enough… seams in it… to give." He leaned up and back, looking at the shape of her body in an entirely mechanical sense.

"They tailor it to you, specifically," Stasia said. "But, no, it feels like wearing your own skin."

"That's kinda gross," Colin said, giving the purple one more playful frown, then tuning back to his drink.

Stasia looked over her shoulder.

"Are you guys going to help them or anything?" she asked.

"Nope," Colin said.

"Colin and I won the flip to be the ones to run the last guys out of here," Sterling said.

"And Jasper is above doing manual labor," Colin said.

"Careful, or I'll change the rules on you," Jasper murmured, and Colin grinned.

"So how long you been in town, Stacy?" Colin asked.

"Landed four days ago," Stasia answered.

"How do you like Verida?" Sterling asked. She wrinkled her nose and then sighed.

"It doesn't have much to say for itself, if I'm honest," she answered.

"Verida has everything to say for itself," Jasper said, turning his back to the bar to watch the other two men work.

"It's a city of cities," Sterling said. Stasia wasn't sure if he was agreeing with Jasper or adding new information, but she didn't get it, either way.

"If he brought his spinstress daughter, it means he's planning on settling," Colin said. "We just looking for a change of scenery?"

"Spinstress?" Stasia asked, too amused to be outraged, but faking it well enough.

"You think you're young enough to marry one of the noble boys?" Colin retorted. "They like their chickens *springy*."

Stasia's jaw dropped, mostly to keep Colin from being able to see how badly she wanted to laugh at that.

Sterling slapped him in the back of the head.

"Are you staying as a guest to the Gormand family, or are you planning on settling in your own holdings?" Jasper asked. "We might be able to direct you to some appropriate ones that might be interested in being on the market."

"Might we?" Sterling asked, and Jasper nodded.

"The king has taken an interest in Minstrel, specifically," Jasper said. "If it helps convince them to stay permanently, he would be happy to help with internal social knowledge."

"Huh," a voice said from behind, and Stasia looked over her shoulder, not sure which of the cleaning men had spoken. The big one straightened slightly, seeing she'd looked at him, and he shrugged.

"The king is running a war and a kingdom," he said. "He doesn't usually take an interest in a single immigrant family."

It was said matter-of-factly, without malice, and Stasia nodded, taking it for what it was.

The other man, much younger and with long black hair, shoved together a pile of debris and straightened to address her formally.

"I'm Matthias," he said. "This is Babe. Welcome to Verida. Somebody ought to say it."

"Thank you," Stasia answered, spinning on her stool to face the room. "I'm not actually interested in staying, so I'm not much use to any of you. I'd rather go back to Boton."

"Birch," Colin corrected without looking at her, and she shot him a look. He grinned, still not looking at her.

"Babe?" she asked. "You actually go by that?"

"Yes, ma'am," the big man answered, pushing the pile toward the front door.

Colin nodded and Matthias glanced over at her, waiting for some kind of reaction.

There was a confidence to a man that size who was okay being called *Babe*.

"I wouldn't ask," Sterling said in a friendly tone through his teeth, and Stasia nodded.

"Seriously, though," Babe said. "You should have someone escort you home, this time of night."

"I told you, I can take care of myself," she answered, watching him.

"Oh, yeah?" he asked, giving the pile a big shove to get it out the door and then leaving Matthias to clean up the scraps. "So if a guy, big guy like me, came up to you in the street, friendly like, and said 'hello, darling', what are you gonna do about it?"

He walked across the open floor, getting close enough to her to invade the socially-appropriate range but without behaving the way men so often did when they approached her on the street like that.

She watched his eyes.

He had thoughtful eyes, not quite kind, but not far off from it, either. A man who had seen danger and had seen violence and who understood the consequences of being soft in the wrong places. She respected that.

She put a hand on his chest.

"Look, friend," she said. "You've got me mistaken for somebody else."

"Oh, no, I don't think so," he said, moving his weight forward without moving his feet forward. She increased the pressure on his chest, drumming on the heavy leather below his collar bone with two fingers.

"Yes, you really do," she said, sliding sideways out of his way and letting him catch himself forward half a step. She stood behind him in the open space where Colin and Sterling had sparred, and she watched him, waiting to see what he would do next.

If he wanted to drive the point home, he could charge her, which meant that she would have normally had a dagger out by now, a disincentive for those not drunk enough yet to ignore it. With the truly drunk, she just had to stay out of swinging range, at this point, but he wasn't drunk at all. Didn't even smell of alcohol, if she made her bet over the background scent of the bar itself.

He turned and looked at her, and Matthias appeared next to her in a sort of a defensive pose, like he was torn between the knowledge that Babe wasn't about to *do* anything and the very real appearance of a woman in danger.

"Where'd you learn that?" he asked.

"Many encounters on just such a dark city street such as those out there," Stasia said, and he shook his head.

"Not that," he said, and she grinned. All three of the guards at the counter turned to look at her, and she shrugged.

"I thought I'd done better than that," Stasia said.

"It'd keep you alive out there," Babe said. "It's that good. Where'd you learn it?"

"What's he talking about?" Colin asked Sterling. Sterling shrugged. Jasper watched Stasia with sharp eyes. He was the one to watch, that one. He saw everything.

Stasia walked over to the bar next to Jasper and dropped the purse onto the wood.

"Next round's on him," she said.

Sterling whistled and Colin laughed.

"You do that often?" Jasper asked, and Stasia shrugged.

"Have to stay in practice," she said. "Figure a man who gets too close is basically asking for it."

Sterling lifted his glass to her and turned back to the bar. Colin grinned.

"Good think you didn't say that in front of the blacks," he said. "They'd haul you off."

"Good thing they hate you guys, anyway," Stasia answered, and Jasper frowned.

"Good thing," he said. He looked over at Babe, who lifted a shoulder, coming to get his purse.

Stasia looked up and down the row, then over at Matthias.

"Look, this has been fun, but I ought to get home, now."

At some point, her father's tolerance really would run out, particularly in a new city.

"Four days," Colin said. "Pretty new to be running around a city by yourself."

"I'm a big girl," Stasia answered.

"Meet me tomorrow," Jasper said. "I'll take you of a tour of the city."

She reflexively wanted to reject it. She wasn't looking for friends, just now - pouting about not being in Birch was still too satisfying - and she didn't like it when people spontaneously showed an interest in her. It was suspicious.

On the other hand, Jasper had a mind in there that was... intriguing. He was reading her, even now, and he dropped his head an inch.

"Consider it me acting in the interests of the king," he said, and she rolled her jaw forward.

"Even knowing that I have no influence over my father and his choices?" Stasia asked. The corner of his mouth came up.

"I must be a great fool, then," he said. "Because I'm going to do it anyway."

She smiled back, then turned for the door. Matthias stepped in front of her.

"Shouldn't someone escort her home?" he asked.

He looked over her shoulder and Stasia followed his glance, finding all eyes on Babe. He shook his head, rolling the soft leather of his purse between his thumb and crooked forefinger.

"No," he said. "No, she's fine."

She met his eye and he nodded.

The lift had impressed him.

She wonder what he'd inferred from it, but she didn't ask. Not having a babysitter take her back to Alyssia's house was worth not pursuing it.

She turned back and Matthias moved aside with a small, friendly smile.

"Tomorrow, here," Jasper called. "Lunchtime."

She held up a hand in acknowledgment.

Going to the door, she paused, finding the debris of the night's fight piled just outside of it. She stuck her hand outside, finding an iron sconce holding up a lamp there beside the door, and she grabbed the sconce, swinging to the brick wall to the side and banking off of it with two feet to land beyond the mess.

She went on, enjoying the night air and the smell of the river, genuinely happy for the first time in weeks.

She wore her dragonskin into town the next day, knowing that the purple of it would attract attention, but feeling more confident in it. Schotzli was happy to be out, and they made their way more slowly, watching the day-people out doing business and trade, socializing and begging and existing.

Verida was a crowded city, during the day, particularly as she made her way past the castle and into the industrial district she'd passed the night before.

The liveryman turned her away, claiming that no amount of silver could change the fact that he was out of stalls, so she rode all the way to the bar, tying Schotzli and standing in the doorway of the bar. She found Jasper sitting in the same corner table as before, with Matthias.

"Two for the price of one," Stasia observed, and Jasper stood.

"Good afternoon," he said. "The king sends his regards."

"You've spoken to him since last night?" Stasia asked, and he shook his head.

"No, but I did speak to the head of taxes and the leader of the merchant's association, and both of them are quite interested in you. When the court is interested in you, it's very accurate to say that the king sends his regards."

Stasia twisted her mouth, then indicated with her head.

"I've got my horse out here and the livery stable is full up. You got any ideas?"

Jasper grunted and came to look, smiling.

"That's a nice animal," he said. "From Kirfall?"

"Bred in Boton," Stasia answered.

He nodded, going past her to admire Schotzli.

Matthias stood in the doorway next to her.

"You drafted, or you need a tour of the kingdom, too?" Stasia asked him, and he shrugged.

"Jasper is taking me under his wing," the kid said. "Showing me what it's like to be a squad leader in the King's Guard."

Stasia would have guessed the kid was sixteen or seventeen. Lanky and taller than she was, already, he was set to be the tallest of the guards in his group when his bones finally stopped stretching. The heft to his shoulders suggested he was going to be a strong man, too, though fine-boned enough that he would never have the sturdiness of figure that Babe had.

"And this is really what you want to be doing today?" Stasia asked him, and he shrugged again.

"I'm on duty," he said. "I do what Jasper tells me to."

She frowned.

"I thought the King's Guard stood around by the walls and made sure no one looked at them funny," Stasia said, and Matthias smiled with genuine humor, if too unconfident just yet to actually respond honestly.

"Those are the palace guard," he said. "Same uniform, different job."

"And what does a King's Guard do?" Stasia asked, and he looked at her funny.

"Do you really not know any of this, or are you making fun of me?" he asked.

"Palace guard is in charge of ground. King's Guard is in charge of *interests*," Jasper answered, turning away from Schotzli. The mare had adored him immediately, which made no small impression on Stasia. "And she's not making fun of you. They don't have a king in Boton."

"Really?" Matthias asked. She shook her head.

"Pretty sure you're a bunch of ignorant cretins, thinking that putting one man in charge of the whole place is a good idea," Stasia said. "We've got a parliament and a system of elections within the parliament to determine committees of leadership."

Matthias blinked at her, and Jasper grinned.

"And that sounds like an awful lot of a shell game, to us," Jasper said. "Too many places to hide graft. Everybody can see the king, anybody can ask what he's been up to and get a reasonable answer."

"And what has the king been up to?" Stasia asked. "Any news about the queen?"

It was pulling his chain, just to see what would happen, but he looked at her with sharp - though not unkind - eyes.

"I know you don't know it, but that was a personal question, not a question of state. Like asking a man if he and his wife are trying to conceive in the midst of negotiation over the price of fish."

"Both relationships are possible," Stasia said, and he nodded.

"But the king is a symbol of state. That is his job. It was an inappropriate question, even if Menda didn't ask it directly. It's information that everyone wants right now, and they're on edge enough that they're willing to go outside of normal social boundaries to get it."

He motioned to Schotzli.

"You can bring her with us. We can put her up at the guard house stable for the afternoon and it won't inconvenience anyone."

"You're sure?" Stasia asked. "I can find another livery with directions."

"I said it and I meant it," Jasper said. "Come on, now."

She untied Schotzli and fell into step with Jasper, Matthias walking on his other side.

"You appreciate horses," she said to Jasper.

"Very much," he agreed. "More than once, I've found that having the right mount is the difference between life and death."

She nodded.

"That's why I brought her," Stasia said. "She's the most important thing I have."

He looked over at her again.

"She's got good bones," he said. "And it's clear you keep her in good shape, though I can see she's lost some muscle at sea. Ought to get her out to the country for some longer rides on good ground, if you can find a noble who will let you on their property."

"People don't say no to me very much," Stasia said, and he smiled, glancing over at the dragonskin.

"I can see that," he said. "Unusual for a woman of your standing to not be in a dress. Two days in a row, no less."

"There are women in the guard in pants," Stasia said. "And women out at the docks."

"Yes," Jasper said. "No one is going to tell you that you can't wear pants because you're a woman. Not here. They will tell you that you can't wear pants if you have money, though. That you ought to find a seamstress who will make a dress to your liking."

"Are there no members of the guard with money?" Stasia asked.

"Not commonly, no," Jasper said. "Whether there has ever been an overlap between money and women within the guard, I couldn't say, but I doubt it. There are better lives for women who can choose them."

"But not the men," Stasia said. He looked over at her, evaluating her again, then smiled.

"No, I suspect that most of the men who walk away from money... are acting with just as much revolt as you are. It's just that women are seldom permitted to rebel like that."

It was bold. Stasia sensed it, even without knowing the rules of behavior in Verida.

Boldness that wanted an answer. Would she rebuff his boldness and emphasize the station of wealth, or would she answer it in kind, a form of solidarity with this... very intelligent man.

"My father has two older daughters," she said. "They married well. His empire will go to them when he dies, and I will be left with... well, likely with a guardianship under one of my brothers in law, truly a spinstress, and one at the mercies of a man who married one of my sisters, no less."

"Better choose well," Matthias said, and Stasia frowned.

"Choose what?" she asked.

"Which brother," Matthias said.

"She probably won't get to choose," Jasper said. "Her father will assign it in his will."

"Can't women inherit?" Matthias asked. "I thought women could inherit property."

"They can," Jasper said, glancing at Stasia. "And for a lot of smaller inheritances, here in Verida, it's normal to split among all of your children regardless of gender." He looked at Matthias again. "But for active businesses, they're mostly going to go to sons who can run them."

"There are women merchants," Matthias said, still confused.

"She's from Kirfall," he said. "They don't… really have women merchants like we do."

Stasia blinked.

There were women who ran market stalls in Boton, but the way he said it, like there was a significant difference between Boton and Verida… there was something important to that.

"Here," he said, motioning. Matthias ran over to raise a wooden crossbeam at the gap in a wooden palisade and Stasia led Schotzli through into a courtyard where a number of guardsmen were talking.

"This way," Jasper said, taking her into a small stable. It wasn't anywhere near as formal or luxurious as the one on the Gormands' property, but it had a warmer, healthier feel to it. Sweet-smelling straw was strewn about everywhere, and a cat strolled past in a saucy sort of way.

Stasia was too busy admiring the stable and the way it smelled despite the humidity and the heat to immediately notice the horses.

The moment she noticed the horses, though, she forgot about the smells.

Matthias offered to take Schotzli's reins as Stasia stopped dead, staring at the most beautiful animal she'd ever laid eyes on.

She loved Schotzli. That wasn't going to change. Not ever. That horse was *hers* and had been for most of her life. But this animal…

The stallion whuffed at her, offering to smell her head, and she stepped forward to let him lip at her hair.

Reaching up over her head, she couldn't have found his ears with her fingers unless he dropped his head some. She wasn't sure her arms would go all the way around his neck.

"Wow," she breathed.

"They're bred up in the hills," Jasper said, appreciating her reaction. He went to lean against the wall and crossed his arms. "Cost a year's wages or more, but we keep a full force of them. They can carry a man in full armor, wearing a full set of armor themselves, and still go over an obstacle as tall as you."

She scratched the horse's chest and he dropped his face to look her in the eye, then pushed his head against hers and turned away to go see if any oats had magically appeared in his feedbox.

"You have more than one?" Stasia asked.

"That's Alfred," Jasper said. "The next one along is Sophie, then Sable, then Gladys and Peter."

Stasia walked along, finding four more horses of extraordinary size in the next four stalls. Each of them was friendly to her in the way of a big dog, too confident to be afraid or insecure.

Peter was a beautiful split-color stallion, black, tan, and white, with a mane that went almost to his knees.

"This is a war-horse?" Stasia asked. "He's beautiful."

"We'd cut the mane back, but someone got the superstitious idea that his power comes from the mane, so now we just have to get one of the newbies in here to braid it all up when he goes out."

"I bet that takes forever," Stasia said, entranced.

"Just the way you'd guess," Jasper answered. "Especially how much the big guy likes to roll."

"Oh," Stasia said, imagining what a spectacle that must have been.

Jasper came over with a carrot for Sable, who had clearly been expecting it, then handed another to Stasia.

"They say I'm a pushover," he said. "But they're the best backup you could ask for, out there."

Stasia nodded. She could imagine.

She went along further, finding horses of much more normal stature and then Schotzli in a stall, tucked into a half-measure of grain.

"She didn't need that," Stasia said. Jasper shrugged.

"Horses that come in eat," he said. "They're working animals. They deserve it."

"This is your doing, isn't it?" Stasia asked, and he nodded, smiling.

"The guard always took good care of them, but I might have tweaked a few policies when they were mine to change."

She sucked on her lips, then smiled.

"Thank you."

He put an arm out.

"We have a tour to get to," he said, and she nodded, following him back out into the sunlight. Matthias was just behind them.

They went around the crossbar and back out onto the street, Stasia feeling light and happy as they walked.

"You were saying something about inheritance," she said after a moment. "How it's different here."

"Mmm," he said. "It's bigger than that, but yes."

Stasia waited for his explanation, but instead he walked across the road to look down at the river.

"Wolfram River," he said. "Comes down out of the Wolfram Mountains, the spine of the world and the wellspring of magic."

"So the river is magic?" Stasia asked, and he shrugged.

"It might be. I don't know. It could be there's magic *in* the river. It isn't really something that humans understand. Like trying to explain the nature of light to someone without eyes. They might be able to feel it sometimes, but we can't understand the nature of magic. What we know is that the mountains are the source of it, and it is tied to the city by the river."

He lifted his face, looking across the width of the river at the castle directly across from them.

"Castle Wyndam," he said. "Home of the queen and king, place of lodging to the king's advisors and court, heart of Veridan government."

Stasia waited, finding after a moment that he was watching her.

"What?" she asked.

"We always refer to the queen and king," he said. "In that order. Because in Verida, they come in that order. The queen is the monarch of the city, while the king is the head of state. It is her line that defines who will be the next monarch, and each queen chooses the king."

"That's interesting…" Stasia said slowly, not getting it.

"In Verida, women have more power than anywhere else in the known world," he said. "There are stories in the fae cities on the back of the continent of true queendoms, but here we have queens who are the legitimization of power. Without the queen's backing, the king would just be another man."

She blinked at this, surprised.

"The royal line is female," she said, and he nodded.

"It's more than that, though," he said. "The queen doesn't *marry* the king. She names him, and he serves at her leisure. Most kings have reached the end of their rule by death, either of pestilence, violence, or age, but a few have been removed and replaced. Lady Wyndam, the noblewoman who founded Verida, understood that being king didn't neatly coincide with being a good husband and father, and she detested the idea of putting both roles onto the same shoulders, so she split it, as she quite well could. To my knowledge, no other civilization on the planet has done as she did, but she did it. The queen's husband has no title. He lives in the castle and takes on whatever industry suits him. They have been blacksmiths and soldiers, managers and advisors. Her eldest daughter will become queen when she dies, and she will name the king within a reasonable period, during which the kingdom will be administered as best as possible by the old king's court and staff, but she does not need to marry until she is certain of her husband, nor must she *wait* to marry until her mother dies. Queen Constance named King Rupert more than thirty years ago, and the kingdom has prospered greatly under their governance."

"But… her only job is to pick the king," Stasia said, and Jasper smiled and shook his head.

"Her only job within the *state* is to pick the king," he answered. "Her role within the *kingdom* is much more whatever she defines it to be. There is a natural… tension there that is often good for Verida."

Stasia blinked again, turning to face the castle once more.

"How interesting," she said.

"So the university here is the Queen's University," he said. "The court is filled with women of power and intellect who are there of their own merit and virtue, not as handmaidens nor as wives of important men. There are women merchants down at the docks seeing off ships. There are women in elite units of soldiers, up in the mountains, fighting the war…"

"The war," Stasia said. "No one talks or acts like there's a *war* going on."

He nodded, turning away from the river and setting off at a working pace.

"No, they wouldn't," he said. "Most of them don't shoulder the cost of it. It's the poor men who need the wage who sign up to go up into the mountains, and many of them make a fine career of it. You won't hear me bemoan it. But within Verida, life is often unaware of the war, outside of the soldiers here on leave or rest and training."

"Who are you at war with?" Stasia asked.

"The mountains," Matthias said softly, and Jasper nodded.

"The fae," he said. "We've invaded a space that may very well be sacred to them, knowing as little as we do about the river and the magic tied to it. They've been trying to push us into the ocean for as long as Verida has existed."

"But they say that there are fae living here in the city," Stasia said.

"There are," Jasper agreed, coming to a bridge and setting across it. "Pixies live here openly. Low elves are... basically everywhere. There are a few high elves, but they hide. The war is with most of the rest of them, though. It's a big, very complicated world up there in the mountains, and it's easier to call it the war with the fae rather than talking about all the tribes of stone elves and the considerations for how the hengewolves are going to react and..." He waved a hand, cutting himself off. "It's frankly all fascinating, but not the purpose of today."

"And what is the purpose of today?" Stasia asked.

"I want to take you to the castle," he said. "Introduce you to the head of the merchant's association. See if there's anything that he can do for you..."

"I told you that I'm not of any use to you, influencing how my dad is going to act," Stasia asked. "He never says no to me, but he doesn't tell me about his business nor his decisions. He told me we were coming *here* basically three weeks before we got on the ship. Found out he'd been discussing it with my sister for almost a year. I'm his *spare* daughter. He's got his two *used* daughters, and they're *very* useful. I'm the spare, I'm the albatross, and... Daddy *loves* me. But the part of his life that is even *aware* of me is minuscule. You shouldn't look at me for any help getting him to stay or go or balance a ball on his nose. The king may send his regards to my father via his advisors and consultants and jesters and whatever, but my *father* does not send his regards through me."

They reached the far side of the bridge and Jasper lifted his chin.

"Where did you learn to lift a coinpurse?" he asked.

"From a guy in the market," Stasia said. "Saw him do it, gave him a coin, he had me doing it… two weeks later, maybe."

"Who else have you paid like that?" Jasper asked, and Stasia snorted.

"Everybody," she said. "I learned how to breed pigs one summer. Don't even know why I decided to do *that*, but I did. I know fourteen styles of dance. I speak six languages. I can paint. I refuse to learn needlepoint, because that would just be giving up. I can mend my own stockings, when I wear them, and I can forge my own daggers, with the right tools. Not *good* daggers, sure, but pointy ones. Oh, and I can climb the castle wall without anybody seeing me do it."

Jasper smiled.

"In broad daylight?" he asked.

She shrugged.

"If you give me an hour, yes," she said.

"An hour."

"An hour," Stasia affirmed.

"Show me."

She frowned.

"No. I'd get in trouble. *Real* trouble."

"Where would you do it?" Jasper asked, and she considered what she'd seen.

"North wall," she said. "Between the second and third extensions."

"You know about the extensions," Jasper said, and she shrugged.

"You can see it in the stonework."

He smiled, a slow, spreading shape that had an awful lot of ideas in it.

"Matthias, you know where the third extension starts on the north wall?" he asked.

"I can ask Bartamaeus," Matthias answered, and Jasper nodded.

"Have him show you," he said. "And then stand there. If she comes up and over the wall, make sure that she walks back out with you, without being stopped."

Matthias boggled.

"You want her to break into the castle?" he asked.

"The palace guard is accustomed to calm times," Jasper said. "They've gotten lax. Where they fall short, the interests of the king are compromised. This is a part of our job. Go do it."

Matthias hesitated a long time, then finally turned and left. He had his hair up in a stylized tail today, woven close against his head where it wouldn't have been grab-able in the event of a fight.

"You believe he can get me out of there if I pop up out of nowhere?" Stasia asked.

"I believe he needs to prove himself," Jasper answered. "And this is a test that is fully up to his capabilities."

Stasia rolled her chin to the side.

"You know that me getting in trouble *inside* the castle is a really bad way to start things off with my father," she said.

Jasper nodded.

"I understand," he said. "But if you aren't of use to me as an emissary of your father's business empire, do you disagree with me using your other talents, as I find them?"

"I do if you don't pay me for them," Stasia said.

He looked at her carefully once more.

"Yes, of course," he said. "It's only fair. You're taking a risk and using skills that are… potentially unusual. I will be sorely disappointed if you fail straight away," Jasper said.

"Merchant's rule," Stasia answered. "Half up front, half on delivery. Six coppers."

It was a trivial sum, but so was climbing the wall. It meant something, and she saw him adjust to the point of it.

He reached into his pocket and produced the three coppers - they'd spent more on that on drinks the night before, easily - and she accepted them, tucking them away into her purse and then walking with him along the front of the castle.

"This side is better-guarded," Stasia said. "More prestige up here. More people to see when your mind wanders. More awareness of the actual potential for threats."

"The south side will be, too," Jasper agreed. "The market across the way attracts huge crowds of people, and many of them are known to be of less-than-noble intent. If a threat will come, it certainly looks like it would come from that direction."

Stasia nodded.

"And the west?" she asked.

"Thinly patrolled. Would have been my first idea, but it's largely private homes back that way, very wealthy ones, and they have open windows and long noses."

Stasia liked the turn of phrase, tucking it away for later.

"What was your reason for picking the north?" Jasper asked. "Other than that the parade guards are all awarded river-facing slots?"

"I saw it," Stasia said. "So I already knew I could do it."

"You think about this kind of thing," he said, and she nodded.

"I wander around big cities at night by myself," she said. "So long as Schotzli is safely in a reputable barn, I'm free to do as I like. I just have to be able to get away."

"Aah," he said slowly. "So the intent is not ingress but egress."

She nodded.

"Yes. Though sometimes I just see a challenging wall and start charting a course up it."

"It would almost be trivial from horseback," Jasper said.

"I thought that, too," Stasia said. "There aren't men with crossbows up there somewhere, are they?"

He shrugged nonchalantly.

"You were the one who said you could do it."

"I said I could climb the wall," she said.

"You said you could do it without getting caught," he said. "Are you backing out? I can go in and get Matthias if you like."

"No, I'm not backing out," Stasia said, finding that she was grinning. "Tell me more about magic."

"I don't know what there is to say. We can't *do* magic, you and I."

"But can we use it?" Stasia asked. He stopped and she walked past him two strides before she realized he wasn't going to start walking again until she faced him.

"That is one of the most insightful questions I've ever heard anybody ask," he said. "And I was told that women aren't educated beyond the age of *nine* in Boton."

"They aren't educated *formally* beyond the age of nine in Boton," she said. "In Birch, they aren't educated formally at all. They're *tutored*. And a great number of my friends can't read as a result, because their mothers thought that reading novels would rot their minds. It's a shame, really."

"But not you," he said, and she shook her head, frowning playfully.

"Oh, no. Not even Minstrel Fielding's *spare* daughter would make entree into the world without the ability to balance the books and read a bill of goods," she said.

"You have an able mind," he said. "It's a shame it wasn't supported as it might have been."

"Who's to say it hasn't been?" Stasia answered. "That I didn't go to your *queen's* university? You think the tutelage there is more insightful than what you can learn from an old man at any bar in town?"

"A man lives to see the word *old* in this city, he's certainly seen a lot," Jasper acknowledged. "But you could have had formal training."

"What do you think the languages were?" she asked. "I mean, apart from pirate shorthand and thieves' sign language, I didn't *choose* any of them. And three of the dances were pure torture."

He set off again finally, shaking his head.

"I can't argue with that," he said. "We can absolutely use magic, so long as it doesn't *take* magic to actualize it. There are pixies and human merchants all over the castle marketplace who sell magic powders, magic potions, magic *weapons*. Pixie magic is temporary. It will turn your hair blond for a night, or fix the pain from an injury or a headache. Elven magic is capable of being permanent, but it is much more often forged, because it is rarer and often harder to prove whether an item is authentically enchanted. With pixie magic, your headache goes away or it doesn't. Your eyes turn purple or they don't. With elven magic, the sword may or may not shatter in battle. You aren't going to know until it doesn't, and even then you don't know if it was because it was authentic magic or simply good blacksmithing."

"Is there like… a *menu* of things that magic can do, or if you found someone who was very good at it, is it more like working with a seamstress who can do just about anything so long as she can get her hands on the right fabrics?" Stasia asked, and Jasper laughed quietly.

"That sounds like a dangerous question," he said. "Fortunately, the answer isn't anywhere near so dangerous. Pixies will work on household staffs if you are very permissive about everything they do that isn't related to their duties. But they will only rarely work magic in that role. They make things that they have commonly traded amongst themselves for generations, and there's a staggering diversity of what they're capable of doing, but it isn't a custom order situation. Perhaps they might be able to *modify* a spell they already sell, but… They don't work for hire. They sell a product."

"Maybe no one has asked them right," Stasia answered, looking up at the wall.

It was a long way up.

Not scary. Stasia didn't know how high she would have to go, to feel afraid of a wall for its height. But it was extra work, when you were up high enough that just falling back onto your feet would leave you unable to run away.

"I'll pay you an extra copper to tell me what you're seeing," Jasper said, his tone friendly. Almost playful. She suspected that playful wasn't in his repertoire, but he was trying for her benefit.

"Have you ever killed someone?" Stasia asked.

"That's a very cold question to ask," he said. "I put a young man through a window for asking me something so witless, not a week ago."

"No you didn't," Stasia said. "Not unless someone else had already *gone* through the window and you were just throwing him out an open hole. You wouldn't risk killing someone over something so trivial as bad social grace."

"Do you know something about bad social grace?" he asked, and she grinned.

There.

The line between the blue stones and the gray ones. It was subtle, but someone had started going to a different quarry, or had stayed with the same quarry but been buying stone that had been cut out of a different, later section of it. The dressing work was different, too. The stones fit very well to each other, on each side of the transition, but there was a mismatch of style that ran a jagged line up the wall that she could exploit.

Unfortunately, the guard for this section of the wall was not fifteen feet away from it.

She needed to either time her moment for when he was *deeply* involved in his own thoughts - which could take all day to evaluate and exploit - or a moment when he was engaged in something very interesting in another direction.

The problem with taking in everything at once was that it was very visible that you were doing it.

She would need another pass. Coming from the opposite direction, she could easily see what was available to work with in his sight line, but then she would have to come past *again* and set in motion whatever was intended to distract him and get past him in time to get over the wall. Something distracting, but not so *large* a distraction as to capture the interest of the next guard down the wall, about fifty feet.

Three times past him in her purple dragonskin had the potential to attract his notice, even as slack-jawed as he was, standing there watching a wall. Not watching a wall, exactly, but the house across the street from him was little more than a wall with a door in it.

"Don't suppose you're interested in being an accomplice," Stasia said without optimism.

"Not at all," Jasper said. "The interest is in a lone individual managing this. A team of experienced thieves would have a very different goal and a very different time of it."

"You worried about an assassin?" Stasia asked and he hesitated, then nodded.

"Nothing specific," he said very quickly. "I give you my word, I have no *specific* information to indicate that there is a threat to the king. But a lone individual making a decision to end the king's life is one of my ongoing considerations, yes."

"I understand," Stasia asked. "How do you want me to kill him?"

"Don't even joke," Jasper said sincerely, and she swallowed, looking over at the castle wall.

"This is a fine game," she said. "I'm having a great time, I'll be honest. But if you want your information to be useful, you need to tell me how you want me to kill the king, once I get to that side of the wall. If it involves something I need to carry, I have to account for it."

He sighed.

"Very well," he said. "But first, your absolute word that you mean no one any harm with this exercise."

"None," Stasia said. "If you want me to poison him, I'll take a rock that I cannot crush. If you want me to use a crossbow, three sticks that I can't allow to break. It's probably even best…" She took off her daggers and handed them to him. "I'm sure Matthias will have no problem convincing anyone that he has everything under control, but probably best I'm completely unarmed, wouldn't you say?"

"Perhaps this is unwise," Jasper said.

"Oh, no, I have your money," Stasia said. "I'm going for it. Just making sure I deliver the product you're most interested in. How would you do it? If you could get in there and you knew everything about the place that you do?"

His eyes went distant for a long time as they walked. The longer gap between passes didn't bother Stasia any.

"Poison is a risk that comes from someone familiar," he said. "Food preparation is too continuous and too broad for an outside attack. Long-range weapons are unreliable and don't require breaking into the castle. If you were going to use a crossbow, you'd do it when the king leaves the castle."

"You permit that?" Stasia asked, and he smiled grimly.

"I work for the king," he said. "Not the other way around."

"All right," she said.

"No, it has to be a blade. Probably a short blade. There's a long way to go from the outer wall to the inner chambers, but preventing the first step protects the rest. You don't need to carry anything special with you."

She nodded.

She accelerated to turn onto the next road running away from the castle and walked for a way, then turned back, going back the way they'd come.

The guards were just… They were *so* bored.

She would need… twenty-five seconds to reach the top of the wall. If anybody saw her in that time, the guards would be on her. She measured the pace of the pedestrians up ahead, finding that if she and Jasper sped up a bit, the woman coming toward them would pass them just as they got to the mismatched stones and would be less likely to notice Stasia behaving abnormally.

"If you want to watch, you should stop here," she said, indicating a doorway. "Don't draw attention."

"Good luck," he said, and Stasia grinned, going on with quick feet. She passed the woman just when she meant to and glanced over her shoulder to find the road clear all the way to the back of the castle. The sun was just past overhead and the slight misalignment of the castle - forced by the shape of the river - meant that the entire wall was in shadow, but the soldiers were in sun.

This was her moment.

It was absolutely exhilarating.

She stepped into the weedy section of untrampled cobble, putting her foot up onto the largest of the jutting mismatches, then jumped, catching a ledge well overhead with her fingertips. Toes and fingers, stay in close against the wall. Use the whole hand as a wedge, either closed or open, where gaps presented themselves, and keep moving. Momentum fixes small mistakes, but she didn't make any mistakes. It was no more than seven motions up the wall, the mellow color of her cape covering the purple dragonskin as she moved. She pulled the cape up over top of her as she hit the top of the wall and lay flat.

She didn't want to stay up here too long, but she hadn't seen the inside of the castle courtyard before; she needed a few moments to make a plan.

She saw Matthias's head below her, and if the wall was any shorter, she would have just poured herself over the edge down next to him and called it a victory. The problem was that she couldn't land that and walk afterwards, and she knew it.

She needed to climb, and that was going to take time and visibility and handholds that she'd never laid eyes on.

She scanned quickly, counting faces, counting faces, looking for her first toehold. She probably only needed one. If she could get her toes solidly into the stone… and this side ought to be easier. They would have been fitting the outside to match up and shouldn't have been that concerned about the inside.

She should have tied her hair up better.

She'd gotten excited and not planned this part out before she'd gone for it.

Two toe-holds, different levels.

She could make it from there.

Faces.

She picked her moment, the seconds ticking past, and she dropped over the side, the shape of a shadow, a cloud passing across the sun. Smooth and quick, down the rockwork and on her feet next to Matthias.

He looked over at her.

"I was beginning to think you'd backed out," he said.

"Never," Stasia answered with a grin.

He motioned for the front gate and they started for it, Stasia's heart still racing like a purr.

"Guards," a woman's voice called. "Guards, that woman just came over the wall. In the purple. Seize her!"

"No wait," Matthias said, his voice abandoning him as he stepped away from her reflexively. Stasia looked at him indignantly, but she could hardly blame him for it. The entire courtyard changed shape, focusing on Stasia.

Stepping back across her, he put his arm out.

"Wait," he said, "it's not what you think."

It was a strong motion, but it wasn't enough to forestay the guards who set upon Stasia, grabbing at her arms and twisting them behind her back. A woman was walking down the wide front stairs of the castle, holding her skirts out in front of her and looking intently at Stasia as Matthias tussled with the guards.

"She's… with us," he grunted, trying to get back over to her. "With Jasper."

"Your Highness," a voice called. "Your Highness, a mistake. A mistake. Queen Constance, may I present to you Stacy Fielding, daughter of Minstrel Fielding."

The guards collectively hesitated as Jasper came running across the courtyard to the midpoint between the handsome older woman and the cluster of guards surrounding Stasia. Matthias wrenched the men off of Stasia, holding her elbow with an excited pressure that would have otherwise been uncomfortable, but just now was more affirming than anything.

"Come," the woman said, motioning. Jasper looked back at Matthias and nodded, and Matthias escorted Stasia forward with several of the more senior-looking palace guards following closely.

They walked to within normal conversation distance, the palace guards searching Stasia quickly and indicating she was unarmed.

That had been a good call.

"Constance," Jasper said. "I can explain."

"Is she really Fielding's daughter?" the woman asked, the tone of a woman who was very, very accustomed to being obeyed.

"Yes, mum," Jasper said.

She looked over as another guard, an older man with a salt-and-pepper beard, jogged down the steps and across the courtyard to them. He motioned one of the guards away and the other, angry-looking man with shockingly blond hair came to stand flanking the queen with him as Matthias continued to hold Stasia's elbow. She suspected he'd forgotten he was doing it, but his grip was really strong.

"Minstrel Fielding's daughter," the palace guard said to the older guard.

"Just broke into the castle," the older guard said with disbelief.

"Yes sir, at my instigation," Jasper said. "She told me that she'd seen that she could do it, and you know I've been wanting to run a test for some time, now. The courtyard is not secured, and I just demonstrated it."

"Using Minstrel Fielding's daughter," the older guard said, his voice rising without rising.

This was another man who was used to the mantle of authority. His beard was visibly streaking with gray, but his hair was light brown. He had sun-worn skin, but he was still very muscular and straight-postured.

"She has unusual skills," Jasper said. "Clearly. If not for the eagle eyes of the queen, she would have walked back out with Matthias unquestioned."

Matthias nodded, finally dropping Stasia's arm as he remembered himself.

"No one has laid eyes on the Fielding daughter," the older palace guard said. "You have brought in an impostor."

Now there was a funny thought. Without her father actually vouching for her, could Stasia prove the relation? She wasn't sure.

The queen was watching her with very sharp eyes.

Exciting eyes.

This was a woman who knew more than anyone else.

The idea of arrest, questioning, being in *really* big trouble with her father was completely overshadowed by the excitement of standing in front of a woman of this *magnitude*. It was visceral, the reaction of awe and admiration, but that paled to the sense of wanting to sit down in front of a fire with two cups of mulled wine and talk about *everything*. Oh, the things that those eyes could tell her.

"I'm insulted," Jasper said. "I put out inquiries last night after we met her and learned that she disappeared from a party at the

Gormand house wearing just such a costume as she was in last night and wears yet today. I believe all parties present will recognize the *distinctiveness* of that costume?"

"I trust you, Jasper," the queen said, holding up her hand as the palace guard began to argue. "I have spoken," she said sternly, and the man fell - sullenly - quiet.

"I *trust* you," the older guard said, "but I do not endorse this decision. You should have cleared it with myself and Petrault first."

"He has tipped off his guards more than once when I have challenged them," Jasper said. "You needed to know that this was possible, sir. No one believes me, but my men see it with their own eyes. This girl, four days new to the city, told me unprompted out of her own mouth that she could sneak into the castle undetected. The queen is not always available to keep watch."

"Unprompted," the blond guard said disdainfully. "I doubt that."

"It was," Matthias said. "I heard it, too."

Stasia wanted no part of these politics. She was mesmerized watching the queen as she listened to her men argue in front of her.

"You need to control your men, Ben," the blond guard - Petrault - said. "If you won't, I will take it before the king and we will *resolve* it."

"It's their autonomy and ability to react to real situations that…" the older guard started, but the queen's hand ticked and he fell silent, lifting his chin.

"Gentlemen," the queen said. "You will discipline your men as you see fit, and you will work to resolve the issues that today's incident has exposed. But I am not going to tire this girl with your long-winded ways of doing so. Miss Fielding, if you would."

She put her arm out and Stasia realized half a beat late that it was an invitation. She wasn't entirely sure what she was supposed to do as the queen turned away from her, and she shot a desperate glance at Jasper, who motioned a deep scooping motion with his flat forearm.

Aha.

She went to put her arm under the queen's, and the woman leaned on her for just a hint of support as they recrossed the courtyard and started up the stairs toward the castle.

"Jasper and Matthias won't get in trouble, will they?" Stasia asked. "I don't think they did anything wrong. I was just talking about how easy it would be to climb the wall while nobody was looking…"

"No child," the queen cut in gently. "Benjamin and Petrault are peers at court, neither has authority over the other, and while they do go out of their way to undermine and embarrass each other, the king knows that keeping both of them strong is in his own best interest. And Benjamin will fight for his men. Your friends will weather this well, and Jasper may earn a very quiet commendation."

"It wouldn't be that hard to fix it," Stasia said, hearing it even as the giddiness poured out of her and unable to contain it. The thrill of permitted breaking-in and the ongoing rush of being captured and released just mixed with the presence of this *woman* in a way that she didn't understand, and the words kept coming even as her well-proven conditioning as a wealthy man's daughter knew better. "Just some mortar on top of the stones at the borders, and not even I could climb them. Well, and the one crack up near the top, but you don't even have to mortar that, because you can't reach it unless you started from horseback."

The woman looked over at her and Stasia finally fell silent. It was like the look gave her permission, strangely, and Constance smiled.

"Tell me, child, why do you know of things like mortaring stone and climbing castle walls? Your sister, Lady Gormand, has been presented to me, and I found none of those things in her."

"No," Stasia said. "She's a good daughter. I'm something else."

"I disagree, but let's not digress. We have heard many stories of your father, and Rupert and the court have been very eager to meet him."

"You're not married to the king," Stasia said, and the queen's eyebrows went up, then she shook her head slightly.

"Does that disturb you?" she asked.

"No, I think it's… smart," Stasia said. "You wouldn't marry your business partner, but that doesn't make them not the best business partner."

"Most of your countrymen cannot fathom our system of government," the queen said, pausing as a pair of guards opened the grand front doors of the castle. She waited until the doors were all the way still to step through. "You elucidate it quite elegantly."

"I don't really like the idea of having a queen," Stasia said.

"Fortunately, being queen does not require your approval," Constance answered with a rich, quiet humor.

They walked across a wide court room with a pair of ornate thrones up on a slight rise of stairs. Stasia stared at them as they went past, and the queen paused, looking up at them.

"I used to think that that was the highest honor of my role, here in the castle," she said. "To name the king and sit next to him as he presides over the public. I think differently, now."

"What do you think, now?" Stasia asked.

"Come," she said. "This is where your friends will find you when they resolve their differences for today."

She went to a much more modest door and paused.

"I hate to tell you, but by tradition, I am not supposed to open doors for myself. The first servant or guard who sees us will come running, but I have sometimes stood at a door for a quarter of an hour, in quieter sections of the house."

"I hope your bathroom doesn't have a door, then," Stasia said. "I think that's silly."

"I do, too," the woman said.

"I can open it, though, right?" Stasia asked.

"Yes, of course."

Stasia left the queen to go open the door, holding it as the woman glided through.

Stasia followed, finding herself in a dim but comfortable room with stone chairs around a large table that appeared to have been cut from a single tree. There were fourteen chairs around the table and one in the corner.

"That is my most honored role," Constance said, indicating the chair in the corner.

"What?" Stasia asked as the queen pulled a chair along a dense rug to sit down at the table, indicating the next one over.

"This is the table of state, where King Rupert sits with his advisors and his administrators and the key members of court to discuss the kingdom and its needs," she said as Stasia sat down.

"And they make you sit in the corner?" Stasia asked, and the queen smiled.

"Yes," she said. "I am not a member of the state government. I am *outside* of it, and it is a role that I have learned to cherish, because there is a freedom to see the problems without being constrained by the solutions of state. I have symbolic authority and I have considerable resources at my disposal, and I may quietly step in wherever I choose. Sometimes I inform Rupert and sometimes I don't. This is an opportunity to make right wrongs large and small that I do not take for granted."

Stasia looked around the room, considering it.

"I think maybe I understand that," Stasia said.

"How old are you?" Constance asked.

"Twenty-three," Stasia answered, understanding exactly what that told the woman about herself.

"And why aren't you married?" the queen asked her.

"Because I don't need to be," Stasia answered. "There isn't a boy anywhere who can authentically say that he wants to wed me for myself and not my dowry, and frankly there isn't a boy anywhere that I've had anything more than a passing interest in him. Men are dull and they expect me to make myself nothing for them, and my father told me when I came of age that it was my decision."

"Your prospects for marriage are narrowing," Constance said. "Does that concern you? No desire for children?"

"My sister in Birch has three children," Stasia said. "I feel like I speak a different language from them. I don't have any interest in disappearing into motherhood."

The queen frowned.

"Many women will tell you that it's different when they're your own child, as though *possessing* them is what makes the difference. I have observed it is different because they come of your own blood. They have passions and capacities that are naturally fitted to your own, and nurturing those things, often where they would be stunted by others, is quite fulfilling. Building something that will build the future. But it is a presence that it is fine not to regret, if it never exists. Does your father look to settle here? Buy land and engage in active trade?"

"He doesn't tell me," Stasia said.

The woman set her mouth, then nodded.

"Perhaps it is best. You are very new to the city. Tell me, how are you filling your time?"

"Poorly," Stasia said. "I go for rides, but I'm not supposed to leave the Gormand property, and Schotzli likes to run. We hit the boundaries almost immediately. I would like to go out to the country, but they tell me that the land out there is all owned, too, and protectively, and that beyond that there are monsters that I wouldn't understand."

Queen Constance snorted.

"The hill country would not put up any barriers that a woman such as yourself would struggle to overcome, as long as you didn't stumble across something particularly unexpected, but I can understand why they say it. What did you do when you were in Kirfall?"

"Went for long rides, visited friends, went into Boton and just… watched things. Met people. I liked going out to the docks and watching the boats come in."

"Where did you learn to climb like that?" Constance asked.

"From a man that I saw do it," Stasia answered.

"You have a lot of skills like that, don't you?" Constance asked, and Stasia shrugged.

"Am I in trouble?" she asked.

"No," the queen told her, shifting in her chair and settling her hands into her lap. "I very much want your father to choose to remain here. It would be good for Verida, even if you went back to Kirfall on your own. But you are from outside in a multitude of ways, and I sense that you might be able to take action that those constrained to the system would not be able to. It is much to ask of a woman your age, with your life just beginning and all of the opportunities possible, yet, but I'd like you to think about it."

"Think about what, exactly?" Stasia asked.

"Taking on some special roles, from time to time, when someone with an outsider's perspective and skills would be uniquely applicable," she said.

The door opened.

"There you are," Jasper said. "Excuse me, mum."

"Come on, Jasper," Constance said. "Close the door."

He looked back at Matthias standing in the doorway and Matthias took a quick step back to not have the door closed in his face. The queen gave a deep, quiet laugh.

"The young man can join us, but he will have to sit in my chair for the time being."

"Yes, mum," Matthias said, darting through the doorway and giving her a little bow. "Yes, mum. Yes, mum."

He went and sat in the corner, clamping his mouth shut.

"Did someone hit you?" Jasper demanded, coming to kneel in front of Stasia and holding her chin between his thumb and forefinger.

"What?" Stasia asked, and only then placed the trace metallic flavor in her mouth. She licked her lower lip, finding it split and swelling. How had she not noticed *that*?

"I'll have heads for that," Jasper said, and Stasia shook her head quickly, drawing her face away from his hand.

"No, no, I hit it on the way down," she said. She knew exactly when she'd done it, as she worked her tongue over it again. Just hadn't thought about it at the time.

He frowned, but went to sit next to her at the table.

"Is everything out there put to bed?" Constance asked.

"As well as it's going to be, today," Jasper said.

"I understand," the woman said. "As far as this young woman's role in it?"

"Any blame will land on my shoulders," he said. "Though I doubt there will be little enough of that. That you were the one who even noticed her has heaped shame on the palace guard. I actually have hope for the future."

"And we all know how little of that you see, of a day," Constance said.

"Yes, mum," Jasper said.

"Tell me about her," Constance said, indicating Stasia.

"Youngest daughter of Minstrel Fielding, unmarried with no established prospects…" Jasper started fearlessly, and Constance shook her head.

"No, no, tell me what's *interesting* about her."

THE QUEEN'S CHAIR   57

"Oh. She lifted a purse off of Babe last night and even he was impressed. She knows her horses and they like her. Matthias is afraid of her. Colin likes her. She says she speaks pirate shorthand and I believe her."

"I thought as much," Constance said. "She's impressed you as much as she has me. Keep tabs on this one. I may have work for her, and I would like to know that you can find her at need."

"She doesn't come cheap," Jasper said.

"That's right; you still owe me," Stasia said.

"I would expect nothing less of a merchant's daughter," the queen said, then rose. Jasper jolted to his feet and came to put his arm under hers, escorting her to the door.

He opened it seamlessly and she lifted her arm from his to walk out on her own. Jasper looked back at her with an amused smile, then motioned that Matthias was allowed to stand, now.

"Well, well, well," Jasper said, coming to take Stasia's hand and needlessly help her to her feet. "You've caught some very important attention today."

"I have no idea what just happened," Stasia answered, and Jasper nodded.

"I understand that. But something just did."

—◆◇◆◇◆—

Stasia spent most of the next two weeks shopping with her sister.

It was exhausting, but Alyssia couldn't seem to get enough of it, riding into town in a carriage, swanning about in one little shop after another where the seamstress's assistants fed her fruit and wine while the seamstress herself took Stasia's measurements in excruciating detail and brought her books of fabrics while they talked about named dress designs that meant nothing to Stasia. One of the women had drawings of what the dresses would look like when they were done, but Stasia didn't have the ability to imagine herself *in* them, so it didn't matter what she picked. She was tempted to let Alyssia make those decisions, but that could only be worse, so she chose at random.

Alyssia paid for everything with an expansive sense of generosity, talking about how much dressing like a Veridan would improve her social prospects, by which Stasia understood Alyssia meant her marriage prospects.

They got lunch at little cafes east of the castle where the proprietors came out and asked Alyssia about her appetite that day and what her mood was when it came to her wine selection. Alyssia thrived under the attention, but Stasia spent the entire time feeling like the dressed up dolly that Alyssia had held tea parties with throughout their childhoods.

Stasia would have gotten Schotzli out and just gone out riding, disappearing, but she'd made the mistake of mentioning at breakfast the morning after the incident with the queen that Schotzli had lost fitness in the crossing, and Alyssia had promised to put an exercise rider on the horse for a few hours a day to help her get back into form. Nothing Stasia had been able to argue had changed her sister's plan, and thenceforward, Schotzli had never been at the stable when Stasia had gone looking for her.

She'd complained to Minstrel about it, and he'd patted her arm.

"I understand you're chafing under your sister's hospitality," he said. "And I know that all of this has been incredibly difficult for you in many ways. But we are her guests, and you were very rude to her peers the night of the welcoming party…"

"My coming out party," Stasia said. "She's trying to marry me off because she thinks you won't."

"She's right," Minstrel said. "And she's trying to do right by you in the best way she knows how. I'm not going to argue with her on that point because, while it isn't her *decision*, in the final, she is absolutely permitted to do each and every thing that she has done so far, and you are permitted to react, which you *have*.

You have made life here very unpleasant for most everyone, and I haven't intervened when she has come to me complaining, either. You two must work it out using the tools you have available to you, just like you always have."

Finally, the dresses started to show up at the house and Alyssia stopped taking her out to order more.

Surprising as it was, that might have been worse, because then Stasia was trapped at the house or limited to how far she could go on foot. She considered absconding with a carriage, but she didn't think that the stable boys would stretch that far. They'd saddle up Schotzli for her, but to just steal a pair of horses that belonged not to Alyssia but to her husband… that was all the way into trouble, and Stasia knew it.

She wandered the gardens to the property line, then wandered back.

She searched Gevalt's library, finding a few books that were of interest to her and reading them, but the servants kept returning them to the library every time she left for a meal, and she eventually gave up. She had a satchel of paints around here somewhere that she could have dug out, but didn't have anyone to stretch and frame a canvas for her, and painting felt like a partial capitulation, so she didn't do it.

Midway through the third week, her father knocked on the door to her room and announced himself.

"Come in," she said, looking up from a sketch she was doing on a stray piece of paper she'd found in the kitchen. She had an inkling it was the cook's unmade shopping list, but Stasia had swiped it anyway because she just couldn't care anymore. Couldn't do it.

"Are you free this afternoon to come with me into town?" Minstrel asked.

"Are you going to unshackle me from the house and set me free?" Stasia answered, and he frowned.

"You used to be so much more cheerful," he said.

"I used to be so much more free," Stasia answered, sitting up on her bed. "Would you like to choose which of the brand new dresses I wear for our excursion? I warn you, if you choose poorly, you *will* have to take your own carriage."

"She said that she gave you total control over the design of them," Minstrel said, and Stasia snorted.

"She gave me a thousand options of the same thing," she said. "It's just a change of color and buttons."

"They *are* more appropriate for state functions," he said. "You need to get used to that, here. There are traditions that come from the top down in a way that we are unused to, in Boton."

"And they treat women *better* here," Stasia answered. "Alyssia just likes finally being able to tie me down and treat me like her ragdoll."

He sighed.

"Will you go with me this afternoon? Please?"

"Yes, Daddy," Stasia answered.

"Good," he said. "I have business at the docks, but I hope to be back by lunchtime and we can go out after that."

Stasia threw her feet over the side of the bed.

"Can I go with you to the docks?" she asked. "Please?"

"No," he said. "I can't watch over you, and they're foreign to you."

"The docks in Boton were foreign to me the first time I went there, and I was twelve."

"Stasia, there is *magic* here. There are *fae*. This place is very dangerous, and I know that you *feel* comfortable in your own skin and that you don't think that you should be forced to fear anything at all, but your sister is terrified what might happen to you, any time you leave the house."

"How is that different from Birch?" Stasia asked. "She never left the house except in a carriage, there, either."

"Please try not to trouble her any more than you absolutely must," Minstrel said. "She has gone out of her way to an extreme degree to try to be a good hostess to us. I know you can't see it, but she really has."

Stasia sighed and rolled back onto the bed, returning to her drawing.

"I will see you at lunch, then," she answered, hearing her door close.

It was unlike her father, really. He'd invented the idea of the spare daughter, truly raised her independent and allowed to make her own decisions. To help Alyssia keep her captive like this suggested that either he really did believe that Verida was altogether different from Boton or that her sister had managed to change how he felt about his permissiveness.

Alyssia had always been afraid of the outside world. It had been dirty and dangerous from before Stasia's first breath, but when their mother had died, it had become the example that Alyssia had pointed at to prove that the world was always on the verge of toppling over and that something catastrophic was always potentially around the corner.

Stasia had asked her nurse when she was nine or ten what Alyssia had been like when she was truly small, and the woman had given her a sad look.

"She lost a lot of herself when she lost her mother," she'd said, and that was all she'd been willing to say about it.

Stasia stayed in her room through to lunchtime, then went down to the table, finding Minstrel and Gevalt talking while the servant poured them coffee.

They fell silent as Stasia sat, and she felt the pressure her sullen attitude put on the room, but she couldn't find the strength to lift it.

She was a prisoner.

There was no one interesting here who was willing to talk to her - she assumed that at least *some* of the staff had lead interesting lives, but they hustled away from her when she tried to pick up a conversation - and the only people that were anything *like* friends to her so far were basically soldiers and an hour's ride away.

"Where is Alyssia?" Stasia asked as the staff began bringing in the food.

"She is with a friend today," Gevalt said. "She asked me to keep you company for the midday meal."

Stasia gave him a little smile. It didn't mean anything, but she hoped it showed an attempt to be polite.

Minstrel and Gevalt picked up a conversation about politics and trade, and while normally Stasia might have had the capacity to listen in and glean some interesting stories, she was just too moody and put out that Minstrel had allowed it to get this way.

They got through the meal and Stasia walked out with her father to find a carriage waiting. He helped her up into it, which was *actually* necessary on account of the dress she'd worn - she couldn't keep it up off of her feet and manage to climb at the same time without better bracing - and they set off.

He handed her a newspaper.

This.

This was stimulating.

"You'll like their newspapers," he said. "Your sister doesn't take any of them, but I plan on taking most of them."

"Most?" Stasia asked.

"Apparently a number of them are very difficult to get. They have limited distribution and limited print runs, and you have to know who to talk to or already be on a distribution list to get them. The ones that are a simple matter of payment, I will procure, and then there are others that simply won't reach us without significant extra effort, so I will have to sample them and see if it's worth it."

"How many newspapers do they *have*?" Stasia asked.

"It seems no one tries to count," Minstrel said. "The queen is quite a curious animal, and she seeks out anything with significant distribution and shuts it down, regardless of what manner of content it prints. It means that they're all printed on…" He shook the page up in the light, demonstrating what low quality of paper it was. "… this sop, and they're generally a scant page apiece, but the sought-after writers can always find print, they print fast, and there is an astonishing diversity of them to pick from. I heard a rumor this morning that the merchant's periodical… here." He shuffled through a stack of papers and held it up. "Is put out four times a day. I do not know if they were indulging my ignorance or not, but from what I've seen, it truly is possible."

The paper was downright transparent, and printed on both sides, but it was crammed with fascinating stories about pixies and fights and sales and things that were happening at court.

"Why does she shut them down?" Stasia asked.

"Apparently she doesn't like the idea of a single voice coming to dominate the news in the city," he said. "I must say, the results are… fascinating. I've been reading them on my ride to the port for the past two weeks, and you find the same writers writing the same stories for dozens of them, you find papers that are basically a reflection of yesterday's print copy for a competitor. Some of them are completely and transparently fabricated. It's chaotic, and I wonder what it must be like for those who don't have but one or two available to choose from."

"How many of them can read?" Stasia asked, and he glanced up.

"Oh, the city is significantly more literate than Boton," he said.

"Really?" Stasia asked and he nodded, looking at his paper again.

"Yes, apparently that's what happens when you teach the mothers to read, too."

She glanced at him, hearing the underplayed tone and exactly what it was intended to tell her.

Yes, he knew that they had fights coming about how he assumed society was going to treat her on account of being a woman. Yes he knew that she had valid points. But hadn't he though - hadn't he? - made sure that each of his daughters was fully literate, thus proving that he had already known the lesson from this particular piece of evidence?

"Who would have thought?" Stasia asked, grinning as she flipped the page over and put it down on the bench to keep the light from rendering it illegible.

They rode in silence in to the city, past the castle and following the river south-ish for a ways and then... well, Jasper had promised Stasia a tour of the city, but she still hadn't seen much of it at all, and she didn't pay close enough attention to the sun to tell when they turned or why, other than that she knew that they did, then the carriage rolled to a stop and Minstrel lifted his head.

"Here we are," he said, stacking the papers that he hadn't yet passed to Stasia and tucking them under the cushion of the carriage. The carriage man came to open the door for them and Minstrel got out first, offering Stasia a hand as she followed.

"What is this?" Stasia asked. "Where are we?"

"This is our new home," Minstrel answered. "I was always happy that we raised you girls out in the countryside, where you didn't have the busy-ness of city life to turn your heads from what you were meant to be, but I think that city life suits both of us better these days, don't you?"

How long ago had they passed the castle?

It hadn't been *that* long, had it?

Maybe thirty minutes, and that by carriage. She was often faster on her own with Schotzli.

"It's a step down from the house in Birch, but what wouldn't be? They hold on to their titled land with some prejudice, so that was never going to happen, anyway, save by buying out one of the merchant row houses, knocking it down, and putting up something new."

"Daddy, I don't care about the house," she said, and he smiled.

"I know," he said. "I'm convincing myself that I don't, either. There was some substantial prestige to being the largest landowner in Birch, but…"

Stasia looked up and down the row of houses.

There was no space to ride here. The property was scarcely double as wide as the house itself and three or four times as deep, but there was a small barn at the back corner that she could just make out around the edge of the house, and Schotzli could adapt to being a city horse. She'd been *born* a city horse.

"Are we allowed to go in?" Stasia asked, and he took a key out of his pocket, handing it to her. She hadn't noticed them coming through a gate as they left the street, but the house was on what appeared to be a man-made hill and overlooked a branch of the river that was a startling blue color.

"They call it the Sapphire River, through here," Minstrel said, coming to stand next to her. "There's not insignificant flood risk, even with the extra feet of elevation, but the house has been here for more than two-hundred years, so they say that the foundations are down deep enough that even the river can't shift them."

"If it floods, Schotzli is coming in the house with us," Stasia said, and he smiled.

"Come see."

She went to the door and unlocked it, opening the wide wooden door to reveal a hosting first floor, but a much less grand staircase up to what looked like a quieter and more private second floor.

"There are six bedrooms to choose from," Minstrel said. "You can pick any one of them that you want, save mine. It restricts how much entertaining we can do with the nobility, but I think I can make that work to my advantage. Within the city, it's normal to leave a party at all hours and just go home, so that means fewer overnight guests, anyway. We'll have to hire in staff for the real parties, but it narrows the normal staff to a head of household, a cook, and an assistant, and I think that might be better. Sometimes you can find all three of those in a single family and really cut down on the issues the staff have with each other."

The floors were marble, the walls were marble, the stairs were marble. Schotzli was going to need a rug, when she moved in to keep her feet dry from the storms.

"It's good," Stasia said.

"Yes?" Minstrel said.

"Yes," Stasia said. It meant they weren't moving back to Boton any time soon. She could see that. And she had a serious part of her telling her that this was *not* the outcome that she wanted.

But at the same time, it was a thousand times better than staying with Alyssia, and Verida was intriguing her, just now.

She genuinely wouldn't mind staying a few months more. Maybe meet a pixie. Learn how to do magic. Be a spy for the queen.

She could get in a few things before she went back.

"Yes," she said. "I'm very happy."

The move consumed all of her energy and attention for almost a week.

Cart loads of luggage and belongings started turning up the next morning, and the housekeeper, an older woman named Tesh, arrived early in the afternoon. By that time Stasia had taken over telling the men where to put things as they arrived, and Tesh went along, overseeing rooms as they began to take shape while Stasia sat in the entry room on her own crate of clothes from Birch and gave the men instruction. Minstrel was working on the more intricate details of setting up his study and businessroom, where every book and ledger needed to be exactly where he expected it to be, at a moment's notice.

The next day, Minstrel went out to procure furnishings where the previous occupants had taken them away, and through the afternoon, furniture showed up on carts pulled by great workhorses. Stasia paid one of the cart boys from her sister's house to watch for Schotzli and steal her away, tied to the next cart load of goods from the Gormand estate. A cook arrived and took responsibility for the kitchen, which was well outside of Stasia's realm of expertise. They had dinner at their own home, that night, just Stasia and Minstrel.

It was almost magic.

She could see the river pouring by before them, and she knew that Schotzli was back in the stable, ready to go out when Stasia finally finished things here.

There were no tapestries on the walls and the floors all tapped and smacked as they walked, bare of rugs and carpets, but the larger furniture was still here, including a very, very nice bed up in Stasia's room at the back of the house, and the kitchen had food, thanks to the cook's collaboration with Tesh, and Minstrel seemed quite happy with the whole thing.

Stasia went to bed each night exhausted, and she slept soundly, but it was work toward a goal of being free and her own once more.

She knew where they were in the city, knew that if she followed any one of the delta rivers up to the main Wolfram, she could follow it down to Port Verida, and then be home. Worst case. There was water every direction until you got to the really big estates up north, and that wasn't likely to be an issue, because she wasn't going to be wandering those parts.

There were too many interesting parts of the city to see, before that.

On the eighth night in the new house, they held a party. Stasia wore a dress, because she wanted Minstrel to see that she really was trying to cooperate and make a place for them in Verida, so that he would let her do her own thing when she wasn't being supportive. She received everyone herself, greeting and curtsying and smiling and hostessing her brains out.

She wasn't good at it. She knew this, but she tried, and Minstrel's social importance sort of covered over the fact that she hadn't actually been responsible for a party in her entire life. She did miss her friends - a lot - and the goofing off that would have happened if they had been there, but the truth of it was that none of them were spare daughters, and they'd been dwindling year by year for a long time. Only two of them remained unmarried, and both of them were in the process of making arrangements for marriage in the next year.

So she'd been headed for this for a long time, and it was time to just go with it. The move to Verida was as good a time as any to deal with it.

She drank wine, she smiled, she listened to people as they talked, nodded encouragingly.

They talked of *nothing*.

The conversation about the Lady Westhauser's black velvet gown was just inescapable, as was conversation about the new ship that had come in at Port Verida from the far side of the continent. It was apparently loaded down with fae merchandise that was difficult to get in the quantities that the known world demanded, and everyone was excited for the cargo to reach the port market so that they could get started distributing it out to the wider world. There was money to be made, and while there were a number of uninterested nobles at the party, the larger portion of the guests were active in trade, and everyone was abuzz with it.

She got to the end of the night and saw the last of the guests away or up to bed, then she changed and went out to Schotzli and rode out to the river, trailing along and enjoying the night air and her independence.

She found herself at the castle, looking at the braziers and the soldiers standing in between them. At least on the river-facing side, she really couldn't see a way into that place.

She crossed the river at the bridge she'd taken with Jasper and Matthias, then rode past the guardhouse and ultimately found herself at the bar again.

There was a pile of debris outside the door, and open air in the window.

"That happened early," she said, leaning down to look inside, finding Colin and Sterling sword fighting.

"There was an incident," Jasper said, leaning back in his chair to be able to see around the edge of the window. "Thought we must have scared you off, after last time."

"Liar," she said. "You knew we bought the house on the Sapphire."

He grinned, then motioned.

"If she can make it around the bits of table, just bring her in."

She heard Babe grunt and get up, coming to push the debris to the side and kicking the last bits out of the way to make room for Schotzli to walk into the bar.

Strange riding a horse through a door. Stasia lay down along the mare's neck, then dismounted.

"Stacy," Colin cried. "Heard you got the palace guard all hot and bothered. You're one of us, now!"

Sterling kissed his fingers and flung them at her, not so much a motion of affection as an effusion of friendly gratitude.

"I heard it was beautifully done," he said.

Babe went to sit in his seat again and Stasia went to sit down next to him, accepting the mug from Marigold and pouring herself a beer out of the flagon at the table.

She looked around the room.

"Does this happen every night?" she asked, and Colin grinned, swinging at Sterling again.

"Only on nights you come," he said.

"It's not every night," Matthias said. "They kind of know when the people they want to fight with are going to come, and they show up because they don't want to miss the fight."

"Don't want to *miss* being punched in the face," Stasia said. "And my faith in your military was already low."

"Ain't the military what's at fault," Babe said.

"Just the police?" Stasia asked, and he shook his head.

"No, it's both of 'em, but it just ain't *all* of 'em."

"Hotheads who won't let bygones be bygones," Jasper said. "How are you finding your new lodgings?"

"Better than the old ones," Stasia answered. "You have anything to do with it?"

He scratched his chin, settling back in his chair and shrugging.

"Who me?" he asked.

"Do the rest of you ever work?" Stasia asked, looking over at Colin and Sterling.

"As little," Colin said, dodging sideways and curling around an imaginary sword, "as possible."

"Wouldn't that be more effective with actual swords?" she asked. "You *are* wearing them."

"Anyone who draws a proper weapon in here gets thrown out," Babe said. "You want to see what they can actually do, ask 'em to go outside."

The window had a seat inside of it, probably used for storage of some kind, and as Stasia turned to watch once more, Colin went vaulting across the window seat and out through the jagged remains of the window, landing on the street with sword in hand. He flicked his eyebrows and Sterling sighed loudly, finishing his glass of wine and jumping up onto the window seat and through the window after him.

Matthias shifted his chair noisily across the floor to where he could see out the window, but Babe settled lower in his chair and crossed his arms.

Stasia watched him for a moment for a clue what she *should* be watching, but he just seemed genuinely disinterested, and she lifted her chair to go sit next to Matthias where she could watch the two men outside fencing as though they were on a stage.

She'd watched soldiers fight in Boton, both in spontaneous exchanges at bars and in training by the docks while they'd been waiting for something to happen. She had no eye for whether they were better or worse than what she'd seen before, particularly because of how much fun the two of them had. Stasia had learned that she had to respect blades, respect edges. A blade in a man's hand was something she could *never* guarantee he couldn't get to her with, so when he brought it out, all of her attention had to go to it and she had to react hard and fast.

Colin and Sterling *played*. Colin preferred big, dramatic arm flourishes and verbal commentary - whether actual words or just vocalizations - while Sterling had feet that wouldn't stay still, not just flat along the ground, but leaping and spinning as they fought.

"This is silly, right?" she asked Matthias. "This is just silly."

"They aren't trying to kill each other," Matthias observed, and Stasia raised an eyebrow. He ducked his head.

She looked over at Jasper, who was speaking quietly with Babe. The man raised his eyebrows like he didn't know what the question was, and she shook her head, watching Colin and Sterling once more.

There was something akin to an agreement between the two of them, and it made the fight into a game, one that they played with an abandon that shocked Stasia.

"Don't they ever hurt each other?" she asked.

Jasper leaned to look out the window, then sighed and leaned back to rest his elbow on the table.

"It's… unusual, certainly, but it takes control to be silly. Soldiers fight commonly enough, and the police are involved in altercations on a regular basis, but the guard may go years without a scuffle. If we're going to keep our edge over people who ambush us or take us by surprise, we have to invent our own methods for doing it."

"And that's the winner?" Stasia asked, and he grinned.

"We all do it our own way."

He looked over at Babe, who sighed.

"Haven't got nothing' else going on, just now, I suppose," he said and stood. Jasper winked and shifted his chair around as Babe made his way out the front door and stopped just down the street from where Colin and Sterling were breaking up their fight to turn their attention to Babe.

Stasia sneaked one more look at Jasper, then Colin roared and he and Sterling set upon Babe.

Babe apparently carried a pair of short swords, not significantly more meaty than long daggers, but he managed to take on both men at once with them, keeping them off of him and away as they hopped and squawked and circled. Stasia had once seen a man in a bar fight who had fought like that, sort of above it and calm in the midst of drunken frenzy, seeing what was going on and only reacting as much as he had to.

Babe threw Colin into Sterling and the two men clattered to the ground as Babe put away his two short swords and made for the door again.

Stasia rose quickly to her feet, making sure that no one was injured, but Colin crowed laughter, and Sterling rose laughing, as well.

"One day, old man," Sterling said, following Babe back into the bar and going back to his bottle of wine. Colin brushed off his leathers and stood straight, sword still in his hand.

"Matthias," he called.

"Oh, no," Matthias answered. "You've had too much to drink tonight for me to fight you."

"Matthias," Colin called again, unchanged.

"I mean it," Matthias answered as Babe threw himself into his chair and crossed his arms again.

"Last time he fought Colin drunk, Colin threw him in the Wolfram," Jasper said cheerfully.

"You people are weird," Stasia said, and Jasper nodded.

"Water finds its own level," he answered.

"Teach me," Stasia said, rising again.

Jasper sat back in his chair, but Matthias stood.

"No," the young man said. "Not tonight. He's having too much fun. They…" He motioned to Sterling and Babe. The sweep of his arm might have included Jasper, but Stasia wasn't sure. "They can keep up with him, but he won't have mercy on you."

"He's got a wicked sense of humor," Sterling said from the bar. "Fair warning."

"I'm not untutored," Stasia answered, looking from Matthias to Sterling to Babe. She approached Babe, holding out a hand. "May I?"

He pursed his lips, then gave her a little shrug and pulled one of the short swords, handing it to her.

"If you go in the river, don't drop it," he said.

"How about I drop it before I go in the river?" she asked, and the corner of his mouth came up.

"Just be certain about it," he said.

"Don't trust the dragonskin," Jasper said as she headed for the door. "If he gets the idea he can actually *hit* you with a sword, he'll do it, and you'll have bruises to show for it for weeks."

"Good tip."

She went out into the street and set herself against Colin, who grinned recklessly, his arm out and above his head in a seagull shape that was openly mocking her stance.

Her stance was correct. She had learned it correctly.

What she was learning here wasn't technique, though, and she sensed that easily enough. What she was learning was something above that.

Confidence, maybe?

Colin circled her, bobbing his head back and forth.

"Sure you don't want to do this in there?" he asked, motioning to the bar. "I can run you through a few times if you like."

"Do your worst," Stasia answered, aware of the glass on the ground and the bits of debris that had rolled away from the pile.

"Oh, no, I always do my best," Colin answered.

"Do not," Sterling called from inside the bar, and Colin laughed, charging her.

It was a reckless charge, sword nowhere near the proper engagement zone, and she should have slashed him for it, if it was a real fight, but instead she jerked her arm away, trying not to hit him by accident as he got close, too close… and then he was standing behind her, his arm around her neck and the base of his sword against her throat.

"Ought to get that thing in a highcollared version," he said playfully.

"Ought to pay attention when your opponent trains with both hands," Stasia answered, and she felt his chest leave her back to look down at the dagger she had poking him in the ribs.

"Fairplay," he said, springing away cheerfully.

The next time, he attacked her properly, but with too much force and at odd angles, never the way she expected him to, and then he kicked her in the back of the knee, dropping her to the ground. The pommel of his sword came down to rest on the back of her neck and she shook her head.

"This isn't what you do with them," she said.

"They don't expose their back and then let me take it," he answered.

He stepped away again, feet doing a funny little jig that would have been elegant if Sterling had done it, but from Colin it was an open taunt.

She attacked him, her form rusty from disuse but as close to perfect as she could make it, and he anticipated her, once more never where she expected him to be and never meeting her strokes with a straight angle.

He was stronger than she was.

She was supposed to anticipate that.

He was older than she was by a couple of years and he trained for this professionally. She *had* to expect his strength.

But the ease with which he deflected her full force, the way he could redirect that force in any direction he liked, like blowing gentle gusts of breath at a live candle to watch it flicker and dance this way or that.

He never dropped the grin, never dropped the sense of *game* or *play*, but in twenty minutes she felt like she'd learned more about swordsmanship than she had in all of her time in Boton.

And she hadn't evaluated him as that *good* compared to either Sterling or Babe. She stepped away from him, letting her sword drop, and he vaulted back through the window, startling Matthias out of the way. Stasia took another big step backwards to where she could see Jasper.

"Are you better than they are?" she asked.

"Babe can take me on experience alone," Jasper said. "But longsword against longsword, I'm better than all three of them put together."

"Why none of us would go up against you like that," Babe murmured as Stasia came in and returned the sword to him. He jerked his chin at her.

"You disappointed?" he asked.

"No," she said. "I learned a lot."

He nodded.

"Didn't show yourself bad, either," he said, giving her another little confirming nod.

Colin raised a mug at her from the bar and Stasia sat back down beside Matthias.

"Where did you learn to do that?" Matthias asked.

She wondered how she compared to him.

"Same place she learned to climb," Jasper answered. "She saw someone do something she couldn't and she convinced them to teach her."

Stasia nodded.

"Helps when you're a pretty girl, getting folk to teach you stuff," Babe said.

"I pay them," Stasia said. "When they go out of their way for me."

"But they'd all do it again, I bet," Colin said.

She looked over at him and he grinned.

"You put up a good fight," he said. "You just don't do it except sometimes for sport."

"And you do it most nights for entertainment while drunk," Stasia said, and he grinned wider.

"Days the king doesn't leave the castle, we do a lot of fun stuff to keep ourselves sharp," he said.

"That's enough," Jasper said. "I'm already in enough hot water with Ben over him thinking I'm giving some foreigner secrets about the castle and the King's Guard."

"I heard the queen liked her, though," Sterling said from above his glass.

There was a quiet in the room, and Stasia got the impression that Sterling had said something forbidden. Matthias looked over at the bartender and Marigold, and then Jasper stood, taking his hat from the table and putting it on.

"And that is the sign of a man too deep in his cups," he said. "Let's go."

Stasia went over to get Schotzli, not having any idea what had just happened, but Sterling tipped his wine back hurriedly and Colin grunted, downing his beer as Babe and Matthias stood to follow Jasper. Schotzli picked her way back out of the bar and Stasia started to mount up, figuring the night was over, but Jasper came and put his hand on the mare's neck.

He looked her in the eye, then nodded.

"I've been asking a lot of questions," he said. "No one seems to know the answers, though. I would prefer to take a chance on someone whose people I know better, but our friend has been adamant. I'd like a word with you, if you please. Someplace more secure."

Stasia blinked at him.

"You're talking like there's a big secret going on here," she said, and he smiled. It was the same kind, friendly, but close-kept smile he'd had with her from the beginning, and she trusted him, but she was just having a real quick check to make sure that wasn't a stupid thing to do.

She didn't know any of these men.

Certainly, she didn't know anybody *else* in the city, either, and they at least had uniforms on and a bar staff vouching for them being legitimate uniforms. The queen knew Jasper, and Stasia was at least as certain that the woman had been the queen as she was certain that she lived in the house on the Sapphire River, today.

She was willing to go with that much.

Did that make them reputable men?

Did guarding the king make you a good person?

Superficially, she would have suspected yes, but then the reality of trade and politics weighed in and she fought vehemently against the idea that any of them were *strictly* good people. You had to be willing to do violent things, and you had to be willing to make sacrifices and compromises, the further you went into a life of significance.

And she had little doubt that Jasper was significant. Babe, too, for that matter.

Colin and Sterling? They were certainly significant to *themselves*.

But did significance lend trustworthiness?

Would they try to use her wealth and position for royal ends, against her father's best interests and her own?

Jasper had honest eyes.

She liked him, in a big brother kind of a way. Could easily imagine throwing herself into his arms as a refuge from violence.

He just had that air to him.

But she genuinely didn't *know* him, and…

He licked his lips and took a half step back from Schotzli, watching her.

He saw so many things. He *knew* so many things.

That was why this was so hard.

She knew better than to get tangled up in whatever complex life he was living, because she was nobody's asset. She was her own, and she'd fought for that her whole life. Not against her father, perhaps, but against everybody else's assumptions.

"She's got good instincts," Babe called from a few paces down the road where the other men had already set off. "Can't mess with those."

"Are you messing with me?" Stasia asked, and Jasper shook his head.

"No. Come with us. Ask me what you want. I'll tell you what I can, and perhaps you can tell me what you will. We should be friends, you and I. Do you sense that?"

Stasia nodded.

"I'm nobody's asset," she said, and he smiled.

"I understand," he said.

"No, you don't," Stasia answered, and he lifted his chin.

"Perhaps I don't," he said, his voice soft. True. "But I hear you. Do you believe that I am someone's asset?"

She looked in his eyes.

It would be so easy to say yes.

Perhaps the closest to truth, too.

He was a tool to be used by the king at will, sent about to risk his life, perhaps without even knowing why, sometimes.

But his eyes were his own. All five of them, they were their own men, doing what they did because they chose it and because they wanted to be there with each other.

She could see the difference, for him, but could she see it for herself?

"Do you believe that you are unsafe with us?" Jasper asked after a moment.

"No," she said truthfully. He dipped his head.

"Do you believe that you are unable to decline anything that anyone might ask you to do?" he asked.

She smiled, turning and burying her forehead against Schotzli's neck, then turned and set off to walk next to him. He appeared to be still waiting for an answer even as he fell into step next to her, and she was trying to find the words that were true and simultaneously find the words she was willing to admit out loud. Finally, she resorted to one set of words.

"I'm afraid that I'm going to have too much fun and stop thinking about whether or not I *should* decline," she said, and he smiled, watching the other four men walk ahead of them. Sterling was walking backwards, telling the others what was happening.

"Then I believe that would make us your assets," he said. "Or have I misunderstood?"

She grinned.

"I think you see everything all too well," she answered, and he looked over at her, openly watching her once more, then nodded.

"Yes," he said. "I think that we will be friends."

She nodded.

"I think so, too."

———◆———

They went back to the guard house, Matthias coming to take Schotzli and stabling her away while the rest of them went up a set of wood steps and into a dining hall of sorts.

There were perhaps half a dozen other men there, but they took up a back corner table and no one bothered them.

"How many of you are there?" Stasia asked, watching the men as they sat at their other tables or leaned against walls and talked.

"More than twenty, less than a hundred," Jasper answered. "The actual answer is… secret, though it would hardly be that difficult to count. We work in groups of four or six, however things work out and however Ben assigns the new recruits each year, and we have a certain amount of autonomy and a certain amount of hierarchical responsibility. Most of us live here at the gate house, though there are a number of men with wives and families who live at home, particularly once they advance to a certain rank and seniority."

The other men were watching him, bored, and Colin leaned in on his elbows.

"We all know that that's not what we came in here to talk about," he said.

Jasper shook his head firmly.

"No. She has questions, and I gave my word to answer what I could. We are strangers to her, and the traditions of Verida are foreign. We owe her the time to figure out whether or not she believes in us enough to even *want* to help us."

"For all she knows, we could be supporting a despot king and a wicked regime," Babe said. "We could be the bad guys."

"No, those wear black," Sterling said, raising an eyebrow at him. Stasia got the impression that this was teasing in some way, but she didn't immediately understand how or why. Babe remained unperturbed.

"Come on," Colin said. "Look at us. Who would believe that *we're* the bad guys?"

Jasper looked over at him placidly.

"If you include people who believe that you could be taken in by a particularly well-told story?" he asked, and Colin pursed his lips indignantly.

"Everywhere I go, I'm the good guy," he said. "Prove me wrong."

"I think Emmett would say otherwise," Matthias said, and Colin pointed at him with an open hand.

"Come on now," he said. "That guy *knows* he's the bad guy. He *knows* it."

There was too much *joy* at the table for them to be wicked, but it didn't rule out scoundrels. She knew plenty of drinking, betting men who told jokes.

Jasper, though.

She looked at Babe.

"You aren't like them," she said.

He rested his chin on his chest, waiting for… something more. It hadn't been a question, she realized.

"Why are you with them when they're so different from you?" she asked.

He frowned, giving it just a moment of consideration, then looked around the table.

"I see four brothers," he said. "*My* brothers. If you're missing the family resemblance, you ain't lookin' hard enough."

He had a slow way of speaking that, superficially, suggested a slow way of thinking, but it wasn't true. It was that the thoughts came from deep.

She looked at Matthias.

"Did you choose them, at all, or did you get assigned?"

He smiled, laughing quietly as Colin gave him a pointy look that very much meant something.

"Every recruit is thrilled to be placed anywhere within the King's Guard," he said. "It's an honor and a life goal. But only a fool would choose anyone other than Jasper as his squad leader, if he had a say in it."

She looked at Jasper, who seemed unmoved by this, though not coldly. He was still watching her.

"I can find nothing wrong with any of you," she finally said. "But this is a new place, and your customs are… as you say, foreign. I don't like to be used and I don't like to be lied to, but most of all I don't like to be tricked."

He took his hat off and lay it on the table between them, leaving his fingers on the rim like a sort of pledge, akin to a salute.

"I give you my word," he said. "I may be a trickster, but so long as you are working with me or for me, I will never trick you."

"Are you a trickster?" Stasia asked, and the other four men nodded in unison with humor.

"But he don't lie," Babe said. Jasper shook his head.

"I find lies tiring," he said. "I gave them up long ago in favor of truth and secrets."

She watched his face, then she nodded.

"All right," she said. "I'm not ready to say I *trust* you, because I still really don't know you, and I certainly don't trust the *queen* all that much, yet, but… let's say I'm willing to just go with all of this for now. What happens next?"

Jasper put his hat back on, looking around the table.

"Now we see if *we're* willing to trust *you*."

The mood at the table shifted. Well, everybody's mood but Babe's shifted.

Jasper leaned onto his elbows, licking his lower lip and watching her, while Sterling and Colin shifted their chairs to point them more directly at Stasia. Matthias literally ducked.

"I've sent letters to men I served with in the pirate wars. I will hear back from them, but I know that Kirfall is a big country, and there's every chance that they've never heard of you. But know that there is *some* chance that anything you tell me will come out as lies, if you embellish or fabricate any of it."

Stasia blinked, then shrugged, leaning back in her chair.

This was a negotiation.

It was a thing that you won or lost, but if both of you knew what you were doing, you both won.

She wasn't afraid of this.

"Oh, they've heard of me," she said. "At least my father, though I've never met someone who has heard of my father who doesn't have *some* opinion of me."

The corner of Jasper's mouth came up and he nodded.

"That's exactly what I'm talking about," he said. "You have a parliamentary system, a very complex one by our reckoning, and have a… native bias against monarchal rule. I can find no reason that your father's interest would be against the monarchy, but I have certainly met those from Boton who cannot submit to the idea of a king."

She'd liked Babe's play at not answering something that wasn't a question, so she waited.

So did Jasper.

"Go on, then," Babe said finally, nudging her chair with his foot. She sighed, glancing at him. His eyes sparkled and he winked, though it was fast enough that she was certain it had been a trick of the light.

Stasia sighed and shrugged.

"Politics for me is about what I'm allowed to wear, where I'm allowed to go, and who's going to sniff at me on the way by. I think it's weird to think that just because this woman came *out* of that woman that she's definitely the one who should pick the guy who's in charge, but… I mean, I guess there are worse ways to do it."

Sterling covered his face with his hand and Matthias looked like he was trying to be shorter than the table. Stasia was unrepentant.

Jasper looked unshocked.

"We're certainly talking about more than a passive disinterest, though, aren't we?" he asked.

She shrugged.

"As far as I'm concerned, no," she said. "She wants to pay me to do interesting things that I find nothing wrong with, I'm in. Always interested in something that will challenge and entertain me. The life of a bored rich girl. Am I signing up to be a soldier? Not hardly."

"What exactly did Constance say to her?" Sterling asked.

Jasper sighed, falling lower over his elbows as he looked around the table.

"The queen has asked that Stacy here act as an outsider in support of actions of the Queen's Chair."

There was a long, broad silence, and Jasper nodded, looking at Stasia again.

"Have you ever done something that was enough against the law that you would have been held for more than a day over, had you been caught?" he asked.

Stasia snorted.

"I've trespassed," she said. "But I've never taken anything that didn't belong to me, I've never broken anything of importance or value, I've never been in a fight that I started, and I've never had income or trade of significance enough to merit taxation."

"They say that you are intractable," he said. "Often rude."

"Are you generally civil?" Stasia asked, and he grinned at that, smoothing the corners of his mouth down with his fingers and collecting himself for just an instant before answering.

"At court, particularly with the queen, candidness has its value, but you have to remember that she is the figurehead leader of Verida. You can't be openly disrespectful, and if members of the court decide that you aren't subordinate and actively respectful enough, they will act to block your access to her. And most of them can, to at least some degree."

Stasia nodded.

"I liked her," she said. "I don't want to be insulting to her. In truth, I don't. I won't tell you that I won't speak my mind, but if you'll warn me to when I do something unintentionally, I'm willing to try to learn."

Jasper nodded.

"Why did your father come to Verida?" he asked.

"Because Alyssia was here? Because there's money here? Because he didn't like how fast his empire on this side of the sea was growing? Because he likes the hats? I don't know. He doesn't tell me that kind of stuff."

"Does he do trade or commerce with men from the underworld or that might get him arrested if it came to light?" Jasper asked.

"Look," Stasia said. "I know that everyone thinks that you can't get rich without cheating, and maybe that's true, but as far as I know, and what I honestly believe, my father is clever, he's hard-working, and he's lucky. What mix of those three things got him where he is today, I haven't a clue, but somebody had to win the game, and he was there when it happened. Every man he trades with comes away richer than he was before. That's what he keeps telling me, all the time. If you want to make a man poorer, you have to do it all at once, because he's never going to come back, but if you make him richer every time, you have a trading partner for life."

Jasper nodded thoughtfully.

"Who do you know, in the city?" he asked.

"Nobody," Stasia said. "I mean, Alyssia and Gevalt, my father, the five of you as much as anyone. We have a new housekeeper named Tesh I've spent a bunch of time with this past week."

"You don't have any other contacts within the city?" Jasper asked.

"I met the queen," Stasia offered insolently, and he smiled.

"There have been parties at both the Gormand estate and your new manor," he observed, and she shrugged.

"I was notably rude at the Gormand estate," she said. "So I didn't make any contacts there, other than the stable boy who probably got in trouble for it. But, yes, I've been formally introduced into the cream of the crop amidst Verida's merchant class."

"And none of them approached you for business or political purposes?" he asked.

"I got two proposals, if that counts," Stasia answered.

"Is that true?" Colin asked, and Stasia sighed.

"I'm worth a third of my father's empire to anyone who can talk me into it," she said. "It's a lot of incentive."

"And I thought that Sterling had a strong track record," Colin said.

"Three," Sterling said. "I have proposed *thrice*."

"Two in a week," Colin muttered.

"Two in an hour," Stasia answered. "It's exhausting, because if I'm being polite, I have to actually *meet* their sons."

"The fathers propose?" Matthias asked, and she nodded.

"They're the one who want the marriage," she told him. "The sons, most of them, have no idea who my father is."

Jasper nodded.

"Do you think that your father will change his mind about an alliance?" he asked.

Stasia shook her head.

"I think if I were very enthusiastic, maybe, but the idea of splitting his empire in three rather than two, when he really did vet Gevalt and Ridge to the point that he doesn't expect to find a better candidate… He would find it to be dilutive, at this point. So long as I don't suddenly decide that's the life I want…" She shuddered. "I'm on my own."

Jasper looked around the table.

"Any other questions?" he asked.

"What did the queen *say*?" Sterling asked.

"What would you be doing if you hadn't run into us?" Matthias asked. Jasper pointed with his thumb, eyebrows up.

"That's good," he said.

"I have no idea," Stasia answered. "Would have eventually bumped into someone else interesting, and maybe I'd be off learning to sing high Veridan… songs."

"Like the soprano ones or the artsy ones?" Colin asked, and Stasia smiled despite herself.

"I can do both," Stasia said. "I'm almost sure."

He grinned back at her and Jasper nodded.

"All right. Well. As long as nobody has any *relevant* questions to add," he said, looking at Sterling, "I'm going to consider her officially recruited."

"Recruited for *what*?" Sterling asked.

"Nothing specific," Jasper said. "And nothing time-sensitive. She just wants us to know how to find her if something specific does show up."

"Have you spoken to her since that day?" Matthias asked, and Jasper nodded.

"Just for a few minutes while we were on duty last week."

"What does that mean?" Stasia asked.

"It means that she's still thinking about how she wants to use you," Jasper said. "She hasn't forgotten about you."

"No, on duty," Stasia said.

"Oh," he said, frowning. "Being an active guard to the king is mentally and physically taxing. Very little rest, almost no sleep, high alert every moment that you aren't asleep. The guards rotate through for brief intervals in order to have time to rest in between, and to train and do the other things that we're supposed to do."

She nodded.

"How long are you on duty, at a time?" she asked.

"That's a secret," Jasper said. "If someone could figure out the guard rotations, they could exploit them."

"And other than that, you're… here?" Stasia asked.

Jasper shrugged.

"We do what we need to do, to do the job," he said. "And then we do the things that make us better at it."

"Like what?" Stasia asked.

"Yeah, like what?" Colin asked. "I just spend all my money."

Jasper closed his eyes with a quiet humor.

"We stay connected to the city," he said. "We meet people. We talk to them. We hear what they're concerned about, what they're excited about. Good people see the brown leathers and they know that they can tell us stuff and it goes to the king." He turned his eyes to Stasia. "But where I could *truly* use you is that you don't wear the brown leathers. You're a rich girl with… a certain amount of latitude with the law. You get yourself in real trouble with the blacks, I can't bail you out, but for smaller things, I can appeal to Ben and he'll walk you out himself, if you prove to be a good source of information."

"What are you saying to me?" Stasia asked.

"He's sayin' he wants you in the dive bars down at the Black Docks to make sure we know where the Rat King's schemes interfere with the king's interests," Babe said.

"The Rat King," Stasia said. "That sounds positively charming."

Stasia looked at Jasper for confirmation, and shrugged and nodded.

"There, among other places."

"I ain't lettin' her down that far on her own 'till I'm sure she knows what she's about," Babe said.

"Oh, I wouldn't send her by herself," Jasper said. "For the Black Docks, you would go with her."

"They all know me down there," Babe protested.

"They know you if you show your face," Jasper said. "You cover your face, like she does, keep your head down unless she needs you, and she can do whatever she wants, knowing that you can get her out of a really immediate jam, if it happens, and I can get her out if she gets herself arrested for being with the wrong people at the wrong time."

Sterling screwed his mouth up to the side.

"How long have you been plotting this, old man?" he asked.

Jasper shook his head.

"Had an itch that it would work, if we went for it, when I sent her over the castle wall. Constance was the one who sealed it for me, though. She's an outsider, no history, no stake in any of this. Uniquely situated to do things that we can't. Go places we can't go, talk to people who would never speak to us in leathers and wouldn't speak to… the rest of us, anyway."

"They'd talk to you," Babe said. "But you can't risk that."

Jasper nodded.

"I can talk to anybody," Colin announced without arguing, and Jasper chortled.

"You can talk *at* anybody," Sterling replied.

"You've got an idea about using me," Stasia said. "What's in it for me?"

"Something to do," Jasper said. "Someplace to go where people look up and are happy to see you, and not for your money. And what you talk to people about while you're about is up to you. We'll send you places you couldn't safely go on your own, to talk to people I bet you've never met the likes of before."

That did appeal to her.

"And I can walk away any time I find something better to do," Stasia said.

"I think you ought to go to the university and forget ever having come here," Jasper said. "If you want my honest advice. But in the meantime, if you *want* to be here, I'll use the talents you've got and the opportunities you present. One of us."

"One of us," Sterling said quickly.

"One of us," Colin crowed.

"One of us," Matthias said after a brief pause, almost embarrassed. They all looked at Babe.

He met Stasia's eye without malice, without unkindness at all, but with genuine consideration and pause.

He nodded.

"One of us."

Stasia smiled just a bit, then grinned.

"One of you."

Babe had been serious that he wasn't sending Stasia out into whatever world there was of Verida to get in trouble in without knowing for sure that she could take care of herself.

She thought that it had been settled, the first night at the bar, but apparently not.

He told her to come back the next day around lunch and he would set to training her himself.

It was exhilarating, having something to *do* the next day, and Stasia could hardly contain herself on the ride home with the prospect of it.

She'd never really *belonged* anywhere. She'd had friends, she'd had a community that knew her, but there had always been this sense of pulling back and holding away until she finally came around and acted right. The men accepting her like they had… it was profound in a way that she hadn't expected.

Schotzli had been light on her toes all the way home, and then Stasia had gone in the back and set up jumps in the pasture out of spare rails in the barn and had gone over the jumps with her until dinner because her heart couldn't *not* fly.

Schotzli loved jumping. She was built for it in every way, even more than the big horses at the guard house, even *if* they could get over bigger and more solid obstacles. Schotzli went over things like she had wings, and Stasia found that the mare was constrained by Stasia's nerve a lot more than her own capacity to clear. She was out of shape, just now, and Stasia could feel it in the way she heaved air at the end of the evening, but once Stasia had washed her down and dried her, she tore into her oats with an enthusiasm that she hadn't had since Birch, and Stasia had gone into the kitchen whistling.

"Now there's a noise I haven't heard in a while," Minstrel called from his study, and Stasia grinned.

"I made friends in town," she called.

"Do I approve of these friends?" he called back.

"Proper and upstanding, Daddy," she answered. She peered over the cook's shoulder for a moment, then found Tesh standing in the doorway.

"We have some things to discuss," the woman said. "Would you like to do so before or after your meal?"

"Tesh, why don't you join us for dinner?" Stasia asked. "We can talk about it then."

Tesh shook her head.

"That wouldn't be appropriate, Miss," she said.

"I don't care," Stasia answered. "So long as we don't have company, it's silly for you to eat by yourself in your room. We have a table that's going to waste. Tell Emily, too."

"Miss," Tesh answered, frowning at the idea of the girl sitting down at the master's table, and Stasia gave her an exaggerated shrug.

"I'm the spare daughter," Stasia said carelessly. "I do a lot of things that no one else is allowed to. And I like you and I like Emily, and I would have Yasmine eat with us, too, if she wasn't going to be the one making sure that the food all turns up in the first place."

She paused.

"Yasmine, if Emily helps, can you eat with us? Sort of… have everything either simmering or whatever or done and ready to come out all at once?"

"Miss, what of the courses?" Tesh demanded.

"What of them?" Stasia answered. "I'm often disappointed I ate too much of an earlier course because the later ones were so good. Let me pick out what I'm actually most excited to eat."

Yasmine looked over her shoulder at Tesh, who still seemed outraged.

This was proof that it could be done.

"Tesh, please fetch Emily and put her at Yasmine's disposal. We will eat together as a household."

"Miss," Tesh said darkly, and Stasia shrugged exaggeratedly.

"I'm going to go up and dress for dinner," she said. "Thank you."

She smiled and went upstairs, whistling as she went.

She couldn't remember the last time she'd been this happy.

<hr/>

She went to the guard house after the midday meal.

Babe met her at the rail and let Schotzli go through, then stood aside as Stasia threw her leg flamboyantly over the mare's neck and hopped down. Matthias took the mare toward the stables, and Stasia noted Jasper, Sterling, and Colin standing up at the rail on the upper floor around the courtyard.

They leaned on their elbows, talking amongst themselves as Babe went to go get a wooden box from on a rail nearby. He brought it to her, a simple enough box, but with an etching on the lid that indicated a brand that Stasia didn't know.

He opened the lid with one finger on each side and looked down into a bed of wadded newspaper where a pair of left-handed daggers lay. They were longer and narrower than the ones she normally carried were, with wide cross-guards that curled up toward the daggerpoints. They weren't the type of weapon that her friends would have had on their walls, lacking intricate decoration and ornate filigrees, but they were solid, soldier's weapons, and they were brand new.

"You didn't have to do that," Stasia said. "I have daggers."

"Not blocking daggers," he said. "Take 'em. I won't fight you otherwise."

She looked him in the eye, then went to the rail and took off her own daggers, leaving them on the wood, purple sheaths and all. She returned to him and took out the two blocking daggers, feeling them out.

They were heavy. More weight in the handle than she was used to, and balanced deep in her palm rather than up near the hilt. Made to hold onto, not for delivering power.

Left-handed daggers were for defense, for blocking a sword when your own sword arm was busy doing something else interesting. She'd trained two-handed, but never against a sword. Men who picked fights with women on the street seldom carried a sword.

She held the two daggers awkwardly, trying to understand what she was going to do with them, when Babe went back to the wall of weapons and took a pair of wooden batons off of it and returned to her.

"You handle blades like I'd handle a live snake," he said. "I believe you're trained. Saw it with m'own eyes, sure enough, but you ain't got the stomach for accidents, and I ain't so sure you got stomach for intent, neither. If you're ever gonna stick a fella, you need to practice meanin' it first."

He tucked the batons under his armpit and put out his hands for the daggers.

A gift given so recently was hard to give up, but Stasia paused, trying to figure out how to flip them so that she could offer them to him hilt-out when both her hands were occupied, and he snorted, just reaching out and closing his hands around them to take them.

His hands were wrapped with white linen, but only once around and tied on the back, and the daggers were new-sharp. He was completely careless with them, like a blacksmith was with a hammer or a fisherman with his gaff. They were an extension of himself, and he was at ease with them.

He went to put them on the rail next to her own daggers, then came back with the batons.

"All right, now," he said. "Hit me."

They were lightweight, mercifully. If they'd been nightsticks, lead-weighted and dense-wooded, she wasn't certain she would have been willing to try, but with the light batons in her hands, she was willing to take a full swing at him.

She'd learned to fight, and she'd learned to fight dirty if that was what it took to escape. Go for the face, the eyes, use her feet to strike, her elbows. She didn't use much of that now, because she wanted to learn whatever it was he was trying to teach her with the batons.

They were close in length to the daggers, maybe a foot or a little less beyond her hands, but it felt like plenty of reach. She could stay out of his range and strike anything that got close.

The problem was that he wasn't getting close.

He raised an eyebrow.

"There a problem here?" he asked. "Hit me."

She put the batons in an X in front of her and nodded, considering.

"Why?" she asked, and he gave her a sideways grin.

"Because I told you to, darlin'."

She shook her head.

"No. What I would *do* depends on who you are and why I feel the need to attack you."

He tipped his head to the side.

"'Cause if you don't kill me first, I'm'a kill you."

She looked at his feet.

"I wager I'm faster than you," she said, and he frowned thoughtfully, teasingly, and he shifted, moving sideways, sideways, circling around her, and then resettling his feet.

"All right, now, you ain't got no away away but *through* me," he said. He'd put his back to the gate.

"I've never started a fight," Stasia said.

He grinned wider.

"Then today's the day you learn somethin' new," he told her.

"I can't beat you," Stasia said. "You're too much bigger than me. Too much stronger than me. All I'm looking for is an opportunity to get away."

He let his shoulders drop a fraction, and she saw her opening but didn't take it. He blinked at her and nodded.

"Smart girl," he said. "I known plenty 'a girls what could best me with them there, me barehanded. Got a lot of anger, them girls do, though. You got anger?"

"No," Stasia said. "Just curiosity and a willingness to stay alive."

He licked his lips, amused.

He nodded.

"Well then."

Something hit her in the middle of the back. Replaying it, later, she would place the sensation as a pair of hands just below her shoulder blades, but it came unexpectedly enough to snap her head back and she took two big steps forward into Babe, as he grabbed at her.

Ambush.

The surge of surprise from the push fueled instinctive reactions.

Fight back hard, fight back fast, fight back decisively, even if you don't know what to do.

She swung.

Babe's hands were everywhere, trying to grab her arms, trying to disarm her. She smashed at his hands, at his forearms, turning sideways to get one arm further away from him and stabbing at him with her heel. He got her arm pinned against her side and she smashed him in the face with the baton, jerking her arm away as he lost his balance momentarily, then dropping both batons in shock.

"I'm sorry," she said as he covered his brow with his hand.

He laughed.

It was the first time she'd ever heard him laugh out loud, and it was a miraculous sound.

He tipped his head back when he did it, a laugh as big as he was, and *happy* with an honesty to it that was almost novel it was so unexpected.

He lifted his head again and grinned at her, motioning at the batons.

"Pick 'em up, girl," he said. "I've gotta see that again."

They trained every day for two weeks.

Stasia's hands grew blisters that popped and wept, and Matthias taught her how to tie the linens around her hands to protect them as she kept on.

He was the one who'd pushed her, and while she was certain he'd done it either on Babe's orders or Jasper's, he was going to pay for it someday, and they both knew it.

She trained mostly with Babe, but Sterling came down sometimes to challenge, her actually teasing her with a sword as she blocked with the two batons, finding that he could place his feet, his hands, and the end of the sword basically anywhere he chose, regardless of what dictates she might have thought gravity and momentum might have imposed on him. Colin came down one afternoon with his odd angles and distracting banter, but she handled him better this time.

Matthias wasn't allowed to train with her because they were afraid he would hurt her, which Stasia found both insulting and deeply troubling. If the other men were holding back so very carefully to avoid injuring her, what was the point of all of this? Was she actually learning anything, or were they just proving that she hadn't?

She'd been in bar fights.

She'd fought off drunks and muggers and worse.

But it had always been an exchange of maybe one or two blows, and then she'd fled. Upwards, usually, where they had a very difficult time following her. Unless you'd made somebody very, very mad, breaking their nose was a good way to convince them that she wasn't the quarry they were after.

But these men fought for a living. They fought to win.

Babe and Jasper had both been in the war. Babe had been up in the mountains, at least, and it sounded like Jasper had been everywhere. They'd talked about the war as it was going on now, once or twice, as she'd sat with them at meals, and there was a hint of an idea that either of them might get called up to go back, if the king's army took key losses, but nobody liked to think about it, so they rarely spoke of it out loud.

There was so much laughter among them and so much belonging, it startled her the day that Jasper told her that they'd been called up on duty and wouldn't be at the guard house for a while.

"I can't tell you how long," he said. "So give us a week and a half before you come back looking for us."

Babe saw her from the railing as he came out of the bunkhouse and held up a hand, calling her to wait. Jasper looked over his shoulder as Colin and Sterling stuck their heads out of the mess hall.

Babe trotted down the stairs and went over to the wall of weapons, coming back with her box of daggers.

"You practice with 'em, while we're workin'," he said. "You do anythin' foolish to fill the time, you wear 'em, you got it?"

She nodded, taking the box from him as he winked.

"How do you know I'll do something foolish?" she asked and Colin laughed.

"What else are you going to do without us here to entertain you?" he asked.

"Don't go to the Black Docks," Babe said.

"Stay out of Highrock," Sterling said.

"Avoid the neighborhood south of the meat markets," Jasper said.

"Greater Highrock is okay," Colin said. "Just don't cross to Lesser."

"Like she can tell where the boundary is," Sterling said.

"Like any of us can tell where the boundary is," Babe muttered.

"Don't go into the industrial districts after dark," Jasper said.

"But other than that, have a great time," Colin said with a grin.

"Highrock, meat market, industrial," Stasia said. "Not making any promises, here, guys."

"Black Docks," Babe said, and she nodded.

"I promise."

He gave her a half a smile and nodded, setting off back up the stairs.

Jasper watched her closely for a moment then shrugged.

"Just on duty at the castle," he said. "We'll see you after a while."

"Sure," Stasia said.

THE QUEEN'S CHAIR   99

"Ought to take that mare of yours up north, give her a good run. I bet your father knows some people who would be glad to be on good enough terms with you to offer to let you ride their land."

She frowned.

"I think that's a great idea," she said, and he smiled, then raised a hand.

"Have a safe week," she said.

"No surprises is the best week," he agreed. "Hard work, still, but there isn't usually all that much going on."

She thought about the court and all of the palace guards, the number of other people around. The size of the castle and the vast swaths of the grounds she hadn't even laid eyes on.

He had to watch all that to keep the king safe.

She pressed her lips in a farewell smile, then he waved her off, going back to whatever he'd been doing.

And then suddenly she didn't know what to do with herself.

She went to the market, riding up and down through rows of stalls, seeing various things that were worth stopping to look at, but not having any place to keep Schotzli while she did it, and not wanting to risk the mare disturbing the rest of the stall while she looked.

Finally, she asked one of the vendors for directions to a good livery stable, and she left the mare within sight of the castle market, going back and taking a full afternoon to look at this, the pinnacle of open commerce in Verida.

Her sister didn't like the market. It wasn't… devoted enough. The market sellers stood there with their tables and crates of goods, taking just anyone who walked past and offering to exchange goods for money. Alyssia preferred merchants who scheduled appointments and who escorted you around charming little upholstered shops and brought you the very thing you were looking for, because you'd told them in advance what you wanted.

Stasia loved the random luck of open markets, the way the whole place breathed chance and prosperity. Not everyone there was rich, but everyone there honestly was going to leave richer than they'd been when they got there that morning. She bought a hairpin with a jewel she'd never seen before from a pixie woman - she actually had real live *wings* - somewhere near the center of the market. She bought a loaf of bread from a very fat man in an apron. Comforting, buying food from someone who very much enjoyed it.

She bought a ledger because she liked the way the leather had been colored for the cover, and because it was always nice to have a gift tucked away for her father for if occasion arose. She found another pixie selling beauty products the likes of which Stasia had never seen before, and she allowed herself to be taken in, buying much more of them than she actually needed in colors she was unlikely to use, but that she wanted to try anyway, based on just the woman's recommendation that they would suit her. It was probably a one-time transaction, but it was ever so slightly possible that she fell in love with semi-permanent dyes and made this a regular stop.

The magic of marketplaces.

She went home around dinnertime and put Schotzli away, going into the kitchen and kissing Yasmine's cheek then sampling one of the sauces for dinner and going in to find her father.

He still worked in his study frequently, but it felt like, with the whole city at his fingertips and Stasia off on her own as much as she was, he was free to leave the house and go out even more than Stasia did. Most evenings she beat him home, and so far she'd managed to hide the blisters on her hands from him. They were almost healed up, and the pixie woman at the makeup stand had given her a salve that was supposed to help. A lot, temporarily, but also accelerating how fast the skin healed even once the magic wore off.

Stasia wasn't certain how that worked, but she was game to give it a try a little and just see.

"Did you have a good day, darling?" he asked.

"Yes, Daddy," she answered, going to throw herself on his couch and look around at the art on the walls that they'd brought from Birch.

She didn't care for most of it. People who meant very little to her, seascapes of courageous boats overcoming great waves. She didn't like to look at the one of her father, her mother, and her sisters sitting in chairs out front of the house in Boton.

Her mother had been beautiful, elegant, and her sisters had been young and rosy-cheeked with a sense of excitement and potential that Stasia had never known in either of them.

She hadn't been born for two more years, after that painting.

Minstrel glanced over at her.

"If I'd known you were going to wear that to the exclusion of all else, I don't know if I would have foregone buying it or bought two."

Stasia smiled.

"It's good for the city," she said. "It washes so easily and I don't have to worry about snagging on rough corners on the way by."

"It marks you as wealthy," Minstrel said, turning forward again.

"Only among people who know what it is," Stasia said. "And they're already rich, too, most of them."

He shook his head, then, finishing what he was working on, straightened and turned in his chair.

"I believe we might have a few minutes before dinner," he said. "What shall we play?"

"Valley Over Jaze?" she asked.

He checked his pocket watch, then nodded.

"Only eight cards, I think, or else Yasmine will get upset at us."

Stasia went to get the deck of cards off of a shelf and pulled the little wooden chair up closer to his desk to deal.

She got a lucky draw at the turn and Minstrel moaned dramatically. He'd be limited at eight, like he said, but Stasia had gotten a six, and had a huge advantage.

In a single-hand game, it was almost silly to even play, but it was a game about quick hands and a quick mind, and Stasia knew as well as Minstrel did that they both kept score in their heads for a lot longer than one game at a time.

Stasia beat him handily, cards strewn all across the desk in front of her by the time she was done, and she looked up to find Tesh standing in the doorway.

"Dinner is ready," the woman said as Minstrel threw his hand onto the desk in an over-excited surrender.

"Bad draw," Stasia said with a wink.

"I'll get you next time," Minstrel said warmly. "Though I think we're reaching the point where I'm just not going to beat you as much as I used to. Fingers are getting slow."

"Never," Stasia teased. "Not you."

He shrugged and they went in to eat.

Meals were lovely with the staff at the table with them. The women chatted happily about things going on up and down the street, around the city, festivals that were coming up and events that Stasia and Minstrel might have never known about, otherwise. Minstrel talked about his day, not the business-y things, but the things that had happened at the port and unusual goods he'd seen go by for sale. Stasia mostly listened, because she hadn't mentioned the King's Guard to anyone, at this point, and she just wanted to keep it to herself, for now. It wasn't the sort of thing she ever would have told her father about, in the past, because Alyssia would have been furious about the permissiveness Minstrel had toward Stasia's activities, and it had just grown up with them.

She had her life, he had his, and she was spare. He wasn't all that worried about what she did with her time.

She finished her dinner and Minstrel went back to his study as Stasia went upstairs.

Briefly.

She hadn't done a lot of climbing, lately, and she was feeling like she was a bit out of practice. While her shoulders and her arms ached with the strain of the training with Babe and the rest of them, they were different muscles than the ones she used to climb, and while the fighting was a worthy tool for getting away from problems, she'd used the climbing much, much more frequently, in the past. She wanted to keep those skills sharp.

She took Schotzli back out again, heading north until she hit more modest housing, a space where the houses were up against each other to save on construction costs, but the streets were still well-kept and Stasia didn't worry about the liveryman letting Schotzli disappear out the back door of the barn. She went downriver a ways, knowing that the livery barns tended to be nearer to the ports and the main river, and eventually finding one. The man took Schotzli and gave her a marker, and Stasia started toward the coast, getting to a small market that was shut down for the evening and climbing up a knuckled drain pipe to stand on the roof of the building, looking out across the city.

She could see the ocean from here, the moon casting a long white trail across it like a door opened to something beyond. Here and there, boats dotted the water in silhouette, tiny little fishing boats out after dark and much larger shipping concerns, a few military vessels with their masses of sails and relatively small bodies.

In Boton, Stasia had seen the boats from Galadine, the capital of Nightik. They were all ocean-going ships, capable of withstanding the moody depths of the Fuelbik Ocean. The Sorbine Sea, what she was looking at now, was calmer, shallower, and protected from the worst of the storms that wrecked ships on the far side of the Altan mini-continent. Minstrel had told her once that, compared to the Fuelbik, you could practically walk across the Sorbine.

The water here was warm most of the year. She understood that the river ran cold a couple of times a year, once at spring thaw up at the mountains and once again at the rainy season late in the year, when they had the worst of their flooding. The rest of the year, the distance from the mountains to the coast and the warmth of the local weather meant that both the river and the shallow sea nearby were very comfortable for bathing in, if only they hadn't been choked with the debris and waste from the city. Everywhere, they threw their refuse into the rivers, and the currents tended to direct it into predictable patterns that meant that there was only one small section of coast where the water was clean enough to get into, in general, and it was somewhere out beyond about a quarter mile of mangroves.

There had been a beach at Birch. Well, a couple miles outside of Birch at a tiny coastal town called Minute, and she had often gone there with her friends during the summer, renting little shacks that opened out onto the water and spending the whole day there, going out wading in the water and enjoying the breeze off of it.

She missed the idea of serene, cooling water that she could go out into in her bare feet, collecting little shells and watching the crabs and shrimp as they scurried around.

Verida was a swamp at its most charming, and the coast did not disappoint in maintaining that mystique.

Up here, above the city, she could almost make out the shape of the castle against the black mountains, and she could hear the way that the city *sighed* at night. Air through the buildings and the grinding roll of carts along streets, but without the strong, powerful voice that it had during the day. It wasn't hushed, because Stasia didn't think that Verida had the capacity to be *hushed*, to be told that its noisesomeness was inappropriate and should be halted, but it was… resting. Taking the deep breath for the plunge into the next day.

It smelled of fish and algae almost everywhere in the city. Stasia watched men fish in almost all of the rivers, pulling out hand-sized silver fish that might keep a child from starving for a day. There were men in little carts who went up and down buying from these men in the more potentive spots, and the really good fishing spots had cartels set up to keep men out of them who weren't paid up with the right petty bosses, but there was too much river and too much hunger, and there were fish bones all along the shores.

Up this high, though, you could smell the ocean, proper, at night. The air came from the north and went south, putting a lot of the cheapest real estate down against the southern edge of the city where they got all of the city stink and smoke all over them, and - as long as you stayed away from the downwind of the meat markets - the air here was almost *clean*. It had a muggy dampness to it that made every surface in the house feel sticky, and that fostered patches of green growth anywhere that didn't have full sunlight on it all day long to finally dry it out and kill it, but…

It was a good place.

She missed home, but she had a sense that her idea of home was something that had been drifting away from her for a long time, and she was almost grateful that the move had shaken that up before she'd gotten stuck in an idea with no reality at all.

She had friends.

She had… this ephemeral idea of a *task*. Something that used *her*, rather than her station or her resources.

The queen.

She tried not to think about the queen too much, because the woman was… antithetical to a lot that Stasia believed about people and the world. Everyone was about the same, raised the same way and given the same resources, and anybody had the ability to accomplish just about anything, if they were willing to make it a narrow enough focus of the resources and knowledge that they had available to them.

Her father had been apprenticed to a traveling merchant when he was very young. His parents hadn't been able to feed him any longer when his mother got sick, and he didn't even know where he was born or where he grew up, before he joined the merchant. He'd seen all of Altan before his teenage years, met Sophia Horne in Eladin, to the south, and married her. The marriage had been the reason he'd stopped traveling. He'd been trading, saving, buying this or that where he saw value and amassing a considerable fortune for a wandering boy, and by the time Sophia had conceived Meglyn, they'd had enough to buy a house in Boton. By the time Alyssia had been walking, they'd bought the biggest house in Birch. His rise had been meteoric, opposed on many sides for his intrusion onto social conventions that didn't harbor change well, and Stasia held no illusions that her mother's noble blood had helped him through the final steps considerably.

But Minstrel Fielding didn't trade on a name. And in Kirfall, nobility was just a party circuit. The power lies with the merchants and the parliament, with significant tension between them, but birth… Birth only told you your eye color and your accent. And you could change your accent.

The idea of a queen repulsed her while at the same time holding a romance for the noble mind of a designated ruler, one who didn't have to squabble through a crowd of clutching rivals, smashing them all back with his heel on his way to power. Queen Constance was an impressive figure in Stasia's memory, and she eagerly looked forward to meeting her again, even though she wouldn't have admitted it to any of her friends in Birch.

She ran along the rooftops, jumping from high to low where it was low enough risk to practice her jumps, finding that while her body needed limbering and retraining, it remembered the *feel* of doing this in Birch and in Boton.

The feel of sliding her leg across a ridge, no weight, no drag, just perfectly at the right height to clear it and no more as she went over the edge of a roof, climbing the pitched roofs and sliding down the back sides of them to spring across a gap and land, looking for the finger and toeholds that she knew would be there.

It was the closest she would ever get to flying, and she knew it.

She reached the next river and followed it in toward the central river, finding herself looking down over an unusual space of open, green and great trees amongst buildings that looked as old and as stately as the castle itself.

She'd heard descriptions, but hadn't yet been to see it.

The university.

Jasper hadn't been the only one who had expected the idea of a formal education to tantalize Stasia. Minstrel had told her shortly after they'd finished the move that he thought she could probably find a way to gain admission at the university and take classes as she wished.

"Women are encouraged to achieve education here," he'd told her, more out of a sense of amazement than information. Certainly they'd talked about it enough at that point that it wasn't news to her.

The space was yawning, a hole in the otherwise dense population of the city, buildings surrounded by gray stone paths and then wide green lawns that were just… The weeds in Verida were tough. Many of them fought back if you wandered into them on accident. The lawns and gardens were hard-fought and rugged, as well. Stasia had seen a creature the size of a small dog burrowing in their front yard last week, and another just smaller the week before that had been tearing up the grass as though hoping to find something underneath it. Nothing was safe, so everything had to fight for the space it got, even if it was tended there.

The university had grass like she'd known in Birch. Grazing grass. Soft, barefoot grass.

The trees were big, tall, with a sense of maturity and wisdom to them that felt… untrue in this soggy-landed city. Like someone had cheated, somehow, to put them there.

Stasia watched the students out, talking, laughing, some serious and intent and others clearly drunk, and she smiled.

Maybe.

She couldn't imagine submitting herself to a place like that for hour after hour every day, but maybe. Maybe she could find a use for it.

She skirted the university and followed the river up to the market, climbing down here and looking across the river at the castle wall.

She'd been out more hours than she'd intended to, and it was going to be a long walk back to Schotzli at this point, but it felt like she'd needed to end up at the castle, tonight.

The market was quiet, dozing like the rest of the city, but not asleep. None of it ever slept completely, as far as Stasia could tell.

Like Boton.

"Would m'lady like to look at hairpins?" a man asked her.

He was closer than she'd expected him to be. She turned and he smiled, coaxing, opening a box with a glass lid for her to look at jeweled hair pins.

Stasia had enormous hair. It was her mother's. Meglyn and Alyssia had gotten Minstrel's thin blond hair and fair skin, but Stasia had Sophia's thick, curly hair and sunkissed skin. She would have lost such a trinket in her tresses, but he seemed adamant.

"Perhaps a mirror," he said, walking backwards toward his stall. She followed him, glancing back at the castle again.

Wondered what the guys were up to.

The man took a purple gemstone out of the box and touched her face to turn it as he tried to put it in her hair. She jerked away, surprised as much as offended, and he held both hands up.

"No trouble, no trouble," he said. "Such a pretty lady."

"You always sell here?" Stasia asked. "In the shadow of the castle?"

He slid the pin in at her temple, pulling a couple of curls over top of it to hide away the brassy pins and stepped away.

"Shadow of the castle," he said. "Hardly casts shade like that. Hot here, anyway. Pretty lady."

"What stone is this?" Stasia asked, looking at her reflection in the mirror.

"Pretty lady," the man murmured, reaching up to touch the stone.

Stasia heard the front edge of a shout, then…

…

She was looking at her reflection in the mirror, unable to see anything else.

She'd worn her mask tonight, because she liked to wear a mask and a cape when she went out climbing. It was silly, in one way, because she fancied that they made her mysterious and elusive, but in another way, they had definitely gotten her out of more than one bind. When she got caught out someplace she wasn't supposed to be, the mask meant that she could just run, and the odds that anyone could figure out who she was were… small. They would have to meet someone who actually recognized the description of her dragonskin. The cape meant that she could hide. Tonight she wore a much heavier cape than she had the night of the party, tied tight around her neck to keep it above her ankles, but with enough extra fabric to close in front of her, and with a cowl that would cover down to her brow line, if she could ever shove all of the hair into it.

And the man with the glass pins was right.

She was pretty.

Not in noble circles. They preferred lighter skin because it kept from confusing them with the outdoor class, and not in aspirational merchant circles, because they thought that their grandkids might marry nobles, buy themselves titles, and that Stasia would scuttle those dreams with her lineage. But she had… bold features. Expressive features. The mask was… silly, and it muted her eyes, but at the same time, it was gold and gilded and bold and… it demanded to be addressed. You couldn't overlook her in that mask.

And then somebody was shaking her.

"Miss?"

She blinked.

How long had she been standing there?

"Miss, I need you to check and see if any of your possessions are missing," someone said. "Miss."

She blinked harder.

It had been just her and the mirror for… hours.

Where was she?

Everything was gauzy and foreign and…

A man in a black leather uniform shook her once more.

"Miss? She's not coming back."

"What happened?" she asked.

"Miss," the man said, relieved. "I need you to tell me if he took anything from you."

Stasia checked her purse, but that was tucked under the armor plate on her thigh where it belonged.

"The marker for my horse," she said. "I had it… here. And…" She drew her head back, looking over at where another of the blacks was holding the man with his arms behind his back. "You took my daggers."

All four of them.

The world suddenly got very clear and very sharp.

"Over there," the man holding him said, pointing. Stasia found an assortment of goods laid out on a table. Purses and jewelry and markers and watches and daggers… She accepted the two purple-sheathed daggers from the policeman who had awoken her, then pointed.

"Those, too," she said, relieved to see that the gifts from Babe were there.

"These, miss?" he asked, and she nodded.

"Yes."

He shrugged and handed them to her, and she slid them into the straps on her legs where they lived.

The weight was interesting, but it hadn't thrown off her balance, climbing, yet.

"What happened?" Stasia demanded.

"Meet Henry Four-Hands," the man said, indicating. "Works the market after dark, pretending to be a legitimate stall-runner after they turn in for the night. Don't often catch him in the act, Miss. You ought to be careful. Not good to be out on your own like that."

"I can take care of myself," Stasia said, feeling very unsure as the words came out of her mouth. "How did he do it?"

"Pixie magic, Miss," the man said. "Don't know more about it than that, but you transfix your victim, you can search them at leisure."

"It's in the hair pins," Stasia said. "He did it with the hair pins."

"I don't think," the policeman said and Stasia shook her head, cutting him off as she went to dig through the box. She tore the pin out of her hair and held it up.

"He put this in my head and then he touched it. That's what he did."

"I believe *that*," the officer said, "but those are just glass."

"Then…" Stasia said, grasping at a reality that couldn't possibly *be*. "How?"

“Probably a powder, Miss,” the man said, looking like he might have actually felt bad for her. “A lot of these guys, they’re pulling old tricks, and they… they distract you so you don’t feel it coming.”

Stasia hadn’t had any clue it was coming.

“Look, lady,” the other man said. “We need to get him back to the police house. Go home, okay? You don’t belong out, this time of night.”

She shuddered.

He hadn’t even touched her.

And she’d completely lost herself.

It was terrifying.

She nodded.

“Yes,” she said.

She was so shaken it didn’t occur to her until halfway home that a man like that was *exactly* the person she needed to talk to about defending herself from that kind of an attack, Henry Four-Hands was, but she was simply slow, not *right*. She didn’t want to be around a man who would do that to her. He could do it again, and she couldn’t stop him any more the next time than the last.

But what she *did* need was somebody who *could* do it, but *wouldn’t*.

She took the major road, then the rooftops back to Schotzli, riding to the house and putting her up, then sneaking quietly up to her room, feeling… chastened… afraid… and very much alive.

There was a whole new universe of things to learn.

And she was behind.

She didn’t leave the house the next day.

Just… needed another day to work up her nerve.

The next morning, she got up on time to eat breakfast with her father, waving a hand at the stack of newspapers he left on the corner of the table for her.

"I saw something somewhere," she said. "About thieves in the marketplace who use magic to stun their victims while they steal all of their valuables."

Minstrel put down his paper and frowned at her.

"I've heard of that," he said.

"Have you asked anybody about how to defend from it?" Stasia asked. "I mean, both of us are out and around the city so much, we ought to be looking into it, right?" she asked.

"They regulate the castle market very tightly," Minstrel said, picking up his paper again. "And it's patrolled routinely. I think you ought to be safe there."

"But what about out traveling?" Stasia asked.

"I travel by carriage," he said. "And as long as you don't stop while you're out, I don't think you're at *great* risk."

"Daddy," Stasia said, and he put his paper down again, sighing.

"Fine," he said. "I will make some inquiries. But, Stasia, are you getting yourself into trouble?"

"Daddy, I want to be able to go out and see people without having to worry about that kind of thing. You know I go out armed. But this is a different threat. I'd at least like to *try* to do something to defend myself."

"That isn't the answer I'd hoped for," he said, then picked up his paper again.

"Daddy?" Stasia asked.

"Yes, Stasia," he answered, not looking up.

"I'd like to take Schotzli out for a run. Do you know anyone up outside of the city who might have some land where they wouldn't mind me running her for a long way?"

"Lord Westhauser came to our party last month," Minstrel answered. "I expect that I could write you a letter of introduction to him and have one of the boys from the market deliver it to him."

It was so tortured.

The vestiges of the staff from Birch they'd left at Alyssia's house because apparently running a house in Verida took training that they didn't have, and while normally Stasia didn't mind having just the three women at the house with them and the carriage man out at the stable during the days, but they'd had messengers and escorts and all manner of staff in Birch, and Stasia didn't properly know how to function here.

On the other hand, people could hardly take offense if she was just a *bit* brash, right?

"Could I take it myself?" Stasia asked.

Minstrel scratched his chin.

"You *have* been presented to them before," he said. "Yes, I suppose that would be acceptable. I don't want you getting lost, though. I think you had better take the carriage and tie Schotzli to the back."

Stasia groaned, but Minstrel was unyielding.

She went up to change into a riding outfit that wasn't the dragonskin. She had a couple that she had ordered for herself from a tailor in town, and she chose a simple brown leather set that had a sweeping green skirt of heavy canvas. The skirt was split up to her ribs in both the front and the back, and it would be easy enough to mount up on her own and the skirt would settle over her feet as she sat astride. It was an odd fashion in Birch, but she saw it on some of the women in town who were on the guard or with the police, and she'd liked it. Feminine but functional.

She waited for the carriage to return from the docks, going to clean and tack Schotzli while she did. If she couldn't be fully ornamented, at least Schotzli would. She'd had a wall of tack for her, in Birch, but she'd only brought the most functional and the most hard-to-replace individual sets of tack. The soft shearling leather on her everyday saddle was a treat, but the purple-and-brass was just… a statement that Stasia enjoyed making.

She took a rag to the mare's coat, smoothing it and shining it, and had set to work on her mane and tail with a pick comb by the time the carriage returned, and she helped the carriage man tie Schotzli's lead to the carriage, then got in, realizing as they set off that she should have brought something to read.

The main roads were clogged heavily at this time of day with foot traffic and carts, little pulling animals or man-powered. There were the transit carts with their teeming loads of people and the small number of carriages with the amount of roadspace that they took up. Stasia knew that there were back routes that might have been faster, but the carriages were almost only on the riverside roads, and Stasia suspected that it was to avoid confrontations with thieves. As she looked out the window, she saw police in their black leathers dotting the roads and intersections.

It was a dangerous city.

Yes, Boton was a dangerous city, full of pickpockets and cutpurses, drunk men with their daggers and the sober ones with theirs. But they were known dangers. Verida had *unknown* dangers, and Stasia needed to find someone who could teach her of *those*.

Why had Babe spent two weeks making her drill with the daggers when a man could come up to her and breathe a word of greeting and make her lose herself? Wasn't that the greater threat?

They passed the castle at perhaps the hour mark of the trip. She might have made better time the night before on foot. Here, the pinchpoint at the market was all shouting and edging forward, but once they crossed to the castle side of the next river branch, they got going and the horses got up to a trot.

Stasia watched the castle go by out the window, the wall blocking all but the highest point of the castle itself at this proximity, and then it was gone. There was a section of higher-end housing beyond the castle, then the beginning of the lesser estates. Stasia had been this far before, but another quarter hour and they were outside of anything that felt like city. The country became rolling and green, with great outcrops of trees in the midst of grazing fields, orchards, vineyards, and dark green crops. Rock walls marked out the edges of fields from the road and each other, and Stasia frowned at them. They were the reason she had to go to all this trouble to go riding.

Yes, Kirfall had fences and boundaries and hedges and walls. What they *didn't* have was the sense of unnoble trespass if someone were to ride across them. The roads were faster, in almost all cases, than riding across the countryside, so Stasia wasn't creating paths any deeper than the cattle themselves did. And so long as she didn't scatter flocks or trample crops, nobody cared if she was there at all.

The country was pretty. The mountains, visible and dominant from the city, became clearer and clearer through the muggy air, and the hills rolled in a way that kept secrets and privacy that didn't happen in cities. In a city, there were buildings and walls, but ultimately someone could always see you and hear you. Especially if they wanted to. Out here…

It was more like traveling in toward the center of Altan from Birch than it was traveling from Boton to Birch, but it was still familiar and sweet, being out here. She could hear Schotzli's footsteps quicken as they got further out into the country. She knew the potential of why they were out here.

They turned, and now the mountains were all out Stasia's window. She leaned her chin on her hand, watching them with awe. Nothing was that big. Just nothing. They were more comparable to waves at sea than anything on land, and she had an instinct to go stand on top of them. She wondered what she could see from up there.

Another thirty minutes or so, perhaps, and they turned off of the narrow road onto an entranceway that was…

Stasia threw herself back in her seat, wrinkling her nose as statues went past outside.

It was elaborate and it was certainly *beautiful,* but it was so self-celebratory.

The entrance road was wider than the road that ran along the front of the property, and it was split so that traffic could go in both directions without passing on the same road. In the middle was landscaping of increasing size and complexity, ending up with trees that were bigger from one side to the other than Stasia was tall. On the outside edges of the road were the effigies. Monument after monument to dead people. Because everyone who had ever been in the Westhauser family was worth remembering forever.

Stasia's opinion of Lord and Lady Westhauser dimmed significantly, seeing it.

They crested a hill and started down toward a lake, following the merged road around the edge of the water toward an enormous house.

It was bigger than their house in Birch by a good bit, and Stasia had long believed that they had the biggest private residence in all of Kirfall.

Clearly anything bigger than the Fielding house in Birch was unreasonably big.

Clearly.

The carriage man pulled the carriage to a stop in front of the grand front doors and came to get the carriage door for Stasia.

All she'd wanted was to go for a ride.

She held the letter from her father, looking up at the building with a sense of pointlessness that was rivaled only by how daunted she was.

One family lived here.

She could hear voices around, men working the grounds, and Schotzli stamped a foot, impatient to be off, devouring the great open ground around them.

She'd come this far.

Stasia went to knock on the door.

A man answered it.

Glancing at the carriage, he dipped his head.

"Good morning. Are you expected?"

Stasia licked her lips.

Brazen. She was here because she was new and important and didn't know better.

"No," she said, holding out the letter from her father. "But I have an introduction from Minstrel Fielding. I am his daughter, Anastasia."

She thought that giving her full name to staff was cruel, so she didn't do it.

"Very good, ma'am," he said, stepping aside. "If you will wait here, please. Someone will bring you refreshments shortly."

She watched after him, then looked around the grand entrance.

It was bigger than the castle.

The big court room in the castle had been big and gray and stony and stoic, and she had genuinely liked it. This was white and gold and brass with lifetimes of artisanry in evidence everywhere she looked. It was gaudy, and it didn't take a merchant's daughter of Stasia's experience to see the cost of it.

A minute or two later a serving girl in a trim black dress came with a tray of drinks. There was a bottle of wine and a decanter of water along with two glasses. Stasia accepted the water, going to sit at a small table and pouring the water for herself. It was hot out, and the water felt really good, going down her throat.

Another five minutes and there was the sound of soft steps from around a corner.

Stasia stood.

"Lady Westhauser," she said. "I'm very sorry to disturb you."

"No disturbance at all," the woman answered. "It's good to have a new face to consider. The Lord Westhauser is out until tonight, at least, but your father's note says that you are looking for a place to ride that's within the queen's territory."

Stasia blinked.

"I'm just looking for green ground where it's not rude for me to have been there," she said. "I don't know what that has to do with the queen, if I'm honest."

Lady Westhauser went to go sit opposite Stasia's seat at the table, pouring herself a glass of water. Stasia went to join her, not sure what to make of the woman.

"We didn't get to speak much, the night of your party in town," Lady Westhauser said, holding her glass thoughtfully. "Though I've heard people speak *of* you considerably more."

Stasia smiled.

"They spoke of you considerably, that night," she said, and Lady Westhauser snorted.

"They speak of fashion and conformity," she said. "Sometimes I do something outrageous just to needle them. I have the instinct that you do the same."

Stasia considered that, smiling.

Lady Westhauser was dressed in a sleeveless black velvet dress that was not entirely different from the one that she'd worn at the party that night. Stasia only remembered because of how much everybody had talked about it. The party dress had been more… structural, embroidered with black thread and with a sweeping gown to it, where this just emphasized the narrowness of the woman's waist and the graceful sweep of her arms.

She wasn't like anyone Stasia had ever seen before, this woman. Her skin wasn't just fair. It outright lacked pigment, and her hair was nearly as white as her skin. Everything about her was just far enough off of marble to be human and no more, including eyes that were only just barely blue enough to qualify as icy and that were framed by white spectacles that gave her an even more intent natural expression.

"I do," Stasia said. "Not as much as they think I do, but I do do that. Mostly I just don't care what they think."

Lady Westhauser dipped her head in acknowledgment.

"A sentiment I very much admire," she said. Stasia looked around the room involuntarily, then jerked her attention back to Lady Westhauser with a sense of guilt.

She was here to ask for a favor.

Lady Westhauser laughed.

It was the laugh that made Stasia see it.

Lady Westhauser was no older than she was.

More elegant, certainly, and in this adorably petite body that was infinitely more attractive than Stasia would ever be, but… there was a sparkle to her that Stasia hadn't seen the night of the party, hadn't had the opportunity to see, that was very familiar.

"I know," Lady Westhauser said, looking around the room. "The old Lady Westhauser, Lord Westhauser's mother, was very proud of her accomplishments in this place. Very proud of the entire estate. Noblewomen are basically tasked with the entire running of the estate, did you know that? It's in many cases as large or larger an enterprise than most of the businesses in the city."

"But a business produces something," Stasia said, wishing she could take it back even as she said it. She did *not* come here to insult this woman. She just… Seeing it in person, it might have been even harder to accept than the idea of a king and queen.

"The estates produce food and wine and a large number of other products," Lady Westhauser told her. "You're right that the manor mostly only sustains itself and a vast swarms of servants. The property, though, is supported by a village about a half a mile from here, and there is all manner of industry. We produce a thousand pounds of woven fabric a month. Two hundred pounds of beeswax a year. There's a tanner and a charcoal man. They dig clay in a section of the property and there are four potters working, in the village. We export lye and candles and wine. My husband, though, sees to the investment of the actual *assets* of the estate. His father left him a considerable wealth beyond the property. My husband admires your father's interest in such things, though he doesn't share it."

"My father believes that trade is the most noble pursuit a man can master," Stasia said.

Lady Westhauser gave her a thin but genuine smile.

"But you do not?" she asked.

Stasia shrugged.

"I'm a spinstress and a spare daughter," she said. "When I was born, all I did was dilute my father's wealth and deprive him of his wife. I don't have beliefs of any significance."

"Oh, I very much doubt that," Lady Westhauser said with quiet humor. "Though I'm sorry to hear of your mother. I write to mine every week, and I can't imagine having been deprived of her through my childhood."

"Many people grow up without a mother," Stasia said, and Lady Westhauser nodded.

"I'm well aware, and I'm sorry for each and every one of them with the same sincerity."

Stasia frowned, trying to absorb this.

At the party, at Alyssia's party, at *all* parties, the wealthy - and the nobles - came together to demonstrate their strict manners and formal relationships. Everything was about catching hold of a string attached to someone else who might be useful to you, someday. Bonus if you actually liked being around them, but hardly a requirement.

"Also, you're hardly old enough to be considered a spinstress. I was married just barely more than a year ago. You could wed if you were of the mind," Lady Westhauser said.

"I'm not," Stasia said. "I don't want to be a merchant's wife. Hard enough being one's daughter."

"What of a nobleman's wife?" Lady Westhauser asked. "There are always plenty around looking for the finance to maintain their estates."

Stasia snorted.

"Hence the dilution of my father's wealth," she said. "I'm not interested in a title. They mean nothing in Kirfall. No. I'm happy enough on my own."

Lady Westhauser nodded, rising.

"I didn't learn to ride, growing up," she said. "I think that I have been negligent. I cannot send you out across the property on your own, for fear that you might get lost or unseated, and I suspect, looking at you, that I cannot keep up with you all day, but if you would be willing to work with me…"

"Yes," Stasia said quickly. "I would love company."

It wasn't the *point*. She still wanted to get Schotzli a chance to stretch her legs out and feel the ground roll away below her, but she liked this woman. Had an instinct to stay here and talk all afternoon, like nothing would make her happier, right now.

Lady Westhauser took Stasia's hand in her own and squeezed it.

"Miss Fielding, I am so glad you came today," she said. "Let me see if I have something I can wear that will be appropriate for sitting horseback, and I will be back with you very shortly. Please don't be shy about a glass of wine if you would like one. It's bottled here on the estate and it's actually quite good."

Stasia nodded, watching Lady Westhauser go, then poured herself a glass happily.

There were voices all over the house, hushed and quick, but there were much *louder* voices a few minutes later, and then Lady Westhauser appeared wearing rolled-up trousers that were too big for her and a linen shirt that tucked into the trousers like a vegetable bag. Her hair was looser, pulled back in multiple tails down her back, and her eyes were wide as a matron of *significant* standing chased her into the entryway.

"Lady Westhauser," she demanded, and the pale woman stretched her eyes at Stasia.

"I won't tell if you don't," Stasia murmured, and Lady Westhauser grinned, rushing for the door.

"I really like that," Lady Westhauser said, fingering the fabric of Stasia's skirts as they went out into the yard where the carriage stood. Schotzli stomped at Stasia again.

"It's modeled on what the female members of the guard wear," Stasia said. "But *I* don't have to wear leather if I don't want to."

"It's pretty," Lady Westhauser agreed. "Leather underneath?"

"For if I fall," Stasia agreed. "Keeps you from getting all cut up in brush."

"Hot, though," Lady Westhauser said, and Stasia nodded.

"It *shouldn't* be any hotter here than in Boton. We're no farther south. But it *is*. It's so much hotter."

"I didn't know that," Lady Westhauser said.

"You wear velvet," Stasia said, and Lady Westhauser laughed.

"If you wear little enough of it, it's tolerable," she said. "And my seamstress is a wizard. She lines the velvet with something that keeps me from suffocating in it. If you don't mind her taking a look at you before you leave…?"

"For the riding skirts?" Stasia asked. "Of course. Your hair is *beautiful*."

Lady Westhauser tossed her head gently, the long smooth tails drifting back and forth across her back like they were in a breeze.

"My head of household hates it," Lady Westhauser said. "Wishes I would dye it brown or black so that I could wear other colors."

"*Why*?" Stasia demanded. "You're the only person like you."

She bit her tongue - literally bit it - realizing that she must feel like she stood out in the same way that Stasia sometimes did. Lady Westhauser noted her self-castigation and shook her head.

"I'm hardly unaware," she said. Stasia looked over at her, boldness overcoming social sense.

"You're *unique*," Stasia said, embracing it. "Why would you want to look like everybody else? *Stand out*. You don't mute your natural advantages. You use them."

Lady Westhauser looked over at her sharply.

"How are you the only one who sees that?" she asked.

Stasia blinked, feeling like the answer was obvious.

"Because merchants live and die by their natural advantages," she said. "And nobles live and die by birth."

Lady Westhauser covered her mouth with her hand.

"Oh, we're going to be friends, you and I," she said. "Marvelous friends."

***

Lady Westhauser was no woman of leisure.

True enough, she had a very hard time finding her seat, and she wiggled a lot on the saddle after the first hour as the stiffness of unused muscle set in, but she had a boldness to her that suggested she was very good at other things, when it came to her physical prowess. Stasia expected that there were noblewoman sports of some kind or another that she probably played aggressively.

Lady Westhauser showed her where the village was, then they wandered the edge of the property for some time, eventually cutting through to a place where their guide - a stableboy in his late teens with a willingness to wander ahead or behind them with his mind elsewhere - said that there was a good place to water the horses and where Lady Westhauser could rest for a bit while Stasia and Schotzli got their exercise.

The pond was lovely and the trees were a kind that Stasia didn't know, with long drooping branches that seemed almost ready to sip at the water themselves. Lady Westhauser dismounted and let the boy tie her horse to a tree nearby while she went to sit at the base of one of the huge trees, tucked down in among its sprawling roots.

"Take as long as you like," she said airily.

"Are you safe out here on your own?" Stasia asked, and the woman gave her a cutting glance.

"I'd like to see someone take me unawares," she said. "Because I'd do it right back to them."

Stasia believed her.

The stableboy set a pace, thinking Stasia would struggle to keep up, but Schotzli leaped out ahead as soon as the idea of a race presented itself, and soon the stableboy and his workaday mount fell behind.

They took in miles, hitting the property marker at the quarter hour or so and turning to race along it, dodging thickets of undergrowth and jumping the wall at the edge of a cow pasture, then turning along another route and jumping their way out. She caught sight of the stable boy as Schotzli finally began to ease of her own accord - she could go on for hours more, if she needed to, but the pent up energy was finally spent - and Stasia decided to follow the social conventions rather than her own instincts for now.

She pulled up even with the stable boy and let him lead them back to the pond where Lady Westhauser was gazing out across the water dreamily. The woman roused herself when she heard them, going to untie her mount and clambering back up into the saddle on her own and they set off again.

"You're both sweaty," she observed.

"Good run," Stasia answered, elated. "Can we do it again?"

"Any time," Lady Westhauser said. "Just let them know down at the stables that you're going out so they can come looking for you if you don't turn up by sundown."

Stasia looked over at her.

"Really?"

Lady Westhauser shrugged.

"You're both sweaty. He isn't. Clearly he didn't keep up with you the whole time. What's the point of asking someone to go out with you when the point is to run the legs off a faster horse?"

Stasia grinned, scrubbing Schotzli's neck.

"She's even braver than I am, too," she said.

"Hard to imagine," Lady Westhauser said.

"What do you do up here all day?" Stasia asked, realizing as she said them that they were the wrong words, but also knowing that there was a magic here that made them into the right words.

"Tell people what to do," Lady Westhauser said glumly. "That way it's my fault if it goes wrong." She straightened abruptly. "Would you like to see the gardens?"

Stasia frowned, surprised that Lady Westhauser would be so delighted at the idea of something as simple as a garden, but she shrugged.

"Okay."

They got back to the manor house and let the boy take all three horses - Schotzli on one side by herself so she wouldn't nip the other two - back to the barn to care for them. Stasia would check in quickly to make sure they got Schotzli adequately cooled before they let her eat, but for now she let Lady Westhauser wind her arm through her own and lead her around the back of the house.

"The front of the house has a plan that the old Lady Westhauser put together," the woman explained as they went. "They're quite fond of it, around here, and I haven't wanted to press my luck, changing anything. The back of the house, though, she only did a very little bit of it because she and her friends would stay on the front patio almost all the time. Only sometimes would they go out back, but they would stay in close to the house. So the back…"

They rounded the far corner of the house and Stasia gasped.

It was *outrageous*.

"Is this what noble gardens look like?" Stasia asked.

THE QUEEN'S CHAIR   127

"No," Lady Westhauser giggled. "They're all very ordered and ornate and well-groomed. Lady Bentmoor has an absolute obsession with *smell*. Her garden is scheduled by season and hour of the day to have coordinated scent."

The colors were eye-gouging, and the plants big and wild and tangled.

"You did this in a year?" Stasia asked.

"The nobles look down on the plants that grow out in the flat," Lady Westhauser said. "But I knew of some that are just… beautiful, though vicious and dominating. So we went and transplanted all of the plants that I wanted to see what they could do, if they were actually given real soil and sun and not have to grow between two bricks at the side of a building, and… well, a lot of them won't live without that kind of challenge, it seems, and others are much smaller in the soil here, but a few of them have truly thrived, and I found a gardener who is willing to play at it as hard as I am. I can't wait to see what we can do with a few more years. Or decades."

The last bit was almost sad, though her eyes were fiercely proud, looking out over the sloping garden.

They went along, following stone paths past fountains and statues and benches, Lady Westhauser's arm wrapped through Stasia's as she pointed at the various plants and told the stories of them.

"How do you know all of the plants down in the city?" Stasia asked. "You spend a lot of time down there?"

"As much as I can," Lady Westhauser said with a personal smile. "Yes."

"I did, too, when we lived outside of Boton," Stasia said. "I was always sneaking down into the city."

Lady Westhauser nodded, then smiled brilliantly.

"Perhaps the secret to it is being able to ride a horse on your own. I've always been dependent on carts and carriages."

"It certainly helps," Stasia said.

"Stay," Lady Westhauser said enthusiastically. "Would you? Can you stay for dinner? I'm hoping Lord Westhauser makes it home tonight, and I would love for him to actually get to meet you outside of the party silliness."

"They *are* silly," Stasia agreed. "But I shouldn't just not turn up at dinner at home."

"And it would mean being here late," Lady Westhauser said. "I understand if you don't like to travel after dark."

"Oh, I don't mind the dark," Stasia said. "I just… I'm not a *free* woman, Lady Westhauser. I need to be where my father expects me, at certain intervals."

"Then let me send word," Lady Westhauser said. "That you'll be spending the night here at Westhauser Manor. I've not met a merchant yet who wouldn't jump at the opportunity to forge ties with the Westhausers."

Stasia couldn't argue with that.

And she didn't want to *go.*

She didn't want to go *into* that silly house, nor deal with the formalities of staying there as a guest, but… She looked over at Lady Westhauser in her rolled-up sleeves and pants.

"I do not want to be a burden," Stasia said.

"I insist," Lady Westhauser said, pressing her hand against Stasia's forearm.

"Then let's go see your wizard seamstress," Stasia said happily, and Lady Westhauser turned them around a loop at the next fountain, heading back to the house.

They spent the rest of the afternoon sitting in the seamstress's studio while the woman took the measurements of Stasia's garb and discussed fabrics and alterations that would make it more suitable for a woman of Lady Westhauser's station.

Stasia was unbothered by the talk of how Stasia's skirts weren't good enough for Lady Westhauser; she didn't have to live up to these standards, and she was indulgent in that knowledge.

They talked of manor life and of town, of Verida and parties and the nobles. Lady Westhauser seemed hungry for details of Stasia's life, and Stasia was free with the details of it, outside of her relationship with the guard.

A woman arrived with folded hands and a stiff posture.

"Dinner, m'lady," she said.

"Any sign of Lord Westhauser?" Lady Westhauser asked.

"His carriage just rounded the curve," the woman said, and Lady Westhauser sprang to her feet, grabbing Stasia by the hand and leading her through the house, up out of the working quarters and into the entertaining spaces, to the front door where a butler was holding the door open for the man that Stasia had met at the party.

At the time, Stasia hadn't cared about anybody in particular. There had been things that she had noticed, certainly, and she'd learned every name the way she'd been trained to since childhood, but he had been just another man at the time, if one that her father had been particularly interested in.

"Husband," Lady Westhauser said. He took off his hat, handing it to the butler and dropped his head in greeting.

"Wife," he answered. Lady Westhauser went to him, leaving Stasia, and he kissed her cheek, but the way that she leaned against him, pushing her face against his, felt more intimate than Stasia had ever seen anyone with money act.

He put his nose into her hair for just an instant, then he straightened and she turned to face Stasia with a bright face.

"Lord Westhauser, may I present Miss Isabella Gabriella Angelina Aurora Renata Anastasia Fielding-Horne."

He gave her a formal, low bow, his shoulders nearly reaching the level of his hips. Stasia was almost certain that it was a toss-up between genuine honor and mocking her, but it was significant one way or the other.

"I didn't tell you my full name," Stasia said, and Lady Westhauser smiled.

"I memorize all of them," she said. "And it's not often there's somebody new."

"Miss Fielding," Lord Westhauser. "It's an honor."

"Fielding-Horne," Lady Westhauser corrected. "Anastasia Fielding-Horne."

"Of course," he said. "I didn't know that you two had met informally."

"She came today looking for a place to go riding," Lady Westhauser said. "She's a very accomplished rider."

Lord Westhauser looked Stasia up and down and nodded.

"I hadn't heard," he said. "I assume you are taking the meal with us."

"She's staying the night," Lady Westhauser said.

Lord Westhauser's eyebrows went up.

"Is that so?"

"Yes," Lady Westhauser said. "And now dinner is ready."

"Well, well," Lord Westhauser said, walking toward Stasia. He offered her his right elbow. "May I?"

She put her hand through his elbow, looking at him carefully.

He looked away, unbothered, offering his other elbow to Lady Westhauser, who put her whole arm through it and leaned her face against his shoulder.

Lord Westhauser was an attractive man. He had angular features that had the parallel advantages of being sharp at the right points and very symmetric. His mouth curled in a pleasant if inscrutable smile. She couldn't tell anything about him but that Lady Westhauser loved him dearly; for right now that was absolutely enough.

They walked into an elegant dining room set for three, and Lord Westhauser escorted Stasia to a chair, pulling it out for her and pushing it in under her, then going and doing the same for Lady Westhauser.

He allowed a butler to push in his chair and adjusted himself at the table.

"I regret that I wasn't able to freshen up before dinner," he said. "I wasn't sure if I would be able to make it at all, until I actually set off."

"Do you often stay in the city?" Stasia asked.

"He has an apartment," Lady Westhauser said. Stasia didn't like the idea of Lady Westhauser being out here by herself all day and all night. It was so lonely.

It only took her a moment to see the irony in that, but still, the way that Lady Westhauser had lit up when Lord Westhauser had walked through the door told her everything she needed to know.

"My heart is always in two places," the man said, reaching over to take Lady Westhauser's hand and smiling again, and she nodded.

"As is mine," she said.

Stasia noticed a scar across the back of Lord Westhauser's neck that looked like the result of real violence, and she frowned, looking at his hands.

Something about him didn't make sense.

He didn't fit.

He looked over at her again.

"You've stirred significant interest in town," he said easily as the kitchen staff brought in their meals. "I must admit I'm profoundly shocked to find you at my table, tonight, though hardly surprised at all that my wife has taken such an interest in you so quickly."

"Now that's a riddle," Stasia answered. "You'll have to forgive me. I'm not used to the culture of Verida, or of nobles in general, so you need to know that whatever subtle information there is in that, it's lost on me."

He laughed, quietly at first, then showing his teeth.

"Yes," he said. "Very well said."

"She calls herself the spare daughter," Lady Westhauser said. "Has no interest in marriage."

"And why should she?" Lord Westhauser asked. "She is wealthy and well-kept, without the demands of husband or household? We should all be so lucky."

He glanced over at her, and there was something… almost wicked in that look.

Stasia looked over at Lady Westhauser, but the woman was changed. It might have been infatuation. It might have been a romantic idea of marriage and devotion. But Stasia had seen it with her own eyes, hadn't she? The way he'd answered her at the door?

"So what interests do you have, if not marriage?" Lord Westhauser asked.

"She rides," Lady Westhauser said. "Her mare is a beautiful animal."

"I'm sure I'll see her tomorrow. I'll ride into town with Miss Fielding-Horne and ensure that she arrives at her father's house safely. It's the least I can do, for so significant a guest."

"No," Stasia said. "That won't be necessary."

"Oh, but I insist," Lord Westhauser said. "Besides, why would I send two carriages into town?"

"I can just ride," Stasia said. "My father didn't want me to get lost on my way here, but it's much simpler, getting home."

He smiled, taking a small bite of his food. Lady Westhauser was looking at him thoughtfully, then she lifted her head.

"Staff out, please," she said.

He sighed, and Stasia frowned.

"You do this too much," he murmured as the servers left.

"They can live with it," Lady Westhauser answered. "Besides, you're making yourself out to be a bully. Please go check them."

He sighed and stood, going to push the door to the kitchen roughly. There was the muffled sound of bodies hitting the floor on the other side of the door, and Stasia covered a smile with her fingers.

"There, now," Lady Westhauser said. "Can we drop *some* of the pretenses, please?"

Lord Westhauser leaned against the door to the kitchen, crossing his arms.

"What do you want me to say, Ella?" he asked.

"I want to hear what you're actually thinking, and I want you to behave better in front of my friend. She thinks you're going to try to seduce her on the way back into the city, for the queen's sake."

He snorted, then sighed, looking at Stasia.

"I've heard various things about you, and while I believe they paint a coherent picture, I would like to be sure before I welcome you into my home so… completely."

"What is it you're afraid I might be?" Stasia asked.

He narrowed his eyes, giving the door one more good shove, then coming back to sit at the table as it swung freely back into its frame. He put his elbows on the table and lifted his chin as he looked at her.

"Less."

"Less of any particular thing?" Stasia asked. "I think I'm tall enough, at least."

Oh, that was guard-level talk. She regretted it immediately, but he smiled at this.

"I see," he said. Lady Westhauser looked particularly self-satisfied. Lord Westhauser took a careful breath and sighed, then nodded. "What you don't understand, being a double outsider as you are, is that acquaintance with the Westhauser estate is highly coveted because it is incredibly *rare*. Your father sent you here, likely innocently on your part, as a speculative play that you might be able to forge a relationship with us where so many have failed, before. I keep closer ties to the merchant class than I do the nobles, but Lady Westhauser has not had an overnight guest to the manor since she has taken her title. I'm not looking to be taken in by a young woman who will giggle and smile and do anything to earn my approval, and while I trust Lady Westhauser's judgment implicitly, I need to check for myself. I hope you'll forgive me."

"Is it so hard to find good friends when you're this rich?" Stasia asked.

"It's always hard to find good friends, no matter who or where you are," Lord Westhauser answered. "Don't ever forget that."

Stasia frowned, and he resumed his dinner.

"Are you satisfied, Wife?" he asked. Lady Westhauser smiled at her own food.

"Very," she said. "I have told her that she is welcome here any time."

"Is it true what they told me outside?" Lord Westhauser asked. "You, yourself, went out riding today?"

"I want a riding outfit like hers," Lady Westhauser said. "Sandra is already working on it."

"No doubt in red velvet," Lord Westhauser said. Stasia boggled slightly at this. It did have a front piece of red velvet.

Lady Westhauser looked entirely unsurprised.

"It's time for me to learn it," she said. "It will give me more independence."

"I trust your instincts," he answered. "Make sure you respect your limitations."

"What limitations?" Stasia asked, and Lord Westhauser smiled.

"You have picked a good one," he said. "I only mean that she shouldn't take the ride into town until she's sure that she can handle both the unexpected *and* the horse. There is literally *nothing* that my wife can't do."

Those were words that struck Stasia profoundly, particularly because he appeared to mean them.

They ate in silence for a few minutes as Stasia tried to watch both of them, catch any signals between them that might tell her something useful about them, and then Lord Westhauser straightened.

"Having dismissed the servants, they can't come bring me my next course," he said.

"Truth is worth the inconvenience," Lady Westhauser answered, smiling, and he reached over to squeeze her hand.

"I wish you could have been in town with me today," he told her. "I've come across a puzzle that your mind would appreciate."

"I'm looking for ways to divest myself," Lady Westhauser answered. "But there is so much complexity to it."

He nodded, then stood, going through the door that the staff had disappeared through.

"You actually love him," Stasia murmured, and Lady Westhauser nodded.

"I actually do," she answered, her voice just as low. "We were lucky, the two of us, that things aligned as they did. I'd never looked for it, and then I found it. The trick is fighting for it once you know it's there."

Stasia shook her head.

Her father had *loved* her mother. She believed that. He had swept her off her feet and convinced her to risk her fortune with him, in point of fact. But he didn't… Stasia couldn't imagine Minstrel Fielding looking at *anyone* the way Lord Westhauser looked at Lady Westhauser when he came to sit back down again. It made Stasia feel like blushing, to even bear witness to it, and she'd seen things in dark corners that ought to have *actually* made her blush, where her reaction had been simple curiosity instead.

This was something very different and considerably more intimate that she was witnessing, and she couldn't tear her eyes away. So she kept staring at her plate because she couldn't imagine how invasive her interest must have looked to them.

"So as long as I am going to give the impression of an economic tie to the Fielding family, I may as well explore the potential of it," Lord Westhauser said as the next course came in.

"I don't know anything about my father's business," Stasia answered. Not literally true, but it captured the situation well enough that it stemmed misunderstandings, she found.

Lord Westhauser played with his knife for a moment, and Stasia found herself captivated by his fingers, seeing once more the discontinuity of persona there without being able to name it.

"It's said that he is very strict in his dealings," Lord Westhauser said. "That he will not dabble in speculation of any dubious nature at all."

"If you're suggesting law-breaking, as far as I am aware, my father does not abide it," Stasia answered, and Lord Westhauser nodded. That was exactly what he'd been suggesting.

"I find that admirable," he said. "If it's true." He let the knife rest on the table and held up his fingers to arrest her reply. "I don't mean to imply that I know or believe otherwise. Simply that I don't know one way or the other, and one must always question. If it is true, I admire it greatly. Too many men rise above the competition through… dark means, shall we say, and then paint themselves white and say that they do not condone such things. But it is said that he is an honest man who does honest trade with a great mind for opportunity. And that that opportunity is what has brought him here."

"Like I said, I wouldn't know," Stasia answered. "He doesn't talk to me about the specifics of his business."

No, they just spent hours discussing the generalities, running thought experiments and playing games of competitors, inventing solutions to imaginary problems. She knew much more than she let on. She just didn't know what was in the boxes or the names of the men counting the money.

And she did genuinely believe that her father abhorred cheaters.

Lord Westhauser's fingers played over the handle of the knife again, not in a way that signaled intent or violence. Stasia wasn't remotely nervous watching it.

And then she saw it.

He handled the dinner knife the way Babe had handled her daggers.

"You're very well-armed for a rich girl," Lord Westhauser said, and Stasia blinked, jerking her eyes up from his hand. How long had she been silent?

"Yes," she said. "I like not having to worry, going out on my own."

"You go out on your own?" Lord Westhauser asked. "In a city like this?"

"In any city," Stasia answered boldly, trying to figure out what it meant. "I want to be prepared, I want to be unafraid, but I ultimately don't want to be *kept*. Do you know what I mean?"

"Perhaps better than you do," he said after a moment. "Ella, you truly have chosen a remarkable one, entirely at random."

"Nothing is random about it," Lady Westhauser answered. Stasia looked over at her, and Lady Westhauser smiled. It was a friend's smile, familiar, and if there was a secret in it, it was a secret that the woman intended to tell her at some point when the situation allowed it.

"I see," Lord Westhauser said. "Well, the Westhauser estate has considerable assets at its disposal, often looking for plausible investments. You may tell your father that I would be... willing to discuss some manner of business with him, if he were interested in such a thing."

Stasia wondered what that meant.

She knew that her father collaborated on various investments all the time, a way of diversifying risk across multiple projects, but she couldn't imagine something that he would seek out Lord

Westhauser specifically to involve him. The Fielding empire didn't require outside capital if it didn't want it. That was the sign of an empire struggling to launch begging capital from outside investors to support a project. Evidently her confusion showed. Lord Westhauser licked his lips and nodded.

"Gormand is a good man, smart and capable. I haven't ever worked with him, specifically, but if you had to choose one of the young men coming up through the trading class, I can't think of one that I would advocate more as a partner. But he doesn't have... access the way that I do. I'm not suggesting anything untoward, but I glide through a different class of people than he could ever hope to, and there are certain things that are only available when you have the quality of connections that I have the reach for."

"If you're talking about bribery," Stasia warned, and he shook his head.

"Not at all. But your father plays games that most people can't even see. Including Gormand. You tell him I'm available. He may or may not have his path already lined up, and perhaps nothing will come of it, but he'll know why I said something."

Stasia sucked on her lips and then nodded.

"I will," she said, and he gave her a dry smile.

"Now," he said. "The boring part is done. Who would like to play a game? Three is so much more interesting than two."

Lady Westhauser grinned.

"Bent Spoon," she said, and he dipped his head.

"Perfect."

❖

Stasia left the table breathless.

Long after the dishes had been cleared, they'd played games. Lord Westhauser had produced a deck of cards from his pocket and they'd played games Stasia had never seen before, new rules, new strategies. She'd played cards with her father since she was very small, but Alyssia and Meglyn had never been interested in them, nor had most of Stasia's friends. They'd played the more casual games, the ones you could hold a conversation while you played, and they were constantly losing track of whose turn it was.

Lord and Lady Westhauser were nothing like that. It was like playing with her father, but the two of them would try to hold a conversation with you with the express intent of keeping you from being able to count cards or plot a strategy. It had taken Stasia an hour, during one particular game, to realize that they kept using topics that were rich in numbers to mess with her. Intentionally.

Even more, though, they messed with each other. Lady Westhauser would play an entire hand without picking it up. Lord Westhauser would play a card, face down, and watch Lady Westhauser for second after second, then pull it back and pick a new card, watching her once more, like not only could he read what she thought of the play, but she knew what was in his hand well enough to have a reaction to a card face-down on the table.

It was incredible.

Stasia never wanted to leave.

If it was possible for her, in her state of life, to have a crush, she had a crush on Lord Westhauser, even as the man made her incredibly uneasy.

She sat in Lady Westhauser's room as the woman put together a sleeping outfit for her. They'd spent most of an hour rehashing the closest or most tactical hands of cards from the night, the fizzy glory of the evening just persisting and persisting, but they'd finally gone quieter, easy and comfortable with each other in a way that Stasia couldn't specifically remember.

"Lord Westhauser," she said, and Lady Westhauser nodded.

"Yeah."

"He's not what he seems," Stasia said, and Lady Westhauser shook her head.

"No. He isn't."

She wanted to ask about the way his fingers knew a knife, but it felt… wrong. Like it invalidated something about the way the night had felt.

Lady Westhauser went and stuck her head out into the hallway, then closed the door to her room, coming back to sit across from Stasia on the bed.

"His life is in the city," she said. "And I'm not going to pretend to know everything about it. More than you know about your father's business, but not like… I can *predict* how he will be, but it isn't because I *know*, do you understand?"

Stasia nodded, not entirely certain that she *did* understand, but willing Lady Westhauser to go on, in hopes of catching up.

"I don't know that you coming here today was random," Lady Westhauser said. "If that bothers you… Well, I don't want it to surprise you, when you figure it out. Because I don't want you to suddenly decide that… We should be friends. And if you discover that Lord Westhauser manipulated situations to make it so that your father would send you here, making something that *looked* random into something that was actually intentional… I don't want you to think that the way that we get along is manufactured or fraudulent. If I hadn't liked you, it wouldn't have come to anything. He would have passed a message to your father or he would have decided that working with Mr. Fielding wasn't worth his effort, and it… It wouldn't have been like this. Lord Westhauser plays games with everything in life, and he plays to win. But who he was tonight with us, who he is with me… that's true. And I haven't enjoyed being around another human being like I have you in years, save him. I genuinely hope that you will come and see me again."

Stasia smiled.

"I really hope to," she said. "I mean, I have to, right? Who else is going to teach you to ride?"

"Will you help me buy a horse?" Lady Westhauser asked. "There's a livestock market I know where they auction horses sometimes, and if I can find out about one…"

"I would love that," Stasia said honestly. "But you should bring someone who knows more about *all* horses than I do. I just know Schotzli, and I know what I find beautiful, but if you're going to buy a horse…"

"An auction isn't the right way to do it, anyway," Lady Westhauser said. "I would want to buy directly from a breeder. But you should come with me to see them."

"Any time you want," Stasia answered, once more feeling breathless. "Absolutely."

Lady Westhauser grinned, then went to get the clothes she'd picked out.

"These will be too short for you, but…"

She shrugged.

"But you went out riding wearing Lord Westhauser's clothes today," Stasia said. "I won't tell if you don't."

"I'm getting better riding clothes for next time," Lady Westhauser said. "I'm so glad you came today. You have saved me from a boredom that I don't have the words to describe."

There was a pause as Stasia realized that tomorrow held the same boredom for the woman once more, then Lady Westhauser put out an arm.

"You must be exhausted," she said. "My guests have special rooms back here, where the only staff who are permitted are my girls. If you need anything, all you need to do is ask."

Stasia followed her down the hallway to a lovely little room with a beautiful bed and very elegant hardwood furniture.

"Sleep well," Lady Westhauser said.

"Thank you," Stasia answered. "And you."

Lady Westhauser closed the door as she left, and Stasia went to lay in the bed, looking up at the ceiling in the dark in genuine amazement.

It was the kind of day that felt like it could change a lifetime.

Stasia got up in the morning feeling exhausted and like she could lay in bed all day.

And then she realized that she wasn't in her room, that she was at Westhauser Manor, and her feet hit the ground before she'd even finished stretching.

She dressed quickly, going and splashing water on her face out of the basin on a dresser and checking her hair. It needed taming, but that was going to take too long, so she split it into a few sections that historically helped, then bound it up on top of her head and left the room.

She found both Lord and Lady Westhauser sitting in the sitting room between their quarters, reading newspapers.

"My father has had a hard time getting the Docker consistently," Stasia said, glancing at the masthead of the one Lord Westhauser was reading.

"Hard to get," he murmured, finishing his article then looking up. "I trust you slept well?"

"You couldn't pay me enough money to move back this far away from the city again, but I'll admit I miss the quiet," Stasia said. He smiled and nodded.

"Nothing is ever perfect. If it is, you've been conned."

"You'd like my dad," Stasia told him and he closed his eyes, dipping his head in genuine humor, then nodded.

"Right up until he discovered he doesn't like me," he said. "I have taken my coffee, so I'm ready to go back to town. Lady Westhauser takes a more leisurely breakfast, these days, if you would prefer to stay on and ride back in on your own."

It was tempting. Potently tempting. But the memory of the man with the hair pins was still a specter she hadn't gotten over, and where she hadn't liked the idea of traveling with Lord Westhauser on his own when he'd proposed it at dinner, the evening of playing cards had forged the idea of him as a friend who respected her as well as a man who was genuinely devoted to his wife, and she was remarkably unhesitant on that front.

"I actually thought I might take a late lunch at the university," Lady Westhauser said, folding her own paper and rising. "So if that makes the decision easier."

"You can leave?" Stasia asked, then frowned. Of *course* she could leave. She wasn't a prisoner here.

Lady Westhauser raised an eyebrow like she knew that Stasia knew better, but went toward the stairs without responding.

Lord Westhauser rose, offering Stasia his paper.

"She has various contacts in town that she maintains regularly," he said. "She is wasted on this place."

"I really liked the gardens," Stasia offered, and he paused, tipping his head.

"I do, too," he answered.

They went down to the front doors and out to find a stable boy tying Schotzli to the back of a carriage. Lord Westhauser had a side conversation with the butler as the carriage man helped first Lady Westhauser and then Stasia into the carriage. Lord Westhauser sprang up into the carriage and sat down next to his wife, folding his hands over his knee.

They took the loop around the front of the house and set off along the edge of the lake, the reflection of the mountains and the rising sun shatteringly beautiful.

"Wow," Stasia murmured.

"Money buys a great many things," Lord Westhauser observed, looking out his window. "Beauty is very much one of them."

Lady Westhauser adjusted her glasses, looking out the window, then shrugging.

"It's a view I thought I might never get tired of," she said. "And then I did."

They swept up away from the lake and over the hill that obscured the house from the main road, and they were off like leaving a dream.

In town, Lord Westhauser's carriage man was much less timid about using lesser-traveled roads, and the trip back to the house on the Sapphire River took substantially less time. Lady Westhauser got out with her and squeezed her hand.

"I hope we see each other again soon," the woman said, then hugged Stasia and accepted Lord Westhauser's hand back up into the carriage.

Stasia watched after them until they turned out of sight, then she went up to the house to bathe and change.

Today was the day she was going to find someone who could teach her about magic.

Or the next day.

Or the next day.

The pixies at the market were friendly enough, in the way of sellers almost anywhere. They were happy to chat with her about what they sold and how it worked, at a functional level, but none of them would speak to her about actual magic.

What was more odd was that the denials didn't appear to be stonewalling so much as confusion. As though they couldn't shape words that would explain it to her, and that they didn't understand her expectation that she might understand it.

She returned to the guard house a little over a week later ultimately defeated in her quest to find someone to teach her how to deal with magic attacks and disheartened that her confidence that she could *do* the things that they thought she could must have been misplaced.

Babe met her at the barrier with a grin that she couldn't help but mirror, but she went upstairs with him to the mess hall with a heavy heart. She was here to tell them that she couldn't do it, that she was too exposed and vulnerable and that, while she would have been completely confident to do it in Boton, she wasn't the one to do it in Verida.

Was she so proud?

She'd wrestled with it for days.

In Boton, she had felt like she had a lid on how much risk there actually was to her person, to her life. She could take actions that would protect her, that would reduce her risk. So she could do stuff that her father might not have approved of, because she was *ready*.

She'd appreciated training with Babe and the rest of them because it had had the same sense of *preparing*.

But if anyone, anywhere in the city could knock her out like that… if they could knock out *anyone* like that… No one was ever safe, and Stasia was falling back on her prosperity and her ability to send other people to take risks on her behalf.

How was the city not in constant turmoil from magic attacks? Stasia couldn't work it out.

Nothing made sense.

A small piece of her wanted to run away and hide at the Westhauser estate, where the magic couldn't get her.

Jasper was sitting at the back table again, his foot up on the chair next to him as he drank something out of a mug, when he saw her.

He stood.

"What's wrong?" he asked.

Babe turned quickly, not having noticed anything, then frowning.

"What's he talking about?" he asked.

Matthias came over with a bowl and a drink, peering at Stasia, then shrugging and going on. Sterling lifted his eyes from a book that he was reading, then went back to the book again, sticking his finger into the page and closing it as Stasia came to sit.

Jasper did not sit.

"Where is Colin?" she asked.

"Still sleeping," Babe said. "Takes his days off serious. What's he talking about?"

Stasia licked her lips.

How had Jasper known?

She met his eye.

They were going to kick her out.

It would be kindly, but if she had no value to them, this would be over, and she didn't *want* it to be over. She liked having a place to go and people who were eager to see her. Lady Westhauser was a good friend, potentially, but it was a social contact that she had to be aware of how often she exploited it. She couldn't go up there every day. She would make herself a burden.

Here, she'd been a part of something where she was needed, at least the way they'd talked about it. They'd *wanted* her to be here.

She wasn't ready to give it up, but she wasn't going to lie to Jasper.

Could she just… go for it? Just *do* it? Accept that that was the risk of living in Verida, that all of them apparently dealt with all the time, and…

Was she a coward?

Jasper was still watching her intently, waiting for her to answer him.

Was she a coward?

After everything?

"I can't do this," she whispered.

He pressed his lips, something like compassion, understanding, and he nodded, sitting down.

"I thought that some time to think about it might bring you there," he said.

"I'm sorry," Stasia said.

"No one is going to force you to do anything you don't want to," Sterling said. "But I'll admit I'm surprised."

"Wait a minute, now," Babe said, sitting down next to her and pushing the back of her chair away from him to spin her to face him. "Now wait a minute. You ain't the type to back down from a thing 'thout a good reason."

Stasia blinked, finding her eyes stung.

"I'm afraid," Stasia said.

"That's reasonable," Sterling said.

"No, it ain't," Babe said, his stare intense.

"What happened?" Jasper asked.

Stasia swallowed.

"You guys take such risks," she whispered, unable to look away from Babe. "I had no idea."

"What happened?" Babe echoed.

"I went to the market, one night. I was practicing climbing and that's just where I ended up, and I was walking through and a man put a hair pin in my hair and I looked in a mirror and just…" She shook her head. "I lost myself. If the police hadn't noticed it, he would have taken everything I had. Could have done anything to me. I can't imagine going out there every day knowing that someone could *do* that to you… and nobody will sell me anything to defend against it. I just… How do you do it?"

Babe grinned, then laughed, one of his big, genuine laughs.

"Is that all?" he asked.

"We should have seen to that before now," Jasper said, standing and starting across the room. "You forget the things you learn, growing up here."

"Is that *all*?" Stasia demanded.

"It's a con," Sterling said. "He underestimated you because he got greedy, but then he got lucky because you didn't know how to see it coming or respond to it."

Babe was still grinning.

"Stop it," Stasia said. "How can you go out there every day like that?"

Babe shook his head, finally wiping the smile off his face and nodding, indicating Sterling.

"He's got it," he said. "'Bout it bein' a con. Won't work without a distraction."

"The mirror," Matthias said, returning to his soup, and Babe nodded.

"Probably a skillful one, to have got you, anyway."

"Here," Jasper said, handing Babe a small bottle and returning to his seat.

Babe nodded, drawing Stasia's attention back over with a finger.

"Lookin' at me, now," he said. Stasia blinked. She *was* looking at him.

"No, really lookin' at me," he said.

She settled, looking him in the eye, letting her awareness of the rest of the room dip and then drop away. He nodded.

"Right. Now. Watchin' my fingers."

He held up his hand, a coin in his fingers. It wandered back and forth, weaving a pattern through thick, calloused fingers that were strikingly clever.

"You'll feel it happen," Sterling said, his voice gentle. "He's got you now. Do you feel it?"

The world had gone gauzy, the way it had in the mirror, her focus narrowing, watching the way his fingers moved, the texture of the coin, the nick in the edge…

She blinked, drawing back, and Babe grinned.

"And that's how it's done."

She looked over at Jasper, who lifted a shoulder.

She blinked quickly, looking back at Sterling, who settled back into his chair.

"Pixie magic is friendly magic," the man said. "Playful. If you aren't going to go along with it, it isn't going to push you into

THE QUEEN'S CHAIR 149

anything. Even if they mean it for malice, it's just not that powerful, because it's temporary by nature. The trick is to keep your wits about you and recognize when something is trying to drag your focus away from you like that."

"You said he underestimated me," Stasia said, and Sterling laughed quietly, nodding.

"Anyone from Verida knows about the ways that a pixie can manipulate you," he said. "And anyone with a modicum of focus and awareness can feel it coming on and break it if they want to. There are a lot of them that you can use recreationally or professionally, if you want to, that also have use in street crimes, so not everyone selling them is a criminal."

"Most of them have legitimate use," Jasper said.

"What do you use *that* for?" Stasia asked.

Babe put the coin away, turning forward, and Sterling chuckled, returning to his book. Stasia looked a demand at Jasper, who shrugged.

"What would you do with it?" he asked. "If you had a bottle of it sitting on your vanity or in your library?"

Stasia realized that Matthias had buried his face into his bowl and appeared to be blushing furiously.

"This is about sex, isn't it?" Stasia demanded, and Jasper's lip wiggled with humor, but he didn't deny it.

"First thing about everything is always about sex," Sterling said, turning the page.

"Students use it to study," Jasper said. "Artists use it while they're painting or sculpting. It just narrows your focus and lets you really see and think about the thing in front of you."

"There are other kinds, though?" Stasia asked, and Jasper nodded, a sturdy rock of unabashed thinking as Babe, Matthias, and Sterling refused to look at her.

"We'll work through all of them as you're ready," Jasper said. "You'll want to recognize all of their effects before you do anything unsupervised. Assuming you would change your mind, if you could control them…?"

"Yes," Stasia said. "How was it that nobody told me about this?" she asked. "I spent days at the market trying to get someone to teach me how they work."

"Who were you talking to?" Jasper asked.

"Sellers," Stasia said.

"Pixie ones?" Jasper asked.

She considered.

"Yes."

He nodded.

"They don't understand magic the way that we do. They couldn't possibly explain it to you, even if they wanted to. Any human from Verida could have told you, though."

"How do they not all hang out, down at the docks, just dosing every sailor to come into port and taking all their stuff?" Stasia asked.

"Illegal," Babe said, and Jasper nodded.

"They certainly *try*, but it only works once or twice on the really *new* sailors, and then on the really *drunk* ones, and the police are really rough on the people who do it, particularly in the legitimate markets and at Port Verida."

"You want to go after 'em?" Babe asked, finally looking at her again.

"What?" Stasia asked.

"That's not bad," Jasper said. "I wouldn't want to do it on our own, but I've got a buddy with the blacks who might be willing to set something up."

"Nice, safe way 'a startin' out," Babe said, and Stasia shook her head.

"I don't understand," she said. "They arrested the man who got me."

"But it'll be a gang running it," Jasper said. "If they've got a potent brew of the potion and some skilled guys running the con, boots on the cobble…"

"Henry Four-hands?" Stasia asked. It had stuck with her, and he frowned, impressed.

"They've got some real credibility, if they've convinced him to join on," Jasper said. "Let me think on it for a day, talk to my friend. It could be a pretty safe way to get you started out."

"Is that… really it?" Stasia asked.

"Should there be more?" Jasper asked.

"I've been afraid all week that I couldn't do this," Stasia said.

"Darlin', I suspect the list of things you can't do is a lot less than most anyone'd figure," Babe said. "You got doubts, you let us know, but I'd bet we can beat most of 'em."

Stasia resettled, then nodded.

"I want to do this," she said. "But I want to know how all of it works. Who can teach me what I need to know about magic?"

"It's a lifetime," Babe said. "But we can start with what we got, and you ain't never goin' into one of these on your own."

Sterling shook his head.

"Babe isn't the only one who can blend in if he needs to. Outside of the Black Docks, any of us can make sure you're safe."

"Then why can't we *do* it?" Matthias asked. "Why do we have to put her at risk at all?"

"You mean what's the point of being a King's Guard if you spend all your time standing around watching people do important things and never doing any of them yourself?" Jasper asked and Matthias gave him an exasperated, impatient look.

"Exactly," he said, and Jasper nodded.

"Time's coming, kid," he said. "Things are good now, and the fact that we haven't seen any action in a couple of years makes it feel like we haven't got any point, but you stay ready because the good times never last, particularly if you assume they will."

Babe nodded, and Stasia wondered what the two of them had seen that they were thinking about.

"Still, why can't we do it?" Matthias asked.

"They know us," Jasper said. "We walk around in our uniforms all the time so that people know that we're the King's Guard and we're the good guys. If we're going to use Stacy to stop things before they happen, we're going to have to be clever about it, so that they never know we're involved. She's got to stay *just* a merchant's daughter, as far as the city is concerned."

"And the fact that I come here every day?" Stasia asked.

He smiled thoughtfully and nodded.

"I thought you were doing it on purpose," he said. "There's no real keeping it from the organized groups, because they've got guys out here spying on us and everyone else all the time, but the smaller groups, the gangs and the one-off plots, the thieves and the cons… We can keep you separate from us. You wear that dragonskin down at the Black Docks and around Highrock because it keeps you safe, and they'll never recognize it because they don't come up here, but if you're talking about the people who might happen to see you coming here every day, they'd never recognize you dressed as a merchant's daughter. It's a question of separation. We can keep how you look separated, depending on where you're going."

"Is that it?" Stasia asked. "A dress and a hairdo and I'm a whole new person?"

He touched his cheek.

"And a mask. If you wear the mask all the time when you come here, no one will ever recognize you in a dress without it."

"Though most of 'em ain't lookin' at your face well enough to mark it, anyway," Babe said.

"Oh, that's flattering," Stasia said, and Jasper shook his head.

"No, it's true. A mark isn't really a person, and they won't remember you again unless you make a real impression." He paused. "And the point is that they shouldn't see you again. You need to be a very careful weapon for us, one that we only use for very targeted things."

Stasia was feeling bolder with the idea that she could overcome the magic that had hit her at the marketplace, and she shook her head.

"No," she said. "That's too limited."

Jasper raised his eyebrows at her, and she grinned.

"If I can master magic and I can master daggers and I can climb my way out of problems, then I should be in it. I should be all over the city, getting to know people, listening to stuff, making friends. If the problem is that you can't talk to the people who know interesting things, and I can, then why wouldn't I do it as much as I can?"

He considered, then nodded.

"We'll see how it looks once we've done it once. Why don't you two go get warmed up and make sure you haven't forgotten anything, and I'll see what I can work up in terms of the castle market and a plan."

Babe grinned, wiggling his eyebrows at Stasia.

"This has the markings of a good one," he said, and Stasia nodded, pulling her daggers and standing.

"I've been bored without you guys around."

He grinned, pushing himself up out of his chair and heading for the door.

"Well, let's fix that, shall we?"

He passed Colin on his way into the mess hall.

"What'd I miss?"

They sparred all afternoon. Jasper left early on in the afternoon, coming back with a man in black leathers a few hours later, and they went up to the upper railing, leaning there and talking while Stasia fought with Colin and Babe. Babe was going easy on her, but Colin was having a great time. He was playing and talking, telling some kind of story about a girl that he had fought with when he was a kid who had liked to push his face into the mud any time she beat him, and how in the end he had taken his revenge by coating her hair with mud while she'd slept at school.

Stasia had marveled for an instant that they actually sent their young girls to school, not just the boys, and he'd hit her in the middle of the back with his sword-butt, knocking her to her face and putting his heel on her neck to push her face into the dust, just for a moment.

"Yup, that's how she'd do it," Colin said. "But, you know, we were eight."

He was trying to make her angry.

It worked.

She unleashed a torrent of strikes at him that he blocked like she was throwing eggs at him, howling with laugher.

Babe caught her around the hips on the way past and threw her at the rail, her feet actually leaving the ground as she flew into it, her back up against a post and just enough time to slow herself down before it actually hurt her.

"Don't lose control," Babe said. "Don't care how big an idiot Colin is, there are worse out there. They'll steal your focus, keep you from doin' the thing you came for."

"Hey, I resent that," Colin said. "Wait, do I?"

Stasia nodded at Babe, steadying herself, and he nodded, straightening.

"All right, give 'em to me."

"What?" Stasia asked, pulling the batons away from him. She hadn't *lost* had she?

"If he's up there talkin' like sendin' you out is actually gonna happen, you gotta know what a real blade in your hand feels like."

She hesitated, then handed over the batons and took out the daggers.

They'd sparred with them some, at this point, but it had all been slow, talking about how to use them effectively, the strategy associated with the length of the blades, the weight, the handle guards. Babe was still very limited in the words that he used, but every one of them was useful.

Babe took a step back and pointed up at Sterling. Stasia wasn't sure how long he'd been up there, but the man was standing up with Jasper and the policeman. He jerked his chin and resettled his hat, coming down the stairs and drawing his sword.

"I'm not supposed to be up against a guy with a sword," Stasia said. "I run away from a guy with a sword."

"So?" Sterling teased, his feet moving like they weren't particularly required in holding himself up. "No better time to learn it than when the other guy isn't trying to kill you."

Babe grunted and went to lean against the lower rail, crossing his arms across his chest.

Stasia held the two daggers out in front of her, crossed at the midpoint with a slight tension against each other. Babe preferred to stand with his arms all the way out, and Stasia could see his point, but it looked like an invitation to her - it probably was - whereas she preferred the physical barrier between herself and her opponent.

Sterling held out his sword, a question. He had kind eyes, and Stasia couldn't actually understand how he'd ended up here, in a role that was almost by definition bound to be violent, but she was glad he was on her side. She nodded, and he swung.

She blocked and stepped, and he swung again.

It felt to her that the blocks should have done *something* to set him off balance, or stopped his momentum or *something*, but he moved like she wasn't even there, and like every motion he made was exactly as he'd intended it.

He was so much *faster* than she was, and she was dismayed at the idea of gaining enough advantage to actually attack him back.

Babe liked to see her attack, liked to exercise different methods of attack and defense intentionally.

Sterling just… showed her up. Over and over again.

He never did get an actual strike on her, the way that Colin had, but he wasn't working that hard at it, either. She knew that at any moment he could have slashed her face or stabbed her chest and she wouldn't have had the speed to stop him.

"You see what you need to?" she heard Jasper ask.

"I'm impressed," the other man said. It was the first time he'd spoken loudly enough for Stasia to hear him.

Sterling relented his attack, putting his sword back away, and Stasia looked at the daggers in her hands.

She wasn't impressed with herself in terms of being able to beat Sterling. Or Colin. Or even Matthias, much less Jasper or Babe. But she had just done that, she realized. At full speed with real live blades.

"Not lookin' for you to be able to kill some guy," Babe muttered from behind her, just for her benefit. "Just for him to b'lieve you'd do it."

She nodded as Jasper and the man in blacks came over.

"Stacy," Jasper said. "I want you to meet Placid. He works with the police and is in charge of the region around the castle. He and I served together against the stone elves. You can trust him. Placid, this is Stacy Fielding. She's not one of the guard, but she's going to be working with us around the city some, trying to deal with issues that rise to the level of meriting the king's attention."

"Mmm hmm," Placid said, sounding as though he knew Jasper too well to take him at his word. The man stepped forward, offering Stasia a handshake, and she tucked her daggers away quickly to answer it.

"I thought the blacks hated the browns," Stasia said, and Placid shook his head.

"What gave you that…? Oh. I'd forgotten about the bar up here. No. Menda is just the only keeper in town who will put up with that nonsense. And your boys here are the only ones who turn up for that beating night after night."

"Speak for yourself," Sterling said.

"We never take any beatings," Colin said from over where he'd joined Matthias against the stable wall.

"Only dish 'em out," Jasper agreed.

Placid grunted, evaluating Stasia.

"How'd they rope you into this business?" he asked.

"Which part?" Stasia answered.

"The part where you want to try to take down the crew that Henry Four-hands is running with," Placid said.

"I got taken in," Stasia said. "Almost robbed, if not for your people. I don't like feeling like that, and if I can help stop it from happening again, I'm in."

Placid raised an eyebrow.

"And how did you find a way into the guard house in the first place?" he asked.

She shrugged.

"I like interesting people," she said.

"Oh, they're interesting, around here," he said, rolling his jaw to the side. "All right, so let's say that I believe you actually care about this, that I even buy that maybe you're going to see it through without tipping them off that we're trying to root them out. What skills are you bringing into this other than a fierce devotion to the idea that nothing in the world is capable of stopping you?"

"Is that not enough?" Stasia asked innocently.

He didn't appear to like that answer, and Stasia shrugged.

"I've grown up in markets and around traders. I know people. No one here knows me, and I can talk to people that you can't. I think that, ultimately, I'm going to be hanging out in underworld markets, finding ways to get gossip that these guys have no hope of picking up on, but they're all worried I'm gonna get myself killed so this is the practice run to see if I can actually pull it off."

Placid pursed his lips, looking back at Jasper.

"That sounds a lot more plausible and a lot less patronizing than any of the explanations I'd heard so far," he said.

"Lying better is up next on the training plan," Jasper said cheerfully.

"Hope you aren't the one doing it," Placid said, facing Stasia once more. "He's got a lot of faith in you, if he's volunteering you for something like this, but I need to decide if I even think it's your job. My guys do a good job, monitoring the market, and saying that the King's Guard need to step in to help us do this job is conceding something I'm not ready to sign off on."

"You mean that it's the king's interest that visitors to the city feel safe enough to shop at night?" Stasia asked. "Or that women feel safe being out on their own after dark? How often does this happen? I've been here in the city just a couple of months and it happened to me. And I must say, the market was all but closed, as I was there. It gives the impression that this is a common enough issue. That isn't within the scope of the king's interest?"

She was guessing, but Placid's sour look gave her a hint that she wasn't far off.

"I am in a great debt that your men stopped the crime as it happened to me," Stasia said. "They were there in the moment that I needed them. I just want to see that it doesn't continue to happen to other people."

"Or we could just not mention our involvement," Jasper said easily. "I'm not looking for points, Placid. You know my problem isn't with you. I've got an issue with the palace guard, but the police are running a big city with a lot of poverty and a lot of opportunity for crime. You've got your hands full and there's no fixing it and none of it is your fault. I just want the experience. For her and for us. I've got an idea, and this is the trial run of it. I could have gone on without saying anything to you at all, but we're friends and I didn't want to go that route."

Placid looked at Stasia again.

"And this is the one you're going to hang your hopes on, here? This goes wrong, I will hang the whole thing on you, Jasper."

"Goes wrong how?" Stasia asked. "If they get away, what's going to happen? They'll *still* be doing it?"

"If you get caught and torn up by a gang looking to prove that they don't like it when the wrong people try to manage their business," Placid said. "Four-hands doesn't run with *forgiving* people. She isn't one of us, boys. They catch her, they're going to make an example of her. To us and to everyone else."

"She is one of us," Jasper said, moving forward slowly, but with a subtle power. "They just don't know it. And the people who are a real threat to the king and the city? They're a lot worse, now aren't they? This is where we figure out if *all* of us are up for this."

Placid sighed.

"You aren't asking for my involvement, here. You're asking for my permission."

"Oh, no," Jasper said. "You're a part of this. We need your information. But, yes, I also want your permission."

"All the glory if you win and none of the loss if you lose? You're a fool to offer those terms, but I'd be a fool to turn them down," Placid said. "Right up until I decide that this is predestined to fail. If you can't prove to me that you've got at least a *shot* of pulling it off, I pull the plug, and you respect it."

"I can agree to that," Jasper said. Placid nodded.

"All right, then," he said. "Let's talk."

⊸⊷⊱◆⊰⊶⊶

They went to the bar.

It was still early and daylight for bar drinking, but all seven of them crowded around the table in the corner. Jasper ordered a flagon of beer and sat down in the corner with his elbows on the table as everyone settled, pulling chairs from other tables as they needed them.

"All right," Jasper said. "So tell us about how this thing works."

Placid shook his head.

"How far back do you want me to start?" he asked.

"How about which players do you know are involved, which ones do you know *must* be involved, categorically, and who you most need to catch to improve the situation," Jasper said. Placid nodded.

"All right. Obviously they've got a pixie mixing the magic up for them. We know that it's a potent brew, because they've been taking in people who really should know better, not just preying on the easy targets, if you'll forgive me saying it, Miss."

Stasia shrugged. She was over that part.

"Do you know who's cooking it?" Jasper asked, and Placid shook his head.

"And the thing with the pixies is it's tricky, because if you arrest one of them, they all disappear and stop selling. They don't put up with it unless and until we get to the more influential ones and convince them that we're doing the right thing."

"It doesn't work like that," Stasia said, and Placid looked at her.

"I assure you it does," he answered.

"Then why do they sell at all?" Stasia asked. "If it's so easy to walk away from a day of sales, why are they out here all day every day selling? If they make that much money at it."

Jasper turned an interested face toward her, but Placid was dismissive.

"We've been through this enough times before," he said. "They shut down when we arrest one."

"They compete with each other," Stasia said. "Drives down prices, even when they're competing with friends, and it puts them at a level where everybody can afford to keep a stall open, but nobody's really getting filthy rich. Otherwise, more people would come and start selling."

"But pixies are the only ones who can do it," Jasper said, not dismissing her. "They're the only fae vendors in the market."

"Is every pixie in the city selling potions?" Stasia asked.

They looked at each other.

"No."

"Well, if they made a thousand villings a day, how many of them would figure out a way to come open a stall?" Stasia asked, picking the first big number that came into her head. It was more than any of them made in a year. On a very good day, Minstrel Fielding might make a thousand villings profit.

They looked at each other again, and Stasia sighed.

"The less they charge, the more people they sell to. One of them, owning the market by himself, might keep prices higher because he makes more profit off of fewer customers, or because he can't meet the demand on his own, but a global shutdown is… they aren't making that kind of money unless there really is some kind of artificial constriction on how many magic goods are created or sold here in the city. I passed a dozen vendors when I went through there, the other day, and I bet they're selling on street corners and in other markets, and in little boutiques all over the city, too, am I wrong?"

Placid licked his lips, then frowned and planted his elbow on the table, resting his temple against his fist. He licked his lips again.

"Okay, so let's say you're right and I'm wrong and they *don't* shut down for a day when I catch a pixie red-handed…"

"I'm not saying your eyes are lying to you," Stasia said. "If they shut down for a day or two, the demand backs up and they just fill it after they open again. Nobody gets hurt by that but the people who needed the products in the meantime. Well… there will be some aggregate loss to demand, but… it's small. They like the power enough to flex it over you. I believe that. But you cave. If you broke them, either by waiting for their emergency resources to dry up or by convincing a few of them to stay open and reap the benefit of breaking with the rest of the community, if you managed it, you'd get the power back to be able to punish them adequately when they break your laws."

Jasper gave Placid a quiet I-told-you-so look, and Stasia shook her head, astonished.

"This is what we talk about at the dinner table at my house," she said. "Breaking cartels and inefficient markets and taking value out of it. What do *you* talk about at the dinner table?"

"Mostly I just eat," Babe said, just the hint of a smile at the corners of his mouth.

"Regardless," Placid said after a moment, pointing at her, "and I'm willing to hear that there's opportunity there. I might come back and find you to talk about it, if it turns out you actually know what you're doing here, but regardless, there's a tension between us and the pixies, and they don't like us trying to take over how they live and work. They *will* do something about it. But more than that, we can't keep a pixie in a cage. They die. The king won't put up with prisoner fatalities above a specific level, heads start to roll, and the jail won't take pixies because they're *going* to die. Hard enough to keep them on a staff at a house. So we can't arrest him, whoever he is."

"What would you do about it, if you knew who it was?" Jasper asked, and Placid gave him a sideways smile.

"Station a dozen of my guys at his stall, follow around any of his major buyers and any of his *wealthy* buyers, make sure that it's a pain to stay in business."

"Make him even more dependent on his gang and his illegal activities," Stasia said, and Placid gave her a dark look.

"You got a solution to that one, too?" he demanded.

"It's not bad," Stasia said, regretting it as she said it for how patronizing it was. He was probably ten or fifteen years older than she was, an experienced soldier and a man with some significant responsibility within the police force, and she was talking to him the way her father spoke to her when she spouted a less-than-optimized idea at dinner. "Look, I don't know why people turn to crime. Okay? It doesn't make sense to me, but clearly it happens a lot. Maybe it really is a cheaper way to live than honestly, and maybe honest living isn't possible for everybody. My father says that you have to respect the volume of things that you don't know if you're ever going to profit from the things that you do know, and I *know* I don't know why people turn to crime. So maybe it's impossible to stop it. And you have to punish them somehow, increase the costs of illegal behavior to above the level of legal behavior. But I would want to break the relationship between the pixie and his gang a lot more urgently than the relationship between him and his legal customers."

Placid frowned at her for almost a full minute, then sat up and looked at Jasper.

"All right, I'm convinced. You actually do have something here I haven't seen before."

Jasper grinned, then jerked his head at Stasia.

"What do you need to know to find the pixie?" he asked.

Stasia sighed, considering the table, her fingers tapping on the wooden surface as she thought.

"How would you do it?" she asked Placid.

He nodded.

"The normal gang is going to have a supplier who may or may not actually be a *part* of the gang. They may have an arrangement with him, they may have leverage on him, or he just may be selling to them in quasi-ignorance. He'll have one or two points of contact within the gang who come to him for supply on a regular basis."

"Pixie magic is always temporary, and it has a short shelf life," Jasper said. "It never lasts more than four or five days at the longest after you use it, and it's rare that it will last in the bottle for more than two weeks."

"Does the duration of the magic depend on how recently it was made?" Stasia asked, and Jasper nodded.

"Old magic is short magic," he said, and she nodded.

It was probably more complicated than that, but it was useful.

"So they're seeking him out frequently," Stasia said, and Placid nodded.

"Though how long they stay under on the jacking spells is not as important," he told her. "And weakness isn't as straightforward. A powerful spell might stay powerful for most of the time, even if it doesn't last very long."

Stasia found herself thinking of the mirror, the hair pin, the man's fingers as he touched it, and she shuddered.

"Go ahead," Jasper said, turning attention back to Placid.

"Right," the man said. "The runners will get the spells to either a central contact point, or they'll be assigned to keep the cons in dust and pull back in the gang's share of the takings. These things will be set up to run themselves, with dust flowing from the pixie to the con and money flowing from the con to the gang."

"How much money are we talking about?" Stasia asked.

"If Four-hands is involved, it's a lot," Placid said. "They'll be watching for my boys, trying to keep him out of sight. Might cause some minor mischief to distract us. Might pay a kid to look out and warn everyone when we go by."

"But you arrested him," Stasia said.

"We did," Placid said.

"You're going to let him go," Jasper said.

"I'm say it again now, what?" Placid answered. Jasper nodded.

"She's good," he said. "And your man is never going to recognize her again. But she can't get in with a gang. Not yet. She hasn't got the skills to sell it, and it would take way too much time to get her moved into position. That's not what we're doing, here. You're going to let him go, and we're going to follow him, figure out who he's handing off loot to, and work our way back up to the source one chain at a time."

Stasia's chest eased.

That did sound like something she could do.

Jasper glanced at her like he knew.

"I'm not letting go of one of the most capable con men in the city," Placid said. "We caught him dead-to-rights, and we can hold him for two years based on that."

"You'll need an excuse," Sterling said. "How he got away."

"Mistake is easiest," Colin said. "Nobody looks ineptitude in the mouth."

"No," Placid said.

"So we just need to let him go in an agreed spot, and Stasia can follow him. We'll switch out which of us are following her, but we want us completely out of sight as much as possible."

"I'll need a dress that doesn't make me a mark," Stasia said, and Jasper nodded.

"We can work that out."

"You're talking about letting him rob more people," Placid said. "Even once you've got his contact, I can't re-arrest him until you've found the rest of them. There's no telling how many people he's going to rob in the meantime."

"And as long as you've got a pixie dealing in potions, willing to sell, you're going to have this problem, it doesn't matter who is doing the con work," Jasper said. "You need to break it up and you need to figure out how to get rid of the pixie. You can't fix the gang kids, but the pixies see to their own. They don't want the city to come after them the way we do elves."

"What?" Stasia asked, and Jasper frowned at her.

"So much you don't know, not growing up here," he said. "We'll talk later."

"The corner two south of the castle market is close enough to the market district for him to disappear, in the middle of the day," Sterling said. "And that's on the path to the prison up north."

"You really think she can keep eyes on him long enough to make her way through the gang?" Placid asked. "If he doesn't even *see* them the first *day*, she's going to stick with it?"

"It isn't going to go a whole day without making any connections," Jasper said. "When he gets loose, he's going to go find safety. We'll follow him there, we'll see who he talks to, we'll start building a network. We don't have to stay on him continually. This may take *patience*. But this is something we can do, Placid. Let us try."

"It's an expensive loss on my part if you guys decide this just isn't what you're good at," Placid said.

"For the king," Babe said. Stasia looked over at her, but his face was smooth and inexpressive.

Jasper nodded.

"I'm sorry," he said. "I know that it puts you in a difficult position with your people. But this is a much bigger idea, and this is where it starts. I need this."

Placid stuck his jaw out.

"Need it, huh?"

Jasper nodded.

"Yes."

"All right," Placid said, standing to lean across the table to shake hands with Jasper. "Just make it good."

"Matthias will check in with you tomorrow for the details on where and when you'll spill him," Jasper said. "We'll be there and ready."

Placid shook his head.

"Most men keep their heads down, Jasper," he said. "Make a good life that way."

"I've never been the kind to keep my head down, and you of all people ought to appreciate it," Jasper said.

Placid nodded and glanced at Stasia.

"Make sure these are the men you want to fall in with," he said. "Either way they'll get you killed but you deserve to at least see it coming."

⸺⬦⬧⬦⸺

Stasia stood at the street corner wearing a linen dress and head wrap, picking through a stall's meager offerings as the accident happened.

A cart tipped over in front of the prison coach, spilling gravel all over the road and stopping traffic as horses refused to walk through it and wheels blocked against it. The prison coach driver got down to argue with the gravel man, and Stasia saw out of the corner of her eye as the man who had accosted her with the hair pin peered out the barred window of the coach.

The volume of shouting went up as more people joined in yelling at the gravel man and the gravel man yelled back. There was a thumping inside the prison coach and a shudder as the bolts on the hinge broke free of the wood. The bottom edge of the door angled out and a large man crammed himself through the gap then took off running.

Stasia watched after him, then turned her eyes down as people around started pointing and shouting after him. The coach guards both went sprinting past and Stasia watched as Henry Four-hands slipped through the door gap and slid under the coach. If she hadn't been watching for him, she never would have seen it happen.

A moment later, a man who had stopped to deal with an issue with his shoe straightened and walked away from the coach, going up the side street away from the river.

Stasia lifted her eyes to where Sterling was watching from just down the street, leaning against a post and eating an apple. He made brief eye contact, then tossed the apple into the air and caught it, taking another dramatic bite of it as he walked.

Stasia followed Henry down the side street, her heart racing as he walked, back straight, never looking back.

She'd been followed enough times in her life to know that he was using any surface he could to track people behind him and how they were moving, including their shadows. She kept her face to the side, looking in shop windows and picking up a bit of fabric or a piece of food. She paid for a loaf of bread and crossed the street, walking like she was going home.

She passed Babe standing in a doorway smoking a pipe, and he winked at her.

Sterling would follow her for a ways, and then Babe would catch up and take over and Sterling would go find Matthias and tell him how to catch them and take over for Babe. They would cycle through following her for as long as they needed to, for Henry to get to a shelter, but Jasper had a bet with Placid that it would be in the first quarter hour.

Jasper won the bet by ten minutes.

Only five minutes out of the coach, Four-hands turned into a building, pulling a bit of wire out of his coat and unlocking the door, then disappearing through it. Stasia made eye contact with Sterling, then went down the alley next to the building and found all of the tools she had come to recognize made a building climbable.

The weather in Verida didn't lend itself to wooden structures, so they tended to build out of stone and brick to withstand a wicked rainy season, humidity, and flooding. Stasia had not experienced anything but the humidity, but she understood that the time was coming.

Well-made brick and stone buildings had relatively smooth sides and were difficult to climb without other features like windowsills and decorative work. The castle wall was very well-built, except where things didn't line up because of the handoff between builders. Fortunately for Stasia, most buildings weren't well-made. The wall was pocked with little flaws that she had the ability to exploit.

She dropped the skirt on the ground for Sterling to come and get it later, climbing in leather leggings and a loose shirt. The head wrap would turn into a draped skirt when she was ready for it, but for now she wanted to make sure that she could see all four sides of the building as soon as possible, to make sure that Henry didn't slip away.

Barely moments before he'd made his way through the front door, Stasia had started climbing the building, and it was only a minute or two for her to get to the roof. She was on so much of an energy rush, she did the climb faster than she would have done it at home on the stairs, though she also had to assume that Henry was in panic mode as well.

He would be moving fast, too.

Stasia walked from corner to corner of the building, trying not to stick her head too far over the edge and draw attention, but not miss anything in the maze of corridors below, either.

Sterling was gone. She didn't know if he'd gotten her dress, but there on the ground it looked like a discarded sack more than clothing.

After an hour, Stasia stopped checking quite so often for signs of Henry, and at two hours, she climbed back down to see where he might actually come out of the building. There were windows on the back, but no doors, so if he left out the back it would be conspicuous.

She was jittery, unable to settle or think straight as she tucked the headwrap into a belt around her waist, forming the draped skirt the way she'd practiced and going back down the street to where Babe was reading a newspaper.

She went to stand in the doorway behind him, leaning there and forcing herself to breathe.

"How you holding up?" Babe asked.

"Did he get away already?" Stasia asked.

"Could be," Babe said, unconcerned. "Or maybe we're doing fine. No way to know yet. Don't sweat it."

She laughed, manic.

"Don't sweat it," she said. "Jasper is risking a lot on me getting this right. I have no idea what I'm doing. Why would he even agree to it?"

Babe snorted.

"Anybody gonna die, you mess it up?" he asked.

Stasia considered that.

There were a lot of merchants who counted their goods in terms of life earnings. That was how many lives were tied up in a shipment of goods. By that metric, yes, people were going to die if she let a thief get away. Their lives' productivity would be stripped away from them, their ability to feed themselves and their families, and if not *their* ability, the ability of the men and women selling *to* them who wouldn't get paid because someone had stolen their wealth away. It was a delicate, thriving system, commerce was, and Stasia's father had always taught her to follow the flow of money if she wanted to understand the health and life of a place.

Thievery was an act of disruption that did ultimately kill people.

Babe looked over at her pointedly and she shook her head.

"No."

He nodded.

"Nope. Take it easy. We got bigger challenges coming, this goes well."

Stasia closed her eyes and forced herself to breathe.

"But what am I supposed to do?" she asked. "What *now*?"

He sighed, turning over his paper.

"Watch who comes, who leaves right after gettin' here, wait. Gonna be fine, Stace. Ain't war."

She wondered why she didn't correct them when they called her Stacy.

Stace.

She actually liked the sound of it.

Her mother had given her all of the names she'd ever imagined giving a daughter, and Stasia had always flourished under the idea that it meant she could be as many people as she wanted to, but the lilting, swishy noise of all of those names reduced to the functional, finite syllables: Stacy. It felt like Verida in a moment. And for Babe to take that and move it to something yet more familiar, more calm… It felt like they were claiming her, and she liked that.

She didn't want to disrupt it.

Her mother had given her all those names and she'd loved it. She liked the idea of embracing even more names, even more people for her to be at leisure.

Babe shifted.

"Now there's a body don't belong."

Stasia walked back out of the entryway of the building, giving Babe a sharp look intended to suggest that he didn't belong there, then she went along, hurrying away from the stranger out front of her building.

There was a young man going into the building down the street from her, the kind who couldn't help but look behind himself as he moved, like he was expecting someone to tap him on the shoulder and ask him what he thought he was doing.

Henry had been much more collected than that. Stasia walked past the building and glanced back to look at Babe again, then she straightened and went on, ducking into the alley at the last moment and climbing the building once more.

This time the fact that she'd done it twice already and the first time she'd done it at a solid sprint actually showed up, and she picked her way up much more carefully.

"Freak accident," she heard a voice say, and she paused. "You saw it. Guy in the cart with me just busted out and the cops took off after him, completely forgot I was in there."

"They're gonna look for you," a younger voice said.

"I know it," the first voice said. Stasia recognized it now, though he'd masked it with a sort of wheedling smoothness when he'd spoken to her at the market. "But you gotta tell Eddie. I'm here and I need him to help me. He's gotta take care of me until they forget some."

The kid whistled.

"Eddie isn't going to like it," he said.

"Don't care," Henry said. "Half the money he's sitting on, I helped liberate. It's time he did something for me, instead."

Stasia's fingers were ready to give, and the last thing she wanted to do was audibly scramble when she moved next - no, actually the last thing she wanted to do was *fall*, but barring that - so she shifted, getting herself up onto the roof and stretching her fingers out, knowing that if Henry walked out the door right that minute, there was no way she could go after him for at least a couple minutes.

She stretched her hands out again, going to look over the front edge of the roof, seeing that Babe was gone again. She couldn't see anybody else, but it didn't mean they weren't around. Maybe ten minutes later, she saw the kid run off again, and she watched Colin detach himself from the side of a building, following along after the kid.

Good.

Someone was doing that.

Stasia was going to stay here and watch Henry.

The first rush of excitement was just finally beginning to wear off, and she went to lean against the top of the roof, putting her chin on her crossed arms and listening hard.

The city was so busy. So much noise.

But she could hear the door below her and the people around her and she thought she would know if something changed.

She settled in to wait.

※

At dusk, as she was getting ready to climb down, she noticed a pair of men coming down the street toward her and she waited, seeing something in the way that they moved, like the kid with his propensity to look over his shoulder, but meaner and with a lot more experience. They weren't *old*, somewhere around Jasper's age or younger, but they moved with authority and… maybe even a sense of violence that gave her pause.

She wasn't afraid, up there on the building. They couldn't get her, and even if they *saw* her and sent somebody up after her, they'd have a seabird's chance in a storm of catching her. The next roof was a good jump away, but she had the legs for it.

It was that she realized - again - for the first time that she was dealing with serious people here. She'd never approached one of these men, and they were too organized and preoccupied to be the type who would approach *her*, and she'd always appreciated that it was easy to keep her distance from this kind of man. She didn't want to learn any of the lessons that he had to teach.

They went into the building and Stasia scrambled down the side to the open window once more, putting her face against the stone to try to keep as much weight off her fingers as she could while she waited.

"Henry," a voice finally said. "Heard it in a rumor and had to come see it with my own eyes."

"Took you long enough," Henry muttered in response.

"Streets are full of cops, what do you think?" the man said. "I was just going to come running over here and point you out to them? Had to make sure things died down before I came. Budgie said that you just showed up here. Escaped out of a transfer cart."

"That's right. Had a bit of good luck, and now I'm looking for you to get me out of here where they aren't going to find me for a good long while."

"Suppose you're going to want me to feed you and entertain you, too," the man said.

"You owe me, Eddie," Henry said.

"I paid you every dime I owe you," Eddie told him. "If I were the type, I ought to be charging you rent for being here all day. I don't keep safe houses up for employees who aren't carrying their weight."

"I didn't tell them a thing," Henry said. "And I'm your best lifter. You don't want me going over to the Highrock boys, now do you? Because they're always looking to buy their way up a bit further."

"You go over to Highrock, you'll watch your back for the rest of your life," Eddie said. "And you won't get anything like the quality potions I've been getting for you, now will you?"

"No, we've had a very good relationship," Henry said. "We have. I'm just looking for you to do right by me, seeing as I got myself picked up working for you."

There was a sound down below her and Stasia looked down with dread. Her fingers were numb and her arms were shaking, and she didn't know if she could make it back up again.

Colin was standing below her, his arms out to either side like a question of what she thought she was doing.

She wanted to stay and listen a little longer, but there was no way.

She climbed down as fast as she dared, shaking out her hands and gasping at the effort.

"Jasper says we're out of here," Colin whispered. "Come on."

"Eddie," Stasia said. "He's working for a guy called Eddie, and he's up there right now."

Colin grabbed her elbow with a quick nod.

"Okay. Come on. I need you to come with me, right now."

"I'm not letting them go," Stasia whispered, and Colin grinned.

"Neither are we," he said. "Matthias is watching the building. Jasper wants to talk to you. Come on."

He spirited her away down the street, walking in shadow almost the whole way, coming to a section of cheap housing with entryway doors every ten feet or so. Colin opened one of them and pointed Stasia up the stairs.

He followed her up on quick feet, opening a door at the top of the stairs and ushering her into a one-room apartment where she found Jasper and Placid sitting at a table with Babe.

"Where's Sterling?" Stasia asked.

"Working," Jasper said. He motioned. "Have a seat."

"I was beginning to worry I was going to have to climb up and get her, myself," Caleb said.

"As if you could make that climb," Jasper answered. Babe looked over at Stasia.

"How are you holding up?" he asked.

"My fingers hurt and I'm bored," Stasia said. "I thought this was going to be dangerous and exciting."

"Boring is always good, in police work," Placid said.

"She was eavesdropping when I caught her," Colin said, throwing himself into another chair as Stasia took the one that Jasper had indicated. "Literally."

"Eddie," Stasia said. "A guy named Eddie came in and was angry at him for being there with the police looking for him."

"I know Eddie," Placid said. "That's useful."

"Matthias will pick him up when he leaves," Colin said.

"What do you know about Eddie's organization?" Jasper asked Placid.

"Some," Placid said. "But it moves around a lot. Kids do little jobs and get bigger ones, move up, decide to set off on their own, Eddie knocks them back down or he lets them go, depending on how they leave it. Could be anybody doing anything, most days."

Jasper nodded.

"Well, we'll stay on Eddie for now, figure out where he's running things from, see if we can't find some of the people they're talking to."

"That's gonna take weeks," Colin said, and Jasper nodded.

"We signed up for it. We'll go through with it."

"What about Henry?" Stasia asked, and Jasper shook his head.

"We want the pixie. The con is just the final outlet. Placid'll round him back up again sooner or later, but for now, we need the *potential* for someone to use the pixie magic, in order for someone to drive a buy. If we can follow Henry, we will figure out where he finally ends up, but we need to stay with Eddie for now to start looking for the pixie."

The door opened again and Jasper stood as Sterling came in.

"Any problem?" he asked, and Sterling shook his head, handing Jasper a leather satchel.

"No, the girl was too sweet for her own good."

Stasia narrowed her eyes at him and he grinned.

"All right. Matthias is following someone, when he leaves the building where Henry hid out. I don't want Matthias ending up on his own. See if you can track him down and one of you report back when the new guy gets back where he's going."

"You got it," Sterling said, heading out again. Jasper motioned at Colin with his chin.

"And you're going to stay on Henry for now."

"All right," Colin said, standing and rushing off to catch up with Sterling.

"Once somebody comes back with where Eddie ends up, you go in for relief," Jasper said to Babe. "Send them for dinner. Make sure you've got a plan for yourself."

"Easy enough," Babe said.

"Is this what's going to happen for the next however many weeks this takes?" Stasia asked.

"If that's what it takes," Jasper said. "But in the meantime, we've been summoned."

"What does that mean?" Stasia asked.

"Get changed," Jasper said, standing and handing her the bag. "I'll meet you downstairs."

"You've still got this?" Placid asked, and Jasper nodded.

"Lucky break that your man Eddie showed up as early as he did. As long as we don't run into our next tour of duty at the castle, we've got nothing better to do with our time."

Placid shrugged and left. Jasper glanced back at Stasia and paused.

"It was a really good start," he said. "A lot of work to do, yet, if we're going to come through like we promised, but if his boss showed up, it means that they don't suspect we're watching him. A really good start."

He left and Stasia looked at the bag.

She genuinely had no idea what to expect of it.

Opening it, she still had no idea what to think.

She found her purple dragonskins and her mask.

"How in the world?" she asked the room at large.

Coming downstairs, she carried the pieces of her dress in the bag. She found Jasper standing outside, leaning against the doorframe. He nodded with approval.

"I figured as long as we're going to go back in there, you may as well keep up the iconic appearance," he said, setting off walking.

He was in his leathers. He hadn't been, earlier today, had he? No.

He'd been in regular clothing, like the other members of the squad had been.

"What's going on?" Stasia asked.

"We've been summoned by the queen," he said. "I got it before lunch. You didn't eat yet, did you? We can stop and get something on our way, if we want."

"And keep her highness waiting?" Stasia asked with sarcasm.

"She asked that we come at our earliest convenience," he said. "I think that counts."

She shrugged, walking quickly to keep up with him.

"What does it mean?" she asked.

"The summons? That she wants to see us," Jasper said.

"But *why*?" Stasia asked.

"With the queen, I've learned better than to guess," he told her.

They stopped at a stall in the castle market and Stasia bought herself a very satisfying lunch, then they crossed the bridge and went around to the front of the castle, presenting themselves at the gate.

"Jasper from the King's Guard, here to see Queen Constance, one guest."

The palace guard let them through and they walked across the courtyard unnoted. Stasia wondered if any of the guards recognized her, but if they did, they didn't say anything about it.

"They mortared the stones on the outside of the wall," Jasper murmured to her. "Don't know if you've gotten a chance to see it."

"I hadn't," Stasia answered, quite pleased with herself.

He nodded, escorting her up the stairs and into the castle itself.

One of the servants took note of them a moment later and came walking over quickly, has hands folded in front of his chest.

"May I help you?" he asked.

"Jasper of the King's Guard, here to see Queen Constance," Jasper said.

"Is she expecting you?" the young man asked.

"We were summoned," Jasper told him, and he dipped his head, scurrying back away again.

Jasper glanced over at Stasia and smiled.

He took a handkerchief out of his pocket and offered it to her, touching the corner of his mouth. Stasia would have just used her hand, but it was such a… tiny gesture of a truly noble heart, she couldn't shame it like that. She wiped her mouth as inconspicuously as possible, finding the red sauce from lunch - at least it hadn't been leafy and green - then tucked the handkerchief away.

"The war has had a few unfortunate turns, recently," Jasper murmured to her. "I don't know how sensitive she is to it, these days, but it may be that she is very preoccupied with other things and doesn't have a lot of spare thought for us."

"Then why would she send for us?" Stasia asked.

"A queen can be preoccupied with the very important and still manage to deal with the otherwise important as well," he said. "It's what makes her a good queen."

"Why is Verida at war?" Stasia asked.

"Because we would like to continue to exist," Jasper answered, then lifted his head and started across the court room as Queen Constance came down a set of stairs at the back corner.

He bowed deeply to her and Stasia faked a curtsy, feeing weird doing it in skins. Maybe she should have bowed, as well.

"Oh, come now," Constance said to Stasia. "It's worse if you do it badly. We both know you aren't a subject. Perhaps an ally, but not a subject. Come."

She took Stasia's hand and they went to the room with the stone table again, Jasper getting the door for them and closing it after, then getting the queen's chair for her. He sat down next to Stasia without horrifying her over her own chair. He was a good man.

"Now," Constance said. "What have they told you about me?"

"Um," Stasia answered. "Almost nothing. I mean, there's *some*, and people are always talking about the queen like there's this woman up on the clouds watching down over them, but… As a person? I learned more sitting with you last time than I have since."

Constance nodded.

"Good. I like making my own impressions. What have you been doing since we last spoke?"

Stasia blinked, looking back at Jasper, who shrugged and nodded.

"Best not to lie to her or keep things back," he said. "She has ways."

"Oh, I do like you, Jasper," Constance said with humor.

"And I you, mum," Jasper said.

"I've been visiting and exploring," Stasia said. "Got myself almost mugged in the castle market after dark, and now I'm helping Jasper and the rest of his squad track down the pixie who is selling the magic they used to get me."

"Surely you aren't susceptible," Constance said.

"Not once we showed her how it worked," Jasper said quickly. "It was her first brush with magic."

"Oh," Constance said. "I might have expected your sister to initiate you. Very well. I hope you weren't injured in the encounter?"

"Only my confidence," Stasia said. "I don't like feeling afraid like that."

"Nobody does," Constance answered. "It takes a certain sort to seek to overcome rather than to hide. I presume you are taking the correct steps?"

"Yes, mum," Jasper said. "I don't think it will be a problem again."

The woman nodded firmly.

"In exploring, what regions of the city have you been in?" she asked.

"Only this side of the river, really," Stasia said. "Other than to go to the guard house and a few things just on the other side of the river, up here."

"I understand you've procured housing on the Sapphire," the woman said, and Stasia nodded. She wondered precisely how many people the queen knew where they lived, in a city this size.

Was this *really* about Stasia, or was this yet another play on controlling Minstrel?

"Yes, ma'am," Stasia answered.

"How do you find it?"

She considered the literal answer, but restrained herself.

"It's a very fine house and the river is beautiful. I love living on the water."

"Has anyone told you it's poisonous?" Jasper asked, and Stasia jerked her head to look at him. He twisted his mouth and nodded quickly. "Should have mentioned that before now. Sorry."

"It's beautiful," Stasia argued, outraged. He grinned.

"Yes, but the reason it's blue is that the magic in the water interacts with something in the soil or the local magic or… something. Someone ever tries to give you a glass of water that has a blue hue to it, they're probably trying to kill you. All of the houses along there drink well water."

"And the wells aren't poisonous, but the river fifty feet away is," Stasia said.

"Unless you're really unlucky," Jasper said cheerfully. "Magic is inscrutable."

Stasia turned to look at the queen again.

"It's a great house, but apparently the water is poisonous."

Constance smiled and nodded.

"I see. And how much supervision does your father assume is regularly required over you?" she asked.

"I leave in the morning and I come back for dinner," Stasia said. "He doesn't ask where I've been."

"And why is that, do you think?" Constance asked.

Stasia considered it.

"I don't really know," she said. "He's never worried about me like that. As long as I'm happy and I don't appear to be injured, I think he's happy."

Constance frowned.

"Does he not care about you?" she asked, and Stasia frowned, shaking her head quickly.

"No," she said. "It's not that at all. It's that… With my sisters, my father never cared what they did all day, either, did he? Because it was at the house and boring. He cared that they were happy and that they were getting a proper education, that they were well-fed and well-clothed. He had people to see to all of those things, and he would sit with us at the table at dinner and ask us how our days were. He still *does* ask that. And if there's a problem, my father would do anything to fix it. But he has full days and a full life, and he is content that I do as well. He doesn't need to know how or why."

The queen dipped her head.

"I need you to go into the city and take lodgings," she said, her voice changing subtly as she got to her point. "Many of them, and all throughout the city. I will provide the funding for it through Jasper, but you must be the one to carry the money, sign documents in the event that they are required, and take the key. I need you to visit each of them at least every few days such that the neighbors up and down the street and in the buildings become accustomed to you being there. You don't have to give reason for being there, and if you're asked, you're free to say anything you like save the whole truth. My name must be kept entirely out of it, and you should never mention the guard, nor have any of them accompany you there."

"I don't like her wandering through the bad neighborhoods on her own," Jasper said.

"I'm very confident that you can prepare her for that, given that Verida is fundamentally no different from any other city in the known world, once you take the magic into account," Constance said. "There are problems coming that may require a safe place to hide before they can ultimately be dealt with. I need someone who is inconspicuous who can come and go from such places such that there is no disruption to the appearance of it, when the time comes for special solutions to urgent problems."

"I can send my men with her out of uniform," Jasper said, and she shook her head.

"There are too many who memorize the faces of the King's Guard even before they memorize the police. The police are predictable and you, with all of your authority and all of your time to use that authority creatively, you are not."

"I do my best," Jasper said.

The woman gave him a quiet smile and dipped her head.

"You know that I value you," she said. "But I need Stacy to do this on her own, if she is willing."

"I'm not sure I understand what you'd be using them for," Stasia said. "Am I hiding people from the *king*? From the *police*? You're the queen. Why would you ever need to hide someone when you could just keep them here?"

Constance licked her lips and nodded, folding her hands on the table and looking directly at Stasia.

"You are a very clever young woman. I've known that since I first met you. Is it such a stretch for you to imagine a circumstance where it is in the king's best interest to *not* know something? For it to pass under his nose, unheeded?"

Stasia considered, then shook her head.

"Only if the kingdom is corrupt," she said. She might have regretted talking to Lord Westhauser like that, but the queen seemed to invite it. Even now, she smiled.

"The world is seldom so simple that corruption flees or vanishes," she said. "The king is a good man who is managing a great many issues of great importance. Corruption exists everywhere, in the heart of every man, and there are many opportunities for good men to exercise their own self-interest in matters of power. Sometimes the wisest thing to do is eliminate that opportunity, do you not agree? Allow the good men who assist the king in governance to *remain* good?"

"That sounds like a good excuse to hide things from the king for your own self-interest," Stasia said.

Once more, the boldness was rewarded with a spark of humor.

"It does," she said. "Or it could be the truth. There are rivalries among the king's court and advisors. How could it be any other way? And when one finds that another's flank is exposed, there is always a temptation to destroy the rival through external means rather than at court."

"That sounds like really bad advisors to me," Stasia said, and the queen smiled merrily.

"Oh, I do like you," she said. "Sometimes I wish that the world were truly that simple, perhaps as it is with the merchants, where you cut off a contact because you discover he is of ill repute, or disavow another because he has demonstrated bad decisions, of late. The king often doesn't have that luxury, as he must decide among the options that exist, rather than the ones he wishes existed. And sometimes those poor options must be... observed carefully and held in equally careful balance."

"Like the King's Guard and the palace guard," Jasper muttered, and she nodded.

"Just so. For, even as Jasper believes his regiment to be heroes of the city and the kingdom, he must understand that there are members of the guard who are unprepared for the responsibility they hold, or who are willing to sacrifice their duty in service to their personal interests. Not every leader has the excellent taste in men that he does, and not every leader has the position to assemble his own squad, much less regiment. We must take the world as we find it, judge those who came before as the world was when *they* found it, and endeavor to improve upon it for those who come after."

"Those are pretty words, but what has it got to do with renting apartments around the city to hide people in?" Stasia asked.

"At the moment, I have no specific action for any of them. But I have had, at times, wished I had the ability to spirit someone away and hold them out of sight and perhaps out of mind for a season while things worked themselves out, and I have also, from time to time, had someone who deserved to disappear and start life over. Verida is a small enough city to seek someone out when they are dispossessed of their options, but large enough to hide in for long enough to get your feet under you and your idea of yourself changed. A ship's captain may mean well, but he has an entire crew to deal with, and any one of them may see the prize of betrayal as more than they can turn down. That's why you interest me so keenly, my dear. Simple coin is unlikely to turn your head. And Jasper is a man of his passions. So long as I hold his faith, I hold his loyalty, after his loyalty to the king himself."

"The day that the queen and king are unaligned is the marking of a bad season for Verida," Jasper observed.

"Wouldn't you just replace the king, if you were really working against him?" Stasia asked.

"Much like the advisors who are available for office, no king is perfect, and no queen is perfect in appointing him. It takes true error in judgment for a queen to have no choice to replace a king after he has been coronated. I may, and I could, but the disruption to the city would be very unlikely to be justified, particularly at my age."

Stasia looked carefully at the woman, chewing on all of it.

"See, the problem is I like you," Stasia said. "My father says to never do a deal with a man you like *too* much, because you'll leave money on the table and you're twice as likely to get taken in. And I think I might even like you too much. I want you to be right. Infallibly right. And once I go along with this, I have a sunk cost telling me that I have to *keep* going along with you, because if you're wrong now, who's to say how many times you've been wrong before?"

"What a charming problem to have," Constance said with a half a smile. "Unfortunately, it is not a problem I can help you solve, because I suspect that acting in a less-desirable manner would be counter-productive."

"That's true," Stasia said. "I've watched con men, and I've caught them trying to lift my purse. I've been lied to and I've lost games to cheats. But I've never lost big, and it makes me… nervous. How can I learn how to not lose big, if I've never done it?"

"Mmm," Constance said. "I rather don't like that one, because I prefer not losing at all."

"Is that possible?" Stasia asked.

"There are always mistakes," Jasper said. "No one gets through an encounter of any importance without them. But I've known men who were never in a battle where their side was routed. Babe among them. He's got scars, but he likes to say that none of them are on his back."

"He won't speak with me," Constance said, and Stasia sat up straighter. That was an important piece of information.

"Why not?" she asked.

"Because he claims he's not worthy to be alone with her in a room," Jasper answered. "He stands guard here and he's attentive and alert, but he doesn't like to be *involved*. He's just a soldier."

"And Colin and Sterling?" Stasia asked.

Jasper lifted his eyes to Constance, who frowned, just a little shrug.

"They are both worthy members of the guard," she said. "And I have no ill will directed toward either of them. But they are Jasper's men, and I will leave them as they are."

"Why Babe, then?" Stasia asked.

Constance gave her a tiny smile that suggested mischief.

"That he won't speak to me, for as much as any other reason," she said. "A man with principles so firm that he rejects an honor simply because he doesn't permit himself to reach so high? This is a man that I would very much like to know better."

Stasia narrowed her eyes.

"You play a lot of games in here, don't you?" she asked. Constance smiled easily.

"They say that playing games is the national pastime of Verida," she answered. "A queen must do as her people do, if at a more queenly level."

It almost tickled, but it was too serious, underneath.

"The story of the queen who picks the king so that the man who fathers her children and the man who rules her country don't have to be the same… that's just a beautiful story, isn't it? The truth isn't anything like that?"

"It is a beautiful story," Constance said thoughtfully. "But it's also one that I have a lifetime of faith invested into. He is a man, and he is surrounded by men, and no man - or woman - is perfect. They make mistakes and they sacrifice their principles on the altar of their interests. Some come in the gate without principles to sacrifice, but they have skills that are unavailable anywhere else. Knowledge that cannot be bought at any price. We must accept that a kingdom made up of men will be as flawed as the men within it, which means that the endeavor is to… to grow better men. It's a challenge I have thought on for a great many years."

"And what have you decided?" Stasia asked.

Constance smiled, shifting in her chair slightly. Jasper stood and took hold of the back of it without pulling it out yet.

"I have decided that perhaps a queen and a king are incapable of doing any such thing by their own force of will, and that they must be allowed to grow themselves by seeking truth and laying hold of it."

"Can secrets be a servant of truth?" Stasia asked, and Constance smiled, reaching over her shoulder and patting Jasper's hand. He pulled her chair out from under the table and she rose slowly.

"Oh, my dear," she said. "What a wonderful mind you have. I think I could spend a great many hours with it, but my time has many burdens on it that compete with those I would choose. Can secrets serve truth? Yes, I believe they can, when the truth itself is under attack. But it is an easy conceit to indulge, just as you see. Will you take the rooms?"

"Yes," Stasia said. She'd known the answer from the moment the queen had told her what she wanted Stasia to do, and yet she had fought it just to hear the reasoning behind it, to convince herself that her first instinct wasn't wrong.

"Very good," the woman said. "I will procure a stipend that Jasper will bring to you. I believe that the sooner you establish a routine at these safehouses, the more useful they will be when I discover I need them. And I will warn you, I rarely let resources lay fallow."

Stasia shrugged.

"Who does?"

Constance beamed at this, then put her hand on Jasper's arm and let him walk her out of the room. He stood in the doorway, watching after her, then looked back at Stasia.

"I think she's got the right idea," he said. "You want to go rent an apartment?"

"I just agreed to it," Stasia said, and he shook his head.

"At the place where we were with Placid," he said. "If Matthias is back and we have a good idea where to find Eddie, I think I need you to suddenly live across the street."

Stasia frowned.

"I can certainly see a lot, like that."

"Not disappointing, using the stairs, instead of the walls?" Jasper asked, and Stasia smiled.

"I can contain my disappointment," she said, and he nodded, putting an arm out.

"Let's go see if we've caught ourselves a hideout."

Matthias was not back at the little apartment when Stasia got there with Jasper. Colin had come back though and reported that Henry hadn't left the building, but that half a dozen people had come and a different three had left. He didn't think that any of them were there to see Henry, but he wasn't capable of climbing a wall to check through the window.

Stasia offered to go, mostly in an effort to tease Colin about it, but Jasper had instead sent her to go shopping for more *common* clothes. She and Colin went through the marketplace, looking at fabrics and the standard versions of low fashion, but while Stasia could pick up a headscarf here and an apron there, even the poor women tended to wear dresses that were made by seamstresses. In great numbers and in great simplicity, yes, but they didn't just come in piles at the marketplace the way many of the men's garments did.

Stasia was actually jealous of how simple clothing shopping for men appeared to be in Verida. Linen shirts and brown canvas pants came in deep stacks and you only had to know two numbers for either one of them. Marvelous.

She took Colin to the clothing district out by the pier where imported fabrics from Boton were turned into textiles, and she bought three dresses there and a number of pieces in different kinds of fabrics and textures that she thought she could mix together to create different shapes and appearances for herself. Pretending to live in an apartment nearby, she wanted them to recognize that it was her every time she went there, but she had an intention of using these for renting apartments all around the city, creating different selves for herself at each of them, such that none of them would immediately recognize her if they happened by her at another of her new residences.

It was going to be quite an undertaking, keeping everything straight and under control, but in truth, her life was made of free time, and if she could procure enough newspapers and enough books to pass the time as she put in her appearances at each of the apartments, it would hardly be wasted time.

Colin was a cheerful companion through the shopping trip, chatting with her about this and that of no particular importance in Verida, talking to the shopkeepers while she browsed in a way that she suspected was intentionally helpful. A shopkeeper who knew his trade could distract you from noticing the deficiencies in a product, calling attention rather to the values that you might not have thought about, and while seeing the values was worthwhile, certainly, Stasia preferred to inspect things with just her own mind for a turn of time before she allowed someone to try to sway her observations.

"So how did you end up in the King's Guard?" Stasia asked Colin as they were headed back to the rendezvous apartment.

"Oh, you know, got told I've got too big a mouth and I'd never amount to anything my whole life," Colin said cheerfully. "Got hit in the mouth an awful lot, growing up, actually, and figured I'd shut 'em all up and make 'em stop hitting me for talking too much all in the same swoop."

"You signed up for the King's Guard because you talk too much," Stasia said, and he grinned.

"Seemed like a good idea at the time. Recruiter put a pen in my hand, told me to sign, and I went with it. Never looked back."

"Is that how you live your life?" Stasia asked. "Just kind of throw yourself at it and not worry about it too much?"

"Seems to me like I'm with a kindred spirit," Colin said, glancing over with humor. "Did I or did I not pull you off a wall just a couple hours ago?"

"But I'm a spare daughter," Stasia said. "I can do anything I want. No one is counting on me and I'm not expected to accomplish anything."

"I'm the fifth of five boys," Colin said. "If I wanted to be heard, at home, I had to shout, usually over and over again. Nobody checks up on me but my second brother and my mom. I can do whatever I want, and I figure, if it's working, why would I worry about it?"

She didn't hate that answer.

They walked back to the apartment where Jasper was waiting with Matthias.

"We've got him," Jasper said. "Are you ready for this?"

"No," Stasia said, glancing at Colin with a grin. "But that's not going to stop me."

Eddie and his crew worked out of a shop only a few blocks away from the meat markets, only just out of sight of the stockyards. The scent was intense, as was the heat. They weren't all that far away from the coast, the fish harbor - actually *called* Fisharbor - but the air tended to come across the promontory that Verida sat on such that most of it was slow-moving and humid, drifting out to sea from here. There were cheaper places to live in Verida, Stasia understood, but not by an awful lot.

The shop was a butcher shop with apartments above it, like much of this part of the city. Some of them were larger operations intended to process meat for other marketplaces within the city, while others were competitive storefronts where people and restaurants who had the freedom to come this far north for their meat could get better prices. Eddie and his crew were in one of the bigger butcher shops on the street, and the meat left in big crates on the back of carts, making the foot traffic in and out of the shop very limited. And very suspect.

Stasia took a room two buildings down the street and across it, filling a pair of crates as though they were a chest and covering them with a board to store her new clothes in them. There was a straw mattress in the corner that reeked of illness and sweat even above the scent of manure and animal bodies. She was tempted to set fire to it, knowing that the walls were made of stone, but she worried about the timbers in the ceiling and the amount of grease apparent on the walls.

Ultimately, she shuffled everything that she had no intent of using into the second room of the apartment, what might have originally been a bedroom, and closed the door, setting herself up as a single room. She went down to a small local market and bought a washbasin and cleaning supplies, a small store of food that she could tuck away that would last for a while, and she ordered a new mattress for delivery. She worried that moving in like that would attract more attention than she wanted, but at the same time, she didn't mind making it look as though she *intended* to be there, rather than hiding about it.

She was thinking through the process of doing this multiple times, multiple places across the city. She had coins in her purse to cover much of this kind of expense, once, but having someone out spending half-villing coins in big numbers might bring more attention than she wanted, and she was realizing that as familiar as she was with dark alleys and disreputable bars, putting together a place to *live* was going to be a different task, even if she didn't really intend to live there. If she was going to keep people that the queen was aware of personally in these places, she needed to get them cleaned up and livable before Constance needed them.

And that was going to take work.

Work that she normally would have paid someone else to do.

She spent several hours cleaning the walls and the floors of the main room of the apartment, leaving the windows open to leave the cleaning cloths out laying in the sun and the open air. In this particular building, there was a small tap in the hallway with clean water that was pumped up from a cistern somewhere under the building or on the first floor. She filled a bucket three or four times out of it and dumped the gray water down a drain in the hallway. By the time she was done, the room at least didn't smell worse than outside, and she'd noted four men who had come and gone at least twice from Eddie's little shop across the way.

She jotted down some notes about them in a little notebook Jasper had given her, basic descriptions and when they came and went, then she tucked it away in her dress and she left, locking the door behind her and going back to the little apartment where she'd met Jasper before. She took a long route to get there, and she unlocked the door, going in to change into her dragonskins before she went home.

Her body was sore in ways that it hadn't been since she'd first learned climbing, in Boton, and she needed a whole night to sit and think about what she'd agreed to with the queen, to make sure she still thought she'd done the right thing and how she was going to go about actually *doing* it, but she was so happy.

She climbed up onto a rooftop just to prove to herself that she wasn't beaten, and because she liked being up there, above the street as the dusk set in.

It was a beautiful city.

Newer than Boton in a lot of ways. Even the tenements had better water than much of old-town Boton, for example. Cheaper than Boton in a lot of ways, because the stuff that had sprung up to support the population hadn't finished falling down yet under the weight of disrepair and poor planning. Boton was sort of in a second cycle, where the decrepit housing was being replaced both with *new* decrepit housing *or* much more expensive housing as neighborhoods that had once been out-of-position economically found new value in the expanded shape of the city, and the poor drifted into better buildings that had similarly fallen out of favor.

She went from rooftop to rooftop until she couldn't find a path forward anymore, then she climbed down once more, considering taking the long walk along the river to the bar to see if any of the guys were there, but deciding against it, instead picking up her pace to get home. If she was going to be out so much more consistently, doing all of the work of letting apartments around the city for the queen, she needed to make sure she took her opportunities to check in at home when she had them, so that her father didn't start demanding that they happened when they were less convenient.

Besides, dinner with her father was never a punishment.

She whistled all the way home.

⟐ ✦ ⟐

Days passed.

Stasia went to the apartment across the street from the butcher shop almost every day, spending hours there watching who came and left, making notes. She went down shopping at the little storefronts and carts along the street, talking to people and listening to the conversations people didn't realize they were having as loudly as they actually were.

It was… novel, really. She'd wandered Boton so much as a teenager, finding people and paying them to teach her to do the things that they'd *actually* learned how to do because this was their reality, day to day. Scraping and scrambling to forge an existence that would extend past today.

She knew that life was hard for the poor. She didn't pretend to herself that she was living an authentic existence, with the coins in her pocket and the purse hidden deeper in her skirts where she could transfer out yet more wealth to sustain herself between shopping trips. But this was the first time that she had been among the sustenance population and been one of them, the way they looked at her, and she appreciated the open window into what another life was like.

She went to the guard house one night perhaps a week later, changed into her dragonskins and wearing her mask, and she found the guys playing cards up in the mess hall.

"You guys just sitting around while I do all the work?" Stasia asked, and Colin jumped up.

"Stacy returns," he crowed. "Come sit. Tell us what you've been up to."

Stasia went to sit next to Babe at the table, glancing over at him. She saw him from time to time, out on the street. He was never truly obvious with being there, despite how physically present he was everywhere he went, and she often had to struggle to not look directly *at* him to verify that it was actually him and not some trick of her imagination, but he gave her a sideways smile now that just seemed to confirm all of it.

He was watching over her.

"What do you have?" Jasper asked, setting his hand of cards face down on the table and resting his elbow on it.

"Nothing specific," Stasia answered, taking out her notebook and sliding it across to him. "Useful, I think, but I'm not here for a specific reason."

Her father was taking dinner down at the docks with a group of merchants who were considering sponsoring a shipment of goods to the far side of the continent, so she had the evening to herself.

He browsed through her notebook, frowning several times.

"This is very good," he said. "I need to discuss it with Placid. Can I keep it for a day?"

"Of course," Stasia said. She'd started including notations about when she expected men to show up and what order they had in the gang's hierarchy, largely based on conversations on the streets and direct observation of the men themselves.

"Any regrets?" Sterling asked. "Not the action you were looking for, I imagine."

"I don't know," Stasia said. "It's been really interesting. Something I wouldn't have ever done, before, really. I've spied on people, but not persistingly and with intention. I'm learning so much."

"Of course you are," Jasper said passively, still reading her notebook. "And that's what you live for, after all."

"Is that backhanded?" Stasia asked, and he glanced up.

"Should it be?" he countered.

"He's in a bad mood," Sterling told her. "The palace guard took over a major part of the castle this week."

"That isn't her business," Jasper said, his tone right on the edge of rebuke.

"I thought she was one of us," Sterling answered mildly, intentionally needling the man. Babe shifted.

"I still don't see how they pulled it off. What are they looking for, Stacy to turn up on a balcony singing drinking songs? We embarrassed 'em once. Ain't that enough to put 'em back?"

"Emeril fell asleep," Sterling said. "And Fabian caught him."

"Emeril," Babe muttered.

"Well, we can't all be you with your soldier's ability to sleep whenever and then not sleep forever," Sterling said.

"Where I come from, sleepin's what gets you killed," Babe said. "Best not to do it when you don't have to."

"Petrault is just generally more to the king's liking, anyway," Sterling said. "Ben doesn't like to say what people want to hear, even if he knows it's true."

Stasia frowned.

"I don't understand," she said. "Doesn't he want to claim the good things when he's within his rights?"

"No," Jasper said loudly. "He likes to point to the distance left to go and the work left to do. He's a wise man, in that way, and a spectacle at court."

He set down her notebook.

"Was there anything else?"

She tipped her head to the side.

"Would the balcony singing thing fix it?" she asked. "'Cause I'll do it."

Babe grinned at his cards.

Jasper closed his eyes.

"Maybe we should just go to the bar," he said. "I'm in the mood for a fight. Even if it isn't with the palace guards, it might do me some good."

Sterling, Babe, and Colin all stiffened. Matthias looked confused.

"But you never fight," the younger man said, and Colin shook his head.

"Because whatever Jasper fights, Jasper kills."

"That's not true," Jasper said darkly. "Whatever I target, I kill, but it doesn't mean I can't end a fight after I've *won* it."

Babe glanced over.

"You ever *done* it? Fought a man what weren't your enemy, somethin' other than practice?"

Jasper looked sideways at Babe, who shifted in the manner of an ox letting you know that he sees you and he's tolerating you, but only at his leisure. Jasper glowered then lowered his gaze to the table again.

"I will not speak ill of the king," he said. "He is my lord and my mission, and his judgment is above my own. But the people he is forced to surround himself with are fools who like flattery rather than success."

"I know those people," Stasia said. "The ones that the success was bought for them with someone else's blood and coin, and they just wear it like a costume."

He licked his lips.

"And what does the merchant's daughter recommend doing with birds of this stripe?"

Stasia considered. There was a very real part of her that wanted to blanch under the dark intensity of his gaze, but Babe's reaction had seemed more right.

"We take their money," Stasia said. "Take their money and compete them out of business. Someone who didn't win what they have is very inept at keeping it."

Sterling smothered a smile behind his hand, and Jasper nodded moodily.

"Unfortunately, what can be done-and-done with commerce is never truly finished at court. The moods and relationships of the king are a complex web that have nothing to do with merit or success."

"Jasper," Sterling warned gently, and Jasper held up a gloved hand.

"The king's judgment is above my own," he said. "I merely wallow in my own ignorance."

Stasia found that difficult to believe, and was struggling to combine it with what the queen had said about the king having to make compromised decisions when it came to the men he kept around him as advisors. They agreed with each other, and yet both Jasper and Queen Constance seemed too clever to put up with it out of a king.

"Is it really so dire?" Stasia asked, looking over at Colin.

He drew a short breath and considered Jasper for a moment, then frowned.

"The war saps the city," he said after a moment. "And it puts everyone on edge. The pirates appear to be working up to a larger presence out in the islands again, and the stone elves are pressing down on the hills anywhere the regiments can't keep them off. Everyone is acting rashly and speaking… imprudently, just now."

"The peace of Verida is coming to a close," Babe said.

"Don't say that," Sterling said, scratching his goatee with his thumb. "You don't know that."

"I've never known anything else," Matthias said, and the entire table turned to look at him thoughtfully.

"What is the peace of Verida?" Stasia asked.

Jasper cleared his throat and sat back in his chair, putting his hand behind his head.

"Fifteen years ago, give or take, a military man called Ebenezer took leadership of the war. He'd been in it for twenty years, himself, but never as a high-ranking officer, and King Rupert discovered him, the stories don't say how, and put him in charge of the strategy of the war with the stone elves. He struck five or six very decisive blows against them and knocked back the pirate infestation at the same time. We study his writing within the guard, but the military is obsessed with it, and every man is required to complete his entire writings before they take the uniform. He was a visionary, and it's likely that just his writing has been enough to keep us under an umbrella of protection for the last fifteen years."

"What happened?" Stasia asked. "Did he die?"

"Assassinated," Babe said.

"There are a lot of theories about who paid for it, and some people think it was a mistake, that the blade was intended for another man at court who had similar features to Ebenezer. But one way or another, a blade pierced his heart and he died on the stone in front of the castle two years after he was brought in to the court. He paid for the peace of Verida with his life, but it can't last forever."

"What are you guys not telling me?" Stasia asked. "There's more to this story. How do you know things are falling apart?"

There was a long silence, then Sterling nodded and leaned out over his elbows.

"The court is reconfiguring itself," he said. "Constance is getting old, and everyone is concerned with how to maintain their power across the gap from one king to the next. It's leading to some destabilizing behaviors that are showing up everywhere."

Like people who might need to hide out for a while so they didn't get themselves killed.

Stasia sighed.

"And what is anyone *doing* about it?" she asked.

"You can't make the queen stay alive forever," Sterling said. "And even if she does have an unexpected decade left, Rupert isn't immortal, either."

"When Queen Constance dies, in a hundred years from now, I hope," Colin said. "They have to coronate her daughter, Melody, and her daughter has to name a king, who has to establish a court and a chain of command among the uniformed services. That can take six months or a year to finish."

"That's why everybody always asks you guys about the queen," Stasia said, and Colin nodded.

"It's rude, asking after her like she's the walking dead," Colin said. "But you can understand how anxious everyone is. Transitions are hard anywhere, but Verida is in the middle of a perpetual war."

"But *why*?" Stasia asked. "How is it not possible to end it?"

"The stone elves believe that we are an abomination on the land," Jasper said. "That we are a sin against magic and that by camping out here on the river like we have…"

"Throwing all our trash in it and the like, no less," Babe murmured.

"… that they have no choice but to attempt to eliminate us."

"Can't do it, though," Babe said.

"No," Jasper agreed. "We're too far from the mountains for them to actually storm the city and push us into the ocean. Too far away and too numerous. But they could certainly come down here with metal weapons and put thousands upon thousands of people to death, if we stopped fighting them up there."

"That's really all that did it?" Stasia asked. "We showed up and they were like, nope, gotta kill 'em all?"

Babe nodded. Jasper looked over at him thoughtfully.

"You've met them, haven't you?" he asked. "Not fighting them, but as real… people."

Babe glanced at Stasia for a moment, then nodded.

"I have."

"How do they get over it?" Jasper asked. "That need to kill all of us?"

"Without grace or tact," Babe answered, unmoving.

"And that's why everybody hates elves," Stasia said, drawing the conclusion, and Sterling twisted his mouth to the side with humor.

"Unfortunately, it's still more complicated than that. We fight the stone elves, but when someone says that they heard a rumor your mama digs skinny men, they're talking about high elves," Colin said.

"Your mother wears her hair too long," Sterling said.

"Longfingers," Matthias said.

"Son of an elf," Babe said.

"There are more than one *kind* of elf?" Stasia asked, and Jasper nodded.

"At least three, but I have a theory that there are dozens that we've just miscategorized."

"Of course you do," Colin said. "For those of us who don't really *care* all that much about how many tribes of high elves there are up sunning themselves on their mountaintops, there are high elves, stone elves, and low elves. And stone elves might be willing to slit your throat any time there isn't anybody looking, it's the high elves that everybody's got a problem with."

"Are you fighting them, too?" Stasia asked, and Jasper shook his head.

"They decline to fight," he said. "The stone elves kill them, too, any chance they get, but the high elves are too powerful, particularly up on top of the mountains where they live, and so they just stay up there and don't involve themselves in the war."

"And… for that they're *worse* than the stone elves?" Stasia asked, having a hard time believing what she was hearing.

"They could tip the war in our favor," Colin said. "Maybe put the stone elves back on their heels so we could actually *stop* fighting for a while."

"We can't ever stop fighting unless we kill 'em all," Babe said. "Fellas in the city, they ain't so bad, no worse than any the others you're gonna meet down at the Black Docks, but up in the mountains? They'll use their teeth to rip your throat out, they happen to drop their knife."

Stasia blinked at Babe, having even *more* difficulty believing any of this. What must he have seen? Or Jasper?

"Boton doesn't get involved in your war," Stasia said. "Why aren't they the bad guys?"

"Because they ain't here," Babe said. "High elves are up there, just watchin' folk die."

But that was better than the creatures doing the killing.

Well, okay.

"How many men are up in the mountains?" Stasia asked. "Fighting?"

"More and more every year," Jasper said. "The peace that Ebenezer bought us is waning, and the strain on the city grows as we recruit the young men who go up and die, and as we tax the rest to pay for the costs of the war. Everybody can feel it. There are tough days to come."

Maybe they hadn't picked the best time to come here.

She and Minstrel could still escape back to Boton if the city collapsed around them; he still owned the manor house in Birch, and Meglyn and Ridge were still there, running that branch of the Fielding empire. But these men were devoted to the king, and they couldn't just run away. The king was trying to keep the city *alive*, at a certain level, and she found it difficult to countenance.

"Not the adventure you signed up for," Sterling said, lifting his eyes to look at her. Jasper flicked his hand of cards closed on the table and gathered up the rest of the deck, tucking it away.

"Definitely a night for the bar," he said. "No more talk of wars and succession. No more talk of the palace guard, or I may go cause a scene there yet tonight. No more talk of pirates and elves."

"What else is there?" Colin asked cheerfully.

"Girls," Sterling said.

"Dice," Babe said.

"Money," Stasia said.

"Training," Matthias said.

"Hope," Jasper said, rising to his feet and indicating the door. "And a fight that we can win."

Stasia walked out of the mess hall with the five of them, the dark and pensive mood lingering as they went down the stairs into the training yard and out onto the street, where the fire cauldrons in front of the castle illuminated tall orange swaths of stone in between sections of black.

There across the river was a king with a kingdom to save and a queen with secrets to hide.

It was complicated in ways that Stasia hadn't anticipated, and she took odd comfort from the mood of the group, both that they weren't treating it like how life in Verida *was*, and in the fact that she was a part of it.

It struck her suddenly and with force, watching the castle as they went along.

She was a part of something.

She'd never done that before.

But she was a part of something, now.

—◈◈◈—

She settled into a routine of sorts. She broke her days into pieces, spreading out the time that she spent up across the street from the butcher such that she covered as many days and as many times of day as possible, but also wandering the city, looking at apartments in the cheaper regions and starting the process of renting them. She was trying to do them one at a time, working on one while she made arrangements for another, and then visiting each of the completed ones at least every couple of days, talking to neighbors and vendors, being familiar without being specific.

She suspected that a number of the men and women she met thought that she was setting up a secret meeting location for a romantic tryst, which offended her at first - why, especially in an enlightened city like Verida where women held important roles in government and were educated right there alongside the men, was it so impossible to believe that a young woman might just be setting out on her own? - but she realized that there were dual benefits to that. If they thought that she was engaged in a romantic entanglement already, she avoided the advances of the young men who noted her, and it also meant that she could arrive with a stranger and simply validate what everybody had already thought of her. No one would be surprised if someone turned up living in the apartment she'd rented.

She put a lot of effort into trying to make the apartments themselves livable, but she was poignantly aware that a lot of the people in the queen's circle might find them simply unacceptable, with the amount of time that Stasia was prepared to put into them each, individually. She left new cleaning supplies at each apartment, rather than carrying them with her, and she stocked them with basic grooming supplies, at least, in hopes of being able to help get any one of them up to par with a little extra time. It was just the first night, she told herself over and over again. Just for the first night, and then they would make things better.

She squared up accounts with Jasper every week, except the week that the guards were in the castle, keeping a careful log of all of her expenses and giving it to him. He gave her the money to compensate what she'd spent, and then there was another villing a week for doing the work. It was too much money, Stasia thought, considering she was just wandering around talking to people and writing down the things she saw, but Jasper told her that it was the amount set by the queen and she should look at it as a sign of value, rather than profligacy.

She went out to the Westhauser estate twice more, taking Schotzli out for long rides, once with Lady Westhauser and once with just a stable boy in tow. It was beautiful country, and provided a staggering contrast to the lives of the people in town that she was interacting with on a daily basis. The air was clean and the space was open, save for the village, a few flocks of sheep, and a large herd of cows, and the mountains in the distance felt clearer and closer and powerful in a way that they just weren't, in the city. Stasia didn't want to live out there, but she was grateful that she got to see it.

One afternoon, Lady Westhauser sent a note to the Fielding house that she would be in town the next day, and Stasia and the woman spent the day at the university library, talking in hushed tones and laughing, going through the vast array of books accumulated there and reading selections to each other as they found them interesting. Lady Westhauser was fascinating to Stasia, not least of all because she had graduated the university and had the hallmarks of a classic education in the way she thought and spoke. Stasia had never begrudged anyone a university education, feeling as though her own had been exactly to her liking, but she realized that there was something else there in the way that Lady Westhauser understood things that Stasia might have been lacking.

"You should at least enroll and sign up for a class," Lady Westhauser told her that evening over dinner. "I think you'd find you enjoy it a lot more than you expect, and it would be something to *do*. I can't imagine how bored you must get, sometimes. There aren't any women in the city *like you*. What do you do with your time?"

"I've made some friends," Stasia said, not certain why she was so reticent about the guard, but her father had always told her that it was better to not say something than to say it and regret divulging a secret, when you weren't sure if it was a secret or not. "I have stuff going on most days and I'm not bored. But you're right. I do think that I should try it, here, and at least see what it's like. Honestly, it makes me a little nervous, because I've never *been* in a class before."

"Never?" Lady Westhauser asked, and Stasia shook her head.

"No. I've only ever been tutored at home."

Lady Westhauser shook her head.

"Criminal, to just disregard all of the girls like that. Why do they get away with it?"

Stasia shrugged.

"It's the way it's always been. The women with money seek out their own interests and the ones without are…"

"Resigned to a life of hard labor and child-rearing," Lady Westhauser said. Stasia nodded.

"Yeah."

Stasia hesitated.

"Have you and Lord Westhauser talked about children?" Stasia asked.

Lady Westhauser took a breath and looked around the room, not exactly scanning it for people who might or might not be there so much as feeling the place and the fact that they existed within it.

"We have," she said. "A few times. He says it's up to me. He isn't concerned with an heir at all."

Stasia blinked.

"Not at *all*?" she asked.

Lady Westhauser shook her head.

"No. He has an uncle whose son will take over the estate if both of us die without children, and he's just… fine with that."

"What about his legacy?" Stasia asked. "What about his assets? Would he just let them all go? He doesn't care *at all*?"

Lady Westhauser smiled, humored.

"He isn't like you think," she said. "He has other things that he thinks about, and all of that stuff really doesn't mean anything to him."

"Like what?" Stasia asked.

Lady Westhauser shook her head.

"He has interests here in the city that he cares about. He spends all of his energy seeing to them, and the estate and his title are more of a burden to him than anything."

"Including you," Stasia said sullenly, still very aware of the idea of Lady Westhauser out at the estate by herself all the time.

"Don't look at it like that," Lady Westhauser said. "It *isn't* like that. We had an arranged marriage, did you know that?"

Stasia gaped, and Lady Westhauser nodded quickly.

"We did. I didn't meet him until the day that we got married, but I fell in love with him so quickly and so hard, it still… I can't even understand it. I wouldn't have ever believed it, if it hadn't actually happened to me. And I tell you, with absolutely no doubt in my mind, he loves me the same way. I know… I wouldn't choose to be the one who is out running the estate every day, and I wish life were different, but I've never been happier in my entire life, and I can't think of anything in my life that has been better than marrying Lord Westhauser."

"Uh huh," Stasia said, and Lady Westhauser laughed.

"Believe me or not, it's true," she said easily. "Maybe you…?"

"Marrying would diminish my father's fortune," Stasia said. "I don't need it, I don't want it, and I have no intention of bearing some man's yoke. I'm free, as I am, and I'm very happy."

Lady Westhauser nodded.

"I'm glad you have that option. I believe you."

"So do you *want* children?" Stasia asked, pushing the conversation back away from herself again.

"I haven't decided," Lady Westhauser said. "I don't know how to decide if someone that doesn't exist today should exist tomorrow."

Stasia frowned at this, working it through, and Lady Westhauser smiled brilliantly.

"I wrote to my mother, asking her for counsel, and she told me that her days were only about survival until my brother was born, and then she had something to fight for that actually meant something to her."

"Because survival didn't mean anything to her," Stasia said, and Lady Westhauser gave her a shrug.

"That was my question, too. I like the way that our life is, and we've only been married for a year. The idea of a baby and being… required to see to it, every single day, for the rest of its life… It feels like a prison sentence to me, but at the same time, the sound of children laughing in the hallways, playing in the garden? It's almost as though the entire manor could gain purpose by being home to them."

"Are there no children out there at all?" Stasia asked, and Lady Westhauser nodded quickly.

"Oh, there are, but they keep them away from me because it would be unseemly for the lady of the manor to ever hear them speak or laugh or run, now wouldn't it?"

Stasia chewed thoughtfully for a moment, then raised her eyebrows, and Lady Westhauser laughed.

"You're better than all of them put together," she said. "We have to do this again as soon as possible."

Stasia nodded.

"I was so glad to get your note. How often do you come into the city?"

"Not as often as I could," Lady Westhauser told her. "The manor requires that someone be there to run it most of the time, but it's hardly an all-day job for me. The staff are capable of taking care of almost everything on their own."

"So, same day next week?" Stasia asked with a smile, and Lady Westhauser nodded eagerly.

"It's a date."

She went back to the little apartment across from the butcher shop and put her things down, unpacking food for the day and a set of towels that she was going to leave there for washing when she came in from other apartments in the middle of the day. One of the problems with her system was that she would spend a significant portion of any given day cleaning walls and floors and washbasins and the like, but there wasn't any place clean to wash *herself*, once she got done, so she was working on getting the second room of the meat district apartment cleaned out - finally - and setting it up as a bathroom where she could get all of the grime and stink off of her skin on days that she came here after working.

The idea of it was an immense relief on an order she hadn't even anticipated, though she still had to deal with all of the debris she'd stashed in the second room initially.

The mattress was a disaster, but she'd gotten less picky about what things she touched, at this point, and it was just a question of dragging it out to the roadside and then sweeping the hallway and the stairs out of a sense of obligation to the building tenants.

Putting the towels on a newly-installed shelf, she went up to the front room again to look out at the butcher shop, wondering what Henry Four-hands was up to, these days, and whether this was ultimately going to prove to have been worth it to everyone.

There was a man down on the sidewalk looking up at her.

She frowned at him.

She was a woman living alone in an apartment in a dangerous district of the city. One where bad things happened to women like her every day. She needed him to know that she saw him and she disapproved of him looking at her.

The door behind her burst in and a pair of men came into the room. Stasia tucked her book away as surreptitiously as she could, but they were already on her, grabbing her by the arms. If she'd had her dragonskins on, or the right set of skirts, she might have climbed out the window, but she didn't have anything to keep the skirts of her dress from covering her feet as she tried to climb, and the man outside was clearly watching for her. She couldn't go up without her feet, and going down wasn't going to help anything.

Just like that, she was caught.

The first man went into her shirt after the notebook, pulling it out and holding it up with the look of a man who had no comprehension of the written word, then he sneered at her.

"Eddie wants a word," he said.

"Who?" Stasia asked.

"Don't play dumb," the other man said, snatching at the book. "Gimmie that."

The first man held it up over his head, jerking Stasia off her feet as he attempted to keep the book from the second man.

"Cal," the second man grunted, jumping as Stasia planted her feet and refused to move forward again under the ill-treatment. "Give it here."

Cal snarled, jerking Stasia forward again and handed the second man the book.

"I found it though," he said. "You tell Eddie I found it."

"Whatever, we came up here because he told us," the smaller one said. "You think he cares?"

Cal snarled again, pulling Stasia through the doorway and down the hallway after him. Stasia jerked her arm away from the smaller man, going along without fighting for now. Better to let them let their guard down and get away once she was outside and had a chance.

Her mind flitted back up to the towels in the bathroom for a moment, thinking how those had been a waste, now, but then she was in the present again.

Watching a butcher shop was *not* the skill that Jasper had singled her out for. She knew how to get away from men who wanted bad things, and she knew how to fight and she knew how to run. The initial jolt of fear was still on its upswing, her heart racing and her hands jittery with the need to do *something*, but she could use that. That was what she knew how to do. It was actually a moment of relative calm as they walked down the hallway toward the front door, then the one called Cal gave a little chirrup of a whistle.

"Hold up here," he said. Stasia hadn't anticipated this, nor did she anticipate it when the big man roughly tied something around her wrist, walking around in front of her to take her other arm from the big man and tie both her wrists together in front of her.

"Ouch," Stasia said, but he ignored her.

"All right," he said.

Now her heart raced harder, the feeling of panic and lack of preparation. They went through the door into the bright light outside, the noise of the street and the livestock yards and two men shouting at each other hitting her hard. She jerked her face away from it, and the big man grabbed her elbow to pull her out onto the cobble, but she instinctively hit him with her two hands clubbed together, first in the stomach, then elbowing him in the side, then hitting him with a dead-lucky blow directly to the face.

The man staggered back and Stasia spun, looking for the second man, but he hit her with his shoulder in the ribs, driving her into the building. She found herself collapsed on the ground, not entirely certain how she'd ended up there, and he had the point of his knife under the corner of her jaw, just standing there.

"I like a woman with spirit," he said. "I like to watch it fade away and die. You want to try that again and see if I can break a few ribs, this time?"

Stasia shook her head, and he put the knife away, lifting her to her feet by the elbow and making a dismissive noise at the big man as he walked her across the street, the man from below Stasia's window falling into line beside her.

The butcher shop was gruesome in ways that Stasia had always tried to avoid knowing about, though she *did* know. They walked her past carcasses and carving tools - weapons, her mind flagged, *weapons* - and into a back room where a man that she recognized was sitting at a small desk. He looked up, then at Cal.

"She give you any trouble?" he asked.

"She's a lively one," the little one said. "Cal's got a broke nose."

Eddie nodded, sighing and coming around to sit on the front of the desk.

"Do you know who I am?" he asked.

"They just broke into my apartment and grabbed me," Stasia said. "I wasn't doing anything."

The little one handed over her notebook and Eddie thumbed through it, then hit her with the back of his hand.

"Don't lie to me," he said. "You're working for *someone*, and I'm going to find out who. I don't like to kill women, but I will if you don't tell me everything."

"I don't believe you," Stasia said, jerking her elbow away from Cal and looking around the room. Four of them, all of them bigger than her. And a door. It was a big ask, and she was going to need the exact right moment, if she was going to pull it off. Her face stung and her ribs and her head hurt from the wall outside, and she was having a hard time mastering her panic, but she had to if she was going to survive.

"What, that I'll kill you?" Eddie asked.

"That you don't like killing women," Stasia answered.

He snorted.

"Lively one indeed. Sit her down, Cal."

Cal shoved her into a chair and stepped away as Eddie went through her notebook more carefully. Stasia hadn't thought about what happened next, if they caught her. What she would tell them.

Eddie put the book down.

"Santiago send you?" he asked.

"Who?" Stasia asked.

Cal hit her.

It felt like it had been a closed fist to her ear, and she blinked, seeing red as she tried to get it back together. She would not cry. She would not cry.

"Blackhelm," Eddie said.

Stasia braced herself.

"Who?"

Cal punched her in the stomach and she doubled over, coughing a sob.

"Highrock?" Eddie asked.

"Highrock?" Cal echoed. "You think?"

"You questioning me?" Eddie asked.

"No," Cal said, and Eddie looked at Stasia.

She coughed again, putting her hand to her face where he'd slapped her and closing her eyes.

"Oh, that's not going to help," Eddie said. "See, I may have a problem killing a woman, but I've got no problem, say, taking a hand. And then another one. Take your feet halfway and then at the ankle. We got the tools out there to do it, you saw."

"I saw," Stasia said. "But you know they'll do worse."

Rivals.

They were talking about rivals.

Stasia recognized the name Highrock as a region.

Eddie was a gang leader.

She hadn't thought that that had a territory to it. Hadn't Placid said something about people leaving the gang for… something?

"Then we'll just have to agree to kill you quick," Eddie said. "Won't we?"

"Or I could join you," Stasia said, thinking fast. Eddie scoffed.

"Little puff like you?" he asked. "Not worth the food to keep you fed."

"I'm good at things," Stasia said. "People don't notice me. I see things."

"I noticed you," Eddie said.

"Johnny noticed her," the big said, and Eddie shot him a dark look.

"So I want to be on your side," Stasia said. "They're all idiots. I don't want anything to do with idiots."

"Where are you from?" Eddie asked. "You talk funny."

"Boton," Stasia said.

"You're a long way from home," Eddie said. "How did Manning get his hooks into you?"

She looked at him, a glare.

"I'm not telling you anything until you agree to make me a better offer," she said.

"You want me to pay for information," Eddie said, and she nodded. He raised his eyebrows. "I never pay for anything I can take for free."

Stasia pressed herself into the chair, turning her face away from him. She needed to *see* him, but he seemed to enjoy the fear. She let him have it.

"But you won't know what's useful until you need it," she squeaked. "Don't you want someone who's been working with them?"

"With *who*?" Eddie pressed.

"I'm not telling," Stasia gasped. "Not until you say you'll take me on. I want to stay alive."

Cal grabbed her face with both hands and forced her to look forward at Eddie. He leered at her with a greed that was staggering.

"Who do you turn this little book over to?" he asked. "How long have you been spying on me, little girl?"

Stasia gritted her teeth and Cal squeezed her face.

"I'm a friend of Henry Four-hands," she said, and he drew his head back.

"The little con man?" he asked. "What's he got to do with this?"

Stasia glared at him.

"He's trying to cut you out," she said. "Says you take half his money and don't give him anything in return. He just needs the pixie that's selling to you, and he can set up on his own."

Eddie's eyebrows went up, and Stasia scrambled, looking for the way to trip him up into telling her about the pixie.

"And you're looking for my supplier?" Eddie asked, and Stasia shook her head. Well, she moved her mouth back and forth between Cal's stony hands.

"Oh, no, he's in on it, too. Henry bought out your runners and then paid me to watch and make sure that no one knew it happened."

Eddie stiffened.

"Little bastard," he said. "That little bastard. Thinks he can get away with cutting me out? Cal, go bring in Zenith. I'd like to have a little talk. Johnny, you go track down Henry. We'll see if they can make their stories match up."

Too late, Stasia realized that she'd given him a complete narrative. She braced as Cal let go of her face, turning to go.

"I know other things, too," she said. "I've been watching you for weeks, and there are things I can tell you that you don't know about your people."

It was actually probably true, if she'd been willing to do it. Even as it was, she felt bad for dragging Henry and the pixie - Zenith? was that a pixie name? - into this, even if they *had* already been involved.

They could die for a lie that she had just told.

"Put her back in the stock room," Eddie said. "I'll talk to her again after I get this sorted out."

The big man that she'd hit in the face picked her up by the armpit and dragged her out of the office, through the butcher shop, and into a back cargo space where boxes and boxes of meat stood stacked against the walls and draining carcasses hung from the rafters. He tied her to a chair roughly as she scrambled to find an opening to attack him and get away, but it never came.

He checked the ropes, then left.

The room buzzed with insects and the cattle just out of sight dripped on the floor. Stasia started to work on the bindings on her wrists, but Cal had used a leather thong to tie her, and it stretched rather than slid when she worked her wrists back and forth. It didn't give her enough slack to get her fingers up to it where she could start loosening it one way or the other and try to get a loop over her hands.

It was dim, almost completely dark, and she couldn't see the ropes that the big man had used to tie her down. She ran her fingers over them, looking for the knots, but they were all out of reach.

There was a quiet grunt and she jerked her head to look at it, but she couldn't see anything. For a moment, she had a sick instinct that one of the cows was still *alive*, but then there was a voice.

"You able to walk?"

Babe.

"I'm fine," Stasia said back, her voice low. "How did you…?"

"Told you I wouldn't let you go into this kind of thing on your own," Babe said. "Jasper didn't like you being out here on your own while we was on duty in the castle, so he had some guys from another squad keep an eye on you."

Stasia let her head hang, struggling to master her emotions.

"The pixie's name is Zenith," she said. She hadn't realized Babe was moving until he stopped.

"You don't ever give up," he said, and she shook her head.

"No."

"Good for you," he said, coming around the last of the hanging cattle and kneeling next to her. He drew a knife.

"Three men outside," he said. "Didn't see me comin' in, but they're agitated now. Somethin' going on with the big boss, right? We're gonna have to fight. You ready for that?"

"Give me a dagger," Stasia answered, and he laughed quietly into the darkness.

"Don't like you doin' this at all," he said, slashing the ropes one by one until they fell into a pile on the ground. "But if it's gotta be someone, ain't nobody better suited than you."

Stasia stood, staggering to the side as her body rapidly adjusted to the level of panic in her system and the fact that everything felt *funny* with as afraid as she had been. Babe grabbed her with an arm around her waist.

"You sure?" he asked. She put her hands on his shoulders, steadying herself, then nodded.

"You hurt?" he asked.

She swallowed, finding her throat had closed.

A hundred times, she had danced with men this close, their arm around her waist, and it had meant *nothing*. A hundred times she had knuckled a man in the stomach or the throat for *trying* to be this close.

Twice, she had actually stabbed a man at this distance.

And yet, she let herself lean against Babe, *sag* against him, if she was being honest, and just breathe for a moment.

"Are you hurt?" Babe asked again, unmoving.

"You see me in the light, you're going to call me a liar, but no," Stasia said. "I'm just… I'm sorry, I've never been like this before."

"Ever feared for your life before?" he asked. "To the moment of it?"

She shook her head, unwilling to move.

"No."

He nodded.

"Comes at everybody different," he said. "Get your breath, then we need to move."

She nodded, forcing herself to straighten. He held her upright until they were both sure her legs were going to take to it this time, then he let her go.

"Give me a dagger," she said, and he pulled his left-handed dagger out of its sheath on his leg and offered it to her.

"Stay behind me as you can," he told her heading for a gleaming light against the ground at the back corner of the building.

Stasia was, for once, glad to do as she was told.

He walked up to two great big wooden doors and shoved one of them, bending it against a bolt somewhere overhead that was holding it closed, but leaving enough room for himself to slide through between the two doors. He grabbed the wood and Stasia leaned against it, using his help to keep the doors split far enough apart to slide through, then the wood jolted back into position and someone was shouting.

Babe drew his sword and Stasia pressed her back against the cart doors, holding the dagger in both hands for one very long, stupefied moment, then she saw that there was another man coming around the back corner of the building, and she squared up to face him, the hours she'd put in at the guard house coming good as she found that she could focus and act even with the weight of dread still hanging off of her from what had happened inside the building.

The man approaching her had a knife that he'd taken out of a sheath on the inside of his ankle, but it was a silly-looking compared to the blocking dagger that Babe had given her, and Stasia held it out, daring the man to actually fight her.

Unfortunately, he wasn't stupid enough for that, but he held his ground, shouting for reinforcements to come help pen them in.

Stasia glanced over her shoulder, trying to stay close enough to Babe that no one would get in between them and surprise either one of them, but without being in follow-through range of that sword.

She wanted to learn how to use a sword, proper.

Maybe she wouldn't ever carry one, true, but it was such a *beautiful* skill, the way he used it.

He drove the two men in front of him back, almost at a full walking pace, and Stasia followed, keeping her dagger between herself and the third man, and then Babe grabbed her elbow and pointed.

"Run," he said.

"Not without you," Stasia warned, and he laughed, stepping deftly around so that all three men were facing him with their backs against the building.

It was his happy laugh, the big, loud, fearless one, and it made her want to shout at the three men with a gleeful sense of victory.

"All that's keeping me here is you, darlin'," Babe said.

Stasia turned and she ran.

"Keep moving, keep moving," Babe grunted at her as she finally slowed blocks later, past the stockyards and in sight of the river that ran past the south side of the castle, somewhere a long way upstream. "Ain't gonna take lightly you walkin' out on them like that."

"You were watching over me," Stasia said, falling into step with him as he scanned the street and the buildings.

"Told you I would," he said. "You even seen me at it."

"Not lately," Stasia said, and he grinned.

"Holed up a long way off and just put my hat down over my eyes, like," he said. "Sleepin' off a night's drink, or waitin' for a friend. You're gettin' hard to follow."

"You've been following me?" Stasia asked. He narrowed his eyes, sweeping the street once more with a glance, then urging her to a faster walk with his hand at the middle of her back.

"Jasper told me to drop it, once you were out of the meat district, but I'm not so good with orders like that, when it comes to friends."

Stasia needed to think about that, given that the queen had *specifically* said there weren't to be any guards around the apartments she was setting up.

"Friends," she said, and he snorted.

"Figure that ain't you?" he asked, and she shook her head.

"No. I actually… I…" It was embarrassing to say out loud, even after he'd been so casual about it. "It's the kind of thing Colin or Sterling would say. It surprised me to hear you say it."

"One of us," he said. "Already claimed you once. Want me to do it again?"

"I'd say you just did," Stasia observed. "You saved me."

He was silent for a moment, and Stasia thought that the conversation was over when he finally spoke again.

"What's a shame is that you stuck your neck out for somethin' that ain't nobody gonna know it's even better, when it's done. They'll see a happy market, safe shoppers, a better city, but they won't know it's because you stepped in and kept it that way. It's the way of most of the good. You see the bad when it happens, but the good tucks in underneath everything about the way things are, and nobody really realizes what's keepin' 'em up out of the muck."

"I think that's too much credit," Stasia said. "He made me angry, doing that to me, and I got even."

Babe grinned.

"It's a good story, at least."

Stasia winked.

"And I'm sticking to it."

He turned at the market and they wove their way through it quickly, stopping in a stall and standing where only a narrow section of the walkway was visible, while the merchant looked at them with some measure of exasperation for taking up his space without even considering buying... fishing tackle. Stasia was actually interested in some of it, because it was a highly complex set of devices at the end of the day, simply to spool up a string and let it back out again, but Babe was moving again and she had frankly lost track of where they were in the sprawling marketplace.

She would likely never be back, and she felt mildly bad about it, but not bad enough to pay any more attention to where they were and any less attention to how Babe was moving.

It wouldn't have been *obvious* to any of the people they were going past. His shoulders were up and his head relaxed, but he stepped through the crowds with a decisiveness that bespoke destination and urgency, and Stasia was following him at some small distance, just because he left a ripple in the crowds that made it easier to walk on her own line.

Finally they reached the wide front gates of the marketplace, and Babe again stepped under an awning, looking out at the crowded street.

"They don't know who you are, do they?" he asked.

"I told them that I was spying on them for Henry Four-hands," Stasia said, and he glanced at her.

"Why would you be doin' that?" he asked.

"Because he's trying to cut them out and work directly with the pixie," Stasia said. He paused, then grinned.

"Oh, you're gonna cause problems," he said. "If they saw us go in the other gates, they ought to be waiting to pick us up here, but I'm not seein' any of 'em."

Stasia paused, then nodded.

"I'll go on my own," she said. "Walk straight past the castle and keep going. If anybody follows me, you'll be able to see."

He nodded.

"All right. I've got your back. So long as we've lost 'em, we'll head to the guard house from here and get the rest of the guys, but if they're followin', I don't know that Jasper wants 'em knowin' who you are."

It was harder than she expected, walking away from him, but she slid the dagger into the waist of her dress, walking quickly for the crowd at the market gate and merging herself into it the best that she could, getting out to the road and dodging between carts and carriages and picking up her pace to match the pulling horses as she walked along the river side of the road.

Past the castle, where the traffic thinned considerably and on to the next bridge across the river. She went and stood at the peak of the first bridge, watching the road. Eventually, Babe came up along the road, just another man out doing a day's work, his build alone standing out just enough for Stasia to identify him. He crossed the bridge without looking at her, and Stasia turned a while after to follow him.

Jasper was the only one at the guard house.

"Where is everyone?" Stasia asked when Babe and he emerged from the bunk house and came walking along the wooden walkway overhead.

"Day off," Jasper said. "We do get them. Are you alright?"

She nodded and he accelerated down the stairs, coming to look at her with concern. He touched her chin with his fingers to coach her face to the side, and he shook his head.

"I'm sorry," he said.

"Would you say that to him?" Stasia asked, indicating Babe with her chin, and Jasper chuckled grimly.

"Of course not."

"Then don't say it to me," Stasia said.

He nodded.

"Okay. What happened?"

"They saw me," Stasia said. "He thought I was spying on him for one of… He asked me about Highrock."

"One of the real crews," Jasper said, glancing at Babe. "He shouldn't be concerned about them. Something's changed that Placid doesn't know."

Babe grunted.

"I told him that I was spying on him for Henry, because Henry was going to cut him out with the pixie and wanted to be sure that Eddie didn't know about it. He sent someone to go get the pixie. Zenith."

"So… the pixie mixing the magic for Eddie and Henry is at the butcher shop right now?" Jasper asked with some measure of disbelief.

Stasia nodded.

"If we're all lucky, you and Placid and whoever else can get there in time to catch him before they hurt him too much."

Jasper nodded quickly, giving Babe a sharp look.

"Watch her," he said, then took off.

Babe watched after him for a moment, then turned his attention back to Stasia.

"You hungry?" he asked.

The smell of the butchery was still in her nose.

"No."

"I could eat," he said, heading up the stairs away from her.

"Why did he tell you to watch me?" Stasia asked, and he looked down on her from halfway up.

"Lot of good soldiers, from training up at the fort, they got promise. Strong, smart, the lot. But they go up against an enemy that first time, see death in the eye, they lock up. Some of 'em never come back from it. Ain't no shame in needin' someone what's been there before to sit with you a time."

"Shouldn't you be going with him?" Stasia asked. "I don't need a nursemaid. I'm *fine*. If he's going to go in there…"

"Jasper knows what he's about," Babe said. "I ain't in the business of second-guessing him. Recommend you don't pick up the practice."

She hesitated, but he continued on up the stairs, and she followed him.

She sat down at the table at the back of the room, looking around at the men at the other tables. They had a variety of ages, few as young as Matthias, but many older than Jasper or Babe, all of them with the look of men who had seen the darkness and come to terms with it. There was happiness there, camaraderie and humor, friendship. They played cards and dice, they ate, they talked. The common language was one of play and jokes, though no one here was casual or rambunctious about it.

Babe came back with a bowl of meaty stew and sat down across from her, eating as though nothing had happened.

Stasia watched for a few minutes, then stirred.

"So what happens now?" she asked.

"What do you want to happen now?" Babe asked around a mouthful of stew.

"With Jasper and Eddie and Zenith," Stasia said. Babe shrugged.

"Police issue," he said. "We figured out who the pixie is that Placid needs to snag off the street. Catch 'im at Eddie's, better yet. But it ain't got naught to do with us, no more."

He glanced up at her again through his eyebrows. "Saw you deck the big guy out in the street. Thought you might have a moment of it, there, where you could still get away."

"The little guy flattened me, instead," Stasia said, and he grinned.

"Yeah, you didn't see that one coming. Weren't a fair hit, anyway."

"No such thing," Stasia said reflexively, then dipped her head. He grinned wider.

"True enough. Surprised to hear you say it, but still true enough."

"Why surprised?" Stasia asked, and he shrugged.

"Most folk like to believe there ought to be rules," he said. "'Specially for women. And I ain't sayin' that's wrong. *Is* wrong to hit a girl, 'less she's willin' to do it right back to you. But the truth of it is, if a guy's willin' to kill you, he ain't so hung up on what he might do, 'tween here and there."

Stasia nodded.

"The man who taught me to hit, in Boton, he told me that I should never assume that anyone would hesitate to take advantage of their physical strength or a weapon that they had, because assuming they *won't* is the thing that would kill me."

Babe chewed thoughtfully for a minute, then nodded.

"There's rules even the stone elves and the pirates will live under, when it comes to war and fightin' soldiers. It's a funny thing that there's fewer rules in Verida than fighting a war, but it's true. Some men'll do right by you even as they rob you blind, but a man what's willin' to do you violence ain't gonna stick to a code."

"But the stone elves will?" Stasia asked, and he nodded.

"Both sides know they don't like the idea of torturin' captives, so they don't so much do it, hopes of keepin' their own side kept well. Execution, sure, but not torture. If a man stops fightin', you give 'im death or you give 'im quarter."

Stasia couldn't imagine.

He had the sense of understanding just how she felt, even if he really *had* been through all of it and could sit there, calm, across from her, eating his stew.

"Hard life, is solderin'," he said. "Much easier to be here in the guard house, knowin' that your only job is to keep the king safe, locked over there in his castle across the river. Some would say Jasper and I took the easy way out, bein' here instead of out there."

"Do you think that?" Stasia asked, and he shook his head.

"I'm a good soldier," he said. "But there comes a time when you got to make a decision whether you're gonna keep killin' and lose what's left of yourself, or if you're gonna let the rest pick up and you come do somethin' else with who you are, and manage to keep some of what it means to be human."

It hurt her to hear him say it, and he looked at her with steady eyes for a moment, then chuckled.

"Don't you pity me none," he said. "I've had it good, compared to the boys I grew up with. My belly was full more than it wasn't. I've got purpose and friends. I come a long way from where I started."

"Where did you start?" Stasia asked, and he shrugged, the corner of his mouth coming up.

"Just another kid in a slum," he said. "Scrambling for food and to keep the other kids from stealin' what was mine. His majesty's army came with a pen and a coin and I made my mark. Don't know what happened to the rest."

"Do you never go home?" Stasia asked, and he shook his head.

"Nothing to go home to," he told her. "Not even a home, really. Just a place with a lot of misery."

"I want to learn to use a sword," Stasia said, and he grinned.

"You ain't mastered a dagger, yet," he said.

"Is that how you learned?" Stasia asked, and he picked up his bowl, tipping it up to drink what was left of his stew and putting it back down on the table, then resting both hands on the table in front of him.

"No, I reckon it ain't."

"What am I doing?" Stasia asked. "This is your day off. You shouldn't have to sit with me all day like this. What would you normally be doing? What is everybody else doing?"

"Sterling is off to see his girl," Babe said. "Matthias goes home to see his ma. Colin has a group of dandies he runs with, when he ain't got not better to do."

"And you?" Stasia pressed. He grinned.

"I sharpen and clean my weapons, top up my healing kit, might read a book. Jasper is much the same. It's a soldier's life for the two of us, and ain't like to change anytime soon."

"How long have you known Jasper?" Stasia asked, and Babe rolled his jaw to the side.

"Sword, you say," he said, and she grinned.

"I want to learn to use a sword."

"I'd say that you ain't got the arms for it, but for how Colin raved about your goin' up a wall. Gotta see that one myself, some day."

Stasia shrugged.

"If I have to be stronger, I'll get stronger. I always have."

He nodded.

"I bet you have."

Jasper arrived back at the guard house a few hours later to find Stasia and Babe sparring in the yard with a pair of bundled reeds, using the same slow method of teaching he'd used to start her out with the daggers. Stasia's forearms were aching and her back was making threats that she *really* needed to listen to, soon, but it was fascinating, watching the way Babe's mind worked when it came to a blade in his hands.

Babe straightened and Stasia looked over her shoulder, realizing that much of the population from the mess hall had come downstairs to watch, and more besides. Jasper was leaning against the front palisade, arms crossed, a half a smile on his face.

"You get the bad guys?" Stasia called, feeling winded and breezy at the same time. He grinned.

"Every last one of them," he said. "Eddie even brought in Four-hands for us to sweep up with the rest of them. Placid has men talking to all of them, but it seems that we caught Eddie at a critical juncture in an organizational change. The timing couldn't have been better."

There was a pause, then one of the men leaning over by the rail began to clap. Another joined, and another, and then they were all clapping. It wasn't effusive - that would have shamed her - but there was a token to it, a sense of respect for what the accomplishment represented. Babe clapped, too, then he put his arm out for the reeds she'd been training with, giving her an excuse to do something other than stand there.

"There's other news," Jasper said, coming in closer to speak with her privately. "The queen wants to see you."

"The queen?" Babe asked, and Jasper nodded. "She shouldn't do anything else exciting today."

"Would you recommend that I ask the queen for a rain check?" Jasper answered. "She's one of us, and if she needs to hold up, she will."

He glanced a question at Stasia, and Stasia nodded.

"I'm good."

"All right," Jasper said, taking a step back and motioning. "You can go home and get changed, if you want."

She looked down at her tousled dress and rolled her jaw to the side.

"I think that would be best."

"You want to ride?" Babe asked. "I could saddle up Alfred and Sable, if you wanted. Long walk."

The giant horses.

How many times had Stasia sneaked into the stables to admire them?

The idea of getting to ride them?

"It is a long walk," Stasia said.

"That's fine," Jasper said, his eyes sparkling with humor, knowing how much it would mean to her. Babe left to get them and Stasia glanced at Jasper.

"You ought to take them out to the country and run them some," she said. "They're gonna get fat and lazy if all they do is stand in a stall all day."

"They go out four mornings a week to a facility at the north of town where they perform military maneuvers and breed-specific training," Jasper said quietly as Babe emerged from the stable with the two great big horses. The mare dragged Babe almost off his feet, coming to smell Jasper's hands, where a carrot materialized literally out of nowhere, Stasia would have sworn.

Babe handed her the lead for the stallion - Stasia was shocked at the idea that they intended her to ride the stallion, but Jasper's attention was on Sable and he showed no particular interest in Alfred as he spoke to the mare and she lipped at his hair.

Babe returned a few moments later with tack. Stasia would have normally taken the saddle and thrown it herself, but the way Babe tipped one way and the other under the weight of the pair of saddles clued her to the weight of them, and she would have had to have gotten it fully over her head to clear the stallion's back.

She took the blankets and threw them over his back as he whuffed at her, lipping at her skirts, then she took the bridle and arranged it in her hands while Babe threw the saddle over Alfred's back.

"He won't run on ya," Babe said as she made to work the halter down the stallion's neck - a hack to keep an ornery horse from refusing a bit and running away - but she was already done. Alfred reached for the bit with the same eager sense that Schotzli did, and a moment later he was tacked, bridle gleaming in the midday light, saddle a work of art over dark purple blankets.

Babe disappeared once more into the stable as Stasia stood next to Alfred and pretend to make a plan on how she was going to get her foot up high enough to reach the stirrup without making a fool of herself. She turned her head to watch Jasper take a running vault from along Sable's shoulder to land astride without the use of stirrups at all.

It was like a man waving a cape, the way he landed on that horse.

She looked up at him with respect, then Babe appeared.

"Let me give you a leg," he said. He had something over his arm, but Stasia didn't ask about it, hauling her skirts up high enough to get her left leg free and letting him grab her by the ankle to lift and throw her over the horse the same way he had the saddle.

"Cloak," he said as she resettled her skirts. It wasn't entirely dignified, but the city wasn't the kind of place that generally cared.

She looked down, the accepted the heavy leather cloak from him, settling it over her shoulders and lifting the hood. She shifted once more, pushing the dress further back behind her so that it was covered by the cloak. Babe took a step back and nodded.

"That'll get you home unrecognized," he said. "Even if they did catch all the important ones, don't want the rest of 'em catching wind, either."

She nodded, letting Alfred follow Sable toward the gate. Babe lifted the barrier and Alfred broke into a wading trot, he was so eager to be out and doing *something*.

"Oh, I know," she said. "Big important horse like you cooped up like that? Who agreed to that?"

Jasper looked back at her.

"You settled?" he asked.

"You insult me," she answered.

"Babe won't be around to get you back up," he said happily as she caught up to ride next to him, Alfred still churning like he was swimming.

"Get me out of these skirts and I won't need him," Stasia answered. He smiled. His entire posture was different, on horseback, she realized.

"Were you in a mounted unit?" she asked. "Up in the mountains?"

He blinked at her, his mouth working twice before the answer came.

"You see it as plainly as that?" he asked, and she shrugged.

"Far as I can tell, you guys don't really have any pastoral communities around here where you could have grown up. Where else would you learn to ride like that?"

"Oh, you haven't seen anything," he said, patting Sable's neck with loud thumps. The mare arched her neck and started to dance on her toes as well. "They want to run. Built for open country, the both of them."

"They're not built for anything," Stasia said. "They shouldn't exist."

He glanced over at her, something… different.

"You see that, too," he said. "No. If you want my opinion, I think they're held together by magic. Bred up in the hills where the stone elves can't drive the truly stubborn back any further, they couldn't exist if they didn't have something special in their bones."

"Are the hill folk giants, too?" Stasia asked, and he laughed.

"No," he said. "But they don't breed with unicorns."

Stasia blinked forward.

She couldn't look at him.

He was making fun of her.

Wasn't he?

He had to be.

Didn't he?

"Unicorns?" she finally asked, barely more than a whisper.

"You didn't hear it from me," he said. "Just a rumor. Can't tell if the hill folk are offended at the idea, or if they're angry that the secret is slipping. I've never seen one and I've never known anyone I trusted who had, but… that's what they say."

"Unicorns," Stasia said, and she heard Jasper grin.

"If I do the math right, unicorns aren't anything like in the stories," he said. "Produce something like this? They're not delicate and fragile at all. Can you imagine, an animal made of magic, this size, coming at you because he's angry? I bet they're terrifying."

"Do they have silver blood?" Stasia asked. She couldn't help herself. She'd once used mud to stick a shell to Schotzli's forehead and pretended the mare was a unicorn all afternoon. And this wasn't that many years ago.

"Like I said, I've never met anyone who talks about them as anything other than a myth. Possible they got tangled up with the hill folk and they're still just a story. Possible… not."

"You think they exist," Stasia said, looking over at him, and he shrugged, turning his head to look back at the mountains behind them.

"I've seen a lot of things that shouldn't be possible," he said. "Hard to believe something as possible as *that*, given everything else."

They rode south to the Sapphire River and then onto the quieter riverfront street to Stasia's house.

"Do you want to come up?" Stasia asked. "I don't think my father will be in, this time of day, but Tesh and Emily are in, and the stableman works during the day."

"Here will be fine," Jasper said. "It's a lovely view. I hadn't seen it myself, before."

"You haven't been here?" Stasia asked, and he smiled.

"I hadn't stopped here and looked at it, before now," he said. "I'll wait."

She turned Alfred up the drive to the post in front of the house, pumping water up into the trough for him out of habit, then she ran around to the back of the house where she could let herself in.

Her dragonskins were up in her room, and went on like a breath of wind, her peasant clothes laying on her bed for her to deal with later.

She dashed back out, putting her mask on and greeted Alfred just for a moment before throwing herself back up into the saddle and riding down to the lane once more.

"That is much better," Jasper said with an easy smile. Stasia appreciated the fresh air in her hair and the great big stallion's eagerness to be off once again.

"Do you know what the queen wants?" Stasia asked, and he shook his head.

"I doubt she'll ever tell us by messenger," he answered.

"You don't even have a guess?" Stasia asked, and Jasper laughed softly.

"With Constance? Never. She never ceases to surprise me nor amaze me. She is constantly evolving and constantly somewhere that you'd never anticipate, thinking about things that no one else is even considering. My loyalty is to Rupert, and I would never follow the queen's orders against the king's, but I think that even he knows the foolishness of that. You don't work at cross purposes with Constance. It's never a good idea."

"The whole thing makes me nervous," Stasia said. "What if I'm doing something in secret that's going to hurt people? Or that I wouldn't approve of, if I knew all the details?"

"I understand that hesitation," Jasper said. "And it's a noble one, too. I believe that. But you have a choice. Are you going to stay above all of the decisions you can't completely understand and away from situations where you should have masterful control, or are you going to throw yourself into something that is so big and so important that you're willing to allow that mistakes are going to happen and regrets are inevitable? Because that's where you are. There will be regrets. There will be loss. But, from about as deep inside of it as you can get, I still believe that the worth of this kingdom, of this city, is there."

"Does anybody ever talk about leaving?" Stasia asked. "I mean, if the elves are all out to kill you and they're never going to stop, and they're angry because you're on their land... I mean, maybe you would all be better off just going back to Kirfall and starting over there."

"Can you imagine the losses?" Jasper asked. "The people who would never recover from being stripped of the few possessions and the shelter they have here to go wander the world somewhere else? I wasn't there when they chose the branch of the Wolfram River for Castle Wyndham. And I wasn't there as the city sprouted and began to grow in number. I wasn't there when the nobles were given their titles and their deeds, nor when the tenements and the apartments swelled with people. I'm here now. In a land where the stone elves *cannot* live, and one where hundreds of thousands of innocent people *do* live. I know that conversation may happen somewhere, sometimes, but I would never be a party to it, because it assumes that things that were done before, by other people, can be corrected by the sacrifice of people who are here now. The stone elves, still this day, do not want to live here. They just want us all gone."

There was bitterness there, Stasia realized - slow. He'd fought to keep the city safe. It would sting him to just walk away from it, though he was also completely right about the loss of life that would happen to uproot the entire city and attempt to transport it somewhere else.

It was a thriving city, by all signs and by all metrics. The trade here was unmatched anywhere else in the known world. Stasia's father came home with a gleam in his eye and great plans, and

Stasia was actually looking forward to a break in her schedule with the guard where she could go wander the docks and perhaps see some of these marvels that Minstrel bought low and sold high.

"I'm sorry," Stasia said. "I didn't think."

"War is a hard place to be," he said. "It's easier to make simple villains out of your enemy than it is to recognize that you've killed a living person who has every characteristic that you hold about yourself that makes you a man, but I think that it spares your soul, leaving it in front of you that they're not monsters. I don't know if I managed or not."

She looked over at him again, but his eyes were on the road ahead.

They made it to the castle, where the palace guard let them into the courtyard and a pair of men came to take the horses.

"Deliver them back to the guard house," Jasper instructed as they dismounted, going to the castle steps and up into the castle.

A servant greeted them a few minutes later.

"We've been summoned by Queen Constance," Jasper said. "I'm Jasper of the King's Guard. She will be expecting us."

"The queen is in her quarters today," the servant said. "I wasn't aware that she was taking audiences."

"Please send word for instruction," Jasper answered, undeterred. "We will wait."

The man looked at Jasper's uniform, then nodded and disappeared through a door.

"This will be a few minutes," Jasper said. "May as well find someplace comfortable to wait."

They went to sit on a pair of wooden chairs against a wall in the court room and Stasia watched as men and women came and went, many of them in formal costume as members of the court, and many, many servants, seeing to the physical needs of the men and women who lived and worked within the castle.

"You said there's an orchard here?" Stasia asked. Jasper nodded.

"They cultivate as much food as they can on the premises," he said. "There's a lovely water garden, a much more functional kitchen garden, and then several acres of orchard. They have a number of uncommon fruits that only grow on marsh, and then the more traditional ones growing on the higher points where the land is better."

Stasia nodded.

"And how many people work here?" she asked. He shook his head.

"I honestly have no idea. Though a foreigner probably shouldn't get caught asking such questions. Boton is a friendly trading partner, but they're not above seeking advantage through surreptitious or outright destructive means."

"Boton isn't organized enough to undermine anything but each other," Stasia said dismissively, and Jasper laughed.

"Do you not know about the pirates, then?" he asked.

"They exist," Stasia said, and he nodded.

"Oh, yes, they do, but they take a bounty from your parliament for every Veridan flag they capture."

Stasia jerked her head to look at him, and he nodded.

"Rumor is that there's a merchant's guild in town paying the same for Boton flags," he said.

Stasia frowned.

"That's a protection racket," she said, and Jasper laughed.

"Yes, it is. You can tip the tide of commerce by outbidding your rivals, certainly, but at what cost?"

Stasia shook her head.

"Fat pirates."

He laughed out loud. Loud enough that several nearby servants gave him chastising looks, though Jasper wasn't the type to be chastised.

He grinned.

"Oh, I needed that," he said. "Fat pirates."

He crossed his legs at the ankle, legs straight, and slouched in his chair, tipping his hat down over his eyes.

"Is it really going to be that long?" Stasia asked, and he shrugged.

"I'm in the castle; I'm not on duty," he said. "I'm going to take my rest where I can. You never know where you'll next be able to sleep."

"Today is your day off," Stasia said. "And you've worked all day instead."

He snorted.

"I don't get days off," he said. "I just get days without the squad to worry about."

She looked over at him, but he seemed quite content, there under the brim of his hat, and she shrugged, watching the castle life instead.

The minutes dragged on and she shifted position several more times before a young woman appeared, walking toward them with quick, intent steps. Stasia nudged Jasper's ankle and he snorted, sitting up and adjusting his hat.

"Queen Constance begs your patience," the woman said. "She is seeing to some delicate personal matters and asks that you wait for her in her personal sitting room. If you'd be so kind as to come with me."

Jasper glanced at Stasia, but there was no alarm there. Stasia rose and followed the woman through a door and up a set of stairs, down hallways and up more stairs, through more hallways and past rooms and rooms of *people* doing *things*. Think what she wanted to about the inefficiency of a place like this, it was industrious.

Finally, the woman opened a pair of tall doors and led them into a huge room that reminded Stasia of the Westhauser manor. The floor was made of cream-colored marble and the pillars were of blue stone with wrought-metal serifs in gold and silver and bronze. The woman indicated them to a set of couches, which were covered in some of the softest leather Stasia had ever felt.

And she was wearing dragonskin.

Maids came through, both of the servant variety and of the handmaiden variety, and Stasia found herself staring at the latter with a sense of disbelief.

These were women who, as she'd been told, had basically dedicated their lives to making sure that the queen was never alone unless she ordered it.

"Are they friends?" Stasia asked Jasper quietly as one of the women left the room.

"Some of them," Jasper answered with rival softness. "Many of them are too aspirational. A queen can help them arrange a favorable marriage. Perhaps when she was younger, more of them would have been her friends, but now they just serve a function."

Stasia wrinkled her nose.

That sounded lonely.

Finally, maybe twenty or thirty minutes later, another pair of doors opened and Constance came in, shooing away the two handmaidens who tried to follow her.

"He's a member of the King's Guard," she said dismissively, then made the shooing motion with her hands again.

"And I'm an old woman," she muttered as she came to sit down across from them. "I'm very sorry to have kept you waiting like this. Today has been... very complex, as I believe you'll understand in a few moments."

She shifted to look at the door, her mouth opening slightly as she did some kind of computation in her head.

"They like to try the keyhole, when they think I'm not looking," she murmured.

"Oh, I can fix that," Jasper said, rising and going to stand in front of the doors, his hands clasped behind his back.

Constance snickered and nodded.

"Very good, Jasper. Thank you."

"Is everything okay?" Stasia asked, and Constance set her mouth delicately, considering.

"Yes and no," she said. "Nothing is different than it was yesterday or the day before that or the year before that. But never is *everything* okay. It is a kingdom at war, and it is a city of a great number of people. Conflict must be expected and dealt with, and such is the nature of today's issue."

"What can I do?" Stasia asked, surprised at how easily loyalty to this woman came for her. She needed to keep an eye on that.

Constance drew a breath, then looked over at the doors where Jasper stood.

"Would you like me to get a rug, as well?" Jasper asked. It sounded like he meant it, if with humor.

"If that you could," Constance said. "The longer this goes on, the more likely it is to get out of hand. Risk now is better than risk later."

She stood and went across the room to open a small door, revealing a pantry of sorts.

Where a man was sitting on the floor.

"Miss Stacy Fielding, Jasper, I would like you to meet Farang Ildawa. Farang, these are the friends I promised to you."

"Constance," Jasper breathed.

"I know," the queen answered. "I have my reasons, and one of my conditions is that you may not ask, not of me now, nor of him later."

"He's an elf," Stasia said, putting it together rather abruptly.

The man unfolded from the floor, rising without using his hands, and gave her an odd, off-balancing look.

"You're not like them," he said, and Stasia shook her head, entranced.

"Nope."

He stepped out of the pantry and walked across the room toward her, looking once at Constance and then over at Jasper, then returning his attention to Stasia.

He stopped in front of her, looking down at her from an absurd height.

"This is the one?" he asked.

"Yes," Constance said.

"Your majesty," Jasper said. "Surely not."

Farang looked over at him with thoughtful eyes.

"He is my guest," Constance said. "But as you might imagine, he isn't safe here."

"He isn't safe anywhere," Jasper answered. "I'd imagined perhaps exposed romantic partners, or family members who were at risk of assassination or kidnap. Not this."

"I had a firm belief that you, of all people, would be willing to take on the risk," Constance said, and Jasper shook his head

"That's not what you're asking, though. You're asking *her* to do it, and she hasn't the first idea what's going on."

"Why do they hate you?" Stasia asked Farang.

He looked at her quietly for a moment, then sat down on the ground in front of her with the same casual folding motion he had used to stand.

"What do you know of my people?" he asked.

"I know that they hate you," Stasia said. "But I also know that their reasons don't make any sense. You aren't fighting them. Right?"

"We take no sides in the war," Farang said, and she nodded.

"See, that's what I don't understand. Why do they hate you, if all you've done is decline to go marching off to battle with them?"

"Because they believe that we have a power that would be capable of setting them free of the need to be at war," he said. "That, if we chose, we could end the entire conflict, and that we choose not to because we prefer that the humans remain at war rather than able to expand into the hills and ultimately the mountains. They believe that we use the stone elves as a shield and silently side with them, and that in our inaction, thousands of their own have died."

"Is it true?" Stasia asked, the corner of his mouth came up slightly.

"I'm sure some of us feel that way," he said. "Just as you must have some people in your awareness who abhor daylight or refuse meat. My people are every bit as... individual as are yours. Would you dare to speak for all of them?"

Stasia frowned, then shook her head.

"Nope. I only speak for me."

He nodded.

"You are different."

"She's not so different," Constance said. "You just have limited exposure to humans. For now. Stacy, I need you to get him out of the castle and hidden away as quickly as possible. I haven't been able to staunch all of the rumors, and there are going to be people who are very shortly going to start tearing apart the entire world to try to find him."

"You knew, when you commissioned her," Jasper said. "You knew that this was coming."

"It could have just as easily been an assassination I was trying to stop," Constance said. "There was never any telling which event would fall apart first. But, yes, I knew this was possible."

"She has no idea the risk you're asking her to take," Jasper said.

"*She* can make a decision on her own," Stasia said, mesmerized with Farang for reasons she couldn't pinpoint. "There's a wide gap between a city that hates you for who you are and a city that's willing to hunt you down and kill you for existing. Why are you special?"

Farang snorted, rising.

"Because I have fallen," he said. "And I have lost my ability to hold myself away."

"There is a theory among certain of Rupert's advisors that the way to gain the next big advantage in the war is to kidnap a high elf and force him to teach them how to fight the stone elves. To make weapons and potions that will be more effective than what they can get from the pixies and the gray market. Farang is the unfortunate target of this first experiment, and I will not allow it."

"Then we can put him in a carriage and drive him up into the hills to the north," Jasper said. "He can return home, from there."

Constance looked sharply at Farang, who sighed, folding his hands.

"I am broken," he said. "My people will not take me back again."

"That's awfully conclusive of them," Stasia said. "Really? You get injured and they just leave you to die?"

"That's not how he's broken," Constance said. "And I don't want the knowledge to get out any further than it already has. It isn't my secret to divulge, and the high elves hold it closely, for obvious reasons. Please just take it on faith that both Farang and I genuinely believe that the rest of his life is going to have to be lived in Verida, if he is going to have any life at all."

Stasia chewed her lip.

"I'll do it," she said. "I'm in. But I know nothing about the feeding and care of elves."

"My needs are nearly indistinguishable from your own, if my understanding is correct. I eat the same foods, sleep in the same way, and I am slain through the same methods."

"Seconds," Constance breathed. "Seconds, Jasper."

Jasper sighed heavily.

"You need to find another solution," he said. "We can keep him hidden for a time, but she isn't capable of understanding the depth of this."

"She keeps him hidden," Constance said. "As I said from the beginning, I do not want the guard involved in this. You are recognizable and Rupert may come to you and ask for help. I need you to be able to search honestly and to reply in truth that you don't know where he is."

Jasper's jaw clenched for a moment, then he nodded.

"Find another way, Constance," he said softly. "This is not going to work for long."

"Many solutions are built on more temporary means than this," Constance answered, going to a beautiful door opposite the one she had entered the room through. "Do you know how to get out, from here?"

"Of course," Jasper said. "I will be in touch."

"Not until I summon you," Constance said. "They'll know you came today. For everyone but the king, you need an answer prepared for why you were here. No one will admit that he's here, out loud, so I don't anticipate anyone will ask you specifically, but they'll be searching for incomplete stories and lies."

"I know how to handle the court," Jasper said. "Are you safe, mum?"

Constance nodded dismissively.

"They'd have to work a lot harder than this to get me cornered," she said. "Go. Go now. I have more appointments today to confuse the track."

Stasia followed Farang out through the doors and down a short hallway to a set of spiraled stairs. Jasper seemed to move like he knew exactly what he was doing, so Stasia took the time to watch Farang.

"Are you sad to be here?" she asked.

"I miss my home with an ache like my heart would freeze," Farang answered. "But I must accept what is. I cannot go back. All there is is forward."

"No more talking," Jasper said, not unkindly. "This stairwell isn't often used, but if people hear us, it will arouse suspicion."

They went down and down and down, passing doors at intervals, but not leaving the spiral staircase as the air grew cooler and gloomier and the torches further and further apart.

Finally, Jasper opened a door and walked them into a gray stone hallway that had no sense of natural light at all. He took a torch from a bin and lit it off of the single torch at the doorway, then led them on.

"Where are we?" Stasia whispered. It echoed chillingly.

"We are under the castle," Jasper answered. "This is where the last stand of the palace guard would take place, and just beyond us is the deep keep, where the king, the queen, and her daughters would be taken in the event of a military breech of the walls."

He turned into a room, going through a doorway without a door, and lifted a heavy leather cloak off of the wall, handing it to Farang. It was almost identical to the one that Babe had given to Stasia for riding out of the guard house, though longer, and it hung to Farang's calves in a way that suggested it was supposed to do that.

"Keep the hood up," Jasper said. "No matter what happens."

Farang complied and they went on, going up a set of steps and through a door into a wide hallway with a thick carpet down the middle.

"Just walk," Jasper said. "Don't need to look at anyone, don't need to justify being here. We are leaving."

They passed servants and people in important costumes, but Stasia kept her eyes on Jasper, doing her very best not to look like she deserved to be arrested.

She was normally better at this, but she'd never sneaked a wanted man out of a castle before, so she cut herself some slack on that.

Out through the front doors of the castle, someone shouted and Jasper stopped, turning back as a man jogged down the steps of the castle to catch up with them.

"Heard you guys were involved with a big thing by the meat market," the man said, and Jasper nodded.

"Trying out a new theory," Jasper said. "It went very well. I wasn't anticipating many people would hear about it, though."

Stasia edged back a step, wanting to be gone. Farang was simply too tall to go unnoticed for that long, wasn't he? A man standing in the courtyard with a leather cloak over his head and his face covered?

There was no one else out here dressed like that. Surely everybody was staring.

Was everybody staring?

"Percival told me," the man said to Jasper. "Don't know where he heard it, just that you were off doing your thing and nobody knew what to make of it."

Jasper laughed quietly.

"You'd think they'd get used to that, sometime," he said. He looked over at Stasia. "You don't have to wait for me. Aaron is on duty, so he obviously has nothing better to do than talk to me."

Stasia nodded as he raised his hand to wave at the palace guards at the gate, then she turned away from him and started toward the front of the courtyard, Farang walking steadily along beside her.

What was she *doing*? If this man really was wanted by the king, if all of these guards were willing to attack the two of them to make sure he didn't escape… Why was Stasia a part of this at all, again?

Yes.

Because the queen had asked her to, and Stasia knew that she could.

She flipped her hair off of her back and shook it out, straightening as she walked. She wasn't skulking and she wasn't hiding. She was going about her business after having been summoned by the queen.

She was an important person.

She had talked to the queen about a favor that the woman wanted her to do, and not just anybody got asked favors by the queen, now did they? The palace guards wouldn't want to get in the way of someone who was in a favor-trading relationship with the queen, now would they?

Would they?

No.

They wouldn't.

The men allowed Stasia and Farang out with scarcely a glance - they were there to keep people *out*, not *in*, and Stasia headed for the market across the river.

This might have been a mistake, she realized after they'd passed the first dozen stalls or so. There were people running around everywhere, and it wasn't uncommon for someone to bump into her or approach her, trying to sell something. If they caught wind of Farang *being* there, she was in the middle of a crowd, and getting out wouldn't be easy.

She turned south, heading for some of the lesser parts of the market as quickly as she could, wondering what Farang was thinking, what he was *feeling* right now.

She'd left Birch sour and unimpressed, but at least she had had family here to keep her safe and in a bed without bugs in it. Farang had lost his family, lost his home, and had no hope of ever going back again. She glanced over at him, feeling a depth of empathy for a moment, then scolding it away again.

She was trying to keep him alive and unimprisoned, just now. She could worry about all of the valid reasons why he might be sad later.

They made it to the south end of the market and went along the main road a bit further, then Stasia realized she was still wearing her dragonskins. She'd never gone to any of the apartments she'd taken for the queen in anything much above her peasant dress. She needed to get home and changed, before she could take him anywhere else. The cloak wasn't enough.

"Shoot," she murmured.

"What is it?" Farang answered, his voice soft and deep, personal.

"I need to stash you somewhere while I go change," she told him. "I stand out, like this, and I need to blend in as much as I can. But I don't know where you should go where no one is going to look at you and the guards won't find you, when they figure out you're missing."

"If I am to be captured, I would like to spend my last hours sitting by the river, if I may," Farang said, and Stasia frowned, then nodded, a plan coming together in her head.

"I can make this work," she said. "I can do this."

She turned around, going back to the market and wandering until she found a stall selling fishing gear. She bought a pole and a bucket with bait, then she went out and found a lightweight waxed fabric cloak that the fishermen sometimes used to keep the sun and the spray off of them. They were particularly common at the coasts, but Stasia did see them sometimes along the river, as well. She slung the cloak over her shoulder and let Farang carry the gear, walking across the first bridge to the Running Man Island, a weirdly-named island just south of the castle that had beautiful paired bridges connecting each bank to the central island. The place was a popular recreational spot, because it flooded in the fall - apparently - and therefore wasn't useful for structures, and great willow trees populated most of the banks.

Stasia walked Farang under one of the willows, where she took the leather cloak from him and helped him put on the fisherman's cloak instead.

"You know how big a mile is?" Stasia asked, and he nodded.

"Yes," he said. "Approximately."

"All right," she said. "I'm going to set off. You follow behind me for about a mile downriver, then find a spot where there's some good open bank down to the river. Some of them are crowded, if you try to pick one of those spots, you'll get run off, so pick an open spot and sit. I'll go home and get changed, and I'll come find you. We'll be in shelter by dusk and we'll figure it out from there."

She was going to be walking at home by herself in the dark.

Awesome.

It would be fine. She would make sure that she was armed, and she knew how to take care of herself.

It would be fine.

She glanced at him again, frowning.

"I'm sorry this is happening to you," she said, and he tipped his head, his form almost spectral under the cloak.

"You are very young, are you not?" he asked, "Very young to have the queen's confidence."

No, she was a spinster.

"I guess," Stasia said.

"Things are as they are," Farang said. "No one can wish them otherwise. I will follow you."

Stasia nodded and ducked between the long, drooping willow branches, setting off towards the other side of the river. She made sure not to look back.

It would be a disaster, if she lost him, she realized.

Still.

Don't look back.

Don't look back.

Don't look back.

———◈◆◈———

She really didn't expect him to be sitting there on the bank, when she got back. For a quarter mile, she watched it, not expecting him, and then sitting down next to a big swamp-rooted tree, she found him with his pole in the water and his head tipped against the tree, his feet - freakishly big feet, as she was actually looking at them - trailing out in the edge of the river. Just here, it was clear between the roots of the tree, but that wasn't a given, everywhere.

"Are you ready?" Stasia asked, coming to sit next to him on the bank.

"It is very hot here," he said. "And worse indoors. Is it your intent that I go indoors and stay there until you and Constance agree that some other plan is palatable?"

Stasia considered that.

"Yes," she finally said. "We need to keep you away from eyes that would turn you in. After that, I don't know what will happen."

"The water cools my soul," he said. "I haven't known it, before, this river, but I find myself bonded to it, all the same."

"I wish I could tell you that it's all going to be okay," Stasia said. "But it's just my job to hide you somewhere where people aren't going to find you. The queen is going to have to tell me what happens next. I don't know how long all of this is going to go on before… it's done."

He nodded, rising.

"How old are you?" he asked.

"Twenty-three," Stasia answered, following him up to the bank to the road and setting off into greater Highrock. She didn't hate this part of the city. It was cleaner than a lot of the neighborhoods to the north, and as long as you stayed close to the main river and didn't drift too far south, the people here were friendly and clean, themselves. She'd taken an apartment a few blocks further south than she would have normally ventured on her own, because it was further away from where the police normally patrolled and the neighbors would ask fewer questions about Farang, when he showed up.

"This way," Stasia said, opening a door and leading the elf up two sets of stairs, then opening a door to the unit at the back of the building.

The walls were crumbly, on this side, but Stasia had climbed the stone on the outside once, after dusk, and she didn't think it was at risk of falling down.

She hoped.

"Washbasin," she said. "Towels. There's a little bit of food in the footlocker by the bed, but I'll bring you more tomorrow once I can get to the market. There's actually a not-very-bad market within walking distance of here, so once I figure stuff out, I can get you fresh food for all of your meals. How many times a day do you normally eat?"

"Once at daybreak and once at dusk," he said. "We carry dry bread in folded cloth with us as we work that we eat throughout the day."

Stasia nodded.

"I'll see what I can find. There are lots of options, if you know where to look. Um. The bed is... okay. I wasn't happy with that one, but I didn't have a lot of time to figure out how to do it better..."

"If you can provide me with a good length of rope and sturdy timbers, plus the tools to work them, I could build my own bed frame, and would just need skins to finish it."

Stasia nodded, considering.

"I can do that," she said. "It might take me a day or two to figure out where to get them from and how to get them here, but... that shouldn't be that bad."

He looked around the room, taking his hood back and just... standing.

"Your ears," Stasia said, just noticing them for the first time.

He put his fingers up to them, touching the point of one between his thumb and forefinger, then he nodded.

"Yes," he said. "I see."

He slicked his hand over the crest of his ear, and it took a new shape, rounded and human-looking. Stasia gawked.

"How did you do that?" she asked.

He smiled painfully.

"Magic," he answered.

"It will stay like that?" she asked.

"For a time," he said. "It depends on how content I find myself to be here."

Stasia went to look out the window. Not all of the apartments *had* windows, so this one was lucky. It didn't have much air-flow, because it backed up to another building that she could all but touch from here, but it was better than nothing.

"Do you need anything to get through tonight?" she asked.

"Oh," he said. "You're leaving me here."

She startled.

"It wouldn't be appropriate for me to stay," she said. "And my father is expecting me home tonight."

She was already going to have a challenge ahead of her, explaining why she was so late and why she was dressed as she was, but she would stay on a few more minutes if they were going to help Farang. Tonight had to have all of the ingredients of a terrible night for him.

"I see," he said. "You are unmarried and therefore uncovered by the laws of your people."

"Is it different with yours?" Stasia asked.

"Our women fight alongside us and work alongside us," he said. "But our settlements are small enough that we don't need considerations for how they behave because everyone is known to everyone. There are no strange men who belong there, day after day, and no reason for them to interact with visitors."

"I have a lot of questions," Stasia said, and he gave her another sad smile.

"I doubt I will answer many of them," he told her, then shrugged, almost as though against the cold, though there was a sweltering heat in the apartment, this time of day.

"There are a lot of things I've heard," Stasia said. "How can I know what's true if no one who knows the truth will tell me?"

"There are many things in the world to be curious about," Farang answered. "But few things that you have a genuine need to know."

Stasia frowned.

"Is there anything I can do for you tonight?" she asked.

"No," he said. "I will… consider my place here tonight and perhaps I will have requests in the morning, but for tonight, perhaps… there is nothing anybody can do, beyond what you have already done."

Stasia gave him a half-hearted smile, then nodded.

"Here's the key," she said. "I don't think you should go out, but… I feel funny having it. It's your apartment, for now. Lock it after I go out and don't answer the door to anyone but me. I'll be back as soon as I can get away in the morning. What do you want for breakfast?"

"I can't consider that, tonight," he said, and she nodded.

"Okay. I'll come here, first. Once I get here, coming and going shouldn't be a problem. I have to make sure no one follows me on my way here, though, so it takes some extra time to get here."

"I understand," he said, going to stand in front of the window. "Thank you for your help."

She nodded and left, going back out the front door of the building and turning the wrong way down the road, away from the river, but not wanting to take too direct a path back up to the main river for fear that someone would already be tracking her and get an idea what road Farang's apartment might be on or near.

The longer it took them to put together the path, the longer he would stay safe.

So she went south into Highrock. After dusk. On her own.

At least she was armed.

She made it two blocks before a group of boys spotted her and attempted to encircle her.

"Aren't you pretty to be out this late," one of them said, coming to lean against the building while his three friends leaned in as close to her as they dared.

Stasia drew one of the daggers from her belt and held it out at him.

"I'm just going home," she said. "Not looking for a fight."

He sniggered.

"We're not looking for a fight, either, are we?" he asked.

"Come nice," one of the other ones said. Another one grabbed at Stasia's skirts and she spun, slashing at his arm with the dagger.

She still couldn't climb in these skirts.

The lead boy grabbed at her elbow and she jerked it away, slashing at another of the boys and drawing her second dagger. The boys laughed.

"Got a lively one tonight," the lead said.

"I like when they have claws," another one muttered. "I like to pluck them out."

She slashed once more at a hand that got too close, then there was a forearm around her neck.

She was going to have to kill him.

That was the only way to prove to them that she meant it.

She flipped one of the daggers over in her palm, staggering back half a step as he pulled her off balance, then the leader chirruped a little whistle and the arm around her throat disappeared.

All four boys melted into the shadows like they'd never existed, and Stasia stood there on her own, her heart racing.

Were they going to come back?

Was this some sick game of cat-and-mouse?

"May I walk you home, miss?" a voice asked.

"Babe," she whispered, then she turned. "You aren't supposed to be here."

He screwed one eye shut thoughtfully as he got close enough for her to see him by a window's dim light overhead. He was wearing a loose linen shirt and tan-colored leather pants. Where was his uniform?

"See, Jasper and me, we got in a big fight when he didn't come back with you," he said easily. "Brought up some real nasty history and he relieved me of duty. Said he didn't want to see me again."

Stasia's eyes went wide.

"Because I didn't walk back across the street with him?" she asked.

He put his arm out and Stasia put her arm through his, walking along the way she had been going, deeper into Highrock. Were they to Lesser Highrock, at this point? The boys seemed to suggest it.

"We fought like this a few times," Babe murmured. "If I read 'im right, and I like to think I do, he thought you needed lookin' after, but he ain't allowed to send me."

"No," Stasia said softly. "It's important that no one see anyone from the guard around here."

Babe sighed.

"Too bad I ain't with the guard no more," he said. "I might be offended by that."

"What did he tell you?" Stasia asked.

"There's a bar not too far from here," Babe said. "If you want, I could buy you a drink and maybe we could sit in a corner somewhere and talk."

She considered that.

There was more to his words than just his words, and she could sense that, but she couldn't exactly tease out what it was.

"Okay," she said. He nodded.

"Right. This way."

She still needed to get home, but the idea of Babe and Jasper fighting over what had happened, as though it had been a bad thing or something out of her control, it bothered her a lot.

A few minutes later, he ducked under a low sign to walk into a dim pub with worn tables and men who were most of their way along to being drunk, already. Babe did, indeed, kick a man out of a corner table and motion for Stasia to sit, before taking the seat in the corner, his shoulders each squared up against a wall.

"Can see who's tryin' to hear, from here," he murmured, crossing his arms. "Ain't like to be nobody takin' special interest in us, what's already here, now, so we just gotta watch the door."

"Oh," Stasia said. "That's clever."

He snorted.

"I'm glad you think so. Now, Jasper didn't have space to tell me much. Just came up and picked a fight with me at mess, and kicked me out through the gate right proper where everybody was watchin', which means I expect he's lookin' for me to come out here in the cold on my own to watch your back, can't figure another reason."

Stasia paused.

She liked Babe.

A lot.

And he'd now saved her twice, just today.

But it didn't mean that she knew him well enough to be certain that he merited the queen's confidence.

Did it?

It was possible he was lying about what had happened with Jasper and had come after her on his own, because someone had already figured out that she was the one who had disappeared with the elf.

She sighed.

"You've gotta give me something," she said. "I trust you with my own life completely, but I'm into politics, now, that I've got no clue about. How do I trust that Jasper actually wanted you to come here?"

He raised an eyebrow.

"Look who's so cynical," he said. "So young. Such a shame."

He didn't seem troubled at all. He put up a hand for two of whatever it was he expected the barmaid to bring over, and the woman arrived a moment later with two beers, casting a curious look at Stasia, then leaving again.

"Jasper said that when I saw you, I should ask for his spare cloak back," Babe said as he twisted the bottle between his fingers, watching her. Stasia grinned, relieved.

"I'm sorry," she said. "I should know that you guys are all on the same side."

He shook his head.

"Don't be. Mostly we're all workin' to the same ends, but there's a lot of opinions out there on how to get there. Right for you to be careful, if what's goin' on is important, which it's got the look to be."

Stasia sighed and nodded.

"I have no idea what I'm doing," she said. "The… woman… asked me to take apartments around the city. I've been working on that."

"I know," Babe said. "It's how I found you. Also why Jasper sent me. He knew I'd know how to find you."

"You've been watching over me all this time," Stasia said, then sat up, alarmed. "But that means a bunch of the other guards know where I've been working…"

Babe shook his head, holding up a hand to slow her down.

"Nothing of the kind," he said. "I'm on my own, for this. Takin' extra hours where the other's play cards or go visitin'. Want to see that you're safe, wanted to know you could see to yourself if you needed to. Saw it tonight, by the way. Would've let you go your own way, from tonight, if it had been just another night."

"What?" Stasia asked, and he nodded.

"You intended to stab the man holdin' you," he told her. "I saw it as I came up. Glad you didn't have to, but glad to know you could. They didn't think you would, and it's a shame you don't get to build a reputation just now as the woman who'll stick you like a slaughterhouse pig for that kind of mistreatment, but there ain't no memory to a woman like you, so it's best you didn't have to do it."

Stasia worked her hands, still feeling the way the dagger had felt in her palm in that last moment, then she nodded and picked up her beer.

"I was," she said. "I was going to."

He nodded.

"Until I knew it, it didn't set right, sendin' you out on your own like that," he said. "But now you've got a new problem, and Jasper saw fit to send me after you until it's done."

"So you aren't actually dismissed?" Stasia asked, and Babe grinned.

"Not on your life," he said. "I know that man like a brother, and he ain't done with me yet."

Stasia nodded, another relief.

"How much should I tell you?" she asked, and Babe settled over his elbows, frowning with thought for several moments.

"Don't know, rightly, just how deep you found yourself today," he said finally. "And I'll admit I'm no fan of politics. But I reckon if you're lookin' for me to help with more than just boys with disrespectful hands, you ain't got the nuance to sort it out and tell me what needs told and not what don't, so… I figure you're best to tell me the lot of it and we'll go from there."

Stasia nodded.

"And you think I'm safe to talk here?" she asked.

"Don't be interestin' enough for the barmaid to tip an ear," he said. "But sure."

She sighed, putting back half her beer and setting it down again.

"The… woman… has a… guest… that she wants me to keep away from her… family and friends," Stasia said. Every one of those words was interesting. She wouldn't have been able to resist trying to eavesdrop someone talking about elves, even when she didn't believe they existed.

"Right," Babe said as though the whole thing were perfectly natural. Stasia went on.

"So I brought him home and I left him there, and I'm going to bring food in the morning, and then I need to figure out how to keep him where the family and friends won't find him for as long as… I guess forever? I'm not sure."

"What kind of friend?" Babe asked, and Stasia paused for a long time, trying to find how to answer that.

"He strikes me as… tall," Stasia said, hoping that wasn't too on-the-nose.

Babe's eyebrows jolted a fraction, then his face smoothed.

"Oh, I see," he said. "Well, ain't that something. He's settled in good for tonight?"

"I hope so," Stasia said. "It was the best I could do."

Babe nodded, settling lower into his chair and picking up his beer to wrest it on the other wrist.

"The folk around feel familiar to you?" he asked. "Like they know you on sight?"

Stasia nodded.

"I've been shopping around here during the day a number of times, and I've spoken to most of the neighbors."

The corner of his mouth came up and he nodded.

"That sounds like you," he said. "And you've always looked like that?"

She nodded.

"Enough."

She wore her hair up tight against her head, and cheap, durable dresses made for physical labor. There were women around who wore pants, instead, but Stasia had cast herself as a service worker rather than an outdoor laborer, which made the dresses more appropriate.

Babe nodded again, his eyes flicking at the door.

"Doubt it's folk from the castle, but we got interest comin' in the door. Keep as you are."

Stasia sighed, tipping her bottle back and leaving it in her hand. She'd rather hit a man with it than draw a dagger, if she got the choice for where to start.

Babe raised his eyes again, this time making firm contact with someone over Stasia's shoulder.

"Ain't a good place to be out where you ain't known," Babe said. "But they know a fight when they see it. You stay like you are."

"I'm sorry," Stasia breathed, and he frowned deeply and shook his head.

"Don't be," he said. "If our friend needs this, ain't no place I ought to be, instead."

Stasia nodded.

"I can be tougher if I need to be," she said. The corner of his mouth came up again, but it looked like he was laughing at the person over her shoulder, not at what she had said.

"We shouldn't stay here," he said. "He's got men out there, could be bringing in others, if they figure us to be carrying anything of value."

"I've only got my purse," Stasia said, and he nodded thoughtfully, still signaling to the person she couldn't see.

"More money than they'd get in any normal score, just there," he said, his mouth hardly moving. Hard to read lips, the way his mouth moved, just now. Stasia needed to learn that. It didn't *look* like he was trying to disguise the shape of his words. That was the genius of it. It was that they simply didn't transmit the way they normally did.

He licked his lips and slid out of his chair, putting his palm - with an awful lot of force - on her shoulder casually as he went by.

She slouched lower in her chair, hooking her arm over the back of it, but not turning around.

"Ain't lookin' for a fight," she heard Babe said.

"You're in the wrong part of town, rat," came the answer.

"Just seein' to a friend," Babe said. "Don't mean no disrespect."

"Marcus says we're friendly with rats," another voice said, and then someone spat violently - opinionatedly.

"Don't care what Marcus says about it, when you see a rat, you stomp it."

"I'd listen to him," Babe said, his tone unconcerned. "You don't want a war."

"Shouldn't be here," the first speaker said.

"He's here with a Highrock girl," another man said.

Stasia stretched her neck to the side, the hair prickling on the back of it as she anticipated the hand that would grab her to pull her into this conversation.

"Seein' to a friend," Babe said. "Nothin' more."

"We'll see to her," the new voice leered, and Stasia stretched her neck to the other side.

"Oh, no, you don't want no piece of that action," Babe said. "She's got claws. Had to stop her gutting a man, just tonight."

Was he talking to her?

Was he telling her to be ready to fight?

Not that she needed him to. She could feel the motion she would make, spinning to bring the bottle down on the head of whatever unlucky man chose to be the one to bring her into this.

Then straight to the daggers.

Would people think twice about messing with her, if she carried a sword?

That was probably too distinguishable, actually. The daggers were tucked away and unremarkable, but a sword would mark her as 'that woman' just as much as the dragonskins would.

But, oh, she was going to start wearing a sword with her skins. That was happening. Just as soon as Babe said she was ready.

If he ever trained her again.

Oh, that hurt.

Why did that hurt?

He'd given up his job, his career, to come see to her, to come watch over her, where she'd already gotten herself in over her head, out here.

"Let me buy you all a round, show I mean well, and we'll go," Babe said. "Ain't lookin' for a fight."

"Let's just…" the second voice said, pleading for sanity.

"I still want to take a look at his girl," the third voice said.

"Marcus wouldn't like this," the second voice said.

Stasia could just picture Babe standing someone down, Babe in his infuriatingly casual way, and the other man furious and looking for an excuse to start something.

"Get out," the first voice said, and Stasia relaxed just an instant, waiting. A moment later, fingers brushed her arm, and she stood. Babe looked at her sideways, then put his shoulder back to indicate she should walk in front of him. There were five young men at the bar, glaring, but the one who had his foot on the ground and his back taut like a bow was the one Stasia would have given anything to watch for a full minute or two.

How could someone that *angry* even exist?

Babe didn't give her the chance, and she was glad for it. She probably wouldn't have been able to resist, on her own. He nudged her forward with his shoulder and she walked on out the door, just walking to put distance between themselves and the bar, at first.

"You know where you're going?" Babe asked, and she shook her head, looking up at the sky for stars, but they were - as was so often true in Verida - obscured by humidity and low-running clouds.

"Not a bit," Stasia answered.

"You want the shortest path home from here?" he asked.

It was truly getting late.

She'd never come home this late before. She'd *gone out* this late before, but never come home this late.

She wondered what her father thought of that.

On the other hand, there were angry men behind her who might very well attempt to follow her, and she wasn't certain what would happen, should they discover that their quarry was actually a rather wealthy heiress in an almost unguarded manor on the river.

"How about the second-shortest route home," Stasia said, and Babe grinned.

"You got it," he said, turning right at the next street. "Ought to walk quick from here to the river."

Stasia nodded.

"I can do that."

"Don't expect no problem," Babe said. "I'm a big target, even if I am a rat." He glanced over at her. "You handled yourself well, back there."

"How?" she asked. "I didn't do anything."

"Hardest part is staying uninteresting until you gotta be interesting," he said. "Knew you had my back, if they tried to jump me, and they didn't know that, did they?"

She glanced over at him and he nodded.

"Left me free to step up to the big guy and put him back down 'thout him gettin' the idea that his buddies would back him. Just pull him out on his own."

"What's a rat?" Stasia asked.

"Hmm?" he asked.

"You said it, too," she said. "He called you a rat like it meant something."

He took a deep breath and nodded.

"'S where I'm from," he said. "Neighborhood controlled by the River Rats."

"How did they know?" Stasia asked.

He tipped his head away from her and put his fingers up to the side of his neck, to a tattoo of a maze of lines intersecting each other at roughly right angles.

"I weren't always a soldier," he said.

"And they saw that from the door?" Stasia asked. If it meant something significant, she couldn't put her finger on it.

"We all see 'em everywhere," Babe said. "Even in a uniform, it's hard to not go for a fella's throat for having the wrong mark."

"You?" Stasia asked, and he grinned.

"Just told you," he said. "Staying still even when your instinct is to act."

"You act like nothing ever bothers you," Stasia said. "Always calm and ready."

He nodded.

"I had a bit of a temper as a lad, got in fights at the fort when I was trainin' up, and my commander, he told me, he said if I couldn't find a way to hold that dog on a chain, I'd run wild and never amount to nothin'. And then he put a chain right 'round my neck, make sure I didn't forget."

"You wore a… you mean figuratively, right?"

He laughed.

"Not a bit," he said. "Mooring chain with a padlock on the back. The day I got sent out to fight, he took it off. Told me I was free and on my own, but that I best remember that, after him, can't nobody control me but me."

Stasia considered that as they walked.

"That's a terrifying idea," she said. "And isn't that the *opposite* of being a soldier?"

The memory seemed to make him happy.

"I had a lot of commanders through the years, true enough, and every one of 'em was there to tell me what to do. But I tell you what, the minute my training commander took that chain off me, I only did what they told me to 'cause I chose it. I control me. Nobody else, yes, but also never lettin' go of that chain, myself. My training commander, he gave me to myself, and I ain't never gonna forget that."

"Were you the only one he did that to?" Stasia asked, and he shook his head.

"Oh, no," he said. "He had all kinds of means to break a man. Had a buddy who wore his wrist shackled to his ankle for most of a year. He had men tattooed to cover their neighborhood markings, when they couldn't get free of 'em, put a couple of 'em in eye patches. But there were a lot of us out of the low neighborhoods wearin' chains. Not many of us made it to the war. He sent a lot of 'em home, and as far as I heard, none of 'em made it more than a couple more years. You can't control yourself, you're gonna make a mistake to get you killed, sooner than later."

"I can't imagine you with a temper," Stasia said. "I mean, I can imagine you just exploding and throwing a table or fighting five guys at once, but I can't imagine you just moody and angry."

"Took a long hard walk to get rid of that man," Babe said. "Don't miss him at all. Weren't nothin' about him but that he was alive that was worth it."

"That's a hard thing to say," Stasia said, and he shrugged.

"Same story as every one of those men back there," he said, indicating behind them. "Won't many of 'em make it long at all, and won't have nothin' to show for a mean, angry life. Women ain't much better, but at least they don't have the killin' to strip the soul out of 'em."

"You believe in a soul?" Stasia asked, and he shrugged.

"Just a word to explain a feeling," he said.

They crossed over the river and his pace slacked considerably.

"They warn you about the floods, yet?" he asked.

"How are you so calm?" Stasia asked. "There's a… man being hunted by… important people and somehow *I'm* the one who's supposed to keep him safe and hidden, you've saved my life not once but twice today, and you just got in a bar fight five-on-one. And you want to talk about flooding?"

He laughed.

"You think we sit around at the guard house or watch the king take his tea," Babe said. "True enough, we don't always see a lot of action, but when it's there, we're in the thick of it, Jasper's squad. Jasper sees to it. Part of what keeps you goin' is talk of the river and the sky, feelin' like ain't nothing wrong with normal, you just ain't there. So, yeah, I ask you about what you've heard of the fall floods, because they're comin' right soon, and I reckon you got a need to know about 'em."

"I didn't mean to offend you," she said.

"Not offended," he said, considering, then nodding. "Not as such. It's that you ain't yet seen what's to come, and I have. Maybe this goes clean, you come out lookin' like an easy hero, but maybe it don't, and you got to see what it looks like when a man's life ends, or when there's no win out there, just the choice of best loss. And maybe you even get that part wrong. I'm tellin' you the thing I know, when days are bleak and dark and death is stalkin' everyone around you, fast or slow. Look to the river and look to the sky and know that normal ain't dead and it ain't dyin'. Normal is livin' all over this city on account of you off fightin' the monsters that would gladly tear through this city and suck it into the abyss."

His voice was dark and quiet, and it shocked Stasia, while at the same time it felt like she might have been hearing his true voice for the first time.

"Okay," she said. "So tell me about the flooding."

"Your manor house will be built above the normal flood plain by a good six or eight feet, but it depends on the rains up in the mountains how much flood we actually get, and you gotta remember, this time of year, most storms to hit here don't go up the mountains, and most of the mountain storms, we don't never see nothin' of 'em. But there'll be a lot of rain, here, the next few weeks, just to remind us it's comin'. You can feel it, can't you? In the air?"

The air was sweltering, as it had been all summer, sitting in the apartments or at the manor. It wasn't quite so bad, out riding Schotzli at the Westhauser estate, but even then they came in drenched and ready to suck down a bucket of water apiece, she and Schotzli did.

"It's just hot, to me," Stasia said, and he nodded.

"Don't get the monsoon at Birch?" he asked.

"We get heavy rain," Stasia said. "But there aren't any rivers around and the ocean doesn't really care."

"It's gonna break," he said. "Rain gets here and the heat just dies for the year. We have the Highwater Festival at peak flood. I should be on the honor guard for the queen and king for that, but that ain't lookin' likely this year." He held up a hand. "Don't you go feelin' sorry for me, neither. I'm assigned and I'm content. Don't want your pity. Festival day is gonna be a circus, and it's a blessing and a curse. You want to move a man in a crowd, there'll be crowds everywhere, doin' all sorts of distracting things. You want to get out where there ain't gonna be nobody around? Wait for tomorrow. Festival day is a loss. Roads are packed, folks are drunk, and the bridges are impassible."

"What's wrong with the bridges?" Stasia asked.

"Highwater festival is about decorating your local bridge or goin' to one that means somethin' to you. Some of 'em don't even intend to allow foot traffic across, past midday. Gotta take a poleboat or a rower. Men keep a little dinghy up on the roof of the house all year long to take fares across the local section of the river on Highwater Day."

Stasia was realizing something he'd said.

"My house is only six feet above the peak flood stage of the river?" she asked, and he laughed quietly.

"Lotta water, coming down out of them clouds," he said. "Lotta mountains refusin' to sop it up. Goes down the rocks in sheets, sometimes as deep as your ankle. I seen soldiers swept away. I seen *trees* swept away. Hits the tributaries and the Wolfram itself and all that water comes down through Wolfram Falls, *around* Wolfram Falls… The fort keeps everybody who isn't actively involved in the front inside at the fort through all of it, because up there north of the city, sometimes the river comes wrong way around a hill and can point right at you with nobut a few minutes' warning. Fort's built to stand it, but it'll wash away a man on a horse, even the biggest carriage you've ever seen. Sometimes it's got trees in it, the floodwater up north, whole fleets of 'em like somebody lined 'em up as battering rams. By the time it's down here, the delta has got it all sorted out, and the flood goes on like it's done every year for all of time, far as I'm concerned, but up north, it's a crazy, wild thing."

"How does the rest of the city not wash away?" Stasia asked.

"Houses are built to handle the water," he said. "First floors are built with tiles that you pull off to let the water through, and then you just gotta have somebody in there all day keepin' the holes from getting stopped up, particularly on the leading wall. You get plugged drain holes, you get enough force to take the wall out from under the building, but if you don't stop the water flowin', it don't take no mind of you."

"So the bar," Stasia said. "Where you guys go. The guard house. All of that's going to be underwater?"

"At least two or three feet," Babe said. "If it's a normal year."

"And this is cause for a festival," Stasia said, and Babe grinned.

"So long as everybody does their part to put the water back in the banks when it comes back down, keep the bugs from croppin' up too bad, the city smells clean for a month after the flood. We got cobble and brick roads because dirt'd just wash away every year. We got buildings - the ones lowest down in the city, they don't got walls; they got skins for the walls on the first floor, and you just roll 'em up. Buildings know how to survive a flood. And there's something about the magic. Don't know what it is, but washing the whole city with it every year is important. Yeah. We mark it with a celebration."

"It can't be anything but destructive," Stasia said. "And it sounds crazy."

He laughed his big, happy laugh.

"Darlin', you just described Verida. It's what makes this city different from anywhere else, and the only place I would want to live."

"But I don't have to worry about making sure that we don't get stuff built up against the side of our house?" Stasia asked.

"You'll have a lot of fancy-pants diversionary features in the landscaping, if you look close. The soil will point upriver like a wedge to break up the big stuff coming down the river, and as far south as you are, it'll mostly just be water. The debris flows best down the big channels and just drifts up in the shallows where the nice houses are."

"Why has no one told me about this before?" Stasia asked.

Babe grinned.

"Because then they wouldn't sell the nice houses on the rivers," he said.

"Will I be able to get out?" Stasia asked.

"One way or another," Babe said. "Road might be underwater. But there'll be men running around up and down river in little boats like river bugs, happy to take you where you want to go for the right coin."

"And how much is that going to cost me?" Stasia asked. It sounded hostile, and in truth it was, because she didn't like to spend money on things that were overpriced and inescapable, but it was mostly just an attitude she'd inherited from her father.

"Crossing typically costs a copper," Babe said. "Depends on how fast the river is runnin' and how many men are out doin' it. Going downriver ain't gonna cost a lot more than that, maybe two. Upriver, though, that'll cost you. Here to the castle might be a jagger."

"That's a princely sum for a man who is rowing a boat," Stasia said.

"Told you, they look forward to it all year," Babe said cheerfully. "We call it a token to the river."

But it wasn't to the river. It was to an industrious man who was taking advantage of a predictable natural phenomenon.

"Can I haggle?" Stasia asked. "Will some of them charge me less than others?"

"I'm sure you can," Babe said. "And I bet a lot of 'em'll drop their rates for a pretty girl like you, with a spirit to her. But is that how you want to spend your festival day? Haggling with a boatman?"

"My father says to never pay more than something is worth," Stasia said. "It can be worth more for intangible reasons, but never pay more than it's worth."

Babe considered.

"And a ride upriver when there ain't no streets for all the river ain't worth a jagger?" he asked.

Oh, now that was a tricky one, actually. How many nights had Stasia discussed with her father the intricate machinery that went into setting a simple price at market, all of the things that pushed it up and down, even as the simple woman selling scarves or shoes or fish just used a bit of chalk on a slate to write down a number for the day.

"Depends on how many empty boats are around," Stasia said, and Babe laughed.

"Oh, this city is gonna love you, when it gets to know you," he said. "Might yet break you when I'm not looking, but even so…"

Stasia turned her head.

"Do I hear waves?"

"Gettin' on toward the shore, there," he affirmed. "Port Verida is nice, this time of night."

"Is it?" Stasia asked, and he nodded.

"Overlook the odd drunken sailor, it gets quiet. Blacks patrol often enough that there ain't much thievery at the port, not much goin' on, on the ships themselves. Everybody with money is on shore leave and everybody without is on board, asleep. Like the quiet of it."

Stasia frowned. She never would have expected that.

They reached a coastal road, one with big market stalls on one side and mangroves as far as the eye could see on the other, and they walked along, passing almost no one as they went. Here and there, shopkeepers were doing maintenance work by torchlight, but mostly it was just the light of the intermittent lamps that kept the road from falling into complete darkness.

It really was pleasant. The mangroves had an earthy, salty smell to them that was an improvement from the open rocky shores the rest of the way around Verida, where dead fish seemed to revel in washing up and rotting, untended by anything but the crabs and the seagulls.

"We have friends with an estate up north of town," Stasia said. "And I go riding up there, sometimes. Schotzli needs to stretch her legs sometimes or she gets out of shape. And I love it up there, but it's so far away, and there's no one there. It feels lonely."

Babe nodded as though he understood what she was feeling, not just what she was saying.

"I seen them hills," he said. "Nobody in eyeshot, nobody in ear's length. Even at a fort full of soldiers, it feels empty."

"Yeah. This is…"

"This is what a city ought feel like," he supplemented after a moment. "At its best."

"I love the market," Stasia said. "And when the roads are full and everyone is coming and going. And the blacksmiths. I swear, I could wander through the industrial districts for weeks and never get bored. I love to watch craftsmen work. But…"

She put her arms out, stepping away from him and spinning, appreciating the soft shoes she tended to wear with her peasant outfits. It wasn't that they were delicate. They were just incredibly cheaply made, hard canvas over cuts of leather for the sole. They wouldn't last forever, the way many of her better-made boots would, but you hoped you had enough money for the next pair by the time this one wore out, and no one was going to try to steal them from you.

Now, though, they slid along the cobbled surface like her feet were playing over an instrument, every curve novel and new. It had taken her feet a while to get used to these surfaces - they were physically exhausting until she'd built up the endurance to cope with it all day long - but she thought that it was helping her climbing.

Her skirt swished along her legs and she laughed.

"This is what it should be like, isn't it?" she asked, and Babe smiled.

"Washes off the day," he said as she paused to let him catch up. "Even the bad ones."

"Was today a bad one?" Stasia asked, and he shook his head.

"What would be?" he asked. "We caught Eddie and his pixie and you got yourself a special assignment with the queen. Walked out from under a lot of men who wanted to hurt you, brushed it off like it wasn't nothing at all. I'd say that was a good day, all the way around, except that someone managed to lay hands on you in the middle of it. Still wish I'd been half a block closer to lay 'im out rather than you going in, but it's what got you the win."

She'd barely thought about the butcher shop, since Babe had let her practice with the reeds in place of a sword.

"You still have to teach me swordplay," she said. "I'm not letting you off the hook on that one."

He grinned.

"Might have to wait until we can find a place to do it that won't attract attention," he said. "But I don't expect you to forget it. Still need work on your daggers, though, and that's easier to just do, around."

"I was going to kill him," Stasia said, the momentary elation stilling, and she looked over at him. She didn't know how to feel about that.

"I'm glad you didn't have to," he said. "Lot of death around, you get used to it, the idea that a man might not be here, who's here today, but to actually end him at your own hand… It's different, and it leaves *you* different. The rest of them boys would have had at you, too, I expect. Some places, they'd scatter, leave him for dead but Highrock has a lot of pride. They'd gut you right back, over that. One killing often causes the next. Best to prevent, and if you can't prevent, dominate."

"Or just carry around a member of the King's Guard to growl at them," Stasia said, and he shook his head.

"Just a rat, now," he said. "Gonna be a liability for you in Highrock, if anything."

"So wear a scarf," Stasia said dismissively.

He snorted.

"You think I could pull that off?" he asked, and she shrugged.

"I defy someone to say to your face that you can't," she said.

He laughed out loud.

"Good point."

They came to the bridge over the river that split to become the city's main port. At some point, it would have been another little wedge of land in between the final fingers of the main river, but they'd dug it out and now it was a wedge into the curved edge of the delta's front to the sea, where ships up to a certain draft could dock. It was a huge and a busy port, and the ships out at the piers were truly beautiful to Stasia as she stopped to look at them.

Babe stood next to her for a few minutes.

"How long is the crossing from Boton?" he asked.

"Six days," Stasia said.

"That the longest you ever lived on a ship?" Babe asked, and Stasia nodded.

"And I hated it the whole time," she said cheerfully. He grinned.

"I wasn't much around for the pirate wars," he said. "But I done my turn on a tub. Started out feeling like a caged animal, but by the end, I could see why a man would want to live his life out on one o'them."

"When did you meet Jasper?" Stasia asked.

He looked over at her.

"Oh, personal questions now," he said with humor. "Are we gettin' on to being friends, now?"

"You've only saved my life twice," Stasia answered. "Do you want to wait until we get to three? Or do I have to save your life once, first?"

He laughed.

He had such a good laugh.

"He recruited me to the guard," he said. "Came back from a tour up in the mountains and I found him in the bunk house just waiting for me."

"So you never fought together?" Stasia asked, and he shook his head.

"Nope. But a soldier's a soldier, and Jasper's a true one. He knows them mountains about as well as any man born here in the city, and the pirate islands, too. Somethin' to having *been* there, same as another man, makes you kin of a sort that most people just wouldn't understand."

"Five years," he said after a moment, nodding. "Almost ten years with the reds, five years with the browns."

"And Colin and Sterling?" Stasia asked.

"More recent'n that," Babe said. She looked over at him and he smiled. "Ain't used to tellin' other people's stories."

"Especially not Colin's," Stasia teased, and he grinned.

"Nope. He normally does all his talkin' for himself."

She looked over at him again and he sighed.

"Sterling's father had a fencing school in town," he said. "His grandfather opened it, and they are, were, famous through basically the known world for the quality students they put out. Problem was, so they say, he was better with a sword than with a villing, and they went broke. Sterling and Colin ended up with the guard for something to do."

"They're school friends?" Stasia asked, and Babe nodded.

"They are indeed."

"That explains so much," Stasia said.

"Sterling is one of the best alive," Babe said. "So good he entertains himself by playing. But you shouldn't underestimate him."

"You beat him," Stasia said, and Babe nodded.

"Only 'cause he's never seen fit to take it seriously. The day he realizes that he cares what happens, really cares, he's going to be an unstoppable force."

She didn't see that in Sterling. Truly. Even trying to believe Babe, she didn't see it.

She could see what he was talking about that Sterling always played when he had a sword in his hand. That was obvious, now that Babe had said it out loud. But the idea that there was another depth to him, something that would come out if something truly important happened… She just didn't see it. He was what he was. He was too *honest* for hidden depths.

"How long has Jasper been with the guard?" Stasia asked, and Babe shook his head.

"Nope, that's one you'll have to ask him," he said. "That definitely ain't my story to tell."

She straightened.

"I intend to," she said, and he grinned.

"Hope I'm there to hear the answer," he said. "Tomorrow morning, breakfast time? I'll meet you here again."

"Oh," Stasia said.

"I assume you're fine on your own feet from here," he said, teasing, and she nodded.

"Of course."

"I need to move out of my apartment by the guard house," he said. "Get something somewhere more fittin' my station again."

"Don't do that," Stasia said quickly. "I've got all the places I'm taking care of. You should use one of them."

"Ain't been kept by a woman since I left my ma," he said.

"Wouldn't be me keeping you," Stasia answered. "It would be the queen. And you're working for her, displaced and apparently fired from your career because of it. I think it's a perfectly fair exchange, given that it doesn't cost her anything, anyway."

Stasia considered, frowning.

"I hope he's okay tonight," she said. Babe looked around casually, then nodded.

"Elves ain't helpless," he said. "Far from it. So long as he's only up against the normal problems of Highrock, he can take care of himself."

He gave her a firm nod, and a tension in her stomach that she hadn't known was there suddenly relaxed.

"You ain't carrying this on your own," Babe said. "Jasper sent me, and you know he ain't just gonna forget, either. You're one of us, and we look to our own."

She licked her lips and nodded.

"Thank you."

He shrugged.

"Breakfast?"

"Breakfast."

"Did you have a good evening?" Minstrel asked as she walked in the door.

"I did," Stasia said. "Sorry I wasn't home for dinner."

"Tesh left something on the oven for you when she went to bed for the night," he said, appearing in the doorway to his office.

"Thanks," Stasia said, realizing suddenly that she was hungry.

"Is this how it's going to work, with us living in the city, now?" he asked. Stasia watched him, feeling guilty, but not sure whether that was right.

"You've never stopped me from doing what I want, before," she said.

"I disagree," he answered thoughtfully. "I spent your youth indulging your passions and your interests, but very carefully inspecting your activities to help you decide how to *get* what you wanted out of the things that you did with your time. You've never had free rein to run rampant. You've confused me allowing you to do things that I would have considered too risky or inappropriate for Meglyn or Alyssia with me allowing you to make all of your own decisions."

Stasia looked at the floor for a moment, reflecting.

"I'm doing good things, daddy," she said. "I'm making friends who are teaching me to be stronger and to appreciate living in Verida, and I'm not wasting my time or being foolish. I don't think."

"Is there a reason you're hiding it from me?" he asked.

Boy, those words hurt to hear.

She didn't always tell him the whole truth about the men that she paid to teach her things, in Boton, but she'd told him that someone was teaching her to climb and that she'd found someone to teach her to defend herself if someone tried to take advantage of her on the road.

The guard was hardly something to be *ashamed* of, even by comparison. Why *was* she so hesitant to tell him about any of it?

"I'm a spinster, daddy," she said. "I'm never going to marry."

"I thought you had already chosen that, long ago," he said, troubled, and she shook her head, then nodded, then shook her head again.

"Oh, of course," Stasia said. "I have no want nor need of a husband. But now everybody knows. I am your ward for life, and… they pity me. They haven't known me my whole life, like they did in Birch. The… transition caught me by surprise. I didn't realize I *was* a spinster until the Veridans pointed it out to me."

"Did that injure you?" he asked.

Stasia drew a breath, wondering if that's what that feeling was.

"The men in the city, they still pursue me for their sons," she said. "Your wealth is still worth it to them, even if I am old for marrying. Your wealth, daddy, it changes everything for me. Everything in my life is shaped by you and your significance."

He narrowed his eyes, and she worried for a moment that she'd hurt him, accusing him of something she didn't mean, then he nodded.

"I see. I've always… known that your life would be something other than it might have been, because I've avoided exposing you to real adversity. I don't regret it for a moment, because you can build the life that you want without fear of failing, but it kept you from becoming as strong as you might have otherwise been, perhaps. Meglyn and Alyssia couldn't have conceived of life another way, but you are so very much like your mother. She needed something to defeat or she felt wasted. I've sensed that in you since your youth, and I planned a different path for you, where you could go out and find your battles so that you would have your victories. But that isn't enough, is it?"

"It is, daddy," Stasia said. "I'm not... embittered. I have no regrets for who I am. But I have a new opportunity, here, for a life where... perhaps my life belongs to me in a new way. I want to be something that is not encased by the fact that I am your daughter. I love you, and I am so very fortunate to have you as my father, in great part because of *who you are*, much more than because of your resources. I am grateful. And I'm... sorry that I've simply run away, as I have. I should have talked to you about it. But I want to have a life that is... my own."

Was it selfish? Did it reject him and all that he meant to her?

He smiled.

"You are a woman," he said. "If you'd married a man in Boton, there's every chance you would be running a household virtually on your own, as the type of man who would have satisfied your expectations would have been rigorously employed at the markets each day. I will not ask you to reduce the scale of the life that you're seeking here, and I... understand that I cast a wide shadow. I may not immediately understand how my ignorance keeps you from falling under it again, but I suspect there are many things I can't see from where I am, and I believe you. What I *will* require of you is that if you need help that I can give you, that you won't reject it out of hand. What good is all of this if my daughter won't use it when she needs it?"

Stasia nodded.

"Okay."

He nodded.

"Do you want to play cards?"

She grinned.

"Let me get my dinner, and I'll be in, in a few minutes."

"Bring it," he said. "I sense that my unlimited time with my daughter is waning, and I find myself jealous of it."

"I love you, Daddy," Stasia said.

"I love you, too, Anastasia," he answered.

She showed up early the next morning and found a baker as he was taking fresh buns out of the great oven in the back of the bakery, along the market row by the docks.

The smell here was different, today. Even first thing in the morning, it had a warmer scent, and she was very aware of the amount of wood in the structures around her. Unlike most of the rest of the city, even the market stalls here were built of wood, as though the timber coming in on the ships was suddenly the cheaper material compared to the stones that would have come out of the ground elsewhere. Perhaps it was self-defeating, taking *anything* out of the ground, this close to sea level.

She bought bread and butter, stabbing hunks of butter into the breadrolls and going to the top of the port where she'd stood with Babe the night before and pulling bread apart to eat it.

She sensed the presence next to her and held out a pair of rolls without looking.

"Surprised the birds ain't found you yet," Babe commented, taking the food.

"Oh, they know better than to mess with me," Stasia answered.

"Do they, now?" Babe asked, and Stasia smiled.

"Oh, yes."

He snorted.

"You ready?"

"What does he eat?" Stasia asked.

"Nothin' you ever heard of," Babe said. "But most anything, really."

"Two more of these?" she asked.

"Can buy 'em in Highrock on the way," he said. She nodded.

"I've got another place up by the green river," Stasia said. "If you want to do that, today."

"Let's go see your tall friend first," Babe said. "We'll worry about me when we're sure of him."

They took the same long path along the water into Highrock, crossing the bridge into the region and making their way to a market that Stasia had used a few times, setting up this particular apartment. She bought a selection of foods, not entirely trusting that Babe knew what he was talking about. They all hated elves. Why would any of them pay any attention to what they ate?

She bought a basket to put it all in, Babe buying various other things and throwing them in alongside Farang's breakfast. A razor and a small dagger, a selection of herbs and a pair of shoes. Stasia didn't question any of it

They finally made their way to the apartment, standing outside of it for a good thirty minutes before they went in to make sure that nothing looked amiss.

"Follow me," Babe said, going up the stairs.

She nodded.

"Third floor, back-facing apartment," she said.

She followed him up to the door, then touched his shoulder, going around him to knock on the door.

"Farang?" she asked. "It's me."

The door unlocked and Farang opened it, wearing the cloak that Jasper had given him. It obscured his entire face in shadow, but he could see Babe.

He reacted immediately, putting out a hand toward Babe, his fingers working a shape in the air that had intent to it.

"Friend," Stasia said. "He's a friend."

Farang looked at Babe from under his hood, pushing it off of his head a moment later. His eyes were cold and piercing, and Stasia realized that Babe had known what he was talking about, warning her that the elf was dangerous. Not to her, but to the wrong person, certainly.

"Jasper sent me," Babe said. "Stacy is good, but he wanted you to have backup out here who knows the lay of the land."

"Constance said to trust no one else," Farang said.

"So don't trust me," Babe said. "Trust her."

"Jasper sent him," Stasia said. "I'm certain of that."

Farang nodded skeptically, then turned aside to let them into the apartment.

Stasia handed him the basket, and he took the dagger out of it immediately, tucking it away under the cloak as he went to set the basket down on the floor.

"This how this place was?" Babe asked, sounding surprised by how spare it was.

"Oh, no," Stasia said. "I threw everything out. I owe Farang wood and tools to make a bed."

"I can help with that," Babe said. "Got nothin' but time, just now."

Farang gave Babe a suspicious look, then lifted a roll out of the basket and tore it apart, going to the window to look out.

"You'll need to cut his hair," Babe said. "Long hair is… A man with long hair in Verida is just askin' to be taken for an elf."

Farang looked over his shoulder, but didn't say anything.

"He had pointy *ears* when we got here," Stasia said. "I think he can take care of it."

"If I used my magic to shorten my hair, it would be back by morning," Farang said. "I would reject the transformation. The ears are nothing."

Stasia looked to Babe, who nodded.

"You're gonna have to do it," he said.

"I've never cut hair before," Stasia said.

"Don't have to be neat," Babe said. "Just gotta be short."

She turned to look at Farang, who sighed, pulling a long braid out of the cloak and letting it fall down his back.

She hadn't noticed it before, perhaps because she hadn't known how important it was, but it fell to his thighs. Unbraided it might have gone to the floor.

"At the shoulders," Babe said, offering her a short, thick-bladed dagger. "Sharpened it last night, but it won't be an easy cut."

Stasia stepped forward to Farang. He kept his back turned.

"We can wait," she said. "You shouldn't go out any time soon, anyway."

"Do it," he said. "I cannot go home again. It no longer matters."

She hesitated a few moments longer, then took hold of the thick braid, putting the knife to the back of it just above shoulder level and slicing across it.

Babe wasn't wrong.

She'd expected something dramatic to happen, but it was rather like the hair was tougher than the knife. She hacked back and forth with the blade, seeing hair spring loose of the braid, and settled in to work at it, knowing that the longer it took, the worse it was likely to be.

Finally, several long minutes later, she cut through the last of the hair and found herself holding a braid that was as thick as her wrist and hard to keep off of the floor.

How did he bear the weight of it?

Farang turned, reaching up to pull the remains of his braid loose. His hair looked hacked up in all different lengths, but it was certainly shorter. He put out a hand, and Stasia handed him the braid, feeling deeply guilty.

He wound it into a coil and put it over on the floor in another corner, where the fishing gear lay.

"My old self has passed," he said. "I do not resist."

"Gonna have to learn to talk like a Veridan if you're ever gonna go out again," Babe observed, and Stasia looked at him sharply. He shrugged. "That's the only path for him. Can't go up into the mountains again, so he's gotta play like he's human."

Farang gave him a sharp look.

"How do you understand that?"

"Soldiers learn a lot of things," Babe said, unconcerned.

"I can bring you lumber in small batches, and nails," Stasia said. "I don't know much about carpentry to know what tools you might need."

"I can draw the tools I need," Farang said. "And I don't need nails."

Babe whistled, low.

"You know what you're doin', then," he said, and Farang nodded, looking around the room with wistful eyes.

"I do, and so long as this will be my cell, I may as well make it comfortable."

"I don't want this to be a prison," Stasia said.

"But it is," Babe said, his voice deep. "Just a better one than he'd get, otherwise."

Farang nodded.

"I will be... content, here," he said. "I am unthreatened. I am unharmed. I am well."

"She's landed you here in a bad neighborhood," Babe said. "Folk outside ain't gonna hesitate to take what's yours, and at the point of a knife if need be."

Farang gave him a level look, like a test, and Babe shrugged.

"Just fair warning," Babe said. "I know you can handle yourself, but better if you see it coming."

Farang nodded.

"Very well."

Stasia looked over at the elf, brimming with questions about how he got here and what he was like before, but they all felt cruel.

"If you have to run," Babe said. "Take the fisherman's tunic and go south until you hit the rocks. We'll find you there."

Farang nodded.

"As you say."

"What can I do?" Stasia asked. "To make this feel more like a home to you for the time being?"

"Just give me the tools of industry," Farang said. "It will keep my hands and my mind busy enough to not notice the losses so keenly."

Stasia sighed.

"All right. I'm going to go out and see what I can find easily from nearby, and I'll be back in an hour or so."

Babe went to sit against the wall where the basket was, picking through it after a piece of fruit he was particularly interested in, and Farang looked over at him.

"Will you not be taking him with you?" he asked.

"Better she goes on her own," Babe said. "She's already known, 'round these parts, and she's safe enough, in the light."

Stasia nodded, relieved that he saw it that way. She'd been prepared to fight with him over it.

"If anyone speaks to you in the hallway, tell them that you're a distant relation of mine, here to seek a trade," Stasia said. "I'll deal with it as it becomes an issue."

"Not a lover, then," Babe asked, and Stasia glanced at Farang coolly.

"I was prepared to claim a man as a discrete lover, but not him," she said. "I don't think that's believable."

Babe snorted and put his head back against the wall.

"Everything happens in Verida," he said. "And anything that happens in Verida happens in Highrock."

She frowned at him, glancing at Farang again, but he seemed not to be offended that she wanted him to be family and not romantic. He handed her a piece of paper with various shapes drawn on it, and Stasia peered at it, then assumed she could figure them out when she saw them in person.

Leaving Babe there to keep an eye on Farang, she went back downstairs. One of the women who took in washing to support her two young children was out in the hallway.

"Morning," she said to Stasia. "You're up early."

"Lots to do today," Stasia answered. "My uncle's grandfather's something-or-other turned up on a ship yesterday and they expect me to get him settled in on my own."

"Oh, I hear you," the woman said. "Does he need his washing done?"

"I'll ask," Stasia said. "He hasn't got a wife to do it for him."

The woman nodded, the gleam of greed or need for one more coin blocking out anything else she might have noticed.

Stasia went out, going to another section of marketplace where it was possible to buy more rugged goods, cookware and wood and metal goods, baskets and sheets and small home machines. She bought the lumber she could easily carry, hiring a boy to carry the other end of the long boards back to the apartment. She gave him his half-lily and he scrambled away as Farang stood to the side and let Stasia carry the wood in.

She put the basket of tools down and Farang knelt, picking through it and nodding.

"They're cheaply-made, but they'll do," he said.

"I can smuggle in some nicer things once I know you're safe to stay here for longer, but right now…"

He glanced up at her and shook his head.

"Nothing I would want to carry with me, for now," he said, and she nodded.

"Yes."

He straightened.

"I can work with these," he said.

"Food?" Stasia asked. "Grooming supplies?"

"Your friend knows more than he's letting on," Farang said, indicating a row of spices he had hung from the wall with little tacks that had been there when Stasia had moved in. She didn't like to remember what had been hanging from them, at the time. "These will aid me considerably."

She shrugged.

"I'm glad. Should I get more?"

"This will suffice for now," Farang said.

"Clothes," Stasia said. "You only have what you're wearing on your back, right now."

"I have little need of much," Farang said. "Though a fresh shirt would be a relief."

Stasia nodded, trying to guess how long his pants might be. She'd only ever shopped for pants for herself, and that with a seamstress who took her measurements and returned with a product specifically fitted to her. Even the commodity dresses had been an adventure in re-fitting them to herself.

Babe stood and squared himself off with Farang.

"Ought to be fine in mine, if you'd put up with 'em," Babe said. "Trousers, too, if too short."

"Your trousers wouldn't stay up on him," Stasia said, imagining just how much the shirts would billow, tucked in.

"What a belt's for," Babe said. "'Round these parts, everybody wears his dad's cast-offs, anyway."

She looked at Farang, who shrugged passively.

"I have no pride in clothes," he said, looking over at his braid. Stasia could feel the grind of the fibers as the knife had gone through them, and she felt awful again.

Babe nodded, slapping his thighs.

"Settled," he said. "I got a pair of chests I'll get down here, by hook or by crook, and we'll be set."

"What?" Stasia asked, and Farang nodded.

"We have agreed that Babe will stay with me here to make sure that I don't miss something that might save my life or my freedom."

"Babe," Stasia said. "You don't have to."

"It's done," Babe said. "Same to me. I lived in the bunkhouse full time, anyway. Apartment was just there for the stuff what didn't fit in a footlocker. Don't mind company and don't mind the floor."

Stasia looked at Farang.

Then back at Babe.

"But everybody hates elves," she said. He nodded, frowning thoughtfully.

"Let's just say I know a fella who set my mind straight on 'em, and that Constance is on the right side, here."

Stasia looked at Farang, who watched her placidly.

He'd taken off the cloak to hang it on the wall by the small fireplace, and she noticed for the first time how coiled his arms were. He was thin, no doubt about it, and shockingly tall, but he was strong, the way his neck met his shoulders and the way that his arms moved across the lumber. Under the cloak, she hadn't been afraid of him at all, but seeing what he looked like in his own skin, she realized that this was a man who could overpower her at a thought.

She wasn't specifically afraid of *Farang*, who had been nothing but calm and willing to go along, but if this was what all elves were like? She'd imagined playful creatures akin to bunnies and squirrels. This was a man who could win a fight. Even before he had magic to work with.

How had the castle held him so easily?

She would have fought to the death over what Constance had been suggesting was going to happen to him, there.

Perhaps she had told him not to, to wait for help.

She looked at Babe again, who nodded.

"It's settled," he said. "I got my chests to move. Gotta hire a cart. You shouldn't be here all day, if you ain't in the habit."

She nodded and they both looked at Farang for a moment, then Babe went to get the door for Stasia.

"I'll walk you up to the river," he said. "Expect you got other things to see to, today, as well."

She nodded slowly.

"Is he going to be okay?" she murmured. He closed the door behind them before he answered.

"Takes a lot out of 'em, bein' this far from the mountains. Best if you can keep 'em near the water, but you had no way've knowin' that, and not much for options, besides. He's strong. He'll keep it together long enough to find his way to ground for good."

"Is that really the best he can hope for?" Stasia asked. He shook his head.

"Don't know nothin' about it, really, but I know an elf can be broke, and once he's broke, stone or high, he can't go back up there again. He ain't got no options but us, outside of setting sail abroad, but that can't be nothin' but worse "

"How miserable is he?" Stasia asked, and Babe shook his head again, getting the front door for her.

"Ain't best to think of it that way," he said softly. "He ain't like you and you ain't like him. He ain't *bad*, certainly, and he don't deserve the way we talk of him, but you can't compare yourself to him and hope to come away understandin'.."

"What did you buy for him?" Stasia asked, and he smiled.

"Bit o' this and a bit o' that," he said. "Stuff I picked up, up in the mountains. He knows what it's for."

"And you're not going to tell me?" she asked.

"Not my secrets to tell," he said. "Gotta see a man about a horse."

He set off in a different direction from her, hands in his pockets and whistling as he went. She recognized the tune, though she knew that they had different words for it, here.

She went the other direction, wandering past the food market stalls that were closest to the apartment and buying a few things, just to have spent the coins and had the conversations. Asked about the boys roaming around at night and whether anyone was ever going to do anything about it, got the same annoyed snorts she always did as the vendors complained that nobody ever did anything about how it was in Highrock. They were on their own, and she was best to never walk alone at night, and if she had to, to carry a knife.

She knew that there were men and women around here who approved of the main gang in the territory, who thought that the Highrock 'family' running particularly the southern end of the region was keeping things in line and making good on opportunities to enrich the community at the expense of those who had gotten wealthy there, but Stasia tried to avoid them.

She was only so gifted at holding her tongue when people said things like that.

She turned north eventually, taking a winding route to another apartment she was working on, where she still had the walls to scrape down and get new plaster put up.

She was getting better at making the apartments livable. It was taking more work, each time, and she took more *time*, each time, to get them where she wanted them to be, but they were clean and relatively clean-smelling, by the time she was done. They had walls that she could paint, if she chose to, and this particular apartment had a separate bedroom from the main room, and a kitchen with a small stove and oven and a few surfaces for food preparation, a few nooks for food storage. She was putting hooks and nails into the walls for storing things, and at some point she was pretty sure she was going to try installing a shelf, just to prove to herself that she could do it.

Beds and dressers and that kind of thing were outside of her capability, though Babe's trunk solution was a good one, and she thought she could get a decent one delivered here, given that many of the craftsmen were working just across the river.

Yes, there had been a sack of straw in the corner when she'd procured the place, but as with all of them, it was a horrific mess of human and animal byproducts, and she'd thrown it away. She had bought a sheepskin from a man by the port and laid it on the floor in the corner, and she was much happier with that, for now. It wasn't big enough - particularly not for Farang - but it was cozy and soft and clean, and it kept her off of the floor.

This was the first time she had gotten a first-floor apartment, and she feared what the floods might do to it, but she'd paid attention as she'd walked, and she was pretty sure that the floor of this building was further above the river than her father's house.

It should be fine.

What it also meant, though, was that the floor was stone rather than wood, and she very much preferred the stone, on some fronts, like the fact that the wood wasn't rotten and stained with use and abuse, whereas stone always washed clean, but it had deep grooves in between the stones that she was still working out what to do about.

She thought that she might see about plastering it and seeing how well that lasted, but she wasn't optimistic. She needed to see what they did at home.

She spent much of the day cleaning and working around the apartment, enjoying the industry of it and pleased with the progress she was making. She had it in mind to take a nicer apartment somewhere north or west of the castle, where she could get one with multiple rooms, running water, and a bathroom, but that was down the road, yet, and she wasn't certain it met with the queen's instructions, specifically.

The sun was beginning to set by the time she was done. She crossed the bridge - the Warbler Bridge, it was called - and made her way toward the castle through the local industrial sector. The men here were tough and tended to live above their workshops, so the Highrock problems almost completely stopped at the river.

It was amazing, how much of a barrier that river constituted.

She paused at a blacksmith's shop where he had a number of iron-bound pieces - a safe and some chests and trunks, among other things - and marked it as a place to come back when she was ready, then she made for the bar where she had first met Colin and the rest of the King's Guard.

She found Jasper there, drinking alone in a crowded room.

Stasia sat down across from him, her back to the room, and he glanced at her.

"Everything going okay?" he asked quietly.

"Where is everyone?" Stasia countered.

"Matthias' mother is unwell, and he is seeing to her in his time off. Colin and Sterling are not speaking to me, just now."

Stasia balked.

"They're mad at you?" she asked.

"I ran off Babe in a fit of temper," Jasper answered. "Of course they are."

Did they not know?

Was he keeping it secret from them out of a lack of trust?

Or was Babe just the one that he *really* trusted enough to send him along after?

Or was it *better* if they didn't know, and the fact that Babe had known where to find Stasia was the reason Jasper had sent him away?

"Is everything okay?" Stasia asked.

"Not remotely," Jasper said. "The king is furious and searching the castle for an escaped prisoner and suspects a traitor in the court. Everyone is very on edge, right now. I was going to go back to the guard house soon in case orders came."

He looked at her once more.

"You should go quietly," he said. "Do you need anything?"

"No," she said. "I don't need anything but to know what happens next."

"I will send Matthias with a note," Jasper said. "Expect it at your father's house. Once things have settled down some and we can make longer plans."

She nodded.

It was good enough.

He looked at her once more, then set down his drink.

"Do you still have confidence?" he asked, and she considered, careful not to look around the room.

"Yes," she said, and he dipped his head.

"Then go. I will be in touch."

He gave her a flicker of a smile and she stood to leave.

She wasn't sure what she had come here for, and she wasn't certain if she'd gotten it, but the whole thing felt sad to her. Babe moving in with a stranger down in a dangerous part of town, Colin and Sterling not speaking to Jasper, Jasper drinking alone.

It had gone wrong, somehow, and it correlated with her showing up.

She wouldn't accept that, but she did at least have to think it.

She didn't know what happened next.

No.

No, that wasn't true.

Next, she helped Farang get his furniture set up, she figured out how to flatten the floor in the new apartment, and she started looking at better apartments where a decent living was more possible.

It was her secret hope that this new apartment she had planned would be the one where Farang eventually ended up, working a respectable job somewhere, doing things that he didn't hate, and living someplace clean and spacious enough for him by himself.

She could hope that, off in the distance.

But, yes, tomorrow had different goals, and she would tackle those first.

She could do that.

She visited Farang and Babe every morning for the next few days, bringing them food and supplies as they identified things that were needed, but with Babe there, and his stuff, the gaps shrank considerably, and she was once more on her own, more or less, working on apartments and even taking a day with Schotzli to go up to the Westhauser estate and ride. Lady Westhauser was there, and they passed a very pleasant afternoon talking about all sorts of things.

Then the rains started.

Babe had warned her that the first of the rains might be up in the mountains where she couldn't see them, and she *did* see signs that the river was inching up on its banks, particularly the further north she went along it within the city. And it did often rain in Verida, but Stasia just put up her hood and went on with her day. She liked the rain. It made things smell clean and it had a sort of cheerfulness to it, the way the world came alive with new pattering noises.

This was entirely different, this rain.

Storms rolled in off of the ocean, great green banks of clouds rolling across the sky as though they were built to devour it, lightning flashing along the horizon as the winds changed and the smell of everything became that of sea churn.

And then they would hit, and Tesh and Alice would run around the house making sure that all of the windows were secure, because the rain came down in violent sheets that were approximately sideways. Any window that wasn't firmly latched - and a few that were - would blow open and buckets of water would pour into the room. Tesh went around with waxed cloth and stuffed it in wherever she could hear air whistling, because it would all eventually leak, and she told Stasia that they would have a mason come in to fix the seals around the windows for next year. It wasn't a sign that the house was poorly made or poorly kept, but seals needed replacing. This was just what it meant to keep a house.

And then Stasia suddenly realized that *Tesh* was the expert she needed to tell her how to set up and keep apartments.

Why it had taken her this long to figure out, she wouldn't know, but she was ashamed of herself for not seeing it.

The trick to it was teasing out the knowledge without tipping her hand, what she was up to. Eventually, she suspected that Tesh thought she had taken an apartment of her own somewhere in town and was fishing for guidance on how to take care of it, and that was perfect. The woman was friendly, particularly as Stasia spent a few days actively following her and helping her with her routine work, and ever since they'd started eating together, Tesh had seemed to develop an appreciation for Stasia's independence.

The Sapphire River came up, foot by foot by foot, over the next few days, spilling over its natural banks by the fourth day and lapping across the green embankment that buffered the road. Stasia took to emptying a bucket she left outside the back door a few times a day, just to watch the water come up in it. She'd never seen such rain.

There were a few open periods between storms, when the sun came out and heated the world, and sometimes it was enough to make the air suffocating with humidity, but mostly the air was beginning to cool enough that - while the sun did make everything humid - it wasn't hot enough to be as uncomfortable as it would have been, any other time that summer. During the periods of sun, Stasia tried to steal away to go check on Babe and Farang, but she felt bad, because there weren't many of these, and she was always in a rush to get out before she got stuck there in the next deluge.

She was perfectly aware that the city mostly went about its business, despite the wind and the rain and the booming thunder, but she had the feeling that if she went out, without her dragonskins, the skirts would take sail and she would blow away. She didn't like being moved by the weather - she was of a mind that she broke the weather, the weather didn't break her - but even opening the front door was intimidating, because the next squall was momentarily going to rip it out of her fingers and slam it against the wall as she scrambled to recover it and get it latched once more.

She couldn't imagine weathering this in one of the flimsy little buildings like the ones the truly poor lived in.

And still the river rose.

It ran all the way across the street. Stasia bought specialized leather boots from a cobbler behind the castle, where she had to wrestle with him to keep them as simple as possible, because his normal clientele preferred color and decoration to differentiate themselves. She took Schotzli out in it, just to make sure the mare was comfortable with water running across her hooves. She didn't like it, but she put up with it well enough. Stasia just had to pay extra attention to her, to make sure she didn't walk into anything that was in the flow of water. She unseated Stasia that way, once.

That was embarrassing.

The city began to stir with the approach of the Highwater Festival, and Stasia wondered if it wasn't just to celebrate the fact that the flooding would abate, from there.

It seemed obvious enough to her. None of this quasi-religious explanation about the merit and worth of the river itself. You celebrate the day things are as bad as they're going to get, because from there they're only going to get better.

Obviously.

The trick to it was: how did they figure out when the highwater was?

Stasia began marking the water in the lawn, the highest point that it reached when no one was rolling past in a carriage to throw waves, and it moved up in fits and starts. One day, it crept up the lawn a full six feet, and the next day it went down a foot.

The water was calf-deep on the road, and dangerous to walk on. The horses were still okay, and the men with their carts did okay but the pedestrians walked up in the grass and against the front wall, holding onto the wrought iron fencing to protect against the water taking their legs out from under them. Wheels kicked up tails behind them and doused pedestrians. Getting across the central river now required an act of bravery, or help from someone else. Stasia learned to grab hold of a cart or a carriage to ride it across the deepest ten or fifteen feet, up to where the speed of the water wasn't enough to pull her away.

One upside to the volume of water was that a new style of skirt came out, worn to just past the knees with leather leggings underneath, and tall boots or with shoes worn slung over the shoulder and bare feet. Stasia could do almost anything in a skirt that length, and she wore daggers strapped to her thighs because she actually knew that she could get to them, there, with just the simple length of fabric over top of them.

Babe kept telling her to learn how to grab a cart, a Veridan habit that Stasia hadn't yet worked out. All around the city, going through even the worst of the worst neighborhoods, were carts run by relatively young men. They just drove around at random, as far as Stasia could tell, one man at the reins and another at the back, pulling people on and taking their money. The carts never stopped. If you wanted to get on, you had to get a running start and jump, and then trust that the guy in the back was going to catch hold of you and get you on. But that wasn't even the hardest part. Stasia had done them twice, now, and had both times ended up someplace completely other than where she'd hoped to be. The men shouting were accented and confusing, referring to landmarks and road names that were foreign to her, even if she knew where she wanted to be, and often you had to know by probability where a cart might end up going after their next couple of locations, because that was all they were shouting.

So she used them to get her onto and off of the bridges, but that was about it.

Most of the central islands were underwater, and people had tied ropes from one bridge to the next that pedestrians would use to pull themselves across.

Twice a day, Stasia made the trek across the city, once into Highrock and once back out, and it was a major investment of effort.

"Talk is that this is going to be a high-cresting year," Babe said as she delivered food one morning after a particularly difficult crossing. Her skirts were wet up past her thighs from stumbling halfway across the main river, and her hair was soaked from getting caught by the next round of storms as she got close to the apartment and still needed to get the shopping done.

"Why anyone ever felt compelled to settle this miserable spit of land, I'll never know," Stasia answered, shaking out her cloak and inspecting her skirts. It wouldn't have been so bad, if she'd been in her dragonskins. The water would have rolled off and that would have been it, outside of issues with her hair. But fabric just sopped it up and stayed damp against her for the rest of the day and made her furious at everyone. Furious enough that she almost missed it:

"Wait, who are you talking to, to hear about that?" she asked.

"He goes out every day after you leave," Farang said, straightening from what he was doing.

Stasia had brought him new lumber again yesterday, but he hadn't started working with it, yet, because it was still damp. He had built a pair of beds and two nightstands, a full set of shelves, a handsome chest that Stasia needed to procure hinges for at some point, and crates that he was using to store his tools and his spare spices in.

The room smelled of woodworking and men and rain, and it was on balance a pleasant place to be, as far as Verida went.

Stasia lifted an eyebrow at Babe, who grinned at the bit of wood he was working at with his knife. The goal of this particular bit of woodworking appeared to be the creation of a pile of sawdust, but neither man seemed concerned about it.

"The scarf is over there on the wall," he said, indicating with his chin without lifting his eyes.

"You wear a scarf and go out," Stasia said. "In this weather?"

"Been cooped up now and again my whole life," he said. "Just 'cause I tolerate it don't mean I like it."

"Then why do I risk getting washed away in the Wolfram twice a day to buy you breakfast?" Stasia demanded. "If you just sneak out the minute I leave and go traipsing about a place where if they knew who you were, they'd try to kill you?"

He shrugged.

"Nice to have a friendly face come by every day," he said, and she shook her head. He looked up sharply.

"You do know how to swim, don't you?" he asked.

"Not like this," Stasia complained, looking at her clothes. "In my purple leathers, I'd be fine, but like this? The mass of it would pull me under."

"Once you get away from the land, the river runs pretty smooth. Take the smooth current to get yourself situated, then get to the outside. The closer you get to the banks, the slower it'll run, and you get yourself to where you can feel the ground with your hands below you - *without reachin'* - before you try to stand up. Like as not, somebody'll come fish you out by that point, but don't try to stand before you can feel the ground right up against you, or else it'll just push you down again. Relax, float, and conserve your energy. Only risk is you wash all the way out to sea, but that hardly ever happens."

"Hardly ever," Stasia echoed. "The river rises up and sucks people out to sea. Hardly ever."

Babe grinned.

"Sorts the fools from them worth keepin' on," he said.

"Sounds like it puts the drunks to rest," Farang commented, and Babe nodded exaggeratedly.

"It does that, too."

"I don't know if I can make it tomorrow," Stasia said. "I'm basically just holding on to the rope and dragging myself across, at the river island. Doesn't matter which one I take. I've tried three of them."

"Running Man is the highest," Babe said. "If you stay in, I'll see that we're fed. Bread carts keep rollin', and I can hear 'em comin' with my stomach. All a man needs, really, for a couple days. Hot bread with butter."

"We have food for a week, just in this room," Farang murmured, his hands busy with the detailed work of carving the end of one board to fit to another. Stasia was desperate to sit and watch him work, the dovetailing was so clever, but he seemed uncomfortable with this.

"We need to talk about what happens next," Stasia said. "This is not a life for either of you."

"Don't know about that," Babe said. "We're fed, we're dry, and the washerwoman downstairs don't charge too much. Hear she's lookin' for a husband."

Stasia shot him a hard look, and he laughed.

"Make sure you get out for the festival," he said. "Be a shame to miss it because you're too sore at the water for bein' inconvenient to you."

"I don't think I really get it," Stasia said. "Everybody… goes out? In the midst of the most treacherous travel conditions the city is going to see all year? And they get drunk to celebrate that? I mean… You people are crazy, Babe."

He laughed for a long time at that, then he nodded.

"I suppose that is how it'd look. You go out and see it, then come tell me if it ain't more than you were expectin'."

She went to sit down on the floor, resting her wrists on her knees and frowning at the world.

"It's solid water out there," she said. "I'd need gills to go home, right now."

Babe laughed again.

"Take your time," he said. "Ain't nobody else going anywhere, either."

Stasia looked over at Farang, but he didn't look up.

What was he making, a chair? A chair would be very convenient, in here, though it was beginning to get crowded with all of the furniture.

A bigger, two-room apartment would be just perfect for him.

"You been up to see the Green River since they started explodin' the banks?" Babe asked after a few minutes. "You won't recognize it."

"Why is it called the Green River?" Stasia asked. "It isn't. It's orange."

Farang looked up sharply.

"You have a river here that is orange?" he asked.

Babe shook his head, looking over at Farang with concern.

"Ain't the water," he said. "It's the algae that grows in it. In great big turfs that go up above the water level a foot or more in good weather. It's orange, true enough. Poisonous to most anything 'cept the trees that seem fond of growing in it. I'm told it's the reason the Black Docks are black. It dies or leaks or whatever it is such a thing does, and the water comin' out of the algae turfs is black all the way down to the sea, and poisonous to everything livin' there."

"Doesn't answer why it's called 'green'," Stasia muttered, feeling cranky.

He went out.

Every day.

Despite everything she was doing to keep the two of them hidden away, the conversations she had on her way in and out with neighbors and shopkeepers, so that they wouldn't think of the men in the apartment as abnormal or out of place, should someone come asking around.

And the water kept coming up.

"You need to learn how to use the carts," Babe said, reading her face. "It's called 'green' because it used to be used for agriculture. Same thing what grows the algae is useful on crops. Still folk 'round these parts with rooftop and back-yard gardens who haul water out of the river for waterin', because the rain just don't come close to what the river can grow."

Farang was watching Babe thoughtfully.

"I would like to see this water," he said, and Babe nodded.

"When you're done sulkin', I expect there's a lot about this city you're going to find int'resting," he answered.

Stasia would have *never* accused Farang of sulking, but he didn't argue the accusation.

"Wait 'till you hear about the Sapphire," Babe said loftily, carving another curl of wood off of the piece he was working. Farang's head came up sharply, and Babe grinned, still not looking up.

Rain pelted against the building and thunder rolled in gusts that shook the floor beneath her, and for a moment it was too noisy for conversation. Stasia wondered if she was going to be trapped here all day. Wondered how Babe and Farang managed to live with it, even if Babe *was* going out every day. It was such a small space, and Farang was used to the mountains and a community so small that he knew everybody.

There was the sound of a fight in the next unit over, and something smashed against the wall.

"She's gonna kick him out again," Babe murmured. "Storm and all."

"He deserves it," Farang answered.

"Ain't arguin' that at all," Babe said.

Stasia looked from one to the other, but neither of them explained what was going on.

"What does the court think that they can learn from you?" Stasia asked Farang.

"Magic," he said dryly, fitting two pieces of wood together like they had come apart from the same piece. There was no seam.

"What does that mean?" Stasia asked.

"None of them have the first idea," Farang said.

"What *could* you do to help them?" Stasia asked.

He looked up at her, pale eyes piercing.

"You may be the first human to ever ask me that," he said.

"She's sharp," Babe said.

Farang drew a soft breath, looking out the window for a moment.

"The wellspring of magic is not within you," he said. "You are full of light and heat and frenzy, and that sustains you, but I live off of the wellspring. Perhaps it is easier for me to understand you than it is for you to understand me, and perhaps not. I cannot know. I might forge tools that are more effective against stone elves, or I might brew potions, mix powders, that amplify your strengths or defend you from stone elf magic. But these are tools, and they come out of me to be used by your hands. Of what benefit is that to me? And is truly of benefit to you? Enough to end my life and take me away from myself?"

"Do you resent the humans asking you to fight against the stone elves because they're magic and so are you?" Stasia asked. "Is there a kinship there?"

He shook his head.

"No more than you would be offended if an elf asked you to help in a fight against the pirates."

"You know about them?" Babe asked, and Farang looked sideways at him, but didn't answer.

"Is it harder, to work magic and brew potions and... everything else... than it is to work wood?" Stasia asked. He looked at the wood in his hands and shook his head thoughtfully.

"It is different, but I would not say it is harder," he said.

"And if we were to pay you for your work," Stasia said. "If I handed you coins for the chair that you're making right now, would you feel that I'd stolen something from you? Or that I'd robbed you of the benefit of your labor?"

"Oh, here we go," Babe muttered, going back to whittling.

"You are arguing that the elves should trade with the humans in order to advance the humans' cause at war," Farang said, and Stasia shrugged.

"It's not theft," she said.

"The coins you carry," Farang said. "Show me one."

She took out a half-villing and flipped it to him across the room. He held it in his palm, flipping it over and back a few times in the feeble light from outside, then he held it up between his fingers, showing it to her.

"What is this made of?" he asked.

"Silver," she said. She was almost certain he knew that, and he was only making a point, but she wasn't sure what it was.

"And where do you get your silver?" he asked.

Stasia wasn't sure. On Altan, the silver mostly came from Nightik, but around here, it might be different. She glanced at Babe.

"Mining out of the mountains facing the gulf," Babe said. Farang nodded.

"Out of stone," he said. "What do you do with your silver?"

"Make it into coins," Stasia said, feeling led and unhappy about it.

"What else?" Stasia asked.

"Silverware," she said. "Pretty things. Gilding things. Things where gold is too expensive to use."

"Frivolous things," Farang said, and Stasia shrugged.

She couldn't come up with anything *important* that used silver in it.

"So you offer me a bag of silver so that I might make rings and cups out of it, and you expect me to take a year of my life to compensate you for this?"

"What would you prefer to get paid in?" Stasia asked. "This isn't that hard a problem. You don't like coins because you don't use them as a means for exchange very often. I can understand that. What medium would you *prefer* to exchange in?"

"Food," Babe muttered, and Farang shook his head.

"While that is a more… acceptable offer, there is nothing that a human makes that is of better or more worthy quality than an elf makes, nor easier to get from elves and elven sources. There are exceptions, like some of the raw metal that we might use to make tools and weapons out of, but we hardly have need for these in scale compared to your need for magic."

Stasia twisted her mouth, then nodded.

"I understand," she said.

"Do you, now?" Babe asked, and she shrugged.

"We need to find things of value to them, if we expect them to help us," Stasia said. "Anything else is slavery."

"Oh, that's cold," Babe said, shifting to look at her. He put his elbow up on his knee and rested his temple against his fist. "And it ain't worth it to 'em, just to keep us from dying in our hordes?"

He'd been there.

He'd seen people die.

Even if he believed that Constance was right, trying to protect Farang from the designs of the king and court, there was a part of him who looked at Farang and saw a man who was cool and indifferent to those deaths.

"Asking them to do it out of pity is one thing," Stasia said. "But expecting it? How many high elves are there? Compared to the soldiers of Verida up in the mountains?"

"Ain't nobody goin' around countin'," Babe muttered.

"The people of Verida sprawl across a great plain," Farang said. "The high elves exist in small communities up at the top of mountains. There is no comparison."

"And how many high elves would it take to supply the army with arms, armor, and magic… powdery stuff?" she asked. "If they were *actually* to side with us in the war?"

Farang blinked at her, deciding something.

"It might take a skilled smith a month to forge a sword the likes of which your soldiers desire," he said. "Healing magic is less, modifying magic is more. I might make Babe a superlative soldier for a month, but it would be six months' worth of magic-working that he would consume. Working magic is much like working wood, in that way. I might make you a chair that you can sit on, certainly, in a day or a week, but to form you something that you would put at the table of the queen might take a month or even a year. You demand magic for a queen, a life's existence of magic, but you offer nothing in return but bags of silver."

She looked over at Babe, who had sat forward, and she nodded to herself.

"Supply and demand," she said. "The world runs on supply and demand."

"The world runs on the blood of soldiers who keep the darkness at bay," Babe answered, but he didn't sound offended, like he had before."

"Does the fact that the humans are fighting the stone elves keep the stone elves from attacking high elf settlements?" Stasia asked, and Farang shook his head.

"On his mountaintop, a high elf is a king. No man and no elf may dethrone him."

She wondered at him for a moment, a new tone in that. He was vulnerable, here. He wasn't just *broken*. He was open to attack in a way that maybe he'd never been, before.

"Nothing but time and shame," Babe said softly, and Farang jolted again.

Babe settled back against the wall again, slicing away at the wood.

"Will you speak with me?" Stasia asked. "Some day soon, when there aren't wolves at the door and rain in the streets, to see if there is something that Verida might offer that does merit support from the high elves?"

Farang stared hard at Babe for one more moment, then relaxed his posture and returned to his chair. He nodded.

"Yes," he said. "I doubt your success, but I do not doubt your earnestness. We can discuss such a thing."

She stood, going to the window and looking out. The light had gone to a faint blue, and she hadn't heard thunder in a few minutes.

"They come through hard, but they vanish just as quickly," she said.

"If you're quick about it, you might make it home before the next one hits," Babe said. "Find a cart shouting for queen's market or castle market, then duck off before it turns north."

"How much?" Stasia asked.

"Ought be a half-lily," Babe said. "Water might have driven 'em up to a full copper."

"If they take me to the coast, I'm going to be cross with you," Stasia said, and he grinned.

"They take you to the coast, you hopped the wrong yeller."

She sighed and looked back at Farang once more, but he had already set back to work on the chair. The additional lumber would be dry in the next few days, and he was talking about building a small table that they could sit at, but after the table and one more chair, they would truly be out of room.

He seemed quietly content, but Stasia wondered if she truly couldn't understand him, if everything she read of him was simply false.

She went back out into the gleaming light that reflected off of the entire world around her, dashes of light streaking in puddles and off of wet glass everywhere. A bread cart rolled past, and a woman sat at a small stall across the road selling leather thongs for tying your shoes together, among other small things.

Stasia wondered what was going on at the castle, if the king and his people were still searching for Farang.

She set off toward home, dreading the walk and wondering if today was the day she was going to get the hang of the carts.

The light was dimming by the time Stasia made it to the road that ran - underwater - along the Sapphire River.

This had *not* been the day she'd figured out the carts, and somehow she'd ended up north of the castle on the wrong side of the Wolfram entirely.

In the end, she'd just gone with it, because it had been a lovely tour of the industrial district north of Highrock, along a path she'd never taken by foot because it swung so wide from the river. When the cart turned south again, Stasia had hopped off and found her way to the river, crossing at the Running Man Bridge over an island that was at least only six inches underwater.

"How does it not wash away?" Stasia asked someone as they crossed.

"River leaves six inches of muck as it comes back down," the man told her. "You're not from Verida."

"No," she admitted, ducking into the market to lose him as she went past, then going south along a path that took the best bridge she knew, the one out by the meat market where the flooding covered acres of ground, but ran shallow and slow.

Finally coming into sight of the house, she frowned at the man jumping up and down halfway between herself and the manor. A horse startled and jolted sideways away from him as he splashed, running toward her, and she braced herself for a confrontation, only then recognizing Matthias as he got closer.

"Jasper sent me," he said breathlessly. "We need to meet tonight."

"What's wrong?" Stasia asked as he grabbed her arm and dragged her back toward the house.

"He wouldn't say. He just said to tell you that you ought to come dressed as the queen's chair. He said you'd know what it meant."

"I do," Stasia said. "I won't be long."

"Why are you so wet?" Matthias asked, looking her up and down.

She spread her arms with a sense of outrage.

"How are you not?" she asked, then held up a finger. "Don't answer that. I'll be quick."

She dashed into the house, waving at her father at the dinner table with Tesh, Alice, and Yasmine, then ran upstairs to change.

"Stasia?" her father called up after her. "What's going on?"

"I just got message that a friend needs to see me tonight," she shouted back down, pulling her dragonskins out of her armoire and changing quickly, appreciating the weight of the four daggers as she sheathed them. It was a lot, but all of them had significance to her, and she liked having them with her.

She found her father at the bottom of the stairs, waiting for her. She kissed his cheek.

"I don't like you being out this late in this weather," he said.

"I wouldn't be going out, if it weren't important," Stasia said. "I'm sorry I'm so late getting in. I tried to take a cart and ended up at the noblemen's line by mistake."

The corner of his mouth twitched upwards as he attempted not to mock her.

"I haven't found them intuitive, either," he said. "I could procure you a carriage for getting about town, if you wanted."

She shook her head quickly.

"No," she said. "That's not necessary. Really. I need to move quickly. I'll see you tonight, or if not tonight, in the morning."

"You are keeping very long hours, Anastasia," he said.

"I know," she said. "I'm doing good things, Daddy. I promise. I need to run."

She went out into the dim again, watching the clouds overhead, wondering if there would be another storm tonight.

Matthias was standing down at the bottom of the driveway, calf-deep in the water, as though the property line was a boundary he was required to observe.

She jogged down the drive, sploshing through the shallow water and getting to the gate, where Matthias took her hand and started off ahead of her. Stasia laughed, pulling her hand away.

"I'm as steady on my feet as you are," Stasia said. "It's very noble of you, but I do not need your help."

"The water is deep, Stacy," he called back to her over the everywhere sound of running water. "And it's running fast."

"I need both my arms to keep my balance," she called back. "Better this way. If I fall, you can catch me."

She glanced playfully back at him and he gave her a look like he wasn't entirely certain *how* he would catch her, but wasn't willing to fight with her any further.

They went along the river's front until the first minor street took them away from it, and they headed uphill out of the water and onto dry stones again.

"Jasper didn't tell you anything else about what was going on?" Stasia asked, and he shook his head.

"Just that I needed to fetch you as quickly as possible and bring you to the card room."

"Card room?" Stasia asked, and he nodded, a rabbit-jerk of a motion.

"It's where we go to talk privately," he said, his voice dropping to secret-level. "It's above a bar across from the market, past the castle, and the owner likes us."

"What kinds of things do you go there to talk about?" Stasia asked.

"Please don't ask me that," Matthias answered. "I'm not sure what I'm supposed to say to you and what I'm not."

"Okay," Stasia answered carefully. "Can you tell me what he sees in you, Matthias?"

"What?"

"Jasper," Stasia said. "You see that he surrounds himself with truly remarkable people, don't you?" She suddenly realized the cruelty of what she was saying, but she didn't take it back. "He chose you, did he not?"

"Yes," Matthias said slowly, sensing a trap and not sure what to do about it.

"Then there must be something remarkable about you," Stasia said. There. That was the positive way to ask it, without tearing him down or putting doubts in his head. Poor kid. "Do you know what it is?"

"I don't," Matthias said, as though relieved to be telling someone a secret. "The others… they're amazing, and all he does is teach me things that they all think are simple. He won't fight with me. I just… I follow him around and do what he says, and I don't know why he chose me."

Stasia felt a deep stab of pity, looking over at him, but the way he jerked his head away, he didn't want that.

"I don't see it, either," Stasia said honestly. "But what I do see is a man who knows what he's doing and who has seen a lot more of the world than you or I have, and I have no doubt in my mind that there *is* something very important about you that we're overlooking."

Matthias huffed a little laugh and shook his head.

"Don't patronize me," he said.

Stasia looked over at him.

"I'm not," she said. "Every time Babe opens his mouth, I respect him even more. He is incredible. Sterling with a sword is… I have no measure to compare to, but even my eye can see that he's capable of things I can't imagine. Colin, I assume, has his uses as well…"

Matthias did genuinely laugh at this.

"Jasper sometimes says that he has his doubts," he told her. "Colin seems proud of that."

Stasia nodded.

"That might be it," she said. "That no one can hurt him with words."

As she said it, the importance of something like that sort of resonated within her, and she set it aside to reflect on another time.

"I didn't think it could get worse, and then you showed up," he told her after a moment, and she frowned.

"How did *I* make it worse?" she asked.

"You're not that much older than me, but you're better at so many things," he said. "You make me look bad."

"I do not," Stasia said reflexively.

"Jasper would have never let me go on a secret mission by myself," Matthias said. "You're running around doing all of this… *stuff* and all they can talk about is how cool you are, and all the things you can do, and I'm just boring and stupid, the kid they have to train and the one they send to *get* stuff."

She glanced over at him.

"If you want pity from me, you aren't going to get it," she said. "I worked hard to be able to do the things I can do, and Jasper happened to find use for them. Whatever it is you're good at, he's got a use for it, but I don't feel sorry for you just because it isn't as exciting."

He shot her a glance that might have been a glare, and she shook her head, immune.

"Besides, I'm plenty older than you are," she said. "How long have you been out of school?"

"Two years," he said.

"Yeah, I never went to one, but even then I'm older than you by a bunch. Didn't you call me a spinstress the first time we met?"

"That sounds like Colin," Matthias said, and she raised an eyebrow.

That did sound like Colin.

"But you've thought it, haven't you? I'm so old there's no point to me anymore. Best put me in a quiet corner with the lacework and a needle so my mind doesn't go dull as it ages."

He looked her up and down, not meaning to, and Stasia grinned.

"Break the rules, kid," she said. "I don't mean go against Jasper. That's not a *rule*, that's a force of nature. Never try to break a force of nature. It will break you. But be someone other than what everyone tells you to be. Be *who* you want to be."

"What if I don't know who that is?" Matthias asked.

She blinked.

The idea was simply so foreign to her it took her a moment to address it with words.

"Why are you in the guard?" she asked.

"It's better than the army," he answered easily.

"So you're protecting the king to avoid conflict," she teased, and he shrugged.

"It's a steady income, a place to live, it's something that my family respects me for, and I like Jasper and the rest of the squad."

"But you didn't have Jasper and the rest of the squad when you went through your first round of training, did you?" she asked. "You do that with all of the other new recruits?"

"And Brutus," Matthias said. "They call him the newbie killer. He's never actually *injured* anyone with his own two hands, but if you aren't going to hack it, he takes pride in proving it to you as quickly as possible."

"Lovely," Stasia said. "Glad to have opted out of that one. But you'd never *met* Jasper before that, had you? Why did you stick it out as Brutus was breathing down your neck, waiting for you to fail?"

He looked at his feet as he walked for a minute, frowning.

"It would make my family proud," he said.

"Huh," Stasia said after a minute. "I mean, I guess I wouldn't want to be a giant *disappointment* to my father, but the closest I can really get to that is that I wouldn't want to break his heart. I can't imagine building a life around what someone else thinks I ought to accomplish."

"Obviously," Matthias said, then looked away like he regretted speaking.

"Learn to break a rule," Stasia said. "The dumb ones that no one says and no one enforces and that aren't written down anywhere. And in the meantime, figure out what you want and who you are. There's still time for you."

"Not you?" Matthias asked, an attempt at teasing.

"Oh, no," Stasia said. "No, I'm an old crone with naught to live for but me needlework."

He snorted.

"They're all right about you," he said. "It doesn't help anything, because if they were just… attracted to you or patronizing you, it would feel unfair, but at least it wouldn't be true. They're *right* about you."

"I do try to impress," Stasia said with a quick bow. Boy, did she like bowing in the dragonskins.

"You do not," Matthias answered dismissively, and Stasia considered that.

"No, I actually do," she said. "But only the people who impress me, first."

He frowned thoughtfully.

"I don't know who impresses me," he said.

"Yes, you do," Stasia answered flatly. "You've just never thought about it. You've followed someone around your whole life without thinking about whether or not they were worth it, haven't you?"

"What did Jasper ever see in me?" Matthias asked, and Stasia frowned.

"Maybe you ought to ask him that, someday when you're feeling secure," she said.

"I'm afraid of what he'll say," Matthias asked.

"Whoops?" Stasia suggested, and Matthias laughed.

"That he was doing someone a favor and he's regretted it ever since."

Oh, that was hard. That was really hard.

"You think it's true?" Stasia asked, and he shrugged.

"I can't think of who it would be, but… It's the only thing that makes sense."

"How did you compare to everyone else you went through training with?" Stasia asked. He shrugged again.

"I was near the top on everything. Swordplay, memorization, hand-to-hand fighting, problem solving, horseback riding, marksmanship."

"You guys use bows?" Stasia asked, and he nodded.

"We're trained with them."

"Huh."

He nodded again.

"It's not of much use to the King's Guard, but the palace guard have them, obviously, and the army has a huge archery contingent. So they train us, too."

"There's that much crossover?" Stasia asked.

"I didn't know if I was going to be with the palace guard or the King's Guard until Jasper claimed me."

"Does everybody get claimed?" Stasia asked, and he shook his head.

"No. A lot of them don't."

"He saw something in you," Stasia said. "Search me, what, but he saw it."

Matthias sighed.

"I hope so."

They walked along in silence for a time, passing the western edge of the castle market and crossing the bridge there with great care. In the dark, Stasia's heart actually raced, crossing the surging water, but Matthias strolled across like he did it every day of his life.

"How many kids do they lose to this every year?" Stasia asked as they turned to walk along the castle wall.

"A few," Matthias said. "We learn young how to recognize still water from moving water and how to measure when the water is too deep to stand in safely."

Stasia frowned.

"How long does this flood *last*, exactly?" she asked.

She heard Matthias laugh softly. The water on this side was washing up against the castle wall, and they walked in single-file along it, passing other pedestrians with great care.

"It ought to peak sometime tomorrow, if everyone is right, and we usually are, within a day or so, and then it'll go down slowly over the next two or three weeks."

"Two or three weeks," Stasia demanded, drawing attention from a couple going past. She didn't care. "What do you mean, two or three weeks? This whole place is *insane*."

"We'll get the roads back the first week or so," Matthias offered over his shoulder. "But the river doesn't go back down to its normal level for a while. There's a lot of water up in the mountains to drain back down, with all these storms."

"When do the storms stop?" Stasia asked.

"Any time now," Matthias said. "Or not for a month. Who knows?"

She threw her arms up, astonished that anyone would put up with that, but let him lead on, turning into a bar where two large canvas bags full of *something* were attempting to impede the flow of water across the floor, and a maid with a mop and a bucket was picking up where they left off.

Matthias touched his brow to the man behind the bar and they went around and up a back set of stairs, finding Jasper, Colin, and Sterling sitting at a table with a deck of cards sitting on it.

"Playing cards, I see," Stasia said, coming to sit down across from Jasper.

"Keeping up appearances," he answered. "How are you?"

"Out after dark in the most dangerous city in the known world," she said. "How are you?"

He gave her a phantom of a smile, looking at his hands.

"You don't approve of the flood," he said.

"No, no I'm pretty sure someone should have told it off by now," she agreed. Colin snickered.

"Oh, I would pay to see that," he said as Matthias brought over a spare chair and attempted to put it next to Sterling.

"How is Babe?" Jasper asked. The table went silent. Stasia frowned.

"Turning bits of spare lumber into sawdust with his knife," she said. "I would guess that that meant he was out of his mind, other than that I'm pretty sure he's never actually unhappy."

Jasper nodded.

"Is he helping to keep watch over our friend?" he asked.

"Oh, he's living with him," Stasia said, and Jasper's eyebrows went up.

"Well, that complicates things," he said. "Though I'll admit, it may be better this way."

"What's going on?" Stasia asked. Jasper looked around the table.

"Froide downstairs is going to let us know if anyone shows up, following you, but I have information that suggests that the court has learned of your involvement with this."

"What now?" Stasia asked, and he nodded.

"The politics at court are… delicate, and there is a good chance that if we can extricate ourselves from the situation successfully, they will have no opportunity or reason to continue to pursue you, as you are among the queen's favored, and this is known. What is important is that they do not know *why* you are involved, and I believe that they believe you are involved because of a misguided Botonese romantic sympathy for elves."

"Elves," Sterling said. "Jasper, what are you mixed up in?"

"You haven't told them?" Stasia asked, and Jasper shook his head.

"So long as it was a secret, it was a secret best kept by fewer. They couldn't possibly answer questions to which they didn't know the answers. And I am very good with secrets. Babe, though, knew things that I most certainly did *not* want freely available, and so I sent him away."

"You didn't *trust* Babe?" Colin demanded.

"It wasn't an act of mistrust," Jasper said. "It was an act of *selection*. He was the only one who could find her. And because he could find her, and *because he could find her*, I sent him to her to help."

"You shamed him in front of everyone," Sterling said.

"And you lied to us," Colin said.

"I didn't lie," Jasper said. "I just chose not to tell you the entire truth. He has been dismissed from the guard, and I will have to take special action with Ben to get him reinstated as he was, but that is my intent, and he knew that, leaving."

"You two," Sterling said.

"You couldn't even tell us that part?" Matthias asked.

"You three being furious at me for the last four weeks has been key to his departure not arousing suspicion," Jasper said. "If anything, I think that Stacy's lack of presence at the guard house and the bar may be what ultimately drew attention to her, or that she was spotted with a very tall man in a cloak leaving through the front gate at the castle."

"You walked him out the door?" Colin asked, swinging his attention around to Stasia. "That is the most incredible thing I've ever heard."

"One foot in front of the other," Stasia said, at a loss for something else more clever. Colin howled at it anyway.

"They're following you," Jasper said, drawing attention back to himself. "The location of your house and the unexpectedness of your hours has helped keep you hidden so far, and I don't know how *long* they have been tailing you, but I heard it from a friend within the palace guard who heard it on the courtyard among three men who forget that the palace guard are not empty suits of armor."

"You have friends on the palace guard?" Stasia asked.

"The world isn't brimming with incompetents," Jasper answered. "It just often feels that way. They believe that you will lead them to our friend, and they are going to seize him and return him to the castle, and arrest you for treason."

"What are they intending to *do* with him?" Sterling asked, and Jasper shook his head.

"It begins with torture. I don't know where it ends."

Stasia shuddered.

"We talked about it some, why they don't help. I think there might be ways to make it work, if we're creative…"

"I'm deeply intrigued," Jasper cut in. "But pressed for time right now, and need focus. You are continuing to support our friend through your active and daily intervention, am I correct?"

"Yes," Stasia said.

"You could remove yourself somewhat and rely on Babe to keep them, but that would mean that Babe cannot return to the guard until we have an alternate solution," Jasper said.

"He's in the middle of Highrock territory," Stasia said. "He's not worried about it, but he isn't safe there, either."

Jasper's jaw worked, and he nodded.

"I didn't anticipate that, but I should have," he said. "We need to get them moved, but without drawing attention, and we need a more permanent solution, so that we can withdraw. He is best if he is completely out of contact with us."

Stasia considered.

"He's very good at woodworking," she said. "I think that he could do it professionally and make a good living at it. I had planned on getting him a nicer apartment near here, so that he could furnish it and live… better, but I haven't started the work on it yet."

"No," Jasper said sharply. "No, he is not to come this close to the castle. There are too many sharp eyes. He needs to be hidden as deeply and as far away as possible, if he's going to have any hope of remaining there."

"We need someone else who can help him," Matthias said. "Someone else who isn't one of us."

"That was her," Jasper motioned with his hand.

"No," Matthias said. "Someone who is *completely* unconnected from the castle. Someone who is trustworthy but doesn't care about politics and… maybe who doesn't mind breaking the law, hiding a fugitive?"

"Do you have someone like that hidden up your sleeve?" Sterling asked, not unkindly. Matthias sat back in his chair, and Jasper lifted his chin to scratch his throat thoughtfully.

"They say the Rat King is a good man," Colin said. "Someone who lets people hide when he doesn't think they've done anything wrong, and who keeps his word."

"He doesn't trust the likes of us," Jasper said. "Not that I blame him."

"Who?" Stasia asked.

"The King of the Rats," Colin said, leaning onto his elbow with a sort of between-you-and-me style gossip or intrigue. "Also known as Lord Westhauser…"

There were more words. She could tell. It was Colin. There were always more words.

"I know Lord Westhauser," Stasia cut in. "I've spent the night at his house. His wife and I are friends."

"*You're* friends with the White Princess?" Sterling asked, and she shot him a dark look.

"Don't call her that," she said.

"It's a term she appreciates," Jasper said. "Though I'm concerned if you've never heard her use it, nor mention the Rats."

Stasia opened and closed her mouth.

"I don't know what to tell you," she said. "I had dinner with him, I played cards with him until my eyes were about to shut on their own, and then I drove back into town with him, and I found him fascinating and engaging. She and I have met together several times since then, and I think that she may become a dear friend."

"How interesting," Jasper said. "So if I were to track him down and deliver a note from you, do you believe that that would be enough to get us an audience?"

"I don't know what that means," Stasia said. "And I can't promise it. But he is an acquaintance, and I would be happy to write you a letter of introduction and ask that he speak with you."

"Better if we track him down tonight and she talk to him on her own," Colin said.

"Do we know how to find him?" Jasper asked.

"Wouldn't he be at home?" Stasia asked.

"At home," Jasper said.

"The Westhauser estate," Stasia said.

Jasper looked around the table.

"It's a long ride," Sterling said.

"It just might be worth it," he answered. "The chargers are built for it."

Sterling stood.

"We'll run ahead and get them ready. Make sure she doesn't float away."

Stasia narrowed her eyes at him and he winked back.

"Cloaks," Jasper said. "Everyone."

He indicated a pile of cloaks on the floor in the corner and he pointed at Sterling.

"And one at a time. I don't want anyone from outside following us and figuring out where we're going. We *need* to keep this link hidden, or else our friend is never going to be safe."

"Does it have to be tonight?" Stasia asked, and Jasper paused.

"Are you unwell?" he asked, and she shook her head.

"I'm just afraid my father might try to wait up for me."

"Write him a note to let him know you're going to be out very late," Jasper said. "Matthias will pay someone from the market to deliver it. Say no more than that. If my instincts are right, we may not have much past the Highwater Festival before they finalize their plans to seize our friend and drag him back. I think there is a good chance they already know where he and Babe are."

"You didn't say that before," Stasia said, going to get a cloak.

"You didn't say Highrock before," Jasper answered. "We need to move them tonight, tomorrow at the latest."

"The festival is probably going to be tomorrow," Matthias said, and Jasper nodded.

"A benefit and a curse. We'll take what we can and lose as little as possible. Nothing else to be done about it."

He motioned, and Sterling put on a cloak, then went down the stairs and left.

"You're sure you're good enough friends to risk this?" Colin asked.

"She's just asking for a conversation with me," Jasper said. "Not for anything else. And the Lord Westhauser doesn't take houseguests, much less overnight houseguests. I hear them complain at court all the time about his inhospitality, while in the next breath complaining of his dubious double-life. He can't stand the nobility, but he is a man of his word. If we can get his agreement to assist us, it will be... the best we can offer our friend."

"I can't tell you whether or not he'll do what you ask," Stasia said. "I genuinely don't know him *that well*, but... I hope that he'll talk to you, because I ask him to."

Jasper nodded.

"It's enough. If we do this right, we might be done by tomorrow, sunset, and our friend will be successfully hidden away where he can build a life as he sees fit."

Stasia nodded. He motioned to Matthias and Colin.

"You two together," he said.

They left and Jasper stood, coming to adjust Stasia's cape in a way that she only just barely didn't mind.

"When we get to the guard house, you write your note for your father and give it to Matthias, and then we'll ride. Have you ridden with a torch before?" he asked.

She nodded.

"Yes. The ride from Boton to Birch a few times."

"Much of the road might be deeply flooded," Jasper said. "We might be forging a difficult path."

"You're talking about the big horses, aren't you?"

"You seemed very fond of Alfred, last time," Jasper said with a smile, and she nodded.

"I was."

"They can take on that distance, get a drink, and then turn around and come all the way back and be ready to do it again by dawn," Jasper said. "So we'll push them. There may be lives at stake, here, and I believe that what they're offering Farang may be a fate worse than death."

"I can keep up with you," Stasia said, and he nodded.

"I believe you."

The ride certainly wasn't *easier* than he'd said, but Stasia felt like she'd made a good show of it as they turned down the last curve of the driveway toward the house. A guard stepped out of a shack there and put a pole axe across the driveway.

"State your business," he shouted over the sound of the oncoming storm.

"My name is Anastasia Fielding-Horne," Stasia said. "Please tell Lady Westhauser that I am here and requesting shelter and conversation."

"She has likely turned in for the night," the man shouted at her. "You may take shelter here for the night and I will send word to her in the morning."

"No," Stasia said. "She will want to know that I am here now," Stasia said. "If you don't tell her, she will be very angry."

He hesitated, and Stasia urged Alfred another step forward.

"You would recognize my other mount," she said. "A brown mare with a purple saddle blanket."

He squinted at her, and Stasia held the torch closer to her face.

"Yes, ma'am," he said. "Of course. I'll send word now."

"Thank you," Stasia said. "We will wait."

She backed Alfred up to stand next to Sable as Jasper looked up at the clouds. Another man from the guard shack went tearing down the driveway on foot, disappearing into the darkness after mere moments. Stasia hoped he didn't fall into the lake.

"The lake isn't flooding," Stasia observed, and Jasper shook his head.

"No, it's above the river level. Anything above where they want it to crest will just spill away toward the river again."

Stasia frowned.

If only it were all that simple.

They waited what felt like a very long time as the horses fidgeted at their tack and pawed at the brickwork, then a man rode up from the barn.

"Miss Fielding-Horne," he said. "Lady Westhauser asks you to come down to the house as quickly as possible, before the storm arrives."

The wind was cold and wet, already, and the storm was imminent. Stasia dipped her head and the man turned his mount around, cantering down the rest of the driveway to the house, where lights were coming on throughout it. A pair of stableboys were in the yard, waiting to take their horses, and Stasia and Jasper ran into the front doors as the first sheets of rain started to hit.

"Well," Lady Westhauser said, standing in front of the doors in a beautiful white dressing gown. "With a member of the guard, no less. I am *fascinated* to hear this story, Stasia."

"Is Lord Westhauser in?" Stasia asked, and Lady Westhauser turned her head.

"I am," came a voice as he rounded a corner into view. "I too am quite interested to hear what confluence of events has driven this particular moment."

"If we could have someplace very private to speak, I would love to tell you," Stasia said. He considered her thoughtfully for a moment, then nodded.

"Yes. I can make that happen."

—•◁◦❖◦▷•—

The study was made of books. Stasia hadn't seen this many books in one place outside of a library, before, and her father adored books. They'd had to leave most of them behind in Birch because the sea water would have ruined them, and their baggage was spare, but he did sometimes talk about sending for them to have at the house on the Sapphire, because he missed them like friends.

This was another *league*.

Lord Westhauser caught her gawping at them and waved a hand.

"Don't be impressed," he said, going to sit in a chair and crossing his legs and steepling his fingers. "My father bought paper and leather bindings and employed a bookmaker for a year and a half to create this collection. Nearly all of them are blank.

Stasia turned her head slowly to look at him.

"They're *what*?" she demanded. He nodded evenly.

"Blank."

"Then may I have one?" Stasia asked. "They're beautiful. I'd pay its worth to you."

"They're worth less than the paper bound within them," Lord Westhauser said. "I would be more than glad to make a gift of one to you. Please select any volume you like. If it contains nothing but blank paper, it's yours."

She shook her head, astonished at this, then caught Jasper's flat look and reminded herself that Babe might be in significant danger.

"Another time, perhaps," she said. "If we remain friends after tonight."

Lord Westhauser's eyebrows went up as he rested his lips against his forefingers.

"Is there a risk of some other outcome?" he asked.

Lady Westhauser closed the door with a muffled thud that bespoke significant sound-proofing, probably in large part due to the layer of books that encircled the room. Stasia glanced back at Lady Westhauser, then at Jasper, though Lady Westhauser did not look at all insecure in her place here.

"I suspect it does not matter if she remains or goes," Jasper said. "If my sources are correct."

"I suspect that your sources are rarely wrong," Lord Westhauser answered, his eyes taking on Jasper for just a moment, then returning to Stasia. "I do not know this outfit, but I've heard stories of it. I wonder what it means."

"I need help," Stasia said, coming to sit across from him. "We need help. And apparently you are the only person who is both situated and trustworthy enough to give it."

The corner of Lord Westhauser's mouth twitched as he glanced at Jasper again.

"Oh, those words must have cost you dearly, if they came from your mouth," he said, and Jasper shook his head.

"We all know that you keep your word," Jasper said. "I just also know that you seldom give it."

Lord Westhauser snorted.

"I am discerning with my word," he said, then looked at Stasia once more. "What is it you want from me?"

"First, we want your word that this conversation will not leave this room," Jasper said. "I understand that you may use it tactically in making decisions that are of personal or commercial importance to you, and I won't ask you to recuse yourself from those, but the things that we say tonight *must* remain among the four of us unless I specifically agree to a modification."

Lord Westhauser looked slowly over at Jasper, lifting his chin and poking it with his steepled forefingers for a moment.

"What does the King's Guard want from the King of the Rats that can trust no one else?" Lord Westhauser asked rhetorically. "It's almost worth agreeing to it simply to find out."

"Skite," Lady Westhauser said sternly. "Don't toy with them."

Lord Westhauser glanced at his wife and smiled, then dipped his head.

"So be it," he said. "From now until the time that door opens again, these are nothing but secrets among us. Good that you let Ella stay, or else I would not have agreed to it."

Jasper tipped his head.

"She's that important to you?" he asked, and Lord Westhauser nodded.

"Almost immediately. The right woman, apparently, will do that to you."

Stasia glanced back at Lady Westhauser, feeling out of her depth, but immensely comforted by the calm and pleased expression on Lady Westhauser's face.

"I come not on the king's errand, but the queen's," Jasper said. "She has rescued a person of interest from a very terrible fate for political ends, and she has entrusted this person to myself and to Miss Fielding in particular to see to his safety and to see that those seeking him will not find him."

Lord Westhauser settled deeper into his seat, pursing his lips.

"And what has that to do with me?" he asked.

"They know something of where he is hiding, and we need to move him. Tomorrow. But it is simply postponing the inevitable, so long as Miss Fielding is acting as liaison and support, because they now have good information that she is involved."

"Then find someone else," Lord Westhauser said, and Jasper shook his head.

"No," he said. "Every time we move him, there is a risk of being caught out, and every new location is a temporary solution. What we need is a permanent solution, and that facilitated through someone with no connection to the guards at all."

"And your first thought was of me," Lord Westhauser said. "How flattering."

"There would be a considerable payment made to cover your expenses and to motivate you to keep the location of this individual carefully guarded. We would expect you to personally see to him, setting him up in a way that allows him to live some semblance of an independent life."

"He's capable?" Lord Westhauser asked, and Stasia nodded.

"I believe he could be a well-respected carpenter," she said.

"Well, that's nice, but you don't get *good* furniture that's been made at the Black Docks," Lord Westhauser said. "If he wants to make things from planks of wood, so be it, but he must never develop a reputation."

Stasia thought of the clever work that Farang was doing at the little apartment in Highrock, and her spirits crushed.

Lord Westhauser was right.

That kind of craftsmanship was trackable. All you had to do was find someone who could tell you where they bought it, and Farang would be easy prey.

"You're welcome to explain that to him," Jasper said.

"What is the queen's interest in him?" Lord Westhauser asked, and Jasper shook his head.

"That's none of your concern."

"Oh, but I'm afraid it's my *only* concern," Lord Westhauser said. "If I take in your stray, give him a home and a bowl of water and a blanket at my hearth, I need to know who is going to come kicking down my door to reclaim him, and why."

Stasia looked over at Jasper, who considered for a long moment.

"He is an elf," he finally said.

"High or rock?" Lord Westhauser replied, not missing a beat.

"High elf."

"Has he lost his mane?" Lord Westhauser asked.

"Yes," Stasia said at a glance from Jasper. "I cut it off myself."

"So he's committed," Lord Westhauser said, tapping his fingers against his lip again. "I'll do it. And I'll even do it out of the kindness of my own heart, knowing what Lord Palora would do with such a creature, if he could get his hands on him."

"What's the catch?" Jasper asked. Lord Westhauser nodded.

"My sources are right about you, too," he said. "There are two. He agrees to create magic artifacts for me, for fair payment, without intervention from the guard, and he agrees to fix Hidalga's eyes."

"Hidalga?" Stasia asked.

"The name Lady Westhauser has taken within the Rats," Jasper said. "I will not interfere with you procuring enchanted pieces from him, so long as you continue to guarantee his anonymity, but I cannot speak to the eyes. I don't know what is possible and what is not."

"What's wrong with her eyes?" Stasia asked, looking over her shoulder. Lady Westhauser had a sarcastic look on her face.

"Nothing," she said. "But he's on a quest to get rid of my need for glasses, and nothing will stop him."

"Do you *want* to get rid of your glasses?" Stasia asked.

"Thank you," Lady Westhauser answered. "No, I hold no animosity for them whatsoever, and I like how they make me look."

"Those are my terms," Lord Westhauser said.

"I will not stand by for you to force an unwanted magical procedure on your wife," Jasper said, and Lord Westhauser nodded.

"How noble of you," he said. "Very well, then leave that as a caveat. The elf agrees to fix her eyes, so long as she agrees to have it done."

Jasper nodded.

"Where can we meet you? We'll return to the city tonight, and Stacy will go and get the elf ready to move."

"Should do it under darkness," Lord Westhauser said. "Particularly with the festival on."

"Is it going to be tomorrow?" Lady Westhauser asked, and Lord Westhauser nodded.

"The castle market has decreed it, as of tonight. They'll announce it in the morning."

Stasia glanced back at Lady Westhauser, who caught her eye and mouthed '*Stacy?*', but Stasia just shrugged and shook her head. Unimportant story.

"Where do I meet you?" Stasia asked.

"There's a bar," Lord Westhauser said. "One block north of the Warbler Bridge and two blocks east. It's frequented by craftsmen who care nothing for politics. I have taken all of the rooms on the third floor and occasionally use it for meetings where a neutral ground is required. Be there at full dark tomorrow night."

"I don't want any of your people involved with this," Jasper said. "No one should have interaction with him but you."

"Does that not arouse *more* suspicion?" Lord Westhauser asked, teasing if Stasia read him right.

"I just know that you are a difficult man to bribe and an even more difficult man to threaten," Jasper said. Lord Westhauser smiled.

"How novel to be appreciated for my true virtues," he said.

Stasia looked back at Lady Westhauser, who gave her a subtle smile.

"You two will need to avoid common relation for a time," Lord Westhauser said. "To avoid people making the connection that actually drove the transaction."

"Is it known at court that they are friends?" Jasper asked. Lord Westhauser scratched his chin and let his hands fall.

"In point of fact, it is not," he said. "It is known that the White Princess has taken up a close relationship with Anastasia Fielding-Horne, while the queen has taken confidence with one Stacy Fielding. I am at bated breath to know how *that* has happened, but it is my best understanding that the city of Verida considers these to be two vastly different women. I am honored to receive Stacy Fielding, tonight, but she should not return to my home again."

Jasper looked over at Stasia with a raised eyebrow.

"Anastasia?" he asked. "How did we get *Stacy*?"

"I go by Stasia," Stasia said. Jasper's expression changed.

"Colin."

She nodded.

"Colin. I don't even know if *he* knows."

"Why didn't you say something?" Jasper asked.

She shrugged.

"I like being Stacy," she said. "It was like… becoming something Veridan, I think."

"Oddly, if my ears are correct, Anastasia Fielding-Horne is a mystery. Even as you were announced as Miss Fielding-Horne at your own party, my wife was the only one who remembered. You are dwarfed in importance by your father, and his name is the only one that they recall. The way they say it, I believe that Fieldinghorn is a single word, in their minds, and the ladies are abuzz with who this young woman might be who has found such favor with the Westhauser family. The intrigue is… well, it shall soon be exhausting, but for now it is quite amusing."

Stasia stared at him.

"I'm already exhausted," she said. "I have no interest in two identities."

"There's value there," Jasper warned quietly, and Stasia shook her head.

"No," she said. "It's a *lie*, Jasper. One that I have to remember exactly who knows what for the rest of my life. I have no interest in that."

Jasper gave her a thoughtful frown, and nodded.

"I see."

"Am I wrong?" Stasia demanded, and he shook his head.

"Not at all," he told her. "Just more observant about it than I expected."

"Regardless," Lord Westhauser said. "For the next few weeks, Stacy-Stasia-Anastasia needs to remain invisible as the city moves on from searching for the castle escapee and life returns to normal."

"He deserves a good life," Stasia said, and Lord Westhauser snorted.

"We all do," he said. "The overwhelming fraction of those who fail to achieve it certainly *still* deserve it. Once his existence is no longer notable, he is free to rise as he may. But the next years will be challenging for him."

"It is better than his alternative," Jasper said, rising. "We need to return to the city quickly and get them out of that apartment, before the palace guard converge on it."

"Or worse," Lord Westhauser said, taking to his feet and going to a shelf. He pulled down a large tome, four fingers thick, and turned to offer it to Stasia.

"Suitable, I think," he said. "I will be taking a carriage into the city and I will carry it with me, to spare it the storm, if you agree."

"It's beautiful," Stasia said. The leather was worked more than most of the other books, giving it a softer texture that was made rigid by a much thicker yellow leather on the inside. It was, indeed, completely full of blank pages.

"Someday I will amaze you with what I do with this," Stasia said, and Lord Westhauser looked around the room for a moment at the shelves of books.

"It would not surprise me at all if being in your possession made this the most notable of any book ever to reside in the Westhauser library," he said. "Go. I've instructed the stables to provide you with fresh mounts. We'll smuggle your horses into the city some time in the future."

"That won't be necessary," Jasper said, heading for the door. "We're on hill chargers."

"Is that so?" Lord Westhauser said. "I'll have to see this for myself."

Stasia turned quickly to Lady Westhauser, who grasped her hands and kissed her knuckles.

"Very soon," Lady Westhauser said. "Very soon we shall discuss all of this at length."

"I'll miss you," Stasia answered truthfully, and Lady Westhauser shook her head.

"Oh, no, our fates just got tied together even more firmly. Don't grieve. This is nothing but a wisp of time compared to what we have, now."

She kissed Stasia's knuckles again then they turned and followed the men down the hallway and through the house back to the front doors.

"This is my man Jeremiah," Lord Westhauser said to Jasper at the door. "You can trust him as you would me. Jeremiah, you will forget that these two people were here tonight. We had a pair of wayfarers who showed up, lost and bedraggled, and we saw to them then sent them on their way, tonight. Please be sure that the staff understand what has happened here."

"Yes, sir," Jeremiah said. Lord Westhauser nodded.

"Good. Please fetch their mounts."

"They came in steaming, sir," Jeremiah said, and Lord Westhauser nodded.

"Then the stableboy who gave you his report left out an important detail," he said. "Have them tacked quickly and brought around. Our guests are leaving."

"Yes, sir."

"Do you need anything?" Lady Westhauser asked. "We didn't offer you refreshments."

"Run to the kitchen and fetch them both a cup of hot wine," Lord Westhauser said. "It's a terrible night to be out, traveling this far."

"That's not necessary," Jasper started, but Lady Westhauser was already gone.

There were several pieces of that that startled Stasia, not the least of which that Lord Westhauser would send his wife to the kitchen rather than a servant, but also that the two of them appeared to think that it was a perfectly normal thing to do.

"That wasn't necessary," Jasper said again. "I'm robust to whatever I need to do, and Stacy is remarkably resilient."

"Or," Lord Westhauser said. "You could drink the hot wine that my cook put on the stove the moment you arrived and brace yourself against the wet. I've done this ride at highwater, before, and I know just how treacherous it can be."

Jasper dipped his head.

"Very well," he said. "Thank you."

Lady Westhauser returned a minute later with two ceramic mugs of steaming red wine, and Stasia sipped at hers appreciatively. Her hair was bound up and her dragonskins shed the water without trouble, but the ride had been intense and tiring, and the wine made her feel as though she could relax for a moment and breathe.

The horses appeared out in the rain a few moments later, and Stasia tossed the rest of the wine back, nearly scalding her throat with it, then handing the mug to Lady Westhauser and taking her cloak back from the rack beside the door and throwing it across her shoulders. Lord Westhauser whistled.

"That's a fine pair of mounts," he said.

"The best anywhere in the city," Jasper answered. "Thank you for your time."

Lord Westhauser gave Jasper a little bow, and then they plunged back out into the rain, throwing themselves up onto the horses and racing off into the darkness.

⬥⬥⬥

The torches were nearly spent by the time they reached the guard house. The streets were empty and black, and the storm had finally broken. Stasia put her head against Alfred's chest as he breathed deep and looked around his stall for grain.

"Feed them," she heard Jasper say to someone out in the hall. "Then make sure that they dry well and are covered for the night."

"Yes, sir," a young voice answered, and Stasia turned to find Jasper leaning against Alfred's stall door.

"I'm afraid you aren't going to get much rest tonight," he said, and she nodded.

"I know," she said. "If I'm willing to go out in the dark and they aren't, I win."

He nodded back.

"All four of us will be there for tonight," Jasper said. "In case you're worried about Lord Westhauser."

"He's bringing me a pretty book," Stasia said. "And I think his wife is my best friend."

"He's a criminal," Jasper said. "There is nothing given about tonight's exchange."

"I thought you trusted him," Stasia said, mildly offended on Lord Westhauser's behalf. Jasper tipped his head back as a stableboy struggled down the aisle with a bucket of grain.

"I do," Jasper said, his tone more confidential now. "But not everyone he associates with."

Stasia nodded.

She hadn't considered that.

Jasper stepped out of her way, closing the bar across the stable door behind her as Alfred attempted to follow her out into the aisle.

"He knows there's food out here somewhere," Jasper said with humor. "Tell our friend the terms. If he will not agree to them, do not bring him."

Stasia nodded.

"Okay."

He gave her a little shrug of a smile and she offered him the cloak. He shook his head.

"Keep it," he said. "Maybe after tonight you won't need it anymore."

She looked back at the boy pouring Sable a measure of oats as Alfred tried to make his nose reach the bucket where it sat in the aisle, and she smiled.

"The Highwater Festival will start in a few hours," Jasper told her. "Things are going to get more complicated, from there."

"Then I'll try to be quick," Stasia said.

He nodded.

"Fare well," he answered.

She dodged out of the stable and across the yard, under the barrier and out onto the street, already calf-deep in the river. The yard was made of mud, at this point, but was still mostly above the standing water.

The moon came out overhead and the world once more gleamed, a much more pleasant light than the garish sun when it broke through the clouds and turned everything into daggers of sunlight. Tesh said that she avoided going outside after the heavy rains during the flood because it gave her headaches. She kept the curtains closed in the rooms where she worked most often, and Stasia could understand it. There weren't any safe places to keep your eyes where the sunlight wasn't liable to hit you.

The moonlight was different. It glinted and played and made the world feel as though it were made of silver, or perhaps a higher metal yet, one made of pure white, and nobler than the base coinmetal. Stasia was legitimately exhausted from fighting the water and the situation all day, and she was missing her bed, but Babe and Farang's lives were at stake, potentially, and if they found Babe *with* Farang, it was possible that Jasper and the rest of them would get into huge trouble.

There was only one bridge between the guard house and Highrock. Well, there were three to choose from, but she only needed to cross one.

She went to the Warbler, but she would have been thigh deep in strong-running water before she reached the first rail, so she went on, moving away from the river because the riverside road was under too much water, as well. It had looked to her like the first row of buildings had actually been temporarily abandoned, under the last surge of water.

She went on.

The next bridge along she hadn't used more than once or twice - maybe - and she didn't know its name, but it took a wider stance, as the river was wider here. The land was also a shallower slope, leading down to the bridge, and her boots were underwater before she could make the bridge out in the darkness.

She pressed forward, needing to at least lay eyes on it.

She wasn't sure if she could even make it home, at this point. She couldn't imagine what the bridges would look like that she needed to cross, to manage it. She couldn't imagine how much of the city was actually underwater, right now. The elevation distance between the banks and the normal level of the river was so much smaller, as you went down the main Wolfram.

She began to be able to make out the railings ahead of her as the last line of buildings came into sight and the angle of the river she could see broadened. The spindles holding up the railings had long Vs in white, cresting water behind them, and she wasn't sure how much of the bridge was *above* the water.

The river was above her knees, now, and she could feel the risk of it sweeping her away. And this was with buildings blocking most of the flow. The water was confused, here, a strong cross-current meeting a flow of water that was actually coming mostly from behind her as the river drained *around* the buildings.

How were they still standing?

She went to stand all the way against the building to the side, knowing that she was leaving herself a longer walk to the bridge, but keeping herself in stiller water for the next ten feet as she went to peer around the corner.

The water was in peaks, charging along under its own force, wakes forming behind every building.

She didn't want to walk across that.

But she also didn't want to go downriver to the *next* bridge, because it was much further into Lower Highrock, where her odds of having some miscreant demand her purse and her honor went way up, and also because the last bridge over the Green River was notably more rickety and improvised, compared to the first two, and while she'd never crossed it, she didn't have any reason to believe it would be better off than the first two.

She needed to get across, and this was the place to do it. Going downriver, the chances of accidentally ending up at sea if she messed it up went up substantially. She was in her dragonskins, she was a decent swimmer at Birch beach, and... now. Now was the time to go.

Maybe she should have tried it at the Warbler Bridge.

It didn't matter.

She didn't have the energy to fight her way back upstream to the previous bridge and then do the same thing.

She was further from the bridge, up here, but if she let the water help her...

She climbed her way up out of the water, around the corner of the building, and to where she could reach the doorframe before she dropped back down into the water.

She wasn't prepared for how fast it was running, and she landed on her knee before her grip caught her on the door and kept the water from pulling her further away.

Her knee slipped away, and then she was chest-down on the water, nothing touching the ground trying to keep her face up and out of the deluge.

Pulling herself up closer to the door, she pulled a foot up underneath her, getting it ahead of her shoulders before she pushed it down to find the ground, and putting her full weight on it before straightening.

She couldn't walk in this.

The instant one of her boots didn't make perfect contact with the ground, the river was going to wash her away again.

This was why a poleman was worth a jagger to take you upriver.

She finally understood.

There was only one way to get to the bridge.

She couldn't believe this was actually her plan, but it was. Carefully letting go of the doorframe, she swung her arms and dove across the water, landing on her stomach in it and immediately jerking sideways under the speed of it. Using her feet on the ground to push and swimming hard with her arms, she made for the bridge.

She'd been aiming for the first banister, but that flew past when she was still a bodylength away. Her feet couldn't reach the ground anymore and she kicked hard, grabbing hold of the second bannister and holding on for dear life as the river crested over her shoulders and tried to rip her free.

She had a grim thought that this was the best climbing training she'd ever met.

She pulled her shoulders up to the banister and tucked her elbows over it, hoping that it truly was made to hold up under the weight of river debris at this speed, then, having caught her breath, she grabbed another post two down, and then another, and pulled her body inch by inch around the corner so that the water was pinning her to the railing rather than threatening to drag her away.

She crawled sideways this way for another four posts, then risked trying to find her footing.

The bridge was calf-deep under water at her elbows, but she could pull herself upright with the railing and continued toward the Highrock shore.

Where she realized she had no plan at all.

Where were the ropes?

There were ropes where the river islands were too dangerous to cross without them. Why weren't there ropes here, to get her from the bridge to land?

The entire street was underwater. That was why.

The ropes would go *across* the street, and if the river had come up as much as she sensed it had in the last twelve hours, that street would have been in use by the heavier carriages and carts as the street was shutting down for the night.

She crossed to the upstream railing, then waded down into the water again, eventually hooking her feet through each post to keep herself upright. At hips-deep in the water, the railing went on, but it was going to go underwater, itself, soon, and Stasia couldn't hold against the water any deeper. It was splashing up to her shoulders, as it was.

Her arms were exhausted and her whole body was beginning to shake under the effort of just standing there.

She couldn't stay here and pretend like she was making a good decision. The longer she waited, the more of her strength was gone, just like holding onto a wall without climbing it.

Go back and admit defeat or go on.

She let go.

She had nothing to use as reference on the far side of the street. Everything was shadow and light, but the shapes didn't make sense, and the water roared around her, grabbing moonlight and throwing it at her in confusing shapes.

At one point, she feared she might have gotten herself turned around and might have been swimming the wrong way, but her last gasp of reason pointed out that the river was coming from her right, and so long as it was pushing her from right to left, she was swimming the correct direction.

She *would* hit ground.

Don't try to put her feet down until her hands reached the street without stretching for it.

Babe had said to lay on her back. To relax and let the river take her.

She couldn't imagine that.

Just… drifting along in the darkness, not knowing if she was getting closer to shore or not, vain hope sustaining her.

No.

No, she swam hard.

As she began to fear that something about the current was pushing her away from the shore as fast as she could swim toward it, as she began to expect a bridge to pass overhead and tell her that she was lost and going to end up out at sea, she bumped her fingers hard on something rude below her.

Losing all focus, her head dipped under the water as she reached for it again, and she came up sputtering, having found nothing and having lost her swimming rhythm completely.

She pushed herself onward again.

Don't reach for the ground.

The water noises changed, and she made out the unmistakable shapes of buildings not that far from her. How had she missed them, getting this close? The water was so disorienting, all sound and light and phantom shapes.

She swam on, not looking for the road below her because she knew she likely couldn't stand on it.

At this point, she wasn't sure she could stand at all. She needed to go find the level where she could just *lay* there for a while.

And then the current changed and she got slammed into the corner of a building. At the last instant, her fingers caught hold of a bit of stone, while the river pulled her further along toward the sea, and she was laying against stone, the water crushing her against it, breaking over her shoulders, trying to drown her.

They *celebrated* this?

She got her arm disentangled from her cloak, which had taken a new shape in the different current and suddenly wrapped itself around the side of her body, and she reached up to find another grip near the one her first hand had.

Just like the bridge, right?

Just pull up and over and around.

No.

She didn't have the strength for that.

She couldn't let go. If she let go, she might never find another building to grab hold of, and she probably would wash off to sea.

She knew that with a crushing certainty that bordered on a religious faith.

The river had her, and this was her last moment to escape it.

She choked up her grip with both hands, shifting around to get the cloak to lay flat along her body again then, using the cloak to help shield her, she pulled a foot forward until her knee was under her. She found a toehold that resisted the water and she brought her other foot up, crouching against the side of the building with her head up high enough out of the water now that she wasn't getting her face washed with spray anymore. Two more deep breaths, then she shifted her hand grip upwards and she attempted to shift her body up and out of the water.

The first effort wasn't impressive, but her feet had purchase and the water was actually supporting her in this direction. So long as she kept her shoulders *up*, the flow of the water buoyed her.

She took a new grip with her left hand that was directly above her head, not resisting the current of the water any more, but pulling herself up and out of it.

Astonishing that hanging from her fingers was easier, but it was.

She got new footholds and she was up. Her hands shook, her shoulders shook, her *thighs* shook with the effort, but she was out of the damning current.

She only gave herself a moment's pause, because this wasn't actually resting, then she worked her way around the corner once more and into a very narrow alley where the water was mercifully still. She worked her way along until, of course, she should have seen it coming, quite literally, she hit the back of the next building. It was a blind alley.

That was why there was no current here, and why the water stank of refuse and grime.

She pushed her back against a wall and leaned her head there for a long time, just breathing and appreciating that nothing was trying to drown her. After a while, she walked back toward the mouth of the alley, where the water was cleaner, and she let herself float there, just breathing and letting the power come back into her limbs. The water was cold - not bone-chilling, but cold - and she needed to get out of it before she would get her energy back, but she could rest for now and recover a good bit of what she needed to move on.

She did need to move on, though.

She had no idea how long she'd lost, at this point, and she expected the people coming from the castle would have a better plan on how to get into Highrock.

Boats, at least.

Drawing one big, final breath, she turned and started climbing.

Crossing Highrock on rooftop at night was not only treacherous, but confusing as well. As far south as she was, Stasia didn't want to be on the street level any more than she needed to, but she didn't like trying the jumps, even with the moonlight as strong as it was at a half-moon almost directly overhead.

Dawn was coming.

She climbed down when she finally came to the conclusion that this was not wise, and she was finally in range of the apartment building as the streets began to alight with dawn and people out, setting up market stalls and walking in clumps.

The air was different, socially, as the people laughed and whispered and just… walked. They weren't the sort of people

who were coming and going from important other things. These
had the feel of people who were just enjoying the day.

Stasia stopped, turning to a woman who was selling little
painted shells of dolphins and turtles and great sea fish.

"What do you do with them?" Stasia asked, looking down the
street again.

The man outside of the door.

He wasn't standing right.

"You wear them," the woman said encouragingly, standing to
show here. "Here."

She pushed a pin through the cloak and Stasia looked down at
it.

On a cloak that was supposed to be completely anonymous, it
looked absurd.

As a trinket celebrating the day that the river gave up on
trying to kill her? She kind of liked it, actually.

"How much?" Stasia asked.

"Two coppers," the woman answered. Stasia browsed through
the rest of the designs, but the great fish in purple and blue was
the most fetching, and Stasia paid for it, pulling the hood of her
cloak up and over her head again so that she could watch the
man outside of the building without him seeing her eyes.

"How long have they been there?" she asked.

"You live there, don't you?" the woman asked.

Stasia looked over at her.

"I do. I was told this was a nicer neighborhood than that."

"King Rupert has long fingers," the woman murmured.
"Palace guards."

"How do you know?" Stasia asked. "That's not a uniform."

The woman nodded.

"It's in the shoes, lass," the woman said. "Palace guards and
King's Guards both get the same boots, but the palace guards get
cracked from wear. King's Guards wear out the soles before the
leather gives out."

Stasia frowned, and the woman nodded.

"It's in the boots," Stasia said thoughtfully. "Why are they here?"

"Welcome to ask him yourself," the woman said with a distant tone. "Certainly none of my business."

Stasia frowned, taking a step toward the building.

The woman went back to sorting her trinkets, and something hit Stasia in the arm.

She looked down at the pebble, then up to find Babe standing in the shadow of a nearby alley. He put his finger to his lips, then turned and disappeared.

Stasia went to talk to the next vendor down, one selling little flags of the type that children might love running around streaming behind them, and Stasia bought one of those as well, then went down the alley after Babe.

He was at the back of the building where, mercifully, this one didn't meet up flush with the building behind.

"Is he still in there?" Stasia demanded in a sharp whisper, and he shook his head.

"Got a sense somethin' weren't right and we left before light," Babe said. "Saw them goin' in and figured you might not think to look for us at the shore, day like today, so I risked stayin' on for a bit. He's down along that-a-way a ways, waitin' on me with a breakfast beer."

Stasia blinked at him.

"Has he *had* a breakfast beer before?" Stasia asked.

He grinned.

"If you hurry, you might save him from finding the yolks," Babe said.

Stasia gagged with her tongue all the way out and he grinned wider.

"Come on," he said. "Gotta move."

"I have news," Stasia whispered and he shrugged.

"It'll keep unless it won't."

She turned to follow him, awash with a sudden realization that if he hadn't been here, Farang would have been captured this morning.

"I'm sorry," she whispered.

"For what?" he asked back, shoving a bit of laundry aside. It wouldn't get much sun, down here, but at least it got open air.

"That you had to give up your whole life to be here," Stasia said. "I would have failed."

He snorted and glanced over his shoulder at her not so much *looking* at her as indicating with his head that he would have, if he weren't so busy dodging stuff in the alley.

"This is the job, darlin'," he said. "Go where I'm needed, do what's necessary. Sittin' around in an apartment with a woodworking elf for a few weeks ain't anywhere close to the worst I've done."

He said it so easily. It wasn't just putting on kind words or bravado. He actually meant it.

She followed him through a maze of alleys, crossing one main street once and otherwise sticking to these back pathways.

"How do you know how to do this?" Stasia asked. "I... I've never been on any of these streets."

"Old skill," Babe said. "Plus, I wandered these routes a lot, the last few weeks, just makin' sure I knew 'em. Lot more to the world than the top side you high folks see."

"I don't like being one of the high folks," Stasia said, and Babe snorted.

"'Course you do," he said. "You just want to know what the rest of us know without havin' to live it first."

"Are you saying I have too much pride to live like you have?" Stasia asked, and he turned to face her, stopping abruptly enough that she almost walked into him.

"I ain't sayin' that at all," he said, shaking his head. "I'm saying you don't *want* to have lived like this. Nothin' wrong with visiting, with play-acting at it, but the way you *feel*, living in a place like this, it's got a… a pull to it, like a thousand strings tied to you, all pullin' back. Every step away costs you, and it's a sense that this is where you're gonna land, someday, when you fall down for good. Don't matter how determined you are, this place… this is where you *belong*."

The word had a sense, not of home, but of conviction.

"And there's no way to escape that?" Stasia asked. Babe shrugged.

"Time," he said. "Distance. Good friends who see you for somethin' else. But in the end, no. The minute you stumble, all those threads come back and start pullin' again like they never went anywhere."

He set off again, and she followed him, trailing through another length of alley mazes and coming out by a little shop with tables out front and a man scurrying around trying to keep everyone's tables full of food.

Babe went to sit down next to a strange man who was looking at his beer like it might have bitten him. Babe put his hat down over his eyes and Stasia looked at the stranger.

He was blond. Farang had had fishbelly silver hair and a clean face, but this man was blond with a scraggly goatee and mustache.

"I didn't know you could do that," she said softly as she sat down with him.

Was he *shorter*?

No.

No, he wasn't shorter, she realized as she studied him more carefully. He was just slouched under the table further than her eyes told her. How had he done *that*?

"It's of little consequence," he answered. "Why is this called a breakfast beer?"

"Because they put raw eggs in it," Stasia answered. He nodded.

"I should have guessed that."

Stasia shook her head aggressively.

"Oh, no, they're lunatics for doing it, but for some reason they think that's normal around here."

The corner of his mouth came up under his mustache and he looked over at her with what might have been curiosity, if she was learning to read his face better.

"You found us," he said. "Babe said that you might not even make it today."

"And yet, he hung out to make sure he was there to grab me when I showed up," Stasia said.

"You came from the wrong direction," Babe said. "Turned onto the street at the wrong place. You just go further around?"

"No," Stasia said. "I had a very interesting evening. We should discuss it, but…" She glanced at Babe, assuming he could see her out from under his hat. "I need to know that we're in a safe place to do that. Do you want to stay here or do you want to move?"

"How are the rivers?" he asked. "Storm last night couldn't've helped any."

"They're a disaster," Stasia said. "I think there have to be bridges that are completely underwater."

He nodded.

"Gonna be a trick, getting across like this," he said. "With men looking for us. How did they know where to find us? I'd worried they might've snagged you."

Stasia lowered her voice.

"Jasper said that they figured out it was me and they'd been following me," she said.

"Then you're in trouble, same as him," Babe said.

"I'm not worried, if that's what you're suggesting," Stasia answered, and he shook his head.

"No, it ain't that," he said. "Just that we gotta keep your head down, too."

"If we can keep them from finding him, I'm fine," Stasia said. "There's nothing against me without him."

Babe considered that, then shrugged.

"Don't know if that's true or not," he said. "But I reckon it don't matter, just this minute. My advice is that we stash him someplace where they ain't gonna be lookin' for him, and then you and I stay out here, keep our heads down but keep an eye on what's going on, get back to Jasper after the festival is over."

Stasia shook her head.

"No, that's part of the news. There's a new plan, and we need to get him across the river by dark tonight."

Babe narrowed his eyes.

"That's gonna take some doin', since they'll know which rivers we got options on crossin'."

"We can do it last minute," Stasia said. "But it's really important that we don't show up with anyone watching us or knowing where we've been."

Babe's hat shifted back and forth a fraction and he settled lower in his chair.

"What exactly is this plan of yours?" he asked.

"We're going to take him to someone that Jasper trusts, and we're going to stay out of contact with him, from there," Stasia said, keeping her voice low. She knew better than to mention the King of the Rats around here, at this point. Even a passive audience around them at other tables would start listening at the mention of the rats.

"This is Jasper's plan?" Babe asked, and Stasia nodded.

"Yeah."

"Then I've got no questions," he said. "I stand by stashing him someplace quiet and us keeping an eye out for when the coast is clear to make a run for it."

"Are you sure the boats will be out?" Stasia asked. "The water is *crazy*."

He nodded.

"Oh, the boats will be out," he said. "Your hair is wet."

"There are conditions," Stasia said, turning her attention to Farang. "You need to be willing to do… stuff… for the man who is going to be finding shelter for you. I think you should start doing woodworking, but it is going to need to be low-end for the time being, so that you don't draw attention to you. But he wants… magic."

Farang sighed, then nodded.

"Everyone does."

"He says that he would pay you, and silver coins buy a lot of worthwhile things, here, even if they don't elsewhere."

"I have my limits," Farang said.

"But you aren't *absolutely* against it on principle?" Stasia asked, and he shook his head.

"No."

"Good. I'm going to take that as a close-enough. Then there's his wife's eyes."

"What's wrong with them?" Farang asked.

"Don't know, didn't ask," Stasia said. "He wants you to fix them."

"That may or may not be possible," Farang said. "It depends on many things."

Stasia glanced at Babe, then shrugged.

"Gonna take that as a yes, too," she said. "So we're good to go. You'll try to meet his conditions, and… That's as close as I'm going to get, today. I have… a place… not far from here. I haven't been to it in the last two weeks, so if they only just started following me, they won't know where it is."

Babe nodded.

"All right. They may or may not know I'm here, but our best bet is to split up from here. You take him on a roundabout route to your new safehouse and I'll follow along behind to watch for anyone following you."

The crowds in the streets were growing thicker and louder as the entire population of Highrock turned out to celebrate the river choking the city to death.

"Gonna be hard to spot anyone following you," Babe observed. "But just as hard to follow, so long as he keeps his head down."

Stasia looked at Farang who nodded.

"Easier said than done," the elf said, and Babe nodded.

"Don't I know it," he said. "All right. No telling what they're gonna do, finding the apartment empty. You two get moving, and I'll be along behind you."

Stasia gave him the briefest description of where the apartment was, in case he lost them, then she stood. Farang gave his beer one more odd look, then stood, a new, light brown cape falling to his ankles.

He ducked his head, but there was no way to disguise how tall he was. Stasia and Babe could blend into a crowd, but Farang was always going to be notable. There were other tall men in the city, and Stasia had become more aware of them over the last weeks, but *they* were notable, too, and there just weren't enough of them around for camouflage.

She set off down the street next to Farang, appreciating the crowds, even as they had to weave around and through them to maintain the pace that she wanted to.

Was she doing it wrong?

On her own, she would have dawdled with the crowds, maybe even taken up with one of them so that she was harder to spot. With Farang, she just wanted to go as fast as she could, because anyone watching would immediately look at them.

She jerked.

"Take off your cloak," she said, pulling her hood off and unwrapping her hair. It was a coily mess, after the swim the night before, but it looked like *her* hair.

Farang did as she said, looking over at her with curiosity.

"They're looking for people who don't want to be noticed," she said. "Act like someone who doesn't care if they're noticed, and you aren't the person they're looking for. None of them have *seen* you before."

"This is true," he observed.

They walked more easily, looking at the shops and the crowds. Stasia bought a blue mask from one of the little stands, putting it on, and she bought Farang a black eyeband that she saw a lot of the other men wearing.

Just out enjoying the festival like everyone else.

She crossed the street and ducked through an alley that she did happen to know, switching directions on the other street and doubling back a few blocks before she cut across and walked around a group of six blocks. The crowds here were becoming standing-room only as they attempted to get closer to the river without actually getting their feet wet. Stasia turned the final corner, opening the door to the building and walking Farang to the first door on the left.

She wasn't happy with how little progress she had made on the floor, but it was clean and it was larger than his previous apartment, and it was very, very temporary.

"I'm not staying," she said. "I'll be back as soon as I can."

"The window is interesting," he said, setting the cleaning bucket down upside down on the floor and sitting down. The curtains were thick enough that they couldn't see inside, Stasia was confident, but the brilliant light outside was enough that he could see the crowds going by.

"I'll wave at you before I come in," Stasia said. "Good luck."

"And to you," he answered, and she closed the door again, going back outside and setting off in the same direction she'd been going but milling more, now, as she could blend in as herself better.

She made it three blocks before the hand on her shoulder came.

"You *are* a trick to follow," Babe said into her ear, passing her. She followed him, trying to keep from looking around all the time, to a first-floor stall of bread and fruit and delicate cakes celebrating the highwater.

"Almost didn't recognize you," Babe said. "Should have left the cloak."

"I'm in my dragonskins," Stasia answered. "They kind of stand out."

He nodded.

"That they do. I'm going to go back past the apartment, make sure nobody's got an unusual interest, then I'll meet you on the back side of the block and we can set up a pattern to watch for them."

Stasia nodded.

"Sounds good to me," she said.

"You done good," Babe murmured in her ear on the way past, and then he was gone again.

Stasia got bumped by a man who was already tipsy and his angry girlfriend, and she shoved him back off without malice, checking everything she cared about and a bunch of other spots as well. The pickpocket had taught her to never check her purse first when she thought someone might have lifted her. It was an easy tactic, to run someone ahead to bump into people, seemingly drunk or unwell, and have every single one of them tell you where their purse was hidden so you could do a much more elegant lift of one after the next.

Everything was where it was supposed to be, and Stasia set out opposite Babe, making a wide loop of the block where she'd left Farang. She had her head up now, trying to mime sight-seeing and festival-going, but watching for other people who were there hunting.

There really *was* a lot of hunting going on, but the men she spotted at it were low-level predators, looking for the tipsy and the unware, lifting purses and shoving people into little niches where they could be more thoroughly removed of their valuables. They moved through the crowd like sand through water, intentional and visible, but only just. Stasia made open eye contact with one of them and he deferred course, letting her past with an air of awareness that she'd beat him at his game.

She came to the spot where she was meeting up with Babe and she bought a little roll with bits of frosting and decoration on it, finishing if halfway when he came into view. She offered it to him and he paused, devouring it in a single bite and with obvious pleasure.

"I guess we're not that worried?" Stasia asked, and he shook his head.

"No, the place is crawling with all sorts of problems, but I only spotted a couple men with the trainin' to take a man in. These things might be my favorite thing about Highwater Festival."

"How late do the boats run?" Stasia asked, getting out another coin to buy two more rolls. They really were pretty good.

"'Till most of dawn, why?" he asked.

"They weren't out last night," Stasia said. "And I can't promise I'd manage to get across again, if they stopped at dark."

He stopped chewing for a moment.

"What'd you do?" he asked, and she shook her head.

"I don't think I'd admit it to anybody who didn't see it," she said.

"Which bridge did you come across?" he asked.

"Second one on the green," Stasia said. "The Warbler was too deep."

He looked over at the crowds, then at her again and rolled his jaw to the side.

"Don't take much imaginin' to see that," he said, and she shook her head.

"I'm here," she said. "Didn't know at the time that you had it all under control."

He twisted his mouth and finished his bun.

"Two sets of eyes is a lot better off," he said. "I had no place to go and no plan. Relief to have you turn up, and that's no lie."

She sighed.

"Still," she said. "It could have waited."

He shook his head.

"Another ten minutes and I would've been gone," he said. "Couldn't afford to sit there and wait while they figured we weren't in the building and went looking outside. Day like today, don't know when you would have tracked us down again."

She frowned, then nodded.

"I think you would have been fine, but thanks for saying it."

He grinned and winked, then straightened, sticking his fingers in his mouth one by one to clean them, then wiping his hands briskly on his trousers.

"We need to go see what they've decided to do about the empty place," he said. "You feeling up to some climbing?"

She nodded easily.

"I like this cloak a lot," she said. "It's even better than my cape."

"Not too heavy?" Babe asked, and she shook her head.

"Not at all. Good cover when I'm climbing, but it doesn't get in the way of my feet."

He nodded, glancing around.

"Not as many quiet corners to go up, just now, but I think that's our next move. You get up high and start seeing what there is to look at. Watch out for rooftops with people on 'em. There are some where they can get to 'em, and they'll be watchin' the festival from up there, especially later in the day."

"How do I signal you?" Stasia asked.

He motioned to the hair wrap she'd tied around her waist.

"Put your hand over the side as you go along," he said. "You see somethin' I need to be cautious of, hold that and let it blow in the breeze."

She nodded, wondering if that was enough, but trusting him to take care of himself.

"And what's the goal?" she asked.

"We got a long day," he said. "Gotta get through the whole thing and be *ready* to move as the sun starts to set. Want to cross clean and want to be on our way on the other side without havin' to find a place to hide if we don't have to. We'll leave some time if we need it, but would prefer to duck into a cove somewhere 'tween here and there and just wait for the sun to finish settin'. No runnin' about. Means we need to know which sections of the river have eyes on 'em and what paths get us here to there. First step, to me, is figurin' out how many men are up at the apartment and whether they're spreadin' out to try to find us or figurin' they can track you down and find him again that way, another day."

Stasia nodded.

"All right."

He dipped his head to her and then set off. Stasia gave him a little bit of a lead, then followed, watching the crowds going by with wide attention, trying to look like someone who was just trying to take it all in.

If they saw her, and they knew what she looked like coming and going from the castle, they were going to recognize her. The cloak helped a lot, but if they caught the dragonskins, she was cooked. They'd come and grab her.

Would they?

She needed to think about that.

Maybe they would think that she would lead them back to Farang, and just try to follow her, which at least gave her an opportunity to flee.

Would they consider grabbing her and dragging her back to the castle to make her tell them where Farang was?

Why would that be tenable today and not yesterday? She was *around*, certainly, where they could find her if they wanted her.

They all knew where she lived.

No, they wouldn't do that because they didn't want to anger her father and… maybe even because they had no proof that she'd done anything wrong. It was always *possible* that they would refrain from arresting her because it was simply unjust. Stranger things had happened.

Though she considered it much more likely that they'd leave her alone because she talked to the queen sometimes.

Because in a city that held elves captive to make them teach them the secrets of magic, talking to the queen made a lot stronger defense than right and wrong.

Babe ducked into an alley and Stasia followed him. He grabbed her by the shoulder and slung her around himself and against the wall, shoving his elbow against the wall by her head and ducking his face down to hers.

"Sorry," he muttered. "One of the blacks saw me and showed too much interest when I went back here. Thought I'd cut off the road clean, but when you followed, he…"

There was a shadow across the mouth of the alley and Babe rolled his face down. The shadow went away and Babe glanced through his elbow to make sure the man was gone.

"Is that a dagger I've got poking me in the belly or does your cloak come with funny buttons?" he asked.

"Habits," Stasia answered. He laughed quietly and pushed himself off the wall and away from her while she put the dagger away again.

"And if I'd actually kissed you?" he asked.

"I probably would have *actually* stabbed you," Stasia answered. "At least a little bit."

He grinned.

"And that's why you're the woman for the job," he said. "Get up there and I'll follow along under. You know your way back to the first apartment from up high?"

"If I get it wrong, walk ahead where I can see you and then turn back," Stasia said. "It's different, up there."

"You ain't got no main roads to cross until we're close," he said. "Got some alleys, though."

"I ought to be able to jump them," Stasia said. "I don't remember anything I couldn't touch with both hands."

"That your length?" Babe asked, and she shrugged.

"I know I can do wider than that."

He shook his head.

"Remarkable. Well, no unnecessary risks," he said. "What we do got is time. Get it right, and if it takes makin' a new plan, so be it."

She nodded, looking the wall over, above her head. The morning angles of the sunlight weren't helping her any, but it wasn't *that* hard a climb.

"You want a boost?" he asked, and she gave him a dour look.

"Is that going to make *any* difference at what I'm about to do?"

He grinned.

"Hard not to offer," he said. "Just watchin' you do the hard part, like this. Makes me feel… heavy."

"That's your purpose," Stasia said, taking her first grip and testing it. "You have to come get me when I wash away."

She heard him laugh, but she was already climbing.

Her muscles were not *that* rejuvenated after the efforts the night before, but she wasn't doing anything that overtaxing, just now, and she went up the four stories of the first building without stopping to think about it.

She got to the top and shook her arms out then stretched her fingers and went to the front corner of the building to look below her.

She saw the top of Babe's head as he started down the road across from her, and she could see the various men in uniforms around. There were actually a lot of red leathers around, she noticed suddenly, and she wondered at that. Had the castle called in military backup to help track down the missing elf?

Would they even admit to *having* him to that many people?

As she watched, she realized that none of them were moving like they were *hunting* something.

Babe moved *funny*, but he wasn't searching for something specific. He was just... agitated. Slightly. And she might have been imagining it.

The reds, though, were casual. They were aware of the power their uniforms represented, and she could see the way they expected everyone to move out of their way as they went along, but they weren't *targeted*. They moved like they were just a part of the crowd, though a self-appointed *important* part of the crowd.

There, though.

The man with the blue cape over his shoulder, going from stall to stall and pawing through things without picking them up or even looking at them?

Stasia took the hair wrap off of her waist and put it out over the edge of the building, walking along the front edge and stepping over onto the next roof.

She knelt on the next roof and rested her chin on her hands, continuing to watch. Babe had been right that there were various roofs around that were occupied, and she needed to be careful not to draw attention to herself. Even to her own eyes, she looked like a burglar.

She watched the street for a while longer, not seeing anything more, and she went on, going up two more buildings and pausing before an alley jump to watch again.

Babe was leaning against a building drinking something out of a mug with his hat pushed down low over his eyes. That was *probably* a signal that he wasn't ready to move on again yet, and Stasia was content to just see what she could, from here.

Little by little, they worked their way back across the city. It wasn't that far, walking directly from one point to the next, but working her way from rooftop to rooftop, waiting every time Babe found something worth his interest and every time he had to deviate from her path in order to get rid of attention that he'd garnered, it took until the sun was well overhead to get back to the apartment that Farang had so recently vacated.

Stasia realized, lying on the roof of the last building she was planning on going to - anything else was too close for comfort, and lost visibility of the front of the building anyway - that she was perfectly comfortable sprawled on the roof on her stomach, watching the city and the festival go by below.

She should have been baking under her cloak, but the sun wasn't unpleasant at all, today.

Babe set off again finally, working his way through the crowd with Stasia following him, and then he turned into an alley and stopped. Stasia looked down at him and he tipped his head back to look up at her. He motioned her down with one hand and she scanned one last time, then set off down the wall again, relieved that her arms seemed much more prepared to hold her up, this time.

She got to the ground and Babe nodded.

"What was your count?" he asked.

"Six?" she asked. "The one at the first market stall, the two at the restaurant, the one coming out of the building where the woman was yelling at him, and the two out front of the apartment building down there?"

"Seven," he said. "There was another one watching people going by at a table about halfway along."

"They're looking for us," Stasia said, and he nodded.

"They are."

"I was hoping that they would give up and try to track him down through me again tomorrow," Stasia said and he shook his head.

"Not unreasonable," he said. "But no luck. They're looking, and we need to assume they're going to keep trying."

"So what next?" Stasia asked.

"Do you need a break?" he asked. "Or are you good to keep going?"

"I'm fine," she said, shaking out her fingers and bending them back on each hand. He gave her a skeptical look, but she shook her head and adjusted her cloak.

"I'm fine," she said again. "What's next?"

"Need to go scout the water," he said. "Figure out who's watching and where. Do that a couple times today to get a feel for how they're moving around."

"You think there are a bunch we missed?" Stasia asked, and he nodded.

"'Course," he said. "No way we saw 'em all, takin' the route we did. Fair chance we caught half or more, but there's at least twelve of 'em runnin' around in Highrock lookin' for the two of you and maybe me as well, and all they gotta do is see us once."

Stasia nodded.

"So let's go do it."

"We can stop and eat," he said. "If you need a rest. You ain't slept at all, last night, I figure, and goin' up a wall ain't nearly the same as walkin' up stairs. Rather you take your time and do it right than fall down on my head and kill us both, provin' you're solid."

She grinned and set off walking, enjoying the feel of the cloak trailing behind her but knowing that she needed to slow before she got into sight of the street, because her legs were showing, and above her boots, the dragonskin was just too characteristic.

"Should I try to change?" Stasia asked over her shoulder.

"Can you climb in anything else?" Babe asked, and she shrugged.

"Leather leggings are fine," she said. "But I would need a shirt to go with."

"And something to carry all your weapons in, beside," he said. "I think where you are is our best plan."

She nodded. She thought so, too, but she'd wanted to ask.

She glanced back at him once more, then stepped out onto the street.

Where the man was waiting for her.

The next series of motions was… confused, even in retrospect.

Something hit her from the side, her arms pinned to her side, the world shifting rapidly. Was she falling? Being pushed? Spun? All she knew was that her head jolted to the side and she'd closed her eyes against the way the world hadn't made sense. Had her eyes been open? Probably, but she wasn't seeing through them.

Then she hit a wall. Something had changed. She had a dagger in her hand and she was prepared to *do* something with it, but the way that her arms had been pinned had changed, and there wasn't a threat to go after anymore. She might have actually knocked her head against the wall pretty good, except that her hair was so thick, and she'd managed to hit the wall with the thickest part of her tail, such that she never actually felt the stone. Just the way her hair tie dug into her scalp for a moment, and then she was holding the back of her head in a senseless attempt to explain to herself why her head didn't hurt.

"Moving," Babe said. "Moving."

"What?" Stasia asked, looking over her shoulder. There had been noises, she realized, listening to them again.

Violent ones.

"Did I stab someone?" Stasia asked, looking down at her dagger to see if there was blood on it.

"Just a little bit," Babe said. "Least of his worries. Leathers took the worst of it."

"I just stabbed a palace guard?" Stasia hissed and he grabbed both of her shoulders to keep her moving forward still.

"He weren't in uniform," Babe said. "Wearin' it under his clothes don't count. You thought you was bein' attacked by a bad man in the Highrock district and you defended yourself."

"Just how *vigorously* did I defend myself?" Stasia asked, trying to figure out what to do with the dagger. Surely she didn't just sheathe it again.

Babe took it and wiped it off on his pants, handing it back to her wordlessly. She put it away again.

"What happens now?" Stasia asked.

There was a shout behind them, and Babe dodged her around a corner into an alley.

"Now we run," he said. "You good?"

"I'm good," Stasia said, shaken, but her legs keen to release the sudden jolt of energy surging up and down her body. Babe nodded.

"C'mon," he said. "Move."

She ran after him, rounding a corner and running into a woman carrying stacks of cloth.

"Move," Babe bellowed as Stasia disentangled herself from the woman, running after him faster. He rounded another corner and Stasia followed, running flat into his back and falling down.

There were four men in this alley, and none of them had nice shoes on.

They were dividing up loot, by the looks of it, and they didn't appreciate being interrupted.

"What'd'you think you're doing?" the tallest of the men asked.

"Just takin' a short cut," Babe answered.

The way Babe spoke was different. Just his normal, everyday speech. Stasia suspected that it was somehow characteristic, though she hadn't heard any trace of the accent on Lord Westhauser, who was theoretically from the same place in town… That made no sense, did it? She still didn't understand *any* of this.

But what she did recognize was the way the tall man reacted to Babe's speech.

He strode forward and snatched the scarf from around Babe's neck, tipping his head back as though he'd known what he was going to find there.

"He's a rat," one of the other men said.

"Sharp crew you run with," Stasia murmured.

"Look, just out enjoying the Highwater Festival," Babe said, putting up both hands. "My girl's from around here, and I ended up on this side of the river. Didn't mean no offense."

"Rats are okay with us, now, right?" said another of the young men. The tall one shook his head.

"Not when nobody's looking, they aren't," he answered.

"You don't want to start nothin'," Babe said. "Get the lot of us in trouble. Not on highwater day. Too much money runnin' around to take from the people out there."

"Of course you don't want trouble," the tall man said.

Stasia could hear footsteps approaching behind them.

Babe sighed.

"Last chance," he said. "Walk away or I will."

"What?" the dumb one from the group said, and the tall man shook his head.

"Oh, you're not going to walk away from this, and neither is your girl."

He looked at Stasia with an evaluating eye, and Stasia closed both her hands around her daggers - the longer, fighting daggers that Babe had given her.

They had knives, but none of them were armed with true weapons.

She didn't *want* to cut her way through them, but if the alternative was submitting herself to *that*, she wouldn't even feel regret.

Babe sighed again.

"Step through," he said, and for an instant, Stasia wasn't sure what that meant.

And then he cleared a hole through the men.

The tall one, he grabbed and threw him sideways into the wall, then he took two big strides and punched the dumb one in the face. He lifted his other arm to catch both of the other men and push them against the wall, and Stasia stepped through the gap in the middle, not turning back as she went to the line of bright light where the street lined up with the ever-higher sun. Here before too long even the alleys would be lit.

"Ain't got a problem with you," she heard Babe said. "You need your face broke to prove you're crew?"

"Nope," said one.

"No," said the other.

"Run that way," Babe said.

Stasia heard their feet retreat, and then Babe was standing next to her.

"You won a lot of fights when you were a kid, didn't you?"

"Bein' at the fort put a good fifty pounds on me," he said. "Hadn't had enough to eat my whole life. But I won more than I lost."

Stasia nodded.

"You good?"

"Feel sorry for 'em," Babe answered, grabbing her elbow and turning out into the crowd.

They steered through to the thickest section of crowd and then slowed, Stasia picking up a conversation with a pair of women about what the castle was doing this year to mark the Highwater Festival.

Unlike many of the other festivals, apparently, the Highwater Festival was different every year, how the queen celebrated it, and it was always the talk of the city the next day as the newspapers reported it.

Stasia paused to buy a new scarf for Babe, and he stood, tying it, as a pair of men came running down the street through the crowd, scanning faces.

Stasia turned away, but Babe grabbed her elbow again, shoving her into the back of the shop and through to a little alley behind that Stasia hadn't even noticed.

He shoved at a door and it opened, and he put her through into a little vestibule with three doors and a stairway off of it.

They were trapped, here, if the palace guard decided to check building by building, but Stasia couldn't see any way that they would have the people to do it. Not with the sheer size of Highrock and the fact that they'd lost side of Stasia and Babe for long enough that they might have just kept running in literally any direction, from here.

Babe pushed the door closed and motioned.

"Stairs," he said.

Stasia followed his direction, even though she doubted whether this was the best plan - were they going to break in to one of the apartments up here? - leading the way up the stairs on quiet feet.

"What are they planning on doing if they catch us?" Stasia whispered as they rounded the second flight of stairs.

"They can't admit what they're doing here," Babe answered quietly. "No one will say it out loud. Means if they catch us, they're gonna do anything they can think of to make us talk, and then they make us disappear."

Stasia stopped dead.

"What?" she demanded, and he shrugged.

"What did you think they were gonna do?" he asked. "Walk you back to the castle for the queen to lift you out and send you home again?"

"I…" Stasia started, struggling to contain the sense of betrayal in mere words. "I thought this was a *better* place than that."

"Most units of palace guard wouldn't think of it," Babe said. "Feud with Jasper or not. But there are a few that are put together for doin' stuff most people can't open their eyes to, and Petrault lets 'em do as they're told and not report back. Some of the court use 'em for stuff the king'd string 'em all up for, if we could ever prove it."

"Then let's do it," Stasia demanded. "Why are we chasing around petty thieves in the market if *that's* going on?"

"Believe it or not, there are more important things to do," Babe said, passing her and taking the lead at the next landing. "And Jasper wants to keep you alive. Mixin' you up with the special guard weren't ever his expectation."

Stasia huffed at this, but followed him up again. He hit a door at the top of the stairs and opened it, going out onto a rooftop. There were three families up here, looking out over the city and the Green River sprawling through the buildings visible for blocks and blocks from here.

"Hey," said a boy. "Who are they?"

His mother hushed him, and Babe took Stasia's arm, walking her over to the corner of the rooftop furthest from the river. They peeked over, but the crowd was now too thick to pick anyone out. Everyone was milling and moving faster and faster.

"Lunch time," Babe said. "From here, they get drunk, too."

"Half the city is underwater," Stasia said. "How do we get across?"

"I got an idea, but it's a bad one," Babe said.

"Better than my none," Stasia answered.

"You can climb," Babe said. "And I know this part of town. Most of the palace guard, most of the guard at all, are taken out of the more… established class of folk around town. They don't come from Highrock, and when they do, they come from Greater Highrock. I'm thinkin' maybe we draw 'em down further and further south, go pick up one or two of 'em, take 'em on a little run, then disappear again. They check in with each other, figure out which way we're goin', make to head us off on our way to the ports."

That *would* be one way to get an elf out of Verida.

"So we risk getting caught and disappeared over and over again so that they're all looking for us in one direction…"

"Then we sneak past 'em, come get our friend, and cross on a boat easy as you like."

"Easy as you like," Stasia said, and he nodded.

"No reason anybody would be watchin' for him to go north from here, across the Green, would they?" Babe asked. "You ain't never set up lodgin' up there, have you?"

Stasia shook her head.

"It's not very common to find something for rent," she said, and he shook his head.

"Right. So if we're tryin' to hide him again, we go someplace you've got ready, like we done, but that's gonna be across the Wolfram or across the South Paw, maybe into Cazian territory. I bet they got twelve elves living down there with the Cazians already. Everybody's crazy, anyway."

Stasia considered it for a moment, then nodded.

"I see it," she said. "We've got to move him when no one can spot him in a crowd. Which means that we need to control where they're all looking."

He nodded.

"Yeah."

She nodded back.

"Let's do it."

It had seemed like it might be fun, at first.

Babe would find an exit, and then Stasia would set off looking for one of the men. The first one had taken her by surprise, and she hadn't liked that at all, but now she was watching for them more actively, and there was a victory at finding one of them. She'd do something innocuous, shop or buy a bit of food, maybe stand talking to a vendor or just a stranger on the street celebrating the Highwater Festival, and then there would be shouting and running and Stasia would lead them through the crowds for perhaps a quarter mile, and then she would disappear by one cunning trick or another.

Babe was right that he knew this part of the city. He could tell by looking at a set of windows and doorways whether a building would have roof access, and he once found a building with both roof access *and* a window in the stairwell, and she had literally climbed up to where he was waiting for her, ducked through the window, and then gone up onto the roof with him to go across to the other side of the block, where the guard couldn't see or reach them without going a *long* way around, and they went down another set of unconcerned stairs.

He had a dozen other tricks just like it.

As they went further south, there were fewer and fewer people out - not none, anywhere, but smaller crowds, and fewer of them on the roofs. Babe told her that they preferred to go north where the better vendors and the better street performers would be. Sometime in the early afternoon, he said, the street performers would get going, and they would make two or three months' wages on the day. Verida loved their street performers, and prided themselves on keeping them in the trade, year in and year out.

The clever way that he set up their exits was exciting.

Running away from men who would apparently gladly kill her was exciting, as she knew she was going to get away.

Avoiding the street kids who were increasingly violent and angry was… hard, but it appeared that most of the able-bodied men who were a part of the Highrock family had gone north to steal from the festival goers, leaving mere children to menace Babe for being in the wrong place with the wrong accent.

Babe would menace them back, and they would scatter, but Babe worried about one of them realizing that the palace guard were after them and turning themselves into a tracking web, feeding information to the guard.

"They don't like the guard," he said. "But they'd do it for spite. Highrock has got nothin' if they don't got spite."

Finally, as the sun began to set that evening, they found themselves within smelling range of the ocean.

The problem was that the palace guard had accurately guessed that they were headed for a specific bridge - as designed, yes - but they had an effective net of men searching for them and blocking the streets, and the Highrock children had become too much of a potential threat.

They were stuck, sitting at a window one level below a rooftop, waiting for one of the guards to make a mistake and leave them a hole to sneak out through.

They'd already been here an hour, and Stasia was feeling stressed about making it on time to the meet with Lord Westhauser.

Babe was more focused on getting out at all.

"So you got a boyfriend back home?" he asked, throwing random questions at her from time to time as though to distract her. "Some young man whose heart you broke when you came here?"

"No," Stasia said. "No, I've known for most of my life I never wanted to marry, so boys were always… rather pointless."

Babe snorted.

"I resent that," he said cheerfully, and she shook her head.

"I didn't live in Boton," she said. "I lived in Birch, where all of the young men were looking to their family's interests when they considered marriage. I had one friend who fell in love, but he was her age, and her parents decided to promise her to someone else, because her choice wouldn't be fit to run a family for several more years, and she was at her prime age for a marriage of economic alliance."

"See I've never got that," Babe said. "Why is it that rich girls and noble girls marry when they're twelve or thirteen, and get themselves married to men in their twenties? Ain't right."

"They don't marry at twelve," Stasia said dismissively. "The earliest any of my friends married was sixteen. Yes, the men marry in their early twenties, but that's because they're finishing their studies and beginning their careers, and that is the proper time to wed and cement your alliances."

"And you lot call us animals," Babe muttered.

"I've never implied anything of the sort," Stasia said.

"Marrying off your daughters to adult men," Babe said. "Because the men have power and money. Can't see how you take it so lightly."

Stasia frowned and considered that.

"At sixteen, I was a woman, same as all of my friends," Stasia said.

"And at, what are you now, twenty-one, twenty-two, you're *too old* to marry?" Babe asked. "When that's the *youngest* you would have taken on a wife?"

Stasia smiled a soft laugh at that and shrugged.

"I'm twenty three," she said. "And, okay, I'll see your point there, too. There are just so many duties for a woman that are better if she sets to work on them young."

"You actually believe that, or you just sayin' what you been told?" Babe asked.

She looked over at him.

"You think a woman is better off if she is beginning to learn how to run a household *and* bear children at twenty-two?"

He shrugged.

"Plenty of women I known who done that, and worked a job 'a their own."

Stasia considered for several moments, then shook her head.

"It's no different here than in Boton," she said. "The women marry young, and it was Matthias himself who called me a spinstress, wasn't it? The men marry older."

"Among the nobles, sure enough," Babe said. "And Matthias is an idiot. Shouldn't take too much of what he says to heart."

"What is it like, for the poor?" Stasia asked.

"They say it's right for an older boy to marry a younger girl, because girls come of age younger, that that's the way it's s'posed to be," he said, looking out the window again with a frown. Still more men out and about. They'd cornered themselves. "But there's plenty of folk who just do as they please. Man can provide for a wife and kids, and she chooses him, mostly we all figure ain't none of our business. Parents are happy for a girl to go to a man who ain't gonna beat or cheat, man's family for him to be with a girl who ain't drunk or vacant. Age ain't got near so much to do with it."

"You ever have a girl?" Stasia asked. "Someone you grew up with, if things had been different?"

He glanced over.

"Two or three," he said. "I weren't the type that a family would have welcomed, in those days, and the girls themselves knew better, too. Ran with the street gangs, stole some, hurt some people what didn't have it comin'. None of the girls were the type I'd look in on again after I signed up with the reds. Assume they got on about as well as anybody down at the Black Docks does."

"You don't think about them?" Stasia asked, and he shook his head.

"I got a life, now," he said. "Not the same person I was back then. They wouldn't even know me, to look at me, and I wouldn't, them, either."

"I'm sorry," Stasia said, and the corner of his mouth came up.

"Not a loss," he said. "The life I had back then weren't worth holding onto, and I don't."

Stasia was disoriented. What did it *mean*?

It meant nothing.

They were talking of nothing.

She shook her head.

"We need to go soon if we're going to make it," she said.

He nodded.

"I know it. Think we're just gonna have to risk it. Got time to recover, if they spot us, but don't have the space to set something up. Think we just gotta go. You feelin' ready for a run?"

In truth, Stasia was exhausted, but she nodded.

"I'm going to sleep for two days after this," she said.

"Assuming we find our beds again," he said. "I think this is our best window. You ready?"

She stood and he unfolded himself from the floor in front of the window.

"Ssst," someone hissed, and Stasia turned to find a small boy standing in a doorway. "You hidin' from the takers?"

"Takers?" Stasia asked.

"It's a local word for anyone who hauls off people for legal or political offenses," Babe murmured. Stasia looked at the boy again.

"What if we are?" she asked.

"How long can you hold your breath?" the boy asked. Stasia frowned.

"What do you mean?" she asked. The boy looked over his shoulder into the apartment, then slipped through the gap in the door and closed it behind him.

"Come with me?" he whispered, going down to the bottom floor of the building and pausing at a door there.

"You're not from around here," he said to Stasia, and she shook her head.

"No."

"But he is," the kid said.

"Grew up in a place a lot like this one," Babe said. The kid nodded.

"You'll start hitting waves before you get out," the kid said. "Tunnel's above water, this time of day, but not for long."

Stasia looked at Babe, who nodded.

"Highrock was some of the oldest city, had some early efforts at drainin' water off the hill. Lot of effort, not much result, but where they ain't collapsed, they use 'em around here to get around unseen." He looked at the kid. "Rather go inland than out. Pipe go both ways?"

The kid nodded.

"Building three down, that way," he pointed. Babe nodded, reaching into his pocket and taking out a jagger. "Might have saved a couple lives today."

Kid shrugged.

"Just hate the takers," he said, tucking the jagger away and disappearing up the stairs. Babe opened the door and stepped through. Stasia followed him into a small, windowless space that smelled of mold. He worked at the floor for a moment, then something creaked.

"No light down here," he said. "You good for this?"

"I'm fine," Stasia said, and he shifted.

"Hand."

"What?"

"Give me your hand."

Stasia waved her hand around in the darkness, connecting with his face. He snorted and grabbed hold of her hand, then her elbow with his other hand.

"Watch your step," he said, edging her sideways around the little room. "Sit."

She knelt and found the hole in the floor, then put her feet down into it.

"What am I expecting?" she asked.

"Ceramic pipe, about a three feet wide. Probably water in it from the storm last night. No more'n a few inches, I expect."

She nodded, the fingers of her free hand finding broken pottery. She slid down, her boots finding the curved surface underneath, and she knelt. Three feet was generous.

"Are you going to fit through this?" she asked.

"I'm not a *horse*," Babe said. "How big you think I am?"

Stasia knelt, finding it difficult to crawl through the space with her feet underneath her.

"I mean, you're not going to *plug* it, but this isn't going to be any fun."

"Hey, if I get out alive, I'm happy," he said. "Get movin'. We ain't got any time to waste."

She nodded into the darkness, shifting along foot over foot, her shoulders pressed against her knees. She heard Babe slide down behind her and the trap door close. It was all just auditory; there was no light to go on.

"Okay, this is tight," Babe said. "Small one."

"You've been in these before?" Stasia asked.

"Never without light," he said. "I'm gonna have a heck of a time makin' it backwards if we gotta double back. You should go ahead a ways to make sure it goes through."

"You're going to *wriggle* that far," Stasia said, shaking her head.

"Just keep goin'," Babe said. Stasia dropped her knees to crawl. The bottom of the pipe was littered with stuff. Some of it was sharp and felt like it might have been broken pottery, but mostly it was the heavier part of dirt that came off of the streets, anything that wouldn't wash away in a heavy rain. Once more, she was glad for how easily her dragonskins shed debris and for the fact that she wasn't worried about cutting open her knees on any of it.

She came to a clot of broken pottery where the dirt and filth had built up behind it, and she tried to look over her shoulder, little good though that would have done her.

"It's about a third of the way filled up here," she said, pulling at the pottery with her hands and letting the dirt slide past it with a bit of pent-up water. "Sorry."

"Should be gettin' close," he said. "You'll know you're there when you feel the air open up over your head."

She knew exactly what he meant by that, actually. The air down here was… clean-ish, really. It smelled of mud and of rot, but not of the disgusting things of humanity just above her head. It was humid, but it wasn't overwhelmingly *hot*. But it was breathless. And she had a sense that when the pipe finally opened up over top of her again, she would know it at the first breath.

There was nothing more to do for Babe with the clot of grime in the pipe, and she moved on, on her elbows over top of it and worried once more that he would get stuck, but she couldn't help him.

Another dozen yards along, give or take, she felt the air lift over her head and she stood, taking two big breaths of open air before squatting to look back down the pipe.

"We're here," she said. "How are you?"

He grunted.

She twisted her mouth, thinking about climbing up to see if she could open the trap door, or at least find a place to sit, but sitting down cross-legged instead to wait for him.

"Is there anything I can do?" Stasia asked.

"Keep talkin' to me," he said. "Lets me know how much further I have to go."

"Are you okay?" she asked.

He grunted again, but this time it was half-laugh.

"Appreciate it if you didn't tell the guys about this part," he said. "Thought this'd be simple enough, but I ain't been in one of these pipes since I was a kid, and I remember 'em a lot bigger."

"You get yourself killed later, I'll give them a detailed, moment-by-moment description of the whole thing," she said. "See if I don't."

He laughed like it cost him something, as though he'd quit moving to enjoy the humor of it, then his air went tight again and he was moving again.

"I'll see *to* it that you don't," he answered.

"You think we're far enough away?" Stasia asked.

"I think every house along is a help," he answered. "Pipe go on from here?"

"Don't know," Stasia said. "You want me to check?"

"Nope," he grunted. "Kid knew it would get us here. Didn't say more. These things buckle all the time, get filled in with dirt and left to rot. No tellin' how far you'd go before you found you had to back your way out, or if it'd collapse on you again before you worked out it was broke. We'll take our chances from here."

He was getting close.

"You gonna be fit to run from here?" she teased.

"Think I gotta be, if I'm gonna keep you from tellin' Colin about it," he answered with humor.

"There's the spirit," Stasia said.

"Listen for feet," Babe said. "Even people good at ambush have a hard time keepin' their feet still."

Stasia nodded, closing her eyes.

It didn't change anything, for what she could *see*, but somehow it signaled to her brain that she was *listening* rather than looking.

About a minute later, Babe's huffing got close enough that Stasia stood to make space for him.

Realizing that the hole in the pipe really wasn't quite big enough for both of them to stand there while he worked out the trap door - not modestly, at any rate, Stasia knelt.

"Back up just a couple inches, there," she said. "Let me go on, so that you can be the first one to go up."

"Good thinkin'," he said, shuffling back. Stasia dropped her back and her shoulders, scooting backwards down the pipe facing the opposite direction she had been before, and she heard him shift and eventually stand.

There was a long, slow breath as he decompressed, then the sound of a dagger drawn out of a leather sheath, a noise that was only audible in absolute silence, and then that of hinges further overhead.

"Well, if they're up there, they're disciplined," Babe said. "I don't hear nothin'."

"You waiting to see if they cut your throat when you come up?" Stasia asked.

"Either that or make a fool of myself swingin' a blade around at an empty room," he answered.

"Your choice," Stasia said, and she heard him laugh softly.

"Come on up," he told her.

His feet left the pipe ahead of her and she followed into the open space, finding his hand at about face level and taking it.

"You do remember I've been climbing buildings all night," she said as he literally lifted her up onto the floor next to him. "I'm perfectly capable of doing that on my own."

"Makes me feel like I'm carrin' my own weight better," he answered cheerfully. "Shall we go see whether makin' a break for it is the right plan?"

"Don't know any better way to do it," Stasia answered. He stood and patted around on the walls until he found a door and cracked it open.

The light inside the building would have been dim at midday, and the sun was rapidly approaching the horizon at this point. Even so, the light from outside that room was almost blinding. Stasia blinked at it hard, trying to adjust, and Babe opened the door the rest of the way.

"Gonna go check the front," he said. "Close this after you."

"Right behind you," Stasia said, rolling onto her feet and going out the door.

She stretched for a moment in the hallway, bending her back as far as it easily went to either side, and then tipping forward to wrap her arms around her knees.

"All right," Babe said from the front door of the building. "Now, we ain't *literally* runnin' from here. There's an alley along the way on the right that I think is our best bet to move north, and we only move *fast* when we're exposed."

"We need to move *fast* until we get to the river," Stasia answered. "We're going to be late."

"Once we get to the crowds, we can do more as we like," Babe said. "Don't want to draw attention, here. Move natural and get into cover. Right?"

"I'm with you," Stasia said. "Not going to run off on my own. Hood up or down?"

He considered that for a moment, then nodded.

"I think let's have it up for now. Not sure it's gonna help or hurt more."

She nodded, going to stand behind him.

Lifting his head as a cue, he went out the door and turned north. Stasia followed him, pushing the door closed behind her and walking along the narrow street with him.

It was one of those streets that curved as it went along, mostly without breaks in the houses. Stasia could have gone a long way up on the roofs here, but this stretch didn't have any stairways that went up to the roof, and there was no way for Babe to get up there.

"They get close to surroundin' us, you cut loose and get away," Babe said. "Same as you would in a bar fight. If you go up, they ain't like to be able to chase you."

"Don't like abandoning you," Stasia answered. He shrugged.

"Rather one of us survive than neither," he answered. "If you're quick about it, you might be able to get word to Jasper what happened to me, and he might have means to help."

"You're lying to me to give me a better excuse, aren't you?" Stasia asked, and he grinned.

"Is it workin'?"

They turned into an alley and sped up a bit, still walking, but taking longer, faster strides. Stasia's cloak drifted along behind her.

"They think we were headed to the shore," Babe said softly. "If that's worked, we ought to be out of range of 'em in another few minutes."

Stasia nodded.

"Hold your breath," she said.

"Either it's worked or it ain't," Babe agreed. "Took the risk."

"It was a good trick," Stasia said, and he nodded.

"I think so, too."

⎯⎯•⇔•❖•⇔•⎯⎯

Block by block, Stasia began breathing more normally.

There were no voices behind them, no one shouting for them to stop.

They cut across minor roads and found new chains of alleys, some so narrow that Stasia had to turn sideways to fit without touching the sides, and Babe literally squeezed through.

"What are these for?" she demanded after the third such squeeze.

"Property rights," Babe said. "Exactly where the line is is disputed, so neither side can build all the way up to it. They build as close as they can get without the other guy threatenin' to tear down the building for bein' over the line."

"They could save an entire *wall*," Stasia said. "Why would they do that?"

"People are petty," Babe answered simply, and Stasia couldn't find any argument with that.

The alleys were deep-dark by the time they heard the sounds of crowds and Babe signaled that they would walk on larger streets from here.

"Late, late, late," Stasia murmured.

"They won't leave without the guest of honor," Babe answered. "Keep movin'. We've still got a shot at this."

She went to the apartment where she'd left Farang while Babe kept watch, waving at the window as she went past and hoping that he could actually see her, and that if he *could* see her that he was actually still watching. She'd never planned on being gone *this* long.

Farang opened the door without her knock, dipping his head.

"I assume you aren't coming in," he said as he started out toward her. She shook her head quickly.

"No. No, we're ready to go if you are."

The elf dipped his head again and closed the door. Stasia went back out onto the street, spotting Babe and following him through the crowd.

This time, they were moving with the crowd toward the water, and the voices were louder and tipsier and more celebratory than they had been earlier in the day.

"Has everything gone as expected?" Farang asked.

"I think *expected* might be a bit aspirational, but I'm optimistic, so long as we haven't run out of time," Stasia told him. He nodded as though that were a reasonable answer.

Stasia disagreed, but that seemed counter-productive.

They were wading through ankle-deep water before very long at all, and the crowds were still thick a long way ahead of them. Men carried torches and the street lamps were lit, which gave the crowd a merry orange glow, so at least she could follow the back of Babe's head with reliable consistency. He looked back at her from time to time to check on her, so she was certain that she didn't have the wrong head, either.

There were a lot of red uniforms around, and a few black ones, but no one seemed that interested in a very tall blond man and the woman next to him in purple dragonskins, so at least there was that.

Finally, the crowd began to thin as the water got to knee deep - and Stasia's boots flooded yet *again* - and Stasia saw Babe ahead negotiating with a poleboat man.

What good a poleboat was going to do against the speed of current out in the middle of the river, Stasia had no clue, but there were enough of them around to suggest that they weren't pointless.

She dug into her purse as Babe and the man shook hands.

"Ready to go," Babe said to her as she and Farang got there, and she handed him a stack of coins.

"You deal with that," she said. "I'm tired."

The world was beginning to bewilder her, in fact. That her own feet managed to catch her on each step was remarkable, and at points that had been all she'd been aware of, on the way here. Farang's presence had sharpened her awareness for a bit, but her eyes were glazing again, fixating on flames and reflections rather than on people, and she just wanted to sit and let someone else take care of it from now on.

That wasn't possible, but she wasn't too proud to admit it was what she *wanted.*

She sat down in the boat as Farang arranged himself up on the front point, trailing a hand in the water and watching with rapt attention the crowds visible along the road. There was another block of buildings to go, but there on the street, the front fringes of the crowd was visible for a long way in either direction.

"Ought to see the castle, this time of night," Babe observed, sitting down next to Stasia as the poleman pocketed his money and began to push them through a gap between buildings.

"The reverence is… authentic," Farang answered.

"You bet it is," Babe answered.

The boat bumped and scuffed on the road surface a few times as they went along, at first, but then the cross-currents of the river proper took hold and the depth increased, and they were out on the open river, past the last line of buildings, where the poleman was having a hard time controlling the boat.

And then Stasia saw them.

The ropes.

She'd expected them, the night before, and not found them, but they were out, now, and the poleman grabbed hold of one of the heavy ropes, pulling them across with it. Maybe they *had* been here, and she hadn't noticed, because they were so high above the water.

She couldn't be sure.

She just marveled at them, up where a man had to stand tall to reach them at shoulder level, so a boat going downriver could have gone under without a problem.

"Going upriver, they stick to the shallows," Babe told her.

That made sense.

They reached the point where the boatman switched back over to poling on the far side of the river, and a few minutes later they began bumping cobblestones again.

"Thank you, sir," Babe said, standing and shaking hands with the man again, and they were moving.

"Where's the bridge?" Stasia asked, looking back out at the water. Babe gave her a strange look and pointed at the party going on in the middle of the river.

"Oh."

They waded against the current and into thicker and thicker crowds, then turned away from the river on the bridge street, turning as Lord Westhauser had indicated.

"Give me five minutes," Babe said to her as he disappeared. She nodded, glancing at Farang.

"All of this for the river," he said, and she shrugged.

"Why is that important?" she asked.

"They have no idea," he said.

"No idea of what?" Stasia asked.

"Is it because of the magic in the water that they celebrate, or do they just know there's *something* special about it, but couldn't say what?"

"I still choose to believe that they're celebrating the day the river stops trying to kill them for the year," Stasia said, and the corner of Farang's mouth came up.

Humor?

Had she proven its existence?

She couldn't be sure.

"You are new to the city, are you not?" he asked.

"Absolutely," she said.

"It is why you don't hate me," he said, and she nodded easily.

"Probably."

"It's also why you don't understand the river," he said. "They drink of it every day from their birth. It is *within* them, and they don't even know it. We think of them as parasites, but… I think that we may have been mistaken."

"Well, that sounds like a useful insight," Stasia said, and he gave her a grim smile.

"If only I had a method of sharing it with anyone *else* who might find it useful," he said.

"I'm sorry," Stasia said, and he shook his head.

"No," he said. "Life is long and unexpected. I do not write off any possibility except that of going home."

She looked up at him with pity and he ignored her.

Babe returned and nodded.

"I don't see nobody watchin' careful 'tween here and there," he said. "Move easy, but we should be set to go."

She nodded.

"I'll go first," she said. He narrowed his eyes at her and she shrugged.

"You didn't go through the door," she said. "If someone is going to tip their hand at the last second, you'll be the one to see it, and that will be when it happens. I'll go first."

He nodded and she set off.

One foot in front of the other.

She went down to the bar in question and up the exposed side stairs to the residential door above the bar.

Without looking over her shoulder - that was what Babe was there to do - she went through it.

There were a pair of lamps on the wall to either side, and a pair of doors just further along.

It was a cheerful, dry, clean hallway with a rug on the floor to muffle footsteps. Ahead of her was a set of straight stairs up to the third floor, and the stairs were actually carpeted.

Stasia dashed up them on light feet, peering around, but found no ambush waiting for them up there, either.

Had they made it?

Was it over?

Could she sit in a corner and sleep while the grownups did the rest of the work?

"There you are," Jasper said, sticking his head out a door. "Where are the others?"

Stasia closed her eyes and sighed.

A moment later, before she could have even answered, the residential door opened again and footsteps that could have only been Babe's came in. She looked over at Farang and then up at Jasper.

"It's been a long day," she said.

"It looks like it," Jasper answered. "But it isn't done yet. Come up."

She went up the rest of the stairs again, Babe and Farang following. Jasper held a door open for her and they went into a room with a merry fire and a large red-and-black rug on the floor.

She saw Lady Westhauser sitting in a corner reading a book, then she found Lord Westhauser on another wall with a stack of newspapers on an end table next to him.

"Good," Lord Westhauser said. "We'd begun to despair."

"The palace guard had raided the apartment by the time I got there," Stasia said to Jasper. "Babe got them out and waited for me, but we've been dodging them all day."

"I'd worried about that," Jasper said. "I'm glad you were both there."

"Took both of us," Babe agreed, settling down into a chair.

"Babe, I don't think you've met Lord Westhauser," Jasper said evenly, something in his tone anticipating exactly the reaction he got.

"What?" Babe asked, jolting back to his feet. "No. Nobody told me *he* had a hand in this. Ain't no way I'm goin' along with a Rat scheme."

"I thought you *were* a Rat," Stasia said, confused, and he shook his head violently.

"No, I'm from the Black Docks," he said. "Left before this madman took over. I got a lotta friends dead because of that man, and I ain't gonna sit in a room with him. Jasper."

"I'm not going to pretend that I wasn't glad you weren't there when we made the decision," Jasper said. Lord Westhauser looked remarkably unperturbed by the outburst, but Stasia was still confused.

"You're from the Black Docks," the nobleman said, recrossing his legs. "Joined the army before my time, I assume."

"Only way out that ain't to sea," Babe snarled. 'To sea' was a euphemism, Stasia gleaned.

"Have you been back since?" Lord Westhauser asked.

"Don't care to see what you done with the place," Babe said.

"It's better," Lady Westhauser said from the corner. Babe's eyes darted over to look at her, and he shook his head.

"Your brother ought be ashamed, marrying you to this murderer," Babe said.

"Okay, now *what*?" Stasia asked. "What is *going on*?"

"Babe," Jasper said, his voice even and firm. "This is the solution I have chosen. I know that you are not in uniform, but I still expect your loyalty to my direction. Is that clear?"

"Yes, sir," Babe said sullenly.

"Very good," Jasper said. "Lord Westhauser, this is your new charge."

"Faris," Stasia said. "Faris Horne."

The room turned to look at her, Farang with perhaps the least curiosity of all. Stasia shook her head.

"We need to break all continuity," she said. "Including continuity of name."

"So you link him to yourself instead," Lord Westhauser said, bemused. Farang dipped his head.

"What of this name is yours?" he asked.

"Horne," Stasia said. "It was my mother's."

He nodded slowly, then straightened.

"I am Faris Horne," he said, his voice, his accent changing. "I am from Altan, abandoned by my family, and I have come to Verida for a new life. All I want is a chance to live quietly and by the labor of my own hands."

Lord Westhauser frowned, then nodded.

"That will do," he said. "Now, as to the terms of this. This is my wife, Hidalga. I require that you fix her eyes."

Farang came to stand in front of Lady Westhauser, tipping his head slowly from one side to the other.

"She is… unusual," he said, and Lady Westhauser nodded.

"I am."

"May I?" Farang asked, asking for her hand with an open palm. She lifted her hand into his and he closed his other hand over top of hers, closing his eyes for a moment.

"Who you are is embedded deeply within you," Farang said after a moment. "You aren't rejecting it."

"No," Lady Westhauser agreed simply.

He let her hand drop gently and reached to touch her glasses.

"May I?" he asked.

She took them off and handed them to him easily, taking half a step back as he twisted them gently between two fingers in the light.

"This is all?" he asked. "There is no more ailment than this?"

"No," Lady Westhauser said.

"Then it is both simpler and much more complex. This is not an illness. Your body does not fight it, and apparently neither does your mind. Perhaps if you went without glasses for a time, it would be easier…"

"No," both Lord and Lady Westhauser said at once.

"I can't do that," Lady Westhauser said. "I'm virtually blind without them."

Farang dipped his head.

"Exactly. All the same, I will do what I can."

He turned to Babe, who produced a small leather bag from his belt. Farang took out two even smaller bags from under his cloak and went to sit at a table.

The room leaned in to watch, but Stasia only saw him pour simple herbs out of all three bags and push them around on the table with his finger.

He rose, leaving the herbs sitting on the polished wooden surface, and came to stand in front of Lady Westhauser again.

"Close your eyes," he said, putting his hands out to either side of her face. She closed her eyes and he put his fingertips to her skin, his thumbs floating just in front of her eyes.

Stasia wanted *something* to happen.

Magic words.

An incantation, even better.

A poof of powder or potion or *something*.

But that wasn't how it went.

Instead, Farang dropped his hands and stepped back.

"That is what I can do," he said.

Lady Westhauser opened her eyes and gasped.

Where her eyes had been the color of frost, only just *barely* bluer than the whites of her eyes, they were now an identical color to the Sapphire River, vibrant and just lighter than the color of the sea.

"I can see," she said.

"Not like when the pixies do it?" Lord Westhauser asked, and she shook her head.

"No. It doesn't… feel… *off*."

"It will," Farang said. "You are too… attached to what makes you unique, and the magic will slip away. The more it does, the more you will reject it. I cannot tell you if it will take hours or days or weeks, but I doubt it will be longer than that."

"Elf magic is supposed to be permanent," Lord Westhauser said.

"Elven magic alters the properties of inanimate objects permanently, so long as those inanimate objects remain unaltered," Farang answered. "With the living, it is considerably more difficult, and with humans and fae, it is more difficult yet. Though, there are things that can last a very, very long time."

He glanced over at Jasper, then back at Lady Westhauser.

"If you come back to me, after the magic has left you, and you want it again, I am happy to do it again. It would probably last better if you are actually the one who wants it. But this is the best that I can do, even with all the supplies and all the time in the world."

Lord Westhauser drew a breath, then nodded.

"I will accept it. And as to the second term of the agreement? That you will provide me with enchanted objects as I require them of you?"

"You can't ask for more than a day's labor per month," Stasia said, and Lord Westhauser looked at her sharply, but without malice.

"You speak for him?" he asked. Stasia raised an eyebrow, looking pointedly at Farang.

"I suppose she does," Farang said. "She appears to be my cousin."

"All right," Lord Westhauser said slowly. "Is that all?"

"Nothing whose only purpose is for killing people," Stasia said.

"Unacceptable," Lord Westhauser said. "That rules out all blades."

"Not at all," Stasia said. "A blade is a defensive tool and a preemptive tool. Unless it isn't."

Lady Westhauser giggled, and Lord Westhauser shot her a sharp but playful glare.

"I see," he said. "Is that all?"

Stasia considered.

"You pay him an hourly rate of one jagger an hour plus expenses, and you will provide all required materials so that he doesn't have to shop for them himself. You must allow one week per day of work for delivery. If something is going to take him four days to finish it, you have to give him a month to deliver it. And in good faith, you can't ask him to manufacture something that will be used to take advantage of women."

"Everything is ultimately useful in taking advantage of women," Lord Westhauser said, perhaps an apology, and Stasia nodded.

"I know. That's why I said in good faith."

Lord Westhauser looked up at Farang.

"She's a good negotiator," he said. "It's in her blood. You could do much worse."

Farang nodded.

"I'm learning that," he said. "Queen Constance has always had excellent taste in her companions."

There was a reverberating shock of silence that lasted less than a second, then Lord Westhauser offered Farang his hand.

"I go by Skite," he said. "And I'm ready to take you to your new home if you're ready to go."

Farang turned to Stasia.

"You have been a very interesting and useful young woman," he said. "Thank you for everything you've done."

He went to stand in front of Jasper.

"I can see it in you," he said. "Don't think that I can't. If you have questions, once it is safe, you may seek me out."

Jasper hesitated, then nodded.

Farang turned to Babe.

There was a long moment between them, then Babe grinned and hugged the elf.

"You ever need set straight again, you send word," Babe said.

Farang nodded.

"If you ever need someone to remind you of the gravity of the situation, find someone else," Farang answered, and Babe laughed.

"Goodbye, friend," Babe said.

"Goodbye, friend," Farang echoed. Dipping his head to Babe, he returned to Lord Westhauser and shook the still-offered hand.

"I am ready," the elf said.

Lord Westhauser rapped Stasia's new book where it was sitting on a table, drawing her attention to it, then holding up a hand.

"Good night, one and all," he said, heading for the door. "It's been interesting and profitable, and that's always a good night."

Stasia looked over at Lady Westhauser, who was holding her glasses thoughtfully.

"I'd tried it a few times before, with pixie magic," the woman said. "Sometimes I wonder if he wouldn't have been so concerned about it, if I hadn't done it for the wedding. The first time he saw me, I wasn't wearing them."

"Did I just let something happen that shouldn't have?" Stasia asked, and Lady Westhauser shook her head with a soft laugh, tucking the glasses away.

"No," she said. "It's just very strange to think that I'll wake up tomorrow morning and not reach for these. He might be right. Maybe I could get used to this and decide this is what I've always wanted."

She came to grasp Stasia's elbows, kissing both her cheeks.

"We have a lot to talk about, someday soon," she said. "I'll reach out to you once Skite tells me it's okay to do it."

Stasia shrugged with humor.

"I'll be waiting on Jasper to tell me the same," she said, and Lady Westhauser winked.

"I can't wait to hear your side of this whole thing," she said, and Stasia nodded.

"And I yours," she said.

"Do you require escort, m'lady?" Jasper asked, and Lady Westhauser snorted.

"I'm the sister of the head of the Highrock family, the wife of the King of the Rats. I'm the Queen of the Rats, no less. And I haven't done anything wrong. I think, if anything, I should ask *you* if you need an escort."

Jasper struggled to contain a grin, and Lady Westhauser dipped her head, then went out the door.

Jasper turned to Stasia.

"I'll get Sterling to walk you home," he said. "I think you need to stay indoors for at least two or three days until they give up searching for Farang."

"No. Nope. Wait a minute. Can we just…" Stasia asked, going to sit in a chair and shaking her head. "I need to understand what's going on here."

"You have a safe place to go?" Jasper asked Babe.

"Why do you hate Lord Westhauser?" Stasia asked Babe.

He looked from Jasper to Stasia, then shrugged.

"The Black Docks weren't a great place to be, growin' up, but it was free. Lotta men moved down there because you could do what you liked, and weren't nobody gonna come chasing after you. Black Docks were too dangerous. Lot of bad men, yeah, but…" He shook his head, looking at the door. "That man walked in and took over and suddenly you were with him or you were dead. Set up gangs for raidin' the rest of the city, got good at it. Used to just be squabbles and takin', but now it's a *business*, and he ain't even one of 'em needin' it. Walked in rich as the mountains and just… liked doin' it. Liked killin'. Took an assassin's name, even."

"Skite," Stasia said, and he nodded.

"None of my buddies were assassins, but at the time I left, if you wanted to hire one, the Black Docks was where to find one. Spoiled rich kid walks in and… takes to killin' like a fish to water. He's a bad man, Stacy. I'm struck you don't see it."

Stasia frowned, trying to make it all compute.

"We shouldn't stay here," Jasper said. "Skite was here when I got here, and that was more than an hour ago. Anyone paying attention will easily put together that we were meeting with him."

"And *you*," Stasia said. "What was Faris talking about?"

"I don't owe you an explanation," Jasper said. "I know what he was telling me and I appreciate him saying it, but I'm not going to discuss it further."

Stasia raised her eyebrows at Babe, who shrugged.

Stasia was angry.

"All this, and you're just going to ignore me?" she asked. Jasper turned to face her, hands on his hips, an actual aggressive stance that she'd never seen directed at her before.

"You saved a man's life tonight," Jasper said. "Which was what the queen asked you to do. I and my men showed up to help you because I thought the cause was noble and worthy, and because I love the queen as a loyal subject. I believe that she asked you to do a good thing. What right does that give you to demand answers of me about my personal experience?"

She blinked.

He was right.

Of course he was right.

And for a moment she was deeply chastened, and then in the next moment she was wounded.

She had thought they were friends. They'd gone through something deeply secret and dangerous, and she had had an expectation that that meant that they had moved to a different level of relationship where such secrets were opened.

And then she wasn't embarrassed and she wasn't hurt. They both passed quickly as he stood looking at her with his eyebrow up.

She was a merchant's daughter, and she was her own person. Certainly she cared about Jasper and what had happened to him, but she wasn't just peppering him with questions because she was curious. She shook her head.

"This is your world, not mine," she answered. "Everybody hates elves, but then I meet one and he's perfectly decent and both you and Babe have no problem hanging out with him and helping keep him alive. Lord Westhauser isn't actually a lord, he's a street thug, and the king who everyone loves is willing to enslave a magical creature to help tip the scales in a war that I still know nothing about. Everyone acts weird all the time, and I'm not going to apologize to you for trying to figure out what's going on. Aggressively."

He sucked on his back teeth for a moment, then shrugged and sighed.

"Lord Westhauser is the son of the recently deceased Lord Westhauser. He's a true nobleman. No one has been able to explain to me how he became a power broker in the crime organizations, but both things are certainly true."

Stasia shook her head.

"You people are crazy," she said, standing. "We have guest rooms at my house. Babe will stay there with us until you recall him to the guard, at which point he will receive any and all back pay he is owed for being dismissed by a moody and unreasonable squad leader."

Jasper looked at her flatly, then nodded.

"Very well," he said.

Stasia looked at Babe, who frowned.

"I don't need you to see to me," he said.

"Have you seen what a cheap apartment in this city looks like the day that you rent it?" she asked. "Because I have. A bunch of times. I can either walk you to one of the ones I've set up to get you in, and then you can walk me home to make sure the river doesn't eat me, and then you can come back on your own, or you can just come with me down to the Sapphire and enjoy a few days eating some of the best food you've ever had."

"Ain't never been a guest at a fancy-footed house in Verida," he said. "Don't know how."

Stasia raised an eyebrow.

"Are you sure you're not feeling your strings?" Stasia asked.

"Strings?" Jasper asked.

"Clever girl," Babe said, shaking his head. "All right. I will learn what it is to be a guest in the house of Fielding."

She nodded, then looked at Jasper.

"I'm exhausted," she said. "And I want to go to bed. I'm sorry if I've said anything I'll regret when I get up in the morning."

"I think you've comported yourself admirably," he said. "Perhaps there are things that you do deserve to know. I'll consider it."

She rubbed her eyes, losing the ability to see things specifically again.

"Get her home," Jasper said. "We'll discuss this more when the smoke is cleared."

Babe took her elbow and Stasia found her head on his shoulder as they went down the stairs, the exertion of the previous two days hitting her in force.

"Tough girl," Babe murmured with humor. "You ain't gonna make me carry you home, now, are you?"

"Not exactly," Stasia answered, not lifting her head.

He laughed softly.

"Let's get you home," he said. "Tomorrow's comin'."

"What's tomorrow?" Stasia asked drowsily.

He shrugged.

"Who knows," he said. "Tomorrow's always comin'."

ALSO BY

Anadidd'na Universe (Urban Fantasy)

The School of Magic Survival Series

The Sam and Sam Series

Other Urban Fantasy

The Tell, the Detective Series

About the Author

Chloe Garner is a wanderer with a host of identities in her head fighting each other to get out. Chloe writes about the things that go bump in the night, the future, and all things fantastical. Find her on Twitter as BlenderFiction, on Goodreads and Facebook as Chloe Garner, or at blenderfiction.wordpress.com.

Subscribe to her mailing list for release notices, advance copies, and occasional freebies.

Printed in Dunstable, United Kingdom